P9-EMO-696

SOUTHAMPTON ROW

ANNE PERRY

SOUTHAMPTON ROW

Thorndike Press • **Chivers Press**
Waterville, Maine USA Bath, England

This Large Print edition is published by Thorndike Press, USA and by Chivers Press, England.

Published in 2002 in the U.S. by arrangement with
The Ballantine Publishing Group, a division of Random House, Inc.

Published in 2002 in the U.K. by arrangement with
Headline Book Publishing.

U.S. Hardcover 0-7862-4066-0 (Basic Series)
U.S. Softcover 0-7862-4502-6
U.K. Hardcover 0-7540-1809-1 (Windsor Large Print)
U.K. Softcover 0-7540-9191-0 (Paragon Large Print)

The text of this Large Print edition is unabridged.
Other aspects of the book may vary from the original edition.

Cover design by Carl Galian. Cover art: Grimshaw, John Atkison (1836–93) *Reflections on the Thames*, Westminster, 1880 (oil on canvas), courtesy of Leeds Museums and Galleries (City Art Gallery) U.K./Bridgeman Art Library

Set in 16 pt. Plantin by Minnie B. Raven.

Printed in the United States on permanent paper.

British Library Cataloguing-in-Publication Data available

Library of Congress Cataloging-in-Publication Data

Perry, Anne.
    Southampton Row / Anne Perry.
      p. cm.
    ISBN 0-7862-4066-0 (lg. print : hc : alk. paper)
    ISBN 0-7862-4502-6 (lg. print : sc : alk. paper)
    1. Pitt, Charlotte (Fictitious character) — Fiction.
  2. Women detectives — England — London — Fiction.
  3. Pitt, Thomas (Fictitious character) — Fiction. 4. Police
— England — London — Fiction. 5. London (England)
— Fiction. 6. Police spouses — Fiction.
  7. Large type books. I. Title.
  PR6066.E693 S68 2002b
  823'.914—dc21   2002018039

With thanks to Derrick Graham
for his assistance in research
and for his excellent ideas

CHAPTER ONE

"I'm sorry," Assistant Commissioner Cornwallis said quietly, his face a mask of guilt and unhappiness. "I did everything I could, made every argument, moral and legal. But I can't fight the Inner Circle."

Pitt was stunned. He stood in the middle of the office with the sunlight splashing across the floor and the noise of horses' hooves, wheels on the cobbles and the shouts of drivers barely muffled beyond the window. Pleasure boats plied up and down the Thames on the hot June day. After the Whitechapel conspiracy he had been reinstated as superintendent of the Bow Street police station. Queen Victoria herself had thanked him for his courage and loyalty. Now, Cornwallis was dismissing him again! "They can't," Pitt protested. "Her Majesty herself . . ."

Cornwallis's eyes did not waver, but they were filled with misery. "They can. They have more power than you or I will ever know. The Queen will hear what they want her to. If we take it to her, believe me, you will have nothing left, not even Special Branch. Narraway will be glad to have you back." The words seemed forced from him, harsh in his throat. "Take it, Pitt. For your own sake, and your family's. It is the best you'll get. And you're good at it. No one could measure what you did for your country in beating Voisey at Whitechapel."

"Beating him!" Pitt said bitterly. "He's knighted by the Queen, and the Inner Circle is still powerful enough to say who shall be superintendent of Bow Street and who shan't!"

Cornwallis winced, the skin drawn tight across the bones of his face. "I know. But if you hadn't beaten him, England would now be a republic in turmoil, perhaps even civil war, and Voisey would be the first president. That's what he wanted. You beat him, Pitt, never doubt it . . . and never forget it, either. He won't."

Pitt's shoulders slumped. He felt bruised and weary. How would he tell Charlotte? She would be furious for him, outraged at the unfairness of it. She would want to fight, but there was nothing to do. He knew that, he was only arguing with Cornwallis because the shock had not passed, the rage at the injustice of it. He had really believed his position at least was safe, after the Queen's acknowledgment of his worth.

"You're due a holiday," Cornwallis said. "Take it. I'm . . . I'm sorry I had to tell you before."

Pitt could think of nothing to say. He had not the heart to be gracious.

"Go somewhere nice, right out of London," Cornwallis went on. "The country, or the sea."

"Yes . . . I suppose so." It would be easier for Charlotte, for the children. She would still be hurt but at least they would have time together. It was years since they had taken more than a few days and just walked through woods or over fields, eaten picnic sandwiches and watched the sky.

Charlotte was horrified, but after the first outburst she hid it, perhaps largely for the children's sake. Ten-and-a-half-year-old Jemima was instant to pick up any emotion, and Daniel, two years younger, was quick behind. Instead she made much of the chance for a holiday and began to plan when they should go and to think about how much they could afford to spend.

Within days it was arranged. They would

take her sister Emily's son with them as well; he was the same age and was keen to escape the formality of the schoolroom and the responsibilities he was already learning as his father's heir. Emily's first husband had been Lord Ashworth, and his death had left the title and bulk of the inheritance to their only son, Edward.

They would stay in a cottage in the small village of Harford, on the edge of Dartmoor, for two and a half weeks. By the time they returned the general election would be over and Pitt would report again to Narraway at Special Branch, the infant service set up largely to battle the Fenian bombers and the whole bedeviled Irish question of Home Rule, which Gladstone was fighting all over again, and with as little hope of success as ever.

"I don't know how much to take for the children," Charlotte said as if it were a question. "How dirty will they get, I wonder . . ."

They were in the bedroom doing the last of the packing before going for the midday train south and west.

"Very, I hope," Pitt replied with a grin. "It isn't healthy for a child to be clean . . . not a boy, anyway."

"Then you can do some of the laundry!"

she replied instantly. "I'll show you how to use a flatiron. It's very easy — just heavy — and tedious."

He was about to retaliate when their maid, Gracie, spoke from the doorway. "There's a cabbie 'ere with a message for yer, Mr. Pitt," she said. " 'E give me this." She offered him a piece of paper folded over.

He took it and opened it up.

Pitt, I need to see you immediately. Come with the bearer of this message. Narraway.

"What is it?" Charlotte asked, a sharp edge to her voice as she watched his expression change. "What's happened?"

"I don't know," he replied. "Narraway wants to see me, but it can't be much. I'm not starting back with Special Branch for another three weeks."

Naturally she knew who Narraway was, although she had never met him. Ever since her first encounter with Pitt eleven years ago, in 1881, she had played a lively part in every one of his cases that aroused her curiosity or her outrage, or in which someone she cared about was involved. In fact, it was she who had befriended the

11

widow of John Adinett's victim in the Whitechapel conspiracy and finally discovered the reason for his death. She had a better idea than anyone else outside Special Branch of who Narraway was.

"Well, you'd better tell him not to keep you long," she said angrily. "You are on holiday, and have a train to catch at noon. I wish he'd called tomorrow, when we'd have been gone!"

"I don't suppose it's much," he said lightly. He smiled, but the smile was a trifle downturned at the corners. "There've been no bombings lately, and with an election coming at any time there probably won't be for a while."

"Then why can it not wait until you come back?" she asked.

"It probably can." He shrugged ruefully. "But I can't afford to disobey him." It was a hard reminder of his new situation.

He reported directly to Narraway and he had no recourse beyond him, no public knowledge, no open court to appeal to, as he had had when a policeman. If Narraway refused him there was nowhere else to turn.

"Yes . . ." She lowered her eyes. "I know. Just remind him about the train. There isn't a later one to get there tonight."

"I will." He kissed her swiftly on the cheek and then turned and went out of the door and down the stairs to the pavement, where the cabbie waited for him.

"Right, sir?" the cabbie asked from the box.

"Yes," Pitt accepted. He glanced up at him, then climbed into the hansom and sat down as it started to move. What could Victor Narraway want from him that could not as easily wait until he reported back in three weeks? Was it just an exercise of his power, to establish again who was master? It could hardly be for his opinion; he was still a novice at Special Branch work. He knew almost nothing about the Fenians; he had no expertise in dynamite or any other explosives. He knew very little about conspiracies in quarrel, nor in honesty did he want to. He was a detective, a policeman. His skill was in solving crimes, unraveling the details and the passions of individual murder, not the machinations of spies, anarchists and political revolutionaries.

He had succeeded brilliantly in Whitechapel, but that was over now. All that they would ever know of the truth rested in silence, darkness and bodies decently buried to hide the terrible things that had happened to them. Charles Voisey was still alive, and they could prove nothing against him. But there had been a kind of justice. He, secret hero of the movement to overthrow the throne, had been maneuvered into seeming to have risked his life to save it. Pitt smiled and felt his throat tighten with grief as he remembered standing beside Charlotte and Vespasia in Buckingham Palace as the Queen had knighted Voisey for his services to the Crown. Voisey had risen from his knees too incensed with rage to speak — which Victoria had taken for awe, and smiled indulgently. The Prince of Wales had praised him, and Voisey had turned and walked back past Pitt with a hatred in his eyes like the fires of hell. Even now Pitt felt a cold knot tighten in his stomach remembering it.

Yes, Dartmoor would be good: great, clean, wind-driven skies, the smell of earth and grass on unpaved lanes. They would walk and talk together, or simply walk! He would fly kites with Daniel and Edward, climb some of the tors, collect things, watch the birds or animals. Charlotte and Jemima could do whatever they wished, visit people, make new friends, look at gardens, or search for wildflowers.

The cab stopped. " 'Ere y'are sir," the

driver called. "Go right in. Gentleman's expecting yer."

"Thank you." Pitt climbed out and walked across the pavement to the steps leading up to a plain wooden door. It was not the shop in the back room of which he had found Narraway in Whitechapel. Perhaps he moved around as the need directed? Pitt opened the door without knocking and went in. He found himself in a passage which led to a pleasant sitting room with windows onto a tiny garden, which was mostly crowded with overgrown roses badly in need of pruning.

Victor Narraway was sitting in one of the two armchairs, and he looked up at Pitt without rising. He was a slender man, very neatly dressed, of average height, but nevertheless his appearance was striking because of the intelligence in his face. Even in repose there was an energy within him as if his mind never rested. He had thick, dark hair, now liberally sprinkled with gray, hooded eyes which were almost black, and a long, straight nose.

"Sit down," he ordered as Pitt remained on his feet. "I have no intention of staring up at you. And you will grow tired in time and start to fidget, which will annoy me."

Pitt put his hands in his pockets. "I

haven't long. I'm going to Dartmoor on the noon train."

Narraway's heavy eyebrows rose. "With your family?"

"Yes, of course."

"I'm sorry."

"There is nothing to be sorry about," Pitt replied. "I shall enjoy it very much. And after Whitechapel I have earned it."

"You have," Narraway agreed quietly. "Nevertheless you are not going."

"Yes I am." They had known each other only a few months, worked very loosely together on just the one case. It was not like Pitt's long relationship with Cornwallis, whom he liked profoundly and would have trusted more than any other man he could think of. He was still unsure what he felt about Narraway, and certainly he did not trust him, in spite of his conduct in Whitechapel. He believed Narraway served the country and was a man of honor according to his own code of ethics, but Pitt did not yet understand what they were, and there was no bond of friendship between them.

Narraway sighed. "Please sit down, Pitt. I expect you to make this morally uncomfortable for me, but be civil enough not to make it physically so as well. I dislike craning my neck to stare up at you."

"I am going to Dartmoor today," Pitt repeated, but he did sit down in the other chair.

"This is the eighteenth of June. Parliament will rise on the twenty-eighth," Narraway said wearily, as if the knowledge was sad and indescribably exhausting. "There will be a general election immediately. I daresay we shall have the first results by the fourth or fifth of July."

"Then I shall forfeit my vote," Pitt replied. "Because I shall not be at home. I daresay it will make no difference whatever."

Narraway looked at him steadily. "Is your constituency so corrupt?"

Pitt was slightly surprised. "I don't think so. But it has been Liberal for years, and general opinion seems to be that Gladstone will get in, but with a narrow majority. You haven't called me here three weeks before I start in order to tell me that!"

"Not precisely."

"Not even approximately!" Pitt started to rise.

"Sit down!" Narraway ordered with a suppressed rage making his voice cut like a blow.

Pitt sat more out of surprise than obedience.

"You handled the Whitechapel business well," Narraway said in a calm, quiet voice, leaning back again and crossing his legs. "You have courage, imagination and initiative. You even have morality. You defeated the Inner Circle in court, although you might have thought twice had you known it was they you were against. You are a good detective, the best I have, God help me!" he replied. "Most of my men are more used to explosives and assassination attempts. You did well to defeat Voisey at all, but your turning of the murder on its head to have him knighted for saving the throne was brilliant. It was the perfect revenge. His republican friends regard him as the arch-traitor to the cause." The merest smile touched Narraway's lips. "He was once their future president. Now they wouldn't allow him to lick stamps."

It should have been the highest praise, yet looking at Narraway's steady, shadowed eyes, Pitt felt only awareness of danger.

"He will never forgive you for it," Narraway observed as casually as if he had done no more than remark the time.

Pitt's throat tightened so his answer was scratchy. "I know that. I had never imagined he would. But you also said at the end of the affair that it would be nothing so

18

simple as physical violence." His hands were stiff, his body cold, not for himself but for Charlotte and the children.

"It won't be," Narraway said gently. For an instant there was a softness in his face, then it was gone again. "But he has turned your stroke of genius to his own use, that is his genius."

Pitt cleared his throat. "I don't know what you mean."

"He is a hero! Knighted by the Queen for saving the throne," Narraway said, uncrossing his legs and leaning forward, a sudden passion of bitterness twisting his face. "He is going to stand for Parliament!"

Pitt was stunned. "What?"

"You heard what I said! He is standing for Parliament, and if he wins he will use the Inner Circle to rise very quickly to high office. He has resigned his place on the Appeal Court Bench and taken to politics. The next government will be Conservative, and it will not be long in coming. Gladstone won't last. Apart from the fact that he is eighty-three, Home Rule will finish him." His eyes did not move from Pitt's face. "Then we will see Voisey as Lord Chancellor, head of the Empire's judiciary! He will have the power to corrupt any court in the land, which means in the end, all of them."

It was appalling, but Pitt could already see how it was possible. Every argument died on his lips before he spoke it.

Narraway relaxed fractionally, an easing of the muscles so slight it was barely visible. "He's standing for the South Lambeth seat."

Pitt quickly thought of his London geography. "Wouldn't that take in Camberwell, or Brixton?"

"Both." Narraway's eyes were steady. "And yes, it's a Liberal seat, and he's Conservative. But that doesn't ease my mind, and if it eases yours, then you're a fool!"

"It doesn't," Pitt said coldly. "He'll have a reason. There'll be somebody he can bribe or intimidate, some place where the Inner Circle has its power he can use. Who is the Liberal candidate?"

Narraway nodded very slowly, still looking at Pitt. "A new man, one Aubrey Serracold."

Pitt asked the obvious. "Is he Inner Circle, and will stand down at the last moment, or throw the election in some other way?"

"No." Narraway said it with certainty, but he did not explain how he knew. If he had sources somewhere deep inside the Inner Circle, he did not disclose them, even to his own men. Pitt would have thought less of him if he had. "If I could see where it was coming from, or how, I wouldn't need you to stay in London and watch," Narraway continued. "Throwing you out of Bow Street may prove to be one of their greatest mistakes." It was a reminder of their power, and the injustice against Pitt. Precise knowledge of what he was saying sparkled hard and bright in his eyes, and he made no pretense to hide it. They both knew he did not need to.

"I can't affect the vote!" Pitt said bitterly. It was no longer an argument against losing his holiday and his time with Charlotte and the children, it was helplessness in the face of an insoluble problem. He could see nowhere even to begin, let alone to achieve a victory.

"No," Narraway agreed. "If I wanted something like that done I have more skilled men for it than you."

"It would also make you little better than Voisey," Pitt said with chill.

Narraway sighed, shifting his position to one more at ease. "You are naive, Pitt, but I knew that. I work with the tools I have, and I don't try to saw wood with a screwdriver. You will watch and listen. You will learn who are Voisey's tools and how he uses them. You will learn Serracold's weaknesses and where they may be exploited. And if we are fortunate enough that Voisey has any unguarded vulnerabilities, then you will find them and inform me immediately." He breathed in and out very slowly. "What I may choose to do about him is not your concern. Understand me in that, Pitt! You are not exercising your conscience at the expense of the ordinary men and women of this country. You know only a small part of the picture, and you are not in a position to make grand moral judgments." There was not a shred of any kind of humor in his eyes or his mouth.

The flippant answer died on Pitt's tongue. What Narraway was asking of him seemed all but impossible. Had he any idea of the real power of the Inner Circle? It was a secret society of men sworn to support each other above all interests or loyalties apart. They existed in cells, no one man knowing the identities of more than a handful of others, but obedient to the demands of the Circle. He knew of no instance in which one had betrayed another to the outside world. Internal justice was immediate and lethal; it was the more deadly because one never knew who else was Circle. It could be your superior, or some ordinary clerk of whom you took little notice. It could be your doctor, your bank manager or even your clergyman. Only one thing were you certain of, it was not your wife. No woman was allowed any part in it or knowledge of it whatever.

"I know the seat is Liberal," Narraway was going on. "But the political climate at the moment is turning extreme. The Socialists are not only noisy but making actual headway in some areas."

"You said Voisey was standing as a Tory," Pitt pointed out. "Why?"

"Because there will be a Conservative backlash," Narraway replied. "If the Socialists go far enough, and mistakes are made, then it could sweep the Tories into power for a long time — quite long enough for Voisey to become Lord Chancellor. Even Prime Minister one day."

The thought was cold and ugly, and certainly too real to dismiss. To turn away from it as far-fetched was to hand Voisey the ultimate weapon.

"You said Parliament rises in four days?" Pitt asked.

"That's right," Narraway agreed. "You'll

23

start this afternoon." He took a deep breath. "I'm sorry, Pitt."

"What?" Charlotte said incredulously. She was standing at the bottom of the stairs facing Pitt as he had come in through the front door. Her face was flushed with exertion, and now temper.

"I have to stay because there's going to be a general election," he repeated. "Voisey's going to stand!"

She stared at him. For a moment all the memories of Whitechapel came back, and she understood. Then she closed it from her mind. "And what are you supposed to do about it?" she demanded. "You can't stop him from standing, and you can't stop people from voting for him if they want to. It's monstrous, but it is we who made him into a hero because it was the only way to stop him. The republicans won't even speak to him now, let alone elect him. Why can't you let them deal with him? They'll be furious enough to shoot him! Just don't stop them. Arrive too late."

He tried to smile. "Unfortunately, I can't rely on their doing that efficiently enough to be of any use to us. We have only about ten days."

"You have three weeks' holiday!" She bit

back sudden tears of disappointment. "It's not fair! What can you do? Tell everybody he's a liar, that he was behind the conspiracy to overthrow the throne?" She shook her head. "Nobody even knows there was one! He'd have you sued for slander, or more likely locked up as a lunatic. We made sure everyone believed he practically single-handedly did something wonderful for the Queen. She thinks he's marvelous. The Prince of Wales and all his friends will be behind him." She sniffed fiercely. "And no one will beat them — not with Randolph Churchill and Lord Salisbury as well."

He leaned against the newel post. "I know," he admitted. "I wish I could tell the Prince of Wales how close Voisey came to destroying him, but we have no proof now." He reached forward and touched her cheek. "I'm sorry. I know I haven't much chance, but I have to try."

The tears brimmed over her cheeks. "I'll unpack in the morning. I'm too tired to do it now. What on earth am I going to tell Daniel and Jemima — and Edward? They've been looking forward to it so much —"

"Don't unpack," he interrupted. "You go . . ."

"Alone?" Her voice rose to a squeak.

"Take Gracie. I'll manage." He did not want to tell her how much it was for her safety. At the moment she was angry and disappointed, but in time she would realize he was challenging Voisey again.

"What will you eat? What will you wear?" she protested.

"Mrs. Brody can cook something for me, and do the linen," he answered. "Don't worry. Take the children, enjoy it with them. Whether Voisey wins or loses, there's nothing I can do after the results are in. I'll come down then."

"There'll be no time left!" she said angrily. "Results go on coming in for weeks!"

"He's standing for a London seat. It'll be one of the first."

"It could still be days!"

"Charlotte, I can't help it!"

Her voice was barely controlled. "I know! Don't be so damnably reasonable. Don't you even mind? Doesn't it infuriate you?" She swung her hand violently, fist tight. "It isn't fair! They have loads of other people. First they throw you out of Bow Street and send you to live in some wretched rooms in Spitalfields, then when you save the government and the throne and heaven knows what else, they reinstate you — then throw you out again! Now they're taking your only holiday . . ." She gasped for breath and it turned into a sob. "And for what? Nothing at all! You can't stop Voisey if people are stupid enough to believe him. I hate Special Branch! It seems they don't have to answer to anyone! They do whatever they like and there's nobody to stop them."

"A bit like Voisey and the Inner Circle," he replied, trying to smile very slightly.

"Just like him, for all I know." She met his eyes squarely, but there was a flash of light in hers, in spite of her attempts to hide it. "But nobody can stop him."

"I did once."

"We did!" she corrected him sharply.

This time he did smile. "There's no murder now, nothing for you to solve."

"Or you!" she countered immediately. "What you mean is it's all about politics and elections, and women don't even vote, much less campaign and stand for Parliament."

"Do you want to?" he said with surprise. He was happy to talk about any subject, even that one, rather than tell her how he feared for her safety once Voisey knew he was involved again.

"Certainly not!" she retorted. "But that's

got nothing to do with it!"

"An excellent piece of logic."

She poked a stray piece of hair back into its pin. "If you were at home and spent more time with the children you'd understand it perfectly."

"What?" he said with total disbelief.

"The fact that I don't want it doesn't mean I shouldn't be allowed it — if I did! Ask any man!"

He shook his head. "Ask him what?"

"Whether he would let me, or anybody else, decide whether he could or not," she said in exasperation.

"Could or could not do what?"

"Anything!" she said impatiently, as if it had been obvious. "It's one lot of people making rules for another lot of people to live by, when they wouldn't accept them themselves. For heaven's sake, Thomas! Haven't you ever told children to do something, and they've said to you, 'Well, you don't!' You may tell them they're impertinent and send them upstairs to bed, but you know it's unfair, and you know they know it too."

He blushed hot at one or two memories. He forbore from drawing any similarities between the public's attitude to women and parents' towards children. He did not want to quarrel with her. He knew why she spoke as she did. He felt the same anger and disappointment choking inside himself, and there were better ways of showing it than temper.

"You're right!" he said unequivocally.

Her eyes opened wide for a moment in surprise, then in spite of herself she started to laugh. She put her arms around his neck and he took hold of her, drawing her body to his, caressing her shoulder, the soft line of her neck, and then kissing her.

Pitt went to the station with Charlotte, Gracie and the children. It was a huge, echoing place crowded with people hurrying in all directions. It was the terminus for the London and South Western line, and the air was loud with the hiss of escaping steam, clanging doors, feet on the platform walking, running, shuffling, wheels of luggage trolleys, shouts of greeting and farewell, an excitement of adventure. It was full of beginnings and endings.

Daniel jiggled up and down with impatience. Edward, fair-haired like Emily, tried to remember the dignity of being Lord Ashworth, and succeeded for a full five minutes before racing along the platform to see the fires roaring as a stoker poked more coal into the bottom of a vast engine. The stoker looked up, smiling at the boy before wiping his hand across his brow and beginning again.

"Boys!" Jemima muttered under her breath with a glance at Charlotte.

Gracie, still not much larger than when she had entered their employ as a thirteen-year-old, was dressed up for traveling. It was the second time she had been away from London on holiday, and she was managing to look very experienced and calm, except for the brilliance of her eyes and the flush in her cheeks — and the fact that she clung on to her soft-sided bag as if it were a life preserver.

Pitt knew they must go. It was for their safety, and he wanted to be free of anxiety and certain he could face Voisey with the knowledge they were where he could never find them. But he still felt an ache of sadness inside himself as he called a porter over and instructed him to put their luggage into the van, giving him threepence for his trouble.

The porter tipped his cap and piled the cases onto his trolley. He whistled as he pushed it away, but the sound was lost in the roar of a belch of steam, the sliding of coal off the shovels into the furnaces, the guard's shrill whistle blast as an engine jolted forward and began to pick up speed, pulling out.

Daniel and Edward raced each other along the platform, looking for the least occupied compartment, and came back waving their arms and whooping with triumph.

They put their hand baggage inside, then came to the door to say good-bye.

"Look after each other," Pitt told them after he had hugged them all, including Gracie, to her surprise and pleasure. "And enjoy yourselves. Have every bit of fun you can."

Another door clanged shut and there was a jolt. "Time to go," Pitt said, and with a wave he stepped back as the carriage lurched and juddered, the couplings locked, and it moved forward.

He stood watching, seeing them leaning out of the window, Charlotte holding them back, her face suddenly bleak with loneliness as she was pulled away. Clouds of steam billowed upwards and drifted towards the vast, many-arched roof. There were smuts in the air and the smell of soot and iron and fire.

He waved until they were out of sight as

31

the train curved around the track, then he walked as fast as he could back along the platform and out into the street. At the cab rank he climbed into the first hansom and told the driver to take him to the House of Commons.

He sat back and composed his mind to what he would say when he got there. He was south of the river now, but it would not take him long, even in the mid-morning traffic. The Houses of Parliament were on the north bank, perhaps thirty minutes away.

He had always cared intensely about social injustice, the pain of poverty and disease, ignorance and prejudice, but his opinion of politicians was not high and he doubted that they would address many of the issues that troubled him unless forced into it by individuals with a passion for reform. Now was a good time to reassess that rather hasty judgment and learn a great deal more about both the individuals and the process.

He would begin with his brother-in-law, Jack Radley, Emily's second husband and the father of her daughter, Evangeline. When they had first met, Jack had been a charming man without either title or sufficient money to make any mark in society, but with the wit and the good looks to be invited to so many houses that he enjoyed an elegant life of considerable comfort.

After marrying Emily, Jack had felt an increasing emptiness in that way of existence, until on an impulse he had stood for Parliament and surprised everyone, especially himself, by winning. It might have been the tide of political fortune, or that his seat was in one of the many constituencies where corruption determined the outcome, but he had since become a politician of some thought and more principle than his earlier years might have led anyone to foresee. During the Irish affair in Ashworth Hall he had shown both courage and an ability to act with dignity and good judgment. At the least he would be able to give Pitt information of a more detailed nature, and perhaps more accurately, than Pitt could gain from a public source.

He reached the House of Commons, paid the cabdriver and went up the steps. He did not expect to be able to walk straight in, and was preparing to write a small note on one of his cards and have it taken to Jack, but the policeman at the door knew him from his days at Bow Street, and his face lit with pleasure.

"Morning, Mr. Pitt, sir. Nice to see you,

sir. No trouble 'ere, I 'ope?"

"None at all, Rogers," Pitt replied, grateful he could recall the man's name. "I want to see Mr. Radley, if possible. It is a matter of some importance."

"Right you are then, sir." Rogers turned and called over his shoulder. "George! Take Mr. Pitt up ter see Mr. Radley, will yer? Know 'im? Honorable Member for Chiswick." He looked back at Pitt. "You go with George 'ere, sir. 'E'll take yer up, because yer can get lost in ten minutes in this rabbit warren of a place."

"Thank you, Rogers," Pitt said with sincerity. "That's very good of you."

It was indeed a tangle of passages and stairways with offices at every turn and people coming and going, all distracted with their own business. He found Jack alone in a room which was obviously shared with someone else a good deal of the time. He thanked his guide and waited until he had left before closing the door and turning to speak.

Jack Radley was approaching forty, but a man of very good looks and natural warmth which made him seem younger. Now he was surprised to see Pitt, but he set aside the newspapers he had been reading and faced him with curiosity.

"Sit down," he invited him. "What brings you here? I thought you were going to take a long-overdue holiday. You have Edward with you!" There was a shadow behind his eyes, and Pitt realized with a bitter humor that he was aware of the injustice of Pitt's present position with the Special Branch and afraid that Pitt was going to ask for his help in reversing it. It was something he could not do, and Pitt knew that even better than he did.

"Charlotte has taken the children," Pitt replied. "Edward was full of excitement and ready to drive the train himself. I have to stay here for a while. As you know, there's going to be an election in a few days." He allowed a flash of humor in his face, and then lost it again. "For reasons I cannot explain, I need some information on the issues . . . and some of the people."

Jack drew in his breath.

"Special Branch reasons." Pitt smiled at him. "Not personal."

Jack colored slightly. He was not often wrong-footed by anyone, least of all Pitt, who was unused to political debate and the thrust and cut of opposition. Perhaps Jack had forgotten that the questioning of suspects held many of the same elements, the obliqueness, the study of face and gesture, the anticipation and the ambush.

"What issues?" Jack asked. "There's Home Rule for Ireland, but then there has been for generations. It's no better than it ever was, although Gladstone's sticking to it. It's brought him down once already, and I think it will certainly cost him votes again, but no one can pry him loose from it, though God knows enough have tried." He pulled a slightly rueful face. "But rather less often argued about is Home Rule for Scotland — or Wales."

Pitt was startled. "Home Rule for Wales?" he said incredulously. "What backing is there for that?"

"Not a great deal," Jack admitted. "Or Scotland, either, but it is an issue."

"Surely it won't affect the London seats?"

"It might, if you were arguing for it." Jack shrugged. "Actually, on the whole, the people most against such things are those geographically the farthest from them. Londoners tend to think Westminster should rule everything. The more power you have, the more you want."

"Home Rule, at least for Ireland, has been on the agenda for decades." Pitt set it aside temporarily. "What else?"

"The eight-hour day," Jack replied

grimly. "That's the biggest, at least so far, and I don't see anything else equaling it." He looked at Pitt with a slight frown. "What is it, Thomas? A plot to overthrow the Old Man?" He was referring to Gladstone. There had already been attempts on his life.

"No," Pitt said quickly. "Nothing so overt." He wished he could tell Jack the whole truth, but for Jack's sake as much as his own, he could not. Any betrayal must not be blamed on him. "Corrupt constituences, some dirty fighting."

"Since when did Special Branch care about that?" Jack said skeptically, leaning back a little in his chair, his elbow inadvertently knocking over a pile of books and papers. "They are supposed to be stopping anarchists and dynamiters, especially Fenians." He frowned. "Don't lie to me, Thomas. I'd rather you told me to mind my own business than fob me off with an evasion."

"It's not an evasion," Pitt replied. "It's a particular seat, and so far as I know, it has no Irish dimension, nor any dynamiters."

"Why you?" Jack said levelly. "Is it anything to do with the Adinett case?" He was referring to the murder which had so infuriated Voisey and the Inner Circle they had taken their revenge on Pitt by having him dismissed from Bow Street.

"Indirectly," Pitt admitted. "You are almost at the point where you would rather be told to mind your own business."

"Which seat?" Jack said, perfectly calmly. "I can't help you if I don't know."

"You can't help me anyway," Pitt countered dryly. "Except with information about the issues, and the odd warning about tactics. I wish I had paid more attention to politics in the past."

Jack grinned suddenly, but it was not without self-mockery. "When I think how narrow our majority is going to be, so do I!"

Pitt wanted to ask about the safety of Jack's own seat, but it would be better to find out from someone else. "Do you know Aubrey Serracold?" he asked instead.

Jack looked surprised. "Yes, actually I know him moderately well. His wife is a friend of Emily's." He frowned. "Why, Thomas? I'd stake a great deal he's a decent man — honest, intelligent and going into politics to serve his country. He has no need of money and no desire to wield power for itself."

Pitt should have been comforted, but instead he saw a man in danger from something he would never see until it was too late; he might well not recognize an enemy even then, because his nature was outside Serracold's understanding.

Was Jack right, and in not telling him the truth was Pitt throwing away perhaps the only weapon he possessed? Narraway had given him a task that seemed impossible as it stood. It was not detecting as he was used to it; he was seeking not to solve a crime but to prevent a sin, one which was against the moral law but probably not the law of the land. It was not that Voisey should have the power — he had as much right as any other candidate — it was what he would do with it in perhaps two or three years, or even five or ten, that was wrong. And you cannot punish a man for what you believe he may do, no matter how evil.

Jack leaned forward across his desk. "Thomas, Serracold is a friend of mine. If he is in some kind of danger, any kind, let me know!" He made no threats and produced no arguments, which was oddly more persuasive than if he had. "I would protect my friends, just as you would yours. Personal loyalty means something, and the day it doesn't I want no part of politics anymore."

Even when Pitt had feared Jack courted Emily for her money — and he had feared it — he had still found him impossible to dislike. There was a warmth in him, an ability to mock himself and yet keep the directness which was the essence of his charm. Pitt had no chance of success without taking risks, because there was no safe way even to begin, let alone to conclude, a fight against Voisey.

"Not physical danger, so far as I know," he replied, hoping he was right in his decision to defy Narraway and confide at least some portion of the truth in Jack. Please heaven it did not come back and betray them both! "Danger of being cheated out of his seat."

Jack waited as if he knew that was not all.

"And perhaps of being ruined in reputation," Pitt added.

"By whom?"

"If I knew that I would be in a far better position to guard against it."

"You mean you can't tell me?"

"I mean I don't know."

"Then why? You know something, or you wouldn't be here."

"For political gain, of course."

"Then it is his opponent. Who else?"

"Those behind him."

Jack started to argue, then stopped. "I suppose everybody has someone behind him. The ones you can see are the least worry." He stood up slowly. He was almost the same height as Pitt, but as elegant as Pitt was untidy. He had natural grace, and was still as meticulously dressed and groomed as in the days when he made his way on his charm. "I'll be happy to continue this conversation, but I have a meeting in an hour, and I haven't had a decent meal today. Will you join me?"

"I'll be happy to," Pitt accepted immediately, rising also.

"Be my guest in the members' dining room," Jack suggested, opening the door for Pitt. He hesitated a moment, as if worrying over Pitt's clean collar but crooked tie and slightly bulging pockets. He sighed and gave up.

Pitt followed him and took his place at one of the tables. He was fascinated. He hardly tasted his food he was so busy trying to watch the other diners without appearing to do so. He saw face after face he had seen in the newspapers, many whose names he knew, others familiar but he could not place them. He kept hoping he might see Gladstone himself.

Jack sat smiling, considerably entertained.

They were halfway through a dessert of hot treacle pudding and custard when a large man with thinning fair hair stopped by. Jack introduced him as Finch, the Honorable Member for one of the Birmingham constituencies, and Pitt as his brother-in-law, without stating any occupation.

"How do you do," Finch said civilly, then looked at Jack. "Hey, Radley, have you heard that this fellow Hardie is actually going to stand? And in West Ham South, not even in Scotland!"

"Hardie?" Jack frowned.

"Keir Hardie!" Finch said impatiently, ignoring Pitt. "Fellow's been down the mines since he was ten years old. God knows if he even can read or write, and he's standing for Parliament! Labor Party, he says . . . whatever that is." He spread his hands in a sharp gesture. "It's no good, Radley! That's our territory . . . trades unions, and all that. He won't get in, of course — not a cat's chance. But we can't afford to lose any support this time." He lowered his voice. "It's going to be a tight thing! Too damned tight. We can't give in on the working week, we'd be crippled. It would ruin us in months. But I wish to the devil the Old Man would forget Home Rule for a while. He'll bring us down!"

"A majority's a majority," Jack replied. "Twenty or thirty is still workable."

Finch grunted. "No it isn't! Not for long. We need fifty at least. Nice to have met you . . . Pitt? Pitt, did you say? Good Tory name. Not a Tory, are you?"

Pitt smiled. "Shouldn't I be?"

Finch looked at him, his light blue eyes suddenly very direct. "No, sir, you shouldn't. You should look towards the future and steady, wise reform. No self-interested conservatism that will alter nothing, remain fixed in the past as if it were stone. And no harebrained socialism that would alter everything, good and bad alike, as if it were all written in water and the past meant nothing. This is the greatest nation on earth, sir, but we still need much wisdom at the helm if we are to keep it so in these changing times."

"In that at least I can agree with you," Pitt replied, keeping his voice light.

Finch hesitated a moment, then bade him good-bye and left, walking briskly, his shoulders hunched as if he were fighting his way through a crowd, although in fact he passed only a waiter with a tray.

Pitt was following Jack out of the dining room when they all but bumped into the Prime Minister, Lord Salisbury, on his way in. He was dressed in a pinstriped suit, his long, rather sad face full-bearded, but almost bald to the crown of his head. Pitt was so fascinated that it was a moment before he looked fully at the man a step behind him, but obviously in his company. His features were strong, intelligent, his nose a trifle crooked, his skin pale. For an instant their eyes met and Pitt was frozen by the power of hatred he saw looking back at him, as if they were the only two in the room. All the noise of talk, laughter, clink of glass and crockery vanished. Time was suspended. There was nothing but the will to hurt, to destroy.

Then the present rolled back like a wave, human, busy, argumentative, self-absorbed. Salisbury and his companion went in; Pitt and Jack Radley went out. They were twenty yards down the corridor before Jack spoke.

"Who was that with Salisbury?" he asked. "You know him?"

"Sir Charles Voisey," Pitt replied, startled to hear how his voice rasped. "Prospective Parliamentary candidate for Lambeth South."

44

Jack stopped. "That's Serracold's constituency!"

"Yes," Pitt replied steadily. "Yes . . . I know that."

Jack let out his breath very slowly; understanding filled his face, and the beginning of fear.

CHAPTER
<u>TWO</u>

Pitt found the house uniquely lonely without Charlotte and the children. He missed the warmth, the sound of laughter, excitement, even the occasional quarreling. There was no clatter of Gracie's heels on the floor, or her wry comments, only the two cats, Archie and Angus, curled up asleep in the patches of sun that came through the kitchen windows.

But when he remembered the hatred in Voisey's eyes, relief washed over him with an intensity that caught his breath that they were out of London, far away where neither Voisey nor any of the Inner Circle would find them. A small cottage in a country hamlet on the edge of Dartmoor was as safe as anywhere possible. That knowledge left him free to do all he could to stop Voisey from winning the seat and beginning the climb to a power which would corrupt the conscience of the land.

Although as he sat at the kitchen table

over breakfast of toast he had definitely scorched, homemade marmalade and a large pot of tea, he was daunted by a task so nebulous, so uncertain. There was no mystery to solve, no explanation to unravel, and too little specific to seek. His only weapon was knowledge. The seat Voisey was contesting had been Liberal for years. Whose vote did he hope to sway? He was standing for the Tories, the only alternative to the Liberals with any chance of forming a government, even though the majority opinion was that this time Mr. Gladstone would win, even if his administration did not last long.

He took another piece of toast from the rack where he had set it, and spread it with butter. He spooned out a very good helping of marmalade. He liked the pungent taste of it, sharp enough to feel as if it filled his head.

Did Voisey intend somehow to win the middle ground and so enlarge his share of the vote? Or to disenchant the poorer men and drive them towards socialism, and so split the left-wing support? Had he some weapon, as yet undisclosed, with which to damage Aubrey Serracold and so cripple his campaign? He could not openly do all three. But then with the Inner Circle behind him, he did not need to be open. No one outside the very top of its power, perhaps no one but Voisey himself, knew the names or positions of all its members, or even how many there were.

He finished the toast, drank the last of the tea, and left the dishes where they were. Mrs. Brody would wash up when she came, and no doubt feed Archie and Angus again. It was eight o'clock in the morning, and time he began to acquire more knowledge of Voisey's platform, the issues he was making the core of his appeal, who his open supporters were, and where he was going to speak. Pitt already knew from Jack the bare outline of these things regarding Serracold, but it was not enough.

It was late June and the city was hot, dusty and crammed with traffic of every sort — trade, business and pleasure. Street peddlers cried their wares on almost every pavement corner, open carriages held ladies who were out to see the sights, keeping the sun from their faces with an array of parasols in pretty colors like enormous overblown flowers. There were heavy wagons carrying bales of goods, vegetable and milk carts, omnibuses and the usual hordes of hansom cabs. Even the footpaths were crowded, and Pitt had to weave his way in and out. The noise was an assault on the ears and the mind, chatter, street cries of vendors of a hundred different articles for sale, the rattle of wheels on cobbles, the jingle of harness, shouts of frustrated drivers, the sharp clip of horses' hooves.

He would prefer Voisey to be as little aware of him as possible, although after their meeting in the House of Commons it could no longer be secret that Pitt was watching the campaign. He regretted that, but it could not be undone, and perhaps it was inevitable; it just would have been better delayed, even a short while. Voisey might have been sufficiently absorbed in his political battles and the exhilaration of the campaign not to have noticed one more person's interest in him.

By five o'clock Pitt knew the names of those backing Voisey's candidacy, both publicly and privately, at least those of record. He also knew that the issues Voisey had espoused were the traditional mainstream Tory values of trade and Empire. It was obvious how these would appeal to the property owners, the manufacturers and shipping barons, but now the vote had extended to the ordinary man who possessed nothing more than his house or rented rooms worth above ten pounds a year, and surely they were natural supporters of trades unions, and so of the Liberal Party?

The fact that it seemed an impossible seat for Voisey to win worried Pitt far more than had he seen some opening, some weakness that could be exploited. It meant that the attack was coming from an angle he had no idea how to protect, and he did not even know where the vulnerability lay.

He made his way south of the river towards the docks and factories in the shadow of the London Bridge Railway Terminal, with the intention of joining the crowd of workers at the first of Voisey's public speeches. He was intensely curious to see both how Voisey behaved and what kind of reception he would receive.

He stopped at one of the public houses and had a pork pie and a glass of cider, keeping his ear to the conversations at the tables around him. There was a good deal of laughter, but underneath it an unmistakably bitter note as well. He heard only one reference to the Irish, or the vexed question of Home Rule, and even that was treated half jokingly. But the matter of hours to the working day aroused hot feelings, and some considerable support for the Socialists, even though hardly anyone seemed to know the names of any of them. Certainly Pitt did not hear Sidney Webb or William Morris mentioned, nor the eloquent and vociferous playwright Shaw.

By seven o'clock he was standing in the open outside one of the factory gates, the gray, flat sides of the buildings soaring up into the smoke-filled air above him. The clang of machinery beat a steady rhythm in the distance, and the smell of coke fumes and acids caught his throat. Around him were five or six score men in uniform browns and grays, color worn out of the fabric, patched and repatched, frayed at the cuffs, worn at the elbows and knees. Many of them had cloth caps on, even though the evening was mild and, far more unusually, there was no chill blowing up from the river. The cap was habit, almost a part of identity.

Pitt passed unnoticed among them, his natural scruffiness a perfect disguise. He listened to their laughter, their rowdy, often cruel jokes, and heard the note of despair underneath. And the longer he listened the less could he imagine how Voisey, with his money, his privilege, his polished manner, and now his title as well, could win over a single one of them, let alone the bulk. Voisey stood for everything that oppressed them and which they perceived, correctly or not, to be exploiting their labor and stealing their rewards. It frightened him because he knew far better than to believe Voisey was a dreamer, trusting to any kind of luck.

The crowd was just beginning to get restive and speak of leaving, when a hansom, not a carriage, came to a stop about twenty yards away and Pitt saw the tall figure of Voisey get out and walk towards them. It gave Pitt an odd shiver of apprehension, as if even in all this crowd Voisey could see him and the hatred could burn across the air and find him.

"Come after all, 'ave yer?" a voice called out, for a moment breaking the spell.

"Of course I have come!" Voisey called back, turning to face them, his head high, his expression half amused, Pitt invisible, one anonymous face among the hundred or so men. "You have votes, don't you?"

Half a dozen men laughed.

"At least 'e in't pretending as 'e gives a damn about us!" someone said a few yards to Pitt's left. "I'd rather 'ave a bastard wot's 'onest than one wot ain't."

Voisey walked over to the wagon which had been left as a makeshift platform, and with an easy movement climbed up into it.

There was a rustle of attention, but it was hostile, waiting for the opportunity to criticize, challenge and abuse. Voisey seemed to be alone, but Pitt noticed the two or three policemen standing well back, and half a dozen or more newly arrived men, all watching the crowd, burly men in quiet, drab clothing, but with a fluidity of movement and a restlessness quite unlike the weariness of the factory workers.

"You've come to look at me," Voisey began, "because you are curious to see what I am going to say, and if I can come up with anything at all to justify your voting for me, and not for the Liberal candidate, Mr. Serracold, whose party has represented you as far back as you can remember. And perhaps you expect a little entertainment at my expense."

There was a rumble of laughter and one or two catcalls.

"Well, what do you want from government?" Voisey asked, and before he could answer himself he was shouted down.

"Less taxes!" someone yelled, to accompanying jeers.

"Shorter hours! A decent working week, no longer than yours!"

More laughter, but sharp-edged, angry.

"Decent pay! 'Ouses wot don't leak. Drains!"

"Good! So do I," Voisey agreed, his voice carrying well in spite of the fact he did not seem to be raising it. "I would also like a job for every man who wants to work, and every woman, too. I'd like peace, good foreign trade, less crime, more certain justice, responsible police without corruption, cheap food, bread for everyone, clothes and boots for everyone. I'd like good weather as well, but . . ."

The rest of his words were lost in a roar of laughter.

"But you wouldn't believe me if I told you I could do that!" he finished.

"Don't believe yer anyway!" a voice shouted back, to more jeers and calls of agreement.

Voisey smiled, but the angle of his body was stiff. "But you're going to listen to me, because that's what you've come for! You're curious what I'm going to say, and you're fair."

This time there were no catcalls. Pitt could feel the difference in the air, as if a storm had passed by without breaking.

"Do most of you work in these factories?" Voisey waved his arm. "And these docks?"

There was a murmur of assent.

"Making goods to ship all over the world?" he went on.

Again the assent, and a slight impatience. They did not understand the reason why he asked. Pitt did, as if he had already heard the words.

"Clothes made from Egyptian cotton?" Voisey asked, his voice lifting, his eyes searching their faces, the language of their bodies, the boredom or the quickening of understanding. "Brocades from Persia and the old Silk Road east to China and India?" he continued. "Linen from Ireland? Timber from Africa, rubber from Burma . . . I could go on and on. But you probably know the list as well as I do. They are the products of the Empire. That's why we are the biggest trading nation in the world, why Britain rules the seas, a quarter of the earth speaks our language, and soldiers of the Queen guard the peace over land and sea in every quarter of the globe."

This time the rising noise had a different note to it, pride and anger and curiosity. Several men stood a little straighter, shoulders square. Pitt shifted quickly out of Voisey's line of sight.

Voisey shouted above them. "It isn't just glory — it's a roof over your heads and food on your table."

" 'Ow about a shorter working day?" a tall man with ginger hair called out.

"If we lose the Empire, who are you going to work for?" Voisey challenged him. "Who are you going to buy from, sell to?"

"Nobody's going ter lose the Empire!" the ginger-haired man replied with scorn. "Even them Socialists in't that daft!"

"Mr. Gladstone's going to lose it," Voisey replied. "A piece at a time! First Ireland, then maybe Scotland and Wales. Who knows what after that — India, perhaps? No more hemp and jute, no more mahogany and rubber from Burma. Then Africa, Egypt, a piece at a time. If he can lose Ireland on his own doorstep, why not everywhere?"

There was a sudden silence, then a loud laugh, but there was no humor in it, instead there was a sharp undercurrent of doubt, perhaps even fear.

Pitt glanced around at the men closest to him. Every one of them was facing Voisey.

"We have to have trade," Voisey went on, but now he had no need to shout. He pitched his voice to the back of the crowd, and it was sufficient. "We need the rule of law, and we need mastery of the seas. In order to share our wealth more fairly, we must first assure that we have it!"

There was a murmur that sounded like agreement.

"Do what you do well, no one on earth better!" Voisey's tone held a ring of praise, even triumph. "And choose freely to represent you men who know how to make and keep the laws at home, and deal honorably and profitably with the other nations of the earth to preserve and add to what you have. Don't elect old men who think they speak for God, but in truth only speak for the past, men who carry out their own wishes and don't listen to yours."

Now there was another roar from the crowd, but in many quarters it actually sounded like a cheer to Pitt's ears.

Voisey did not keep them much longer. He knew they were tired and hungry and tomorrow morning would come all too soon. He had enough sense to stop while they were still interested, and more than that, while there was still time to get a good dinner and a couple of hours at the public house to take a few pints of ale and talk it all over.

He told them a swift joke, and another, and left them laughing as he walked back to his hansom and rode away.

Pitt was stiff from standing still, and cold

inside with bitter admiration for the way
Voisey had turned a crowd from hostile
strangers into men who would remember
his name, remember that he had not betrayed them or made false promises, that
he had not assumed they would like him,
and that he had made them laugh. They
would not forget what he had said about
losing the Empire that provided their
work. It might make their employers rich,
but the truth was that if their employers
were poor, then they were even poorer. It
might or might not be unjust, but many
men there were realist enough to know
that it was the way things were.

Pitt waited until Voisey had been out of
sight for several minutes, then he walked
across the dusty cobbles into the shade of
the factory walls and along a narrow alley
back towards the main road. Voisey had
shown at least some of his tactics, but he
had revealed no vulnerability at all.
Aubrey Serracold was going to have to be
more than charming and honest to equal
him.

It was early yet to go home, especially to
an empty house. He had a good book to
read, but the silence would disturb him.
Even the thought of it held a loneliness.
There must be something else he could do

which might be useful, perhaps more he could learn from Jack Radley? Maybe Emily could tell him something about Serracold's wife? She was acutely observant and a realist in the ploys of power far more than Charlotte. She might have seen a weakness in Voisey, where a man, with his mind more on political policies and less on the person, might have missed it.

He leaned forward and redirected the driver of his hansom.

But when he arrived the butler told him with profound apologies that Mr. and Mrs. Radley were out at a dinner party and could not reasonably be expected home before one in the morning at the earliest.

Pitt thanked him and declined the offer to wait, as the butler had known he would. He returned to the cab, and told the driver to take him instead to Cornwallis's flat in Piccadilly.

A manservant answered the door and without question conducted him through to Cornwallis's small sitting room. It was furnished in the elegant but spare style of a captain's cabin at sea, full of books, polished brass and dark, gleaming wood. Above the mantel shelf there was a painting of a square-rigged brigantine running before a gale.

"Mr. Pitt, sir," the manservant announced.

Cornwallis dropped his book and rose to his feet in surprise and some alarm. "Pitt? What is it? What's happened? Why are you not on Dartmoor?"

Pitt did not answer.

Cornwallis glanced at the manservant, then back at Pitt. "Have you eaten?" he asked.

Pitt was startled to realize that he had had nothing since the pie in the tavern near the factory. "No . . . not for a while." He sank down in the chair opposite Cornwallis's. "Bread and cheese would be fine . . . or cake if you have it." He missed Gracie's baking already, and the tins at home were empty. She had made nothing, expecting them all to be away.

"Bring Mr. Pitt bread and cheese," Cornwallis directed. "And cider, and a slice of cake." He looked back at Pitt. "Or would you prefer tea?"

"Cider is excellent," Pitt replied, easing himself into the softness of the chair.

The manservant departed, closing the door behind him.

"Well?" Cornwallis demanded, resuming his own seat and the frown returning to his face. He was not handsome but there was a strength and a symmetry in his features which pleased one the longer one looked at him. When he moved it was with the grace and balance of his long years at sea, when he had had only the quarterdeck in which to pace.

"Something has arisen in connection with one of the parliamentary seats which Narraway wishes me to . . . to watch." He saw the flash of anger in Cornwallis's face, and knew it was because he saw injustice in Narraway's not honoring Bow Street's commitment to Pitt's leave. It added to the outrage of the entire dismissal of Pitt's reposting to suit the vengeance of the Inner Circle. All the old presumptions and certainties were gone, for both of them.

But Cornwallis did not probe. He was accustomed to the solitary life of a captain at sea who must listen to his officers but share only practicalities with them, not explain himself or indulge in emotions. He must always remain apart, maintain as much as possible of the fiction that he was never afraid, never lonely, never in doubt. It was the discipline of a lifetime and he could not now breach it. It had become part of his personality and he was no longer aware of it as a separate decision.

The manservant returned with the

bread, cheese, cider and cake, for which Pitt thanked him. "You are welcome, sir." He bowed and withdrew.

"What do you know of Charles Voisey?" Pitt asked as he spread the crusty bread with butter and cut off a heavy slice of pale, rich Caerphilly cheese and felt it crumble beneath the knife. He bit into it hungrily. It was sharp and creamy in his mouth.

Cornwallis's lips tightened, but he did not ask why Pitt wanted to know. "Only what is public information," he replied. "Harrow and Oxford, then called to the bar. Was a brilliant lawyer who made a good deal of money, but of more value in the long run, a great many friends in the places that count, and I don't doubt a few enemies as well. Elevated to the bench, and then very quickly to the Court of Appeal. He knows how to take chances and appear courageous, and yet never slip badly enough to fall."

Pitt had heard all this before, but it still concentrated his mind to have it put so succinctly.

"He is a man of intense pride," Cornwallis continued. "But in day-to-day life he has the skill to conceal it, or at least make it appear as something less offensive."

"Less vulnerable," Pitt said instantly.

Cornwallis did not miss the meaning. "You are looking for a weakness?"

Pitt remembered with an effort that Cornwallis knew nothing of the Whitechapel affair, except Adinett's trial in the beginning and Voisey's knighthood at the end. He did not even know that Voisey was the head of the Inner Circle, and for his own safety it was better that he never learn it. Pitt owed him at least that much in loyalty for the past, and he would have wished it in friendship now.

"I'm looking for knowledge, and that includes both strengths and weaknesses," he replied. "He is standing for Parliament as a Tory, in a strong Liberal seat. The question of Home Rule has already arisen!"

Cornwallis's eyebrows rose. "And that means Narraway?"

Pitt did not answer.

Cornwallis accepted his silence.

"What do you want to know about Voisey?" he asked. "What kind of weakness?"

"Who does he care for?" Pitt said softly. "Who is he afraid of? What moves him to laughter, awe, pain, any emotion? What does he want, apart from power?"

Cornwallis smiled, his eyes steady on

Pitt's, unblinking. "It sounds as if you are deploying for battle," he said with a very slight lift of question.

"I am searching to see if I have any weapons," Pitt replied without looking away. "Have I?"

"I doubt it," Cornwallis answered. "If he cares for anything apart from power, I've not heard of it, not enough that the loss of it would hurt him." He was watching Pitt's face, trying to read in it what he needed. "He likes to live well, but not ostentatiously. He enjoys being admired, which he is, but he's not willing to curry favor to get it. I daresay he doesn't need to. He takes pleasure in his home, good food, good wine, the theater, music, company, but he'd sacrifice any of them if he had to, to reach the office he wants. At least that's what I've heard. Do you want me to ask more?"

"No! No . . . not yet."

Cornwallis nodded.

"Anyone he fears?" Pitt asked without hope.

"None that I know," Cornwallis said dryly. "Has he cause? Is that what Narraway is afraid of . . . an attempt on his life?"

Again, Pitt could not answer. The silence

was worrying him, even though he knew Cornwallis understood.

"Anyone he cares about?" Pitt asked doggedly. He could not afford to give up.

Cornwallis thought for a moment or two. "Possibly," he said at last. "Although how deeply I don't know. But I think there are ways in which he needs her — as his hostess, if nothing else. But I think he does care for her, as much as a man of his nature can."

"Her? Who is she?" Pitt demanded, hope quickening in him at last.

Cornwallis dismissed the matter with a tiny, rueful smile. "His sister is a widow of great charm and formidable social skills. She appears, at least on the surface, to possess a gentleness and moral sensitivity he has never shown, in spite of his recent knighthood, of which you know more than I." It was not a question. He would never intrude where he knew he had no rights, and a refusal would hurt. He frowned very slightly; it was just a shadow between the brows. "But I have met her only twice, and I am no judge of women." Now there was a slight self-consciousness in him. "Someone more skilled might tell you quite differently. Certainly she is one of his greatest political assets among those in the party with the power and the will to support him. With the voters he has little to rely on but his own oratory." He sounded discouraged, as if he feared that would be sufficient.

Pitt feared it even more so. He had seen Voisey face the crowd. It was a blow to discover that he had a social ally of such ability. Pitt had been hoping that perhaps being unmarried would be Voisey's one weakness.

"Thank you," he said aloud.

Cornwallis smiled bleakly. "Have some more cider?"

Emily Radley enjoyed a good dinner party, most especially when there was an edge of danger and excitement in the air, struggles of power, of words, ambition hidden behind a mask of humor or of charm, public duty or a passion for reform. Parliament had not been dissolved, but it would be any day, and they all knew it; then the battle would be in the open. It would be swift and sharp, a matter of a week or so. There was no time to hesitate, reconsider a blow, or moderate a defense. It was all in hot blood.

She prepared as for a campaign of war. She was a beautiful woman, and she was very well aware of it. But now that she was in her thirties and had two children, it required a little more care than it used to in order to be her best. She set aside the youthful pastels she had once favored for her delicate coloring and selected from the latest fashions from Paris something bolder, more sophisticated. The basic skirt and bodice were midnight-blue silk, but with an overdress of light blue-gray slashed diagonally to swathe up over the bosom and be caught at the left shoulder, and again at the waist, with another deep slash and ties falling from her hip. It had the usual high rouched shoulders, and of course she wore kid gloves to the elbows. She chose diamonds rather than pearls.

The result was really very good. She felt ready to take on any woman who might be in the room, even her current closest friend, the dashing and superbly stylish Rose Serracold. She liked Rose enormously, and had since the day they met, and she sincerely hoped that Rose's husband, Aubrey, would gain his seat in Parliament, but she had no intention of being outshone by anyone. Jack's seat was pretty safe. He had served with distinction and made several valuable friends in power who would no doubt stand by him now, but nothing should be taken for granted. Political power was a highly fickle mistress and must be courted on every possible occasion.

Their carriage drew up outside the Trenchards' magnificent house on Park Lane, and she and Jack alighted. They were welcomed by the footman at the door and crossed the hall and were announced. She entered the withdrawing room on his arm with her head high and an air of confidence. They were greeted by Colonel and Mrs. Trenchard at exactly quarter to nine, fifteen minutes after the hour stated on the invitation that in turn had been received five weeks earlier. It was precisely the correct moment to arrive; they had judged it to perfection. To be on time would be vulgarly eager, whereas it was rude to be late. And since dinner was announced approximately twenty minutes after the first guest arrived, long after that one might easily find oneself shown in when everyone else was already going into the dining room.

Etiquette, which was of immovable rigidity, dictated who should go in with whom, and in what order, or the whole procedure would be thrown into chaos. To be noticed for beauty was always admirable; for wit was usually so, although there were risks attached. To make a spectacle of oneself would be disastrous.

No drinks were served in the brief time before the butler announced dinner. It was customary merely to sit and exchange a few pleasantries with whomever one might know until the procession to the dining room commenced.

The host would lead the way, with the senior ranking lady on his arm, followed by the remainder of the guests, in order of the ladies' rank, followed at the last by the hostess on the arm of the senior male guest.

Emily had time only to speak for a moment with Rose Serracold, easy to see with her ash-blond hair and sharp, straight profile even before she turned her pale aquamarine eyes to regard the latest arrivals. Her face lit with pleasure and she moved swiftly to Emily's side, twitching her flesh-pink taffeta dress. The gown plunged to the waist at the front, over claret-red embroidered brocade, which was echoed in mid-hip panels and an underskirt. It made her slender hips look richly curved and her waist a mere handspan. Only a woman of supreme confidence could have looked so dazzling in such a gown.

"Emily, how delightful to see you!" she

said with enthusiasm. Her glance swept up and down Emily's dress in immediate appreciation, but with a flash of amusement she deliberately avoided saying anything about it. "What a pleasure you could come!"

Emily smiled back. "As if you had not known I should!" She raised her eyebrows. They both knew Rose would have been familiar with the guest list or she would not have accepted.

"Well, I did have just the slightest idea," Rose admitted. She leaned a little closer. "It feels a trifle like the ball the night before Waterloo, doesn't it?"

"Not an occasion I recall," Emily murmured in mock spite.

Rose made a very slight face at her. "Tomorrow we ride into battle!" she responded with exaggerated patience.

"My dear, we have been at war for months," Emily replied as Jack was drawn into a group of men close by. "If not years!" she added.

"Don't shoot until you see the whites of their eyes," Rose warned. "Or in Lady Garson's case, the yellow. That woman drinks enough to drown a horse."

"You should have seen her mother!" Emily shrugged delicately. "She could have drowned a giraffe."

Rose threw back her head and laughed, a rich, infectious sound that caused half a dozen of the men to look at her with pleasure, and their wives to stare with disapproval, before deliberately turning away.

The dining room was blazing with light from the chandeliers and reflected from a thousand facets of crystal on the table and the sheen of silver on snow-white linen. Roses spilled out of silver bowls and long vines of honeysuckle trailed down the center of the cloth, sending up a rich perfume.

At each place setting there was a menu card — written in French, naturally. The guest's name was on the front to indicate where each person should sit. The footmen began to serve soup, according to each guest's preference, the choice being oxtail or bisque. Emily was placed between a Liberal elder statesman on her left and a generous banker on her right. She declined the soup, knowing there were a further eight courses to come, but the banker took the oxtail and began to eat immediately, it being correct to do so.

Emily glanced across the table at Jack, but he was busy conversing with a Liberal member who would also be defending his seat against a vigorous attack. She caught the odd word, indicating that they were concerned with the factions among the Irish members, which would almost certainly make the difference if the main parties were close in number. The ability to form a government might depend upon winning the support of either the Parnellites or anti-Parnellites.

Emily was tired of the issues of Home Rule simply because they had been argued over for as long as she could remember, and seemed no closer to a solution than when she had first had them explained to her in the schoolroom. She bent her attention to charming the rather grand elder statesman to her left, who had also declined a first course.

The second course was a choice of salmon or smelts.

She chose salmon, and for a little while refrained from conversation.

She declined the entrees, not wishing for curried eggs or sweetbreads with mushrooms, and listened to what she could catch of the discussion across the table.

"I think we should take him very seriously," Aubrey Serracold was saying, bending forward a little. The light caught his fair head, his long face filled with seriousness, all laughter gone, even his usual self-deprecating charm for once invisible.

"For heaven's sake!" the senior statesman protested, his cheeks pink. "The man left school at ten years old and went down the mines! Even other miners have more sense than to imagine he can do anything for them in Parliament, except make a fool of himself. He lost in his native Scotland; he hasn't a chance here in London."

"Of course not," said a bluff-faced man opposite who turned around indignantly, reaching for his wine and holding it for a moment before drinking. "We are the natural party for the workingman, not some newfangled creation of wild-eyed fanatics with picks and shovels in their hands!"

"That is just the kind of blindness that will lose us the future!" Aubrey returned with utmost seriousness. "Keir Hardie should not be dismissed lightly. A lot of men will see his courage and determination, and know how he has bettered his situation. They will think that if he can achieve so much for himself he can do the same for them."

"Take them out of the mines and put them in Parliament?" a woman in poppy-red said incredulously.

"Oh dear!" Rose twisted her glass in her

fingers. "Then what on earth shall we burn on our fires? I doubt the present incumbents would be the slightest practical use."

There was a burst of laughter, but it was high-pitched, and too loud.

Jack smiled. "Very funny as a dinner table joke — not so amusing if the miners listen to him and vote for more like him, who are full of passion to reform but haven't any idea of the cost of it — I mean the real cost, in trade and dependent livelihoods."

"They won't listen to him!" a white-whiskered man said with a gesture to courtesy, but his voice was dismissive of the seriousness Jack invested in the subject. "Most men have more sense." He saw Jack's expression of doubt. "For heaven's sake, Radley, only half the men in the land vote! How many miners own their own houses or pay more than ten pounds a year in rent?"

"So by definition" — Aubrey Serracold turned to face him, his eyes wide — "those who can vote are those who prosper under the system as it is now? That rather invalidates the argument, doesn't it?"

There was a quick exchange of glances across the table. This remark was unexpected, and to judge from several of them, also unwelcome.

"What are you saying, Serracold?" the white-whiskered man asked carefully. "If a thing works, change it?"

"No," Aubrey replied equally carefully. "If it works for one section of the people, it is not that section who should have the right to decide whether to keep it or not, because we all have the tendency to see things from our own view and to preserve what is in our own interest."

The footman removed the used plates and, almost unnoticed, served iced asparagus.

"You have a very poor opinion of your fellows in government," a red-haired man said a trifle sourly. "I'm surprised you want to join us!"

Aubrey smiled with extraordinary charm, looking down for a moment before turning to the speaker. "Not at all. I think we are wise and just enough to use power only as it is honestly given, but I have no such confidence in our opponents." He was met with a shout of laughter, but Emily saw that it did not entirely dispel the anxiety — in Jack, at least. She knew him well enough to see and understand the tension in his hands as he held his knife and fork and with dexterity cut the tips off the asparagus spears. He did not speak again for several minutes.

The conversation turned to other aspects of politics. The used dishes were taken and replaced with game — quail, grouse or partridge. Emily still did not accept any. Young ladies were always advised not to, as it might make their breath strong. She had always wondered why it was acceptable for men to. She had once asked her father, and received a look of blank amazement. The inequity of it had never occurred to him.

She declined still, not considering herself old enough to be disqualified from it mattering. She hoped she never would be.

After game there were sweets. The menu offered ice pudding, confiture of nectarines, iced meringues or strawberry jelly, which she accepted. She ate the jelly with her fork, as required by etiquette, an art necessitating a certain degree of concentration.

After the cheese there was a choice of ices, Neapolitan cream or raspberry water, and lastly pineapples, from the glass house presumably, strawberries, apricots or melons. She glanced with amusement at the varieties of skill displayed on the requirement to peel and eat each of these with a knife and fork. More than one person had cause to regret their choice, especially of apricots.

The conversation resumed. It was her job to be charming, to flatter with attention, to amuse, or more often to appear amused. It was the greatest compliment to a man to find him interesting, and she knew few who could resist it. It was amazing how much of himself a man would reveal if one simply allowed him to talk.

Beneath the plans, the assurances and the bravado, Emily heard a deep unease, and it was borne in on her with increasing certainty that those men who had been in government before and knew its subtleties and pitfalls did not wish to lose this election, but neither did they wholeheartedly desire to win. It was a curious situation, and because she did not understand it, therefore it troubled her. She listened for some time until she perceived that each, for his own passion and ambition, wished to win his own particular battle, but not the war. To the victor went spoils they were uncertain how to handle.

The laughter around her was brittle and the voices charged with emotion. The lights glittered on jewels and wine-glasses and the unused silver. The rich odors of food lingered amid the heavy perfume of the honeysuckle.

"It required long experience, a colossal courage, any amount of cool self-possession and a great skill to attack and dispose of it without harm to yourself or your neighbor, he told me," Rose was saying intensely, her eyes glistening.

"Then, my dear lady, you should leave such dangerous quarry to a hunter of courage and strength, a quick eye and a brave heart," the man next to her replied decisively. "I suggest you content yourself with following the pheasant shoot, or some other such sport."

"My dear Colonel Bertrand," Rose answered with shining innocence, "those are the etiquette instructions for eating an orange!"

The colonel blushed scarlet amid the uncontrollable burst of laughter.

"I do apologize!" Rose said as soon as she could be heard. "I fear I did not make myself plain. Life is full of dangers of so many kinds, one steps aside from one pitfall only to plunge into another."

No one argued with her. There was more than one other present who had felt the colonel's condescension, and no one rushed to his defense. Lady Warden giggled on and off for the rest of the evening.

When the meal was at last finished the ladies withdrew so the gentlemen might enjoy their port and, Emily knew perfectly well, have the serious political discussion of tactics, money and trading favor for favor which was the purpose of the evening.

To begin with she found herself sitting with half a dozen other wives of men who either were Members of Parliament already or hoped to become so, or who had money and profound interests in the election outcome.

"I wish they would take the new Socialists more seriously," Lady Molloy said as soon as they were seated.

"You mean Mr. Morris and the Webbs?" Mrs. Lancaster asked with wide eyes and a smile verging on laughter. "Honestly, my dear, have you ever seen Mr. Webb? They say he is undersized, undernourished and underendowed!"

There was a slight titter around the group, as much nervous as amused.

"But she isn't," someone else put in quickly. "She comes from a very good family."

"And writes children's fairy tales about hedgehogs and rabbits!" Mrs. Lancaster finished for her.

"How appropriate! If you ask me, the whole Socialist idea belongs with Peter Rabbit and Mrs. Tiggiwinkle," Lady Warden said with a giggle.

"No, it doesn't!" Rose contradicted, her deep feeling unconcealed. "The fact that a person's appearance may be a trifle quaint should not blind us to the worth of that person's ideas, or more importantly, to appreciate the danger those ideas may present to our real power. We should draw such people in to ally with us, not ignore them."

"They aren't going to ally with us, my dear," Mrs. Lancaster pointed out reasonably. "Their ideas are impractically extreme. They want an actual Labor Party."

The discussion moved to specific reforms and the speed at which they might be achieved, or even should be attempted. Emily joined in, but it was Rose Serracold who made the most outrageous suggestions and provoked the most laughter. No one, especially Emily, was entirely certain how much Rose meant beneath the wit and the keen observation of emotion and foible.

"You think I'm joking, don't you?" Rose said when the group divided and she and Emily were able to speak alone.

"No, I don't," Emily replied, keeping her back to those nearest them. Suddenly she was quite certain of it. "But I think you'll be very well advised to let other people think so. We are at precisely that stage in our understanding of the Fabians where we will think they are funny but have begun to have the first suspicion that in the end the joke may be more against us than with us."

Rose leaned forward, her fair face intense, all lightness gone from it. "That is precisely why we must listen to them, Emily, and adopt at least the best of their ideas . . . in fact, most of them. Reform will come, and we must be in the forefront of it. The franchise must include all adults, poor as well as rich, and in time women as well." Her eyebrows arched. "Don't look so horrified! It must. As the Empire must go — but that is another issue. And no matter what Mr. Gladstone says, we must make it law that the working day is no more than eight hours across all manner of trades, and no employer can force a man to do more."

"Or woman?" Emily asked curiously.

"Of course!" Rose's answer was immediate, a reflex to an unnecessary question.

Emily affected innocence. "And if you

call for your lady's maid to fetch you a cup of tea at half past eight, will you accept the answer that she has worked eight hours and is off duty — and you should get it yourself?"

"Touché." Rose bent her head in acknowledgment, a flush of mortification on her cheeks. "Perhaps we only mean factory work, at least to begin with." Then she lifted her eyes quickly. "But it doesn't alter the fact that we have to go forward if we are to survive, let alone if we are to obtain any kind of social justice."

"We all want social justice," Emily answered wryly. "It's just that everyone has a different idea as to what it is . . . and how to achieve it . . . and when."

"Tomorrow!" Rose shrugged her shoulders. "As far as the Tories are concerned, any time, as long as it isn't today!"

They were joined again briefly by Lady Molloy, speaking largely to Rose, and obviously still turning over in her mind what had been said previously.

"I had better be careful, hadn't I?" Rose said ruefully when Lady Molloy had gone. "The poor soul is quite flummoxed."

"Don't underestimate her," Emily warned. "She may have little imagination, but she is very astute when it comes to practical judgment."

"How tedious." Rose sighed elaborately. "That is one of the greatest disadvantages of running for public office, one has to please the public. Not that I don't desire to, of course! But making oneself understood is the greatest challenge, don't you think?"

Emily smiled in spite of herself. "I know exactly what you mean, although I admit I don't even attempt it most of the time. If people don't understand you, they may think you are speaking nonsense, but if you do it with enough confidence they will give you the benefit of the doubt, which doesn't always happen when they do understand. The art is not so much in being intelligent as in being kind. I really do mean that, Rose, believe me!"

Rose looked for a moment as if she were going to make some witty response, then the lightness drained out of her. "Do you believe in life after death, Emily?" she asked.

Emily was so startled she spoke only to give herself time to think. "I beg your pardon?"

"Do you believe in life after death?" Rose repeated earnestly. "I mean real life, not some sort of general holy existence as part of God, or whatever."

"I suppose I do. Not to would be too awful. Why?"

Rose gave an elegant shrug, her face noncommittal again, as if she had retreated from the edge of some greater honesty. "I just thought I'd shock you out of your political practicality for a moment." But her voice held no laughter, nor did her eyes.

"Do you believe in it?" Emily asked, smiling a little to make the question seem more casual than it was.

Rose hesitated, obviously uncertain now how she was going to answer. Emily could see the emotion in the angle of her body — her dramatic gown with its rich wine and flesh colors, and the tension in her arms where her thin hands gripped the edge of the chair.

"Do you think there isn't?" Emily said quietly.

"No, I don't!" Rose's voice was steady with total conviction. "I am quite sure there is!" Then just as suddenly she relaxed. Emily was certain it had cost her a very deliberate effort. Rose looked at her, then away again. "Have you ever been to a séance?"

"Not a real one, only pretend ones at parties." Emily watched her. "Why? Have you?"

Rose did not answer directly. "What's real?" she said with a tiny edge to her voice. "Daniel Dunglass Home was supposed to be brilliant. Nobody ever caught him out, and many tried to!" Then she swiveled to look directly at Emily, a challenge in her eyes, as if now she were on firmer ground and there was no hurt waiting under the surface were she to misstep.

"Did you ever see him?" Emily asked, avoiding the direct issue, which she was quite certain was not Dunglass Home, although she was not sure what it was.

"No. But they say he could levitate himself several inches off the floor, or elongate himself, especially his hands." She was watching Emily's response, although she made light of it.

"That must have been remarkable to see," Emily replied, unsure why anyone would wish to do such a thing. "But I thought the purpose of a séance was to get in touch with the spirits of those you knew who had gone on before."

"It is! That was just a manifestation of his powers," Rose explained.

"Or the spirit's power," Emily elaborated. "Although I doubt any of my ancestors had tricks like that up their sleeves . . .

unless you want to go back to the witch trials in Puritan times!"

Rose smiled, but it went no further than her lips. Her body was still stiff, her neck and shoulders rigid, and suddenly Emily was convinced that the whole subject mattered intensely to her. The trivial manner was to shield her vulnerability, and more than the pain of being laughed at, something deeper, perhaps having a belief snatched from her and broken.

Emily answered with total seriousness she did not have to feign. "I really don't know how the spirits from the past could contact us if they wanted to tell us something important. I cannot say that it wouldn't come with all kinds of strange sights, or sounds, for that matter. I would judge it on the content of the message, not on how it was delivered." Now she was not sure whether to go on with what she had intended to say, or if it were intrusive.

Rose broke the suspense of the moment. "Without the effects, how would I know it was real, not just the medium telling me what she thought I wanted to hear?" She made a casual little gesture of dismissal. "It isn't what you would consider entertainment without all the sighs and groans, and the apparitions, the bumps and glowing ectoplasm and so on!" She laughed, a brittle sound. "Don't look so serious, my dear. It's hardly church, is it! It's only ghosts rattling their chains. What is life if we can't be frightened now and then . . . at least of things like that, which don't matter at all? Takes one's mind off what is really awful." She swept one hand into the air, diamonds glittering on her fingers. "Have you heard what Labouchere is going to do with Buckingham Palace, if he ever has his way?"

"No . . ." Emily took a moment to adjust from the profoundly emotional to the utterly absurd.

"Turn it into a refuge for fallen women!" Rose said in a ringing voice. "Isn't that the best joke you've heard in years?"

Emily was incredulous. "Has he actually said so?"

Rose giggled. "I don't know . . . but if he hasn't yet, he soon will! When the old Queen dies, I don't doubt the Prince of Wales will do that anyway!"

"For heaven's sake, Rose!" Emily urged, glancing around them to see who might have overheard. "Keep a still tongue in your head! Some people wouldn't know sarcasm if it got up and bit them!"

Rose tried to look taken aback, but her

pale, brilliant eyes were shining and she was too close to hilarity to carry it off. "Who's being sarcastic, darling? I mean it! If they haven't fallen yet, he'd be just the man to help them!"

"I know, but for heaven's sake don't say so!" Emily hissed back at her, and then they both burst into laughter just as they were joined by Mrs. Lancaster and two others who were aching to know what they might have missed.

The ride home in the carriage from Park Lane was entirely another matter. It was after one in the morning but the street lamps lit the summer night, making the way clear, and the air was warm and still.

Emily could see only the side of Jack's face closest to the carriage lamp, but it was sufficient to show a seriousness he had hidden all evening.

"What is it?" she asked quietly as they turned out of Park Lane and moved west. "What happened in the dining room after we left?"

"A lot of discussion and planning," he replied, turning to look at her, perhaps not realizing it cast his face into shadow. "I . . . I rather wish Aubrey hadn't spoken so much. I like him enormously, and I think he'll be an honest representative of the people, and perhaps more importantly, an honest man in the House . . ."

"But?" she challenged. "What? He'll get in, won't he? It's been a Liberal seat for as long as anyone can remember!" She wanted every Liberal to win who could, so as to put the party back in power, but just at this moment she was thinking of Rose, and how crushed she would be if Aubrey failed. It would be humiliating to lose a safe seat, a personal rejection, not a difference of ideas.

"As much as anything is certain, yes," he agreed. "And we'll form a government, even if the majority isn't as large as we'd like."

"Then what's wrong? And don't tell me 'nothing'!" she insisted.

Jack bit his lip. "I wish he would keep some of his more radical ideas to himself. He's . . . he's closer to socialism than I realized." He spoke slowly, considering his words. "He admires Sidney Webb, for heaven's sake! We can't take reform at that pace! The people won't have it and the Tories will crucify us! Whether we should have an empire or not isn't the point. We do have, and you can't cut it loose as if it didn't exist and expect to have the trade, the work, the status in the world, the treaties, or anything else we do, without the reason and the purpose behind it. Ideals are wonderful, but without an understanding of reality, they can ruin us all. It's like fire, a great servant, yet totally destructive when it's master."

"Did you tell Aubrey that?" she asked.

"I didn't have the chance, but I will."

She said nothing for a few moments, riding in silence, thinking over Rose's sudden, strange questions about séances and the tension within her. She was uncertain whether to worry Jack with it or not, but it hung heavily with her, an unease she could not dismiss.

The carriage turned a corner sharply into a quieter street where the lamps were farther apart, shining up with ghostly gleam into the branches above.

"Rose was talking about spiritualists," she said abruptly. "I think you should suggest that Aubrey tell her to be discreet about that, too. It could be misinterpreted by enemies, and once the election is called in earnest there'll be plenty of those. I . . . I think perhaps Aubrey isn't used to being attacked. He's such a charming man almost everyone likes him."

He was startled. He jerked around in the

carriage seat to face her.

"Spiritualists? You mean mediums like Maude Lamont?" There was an edge of anxiety in his voice sharp enough that she did not need to see his expression to know what it would be.

"She didn't mention Maude Lamont, although everybody's talking about her. Actually, she talked about Daniel Dunglass Home, but I suppose it's much the same. She spoke of levitation and ectoplasm and things."

"I never know whether Rose is joking or not . . . was she?" It was not a question but a demand.

"I'm not sure," she admitted. "But I don't think so. I had the feeling that under the surface she cared very much about something."

He shifted uncomfortably, only half because of the carriage's rattling over uneven cobbles. "I'll have to speak to Aubrey about that, too. What is a social game when you are a private person becomes the rope for journalists to hang you with when you stand for Parliament. I can see the cartoons now!" He winced so acutely that she saw the movement in his cheek in the pool of light as they passed under a street lamp and back into darkness again. "Ask Mrs.

Serracold who's going to win the election! Damn it, better than that . . . who's going to win the Derby!" he said in a mimicking voice. "Let's ask Napoleon's ghost what the Czar of Russia's going to do next. He can't ever have forgiven him for Moscow and 1812."

"Even if he knew, he wouldn't be likely to tell us," she pointed out. "He is even less likely to have forgiven us for Waterloo."

"If we couldn't ask anyone with whom we've ever had a war, that would rule out just about everybody on earth, except the Portuguese and the Norwegians," he retorted. "Their knowledge about our future might be rather limited; they probably don't give a farthing." He took a deep breath and let it out in a sigh. "Emily, do you think she's really seeing a medium, other than just for fun at a house party?"

"Yes . . ." Emily spoke with a chill conviction. "Yes . . . I'm afraid I do."

The following morning brought news of a different and disturbing kind. Pitt was looking through the newspapers over breakfast of poached kippers and bread and butter — one of the few things he was quite good at cooking — when he came across the letter to the editor. It was the first one on the page, and given particular prominence.

Dear Sir,

I write in some distress, and as a life-long supporter of the Liberal Party and all that it has achieved for the people of this nation, and thus indirectly of the world. I have admired and endorsed the reforms it has initiated and passed into law.

However, I live in the constituency of South Lambeth, and have listened with growing alarm to the opinions of Mr. Aubrey Serracold, the Liberal candidate for that seat. He does not represent the old Liberal values of sane and enlightened reform, but rather a hysterical socialism which would sweep away all the great achievements of the past in a frenzy of ill-thought-out changes, possibly well-meaning, but inevitably benefiting the few, for a short while, at the expense of the many, and to the eventual destruction of our economy.

I urge all others who normally support the Liberal Party to pay the closest attention to what Mr. Serracold has to say, and consider, albeit with regret, whether they can indeed support him, and if they do, what path of ruin they may be setting us upon.

Social reform is the ideal of every honest man, but it must be done with wisdom and knowledge, and at the pace at which we can absorb it into the fabric of our society. If it is done hastily, to answer the emotional self-indulgence of a man who has no experience and, it would seem, little practical sense, then it will be to the cost and the misery of the vast majority of our people, who deserve better of us.

I write with the greatest sadness,
Roland Kingsley,
Major General, retired

Pitt let his tea go cold, staring at the printed sheet in front of him. This was the first open blow against Serracold, and it was hard and deep. It would damage him.

Was this the Inner Circle mobilizing, the beginning of the real battle?

CHAPTER
<u>THREE</u>

Pitt went out and bought five other newspapers and took them home to see if Major
General Kingsley had written to any more of
them in similar vein. Almost the same letter
was in three of them; there was only a variation of phrase here and there.

Pitt folded the papers closed and sat still
for several minutes wondering what weight
to attach to it. Who was Kingsley? Was he
a man whose opinion would influence
others? More importantly than that, was
his writing coincidence or the beginning of
a campaign?

He had reached no conclusion as to
whether there was a necessity for
learning more about Kingsley, when the
doorbell rang. He glanced up at the
kitchen clock and realized it was after
nine. Mrs. Brody must have forgotten her
keys. He stood up, resentful of the intrusion although he was grateful enough for
her work, and went to answer the increas-

ingly insistent jangle of the bell.

But it was not Mrs. Brody on the step, it was a young man in a brown suit, his hair slicked back and his face eager.

"Good morning, sir," he said crisply, standing to attention. "Sergeant Grenville, sir . . ."

"If Narraway wants to tell me about the letter in the *Times*, I've read it," Pitt said rather sharply. "And in the *Spectator*, the *Mail* and the *Illustrated London News*."

"No, sir," the man replied with a frown. "It's about the murder."

"What?" Pitt thought at first that he had misheard.

"The murder, sir," the man repeated. "In Southampton Row."

Pitt felt a stab of regret so sharp it was almost a physical pain, then a surge of hatred for Voisey and all the Inner Circle for driving him from Bow Street, where he had dealt with crimes he understood, however terrible, and for which he had the skill and the experience in almost all cases to find some resolution. It was his profession, and he was good at it. In Special Branch he was floundering, knowing what was coming and powerless to prevent it.

"You've made a mistake," he said flatly. "I don't deal with murders anymore. Go back and tell your commander that I can't help. Report to Superintendent Wetron at Bow Street."

The sergeant did not move. "Sorry sir, I didn't say it properly. It's Mr. Narraway as wants you to take over. They won't like it at Bow Street, but they just got to put up with it. Mr. Tellman's in charge in Southampton Row. Just made up recent, like. But I expect you know that, seeing as you was used to working with 'im all the time. Begging your pardon, sir, but it would be a good thing if you went there right away, seein' as they discovered the body about seven, an' it's coming up 'alf past nine now. We just got to 'ear of it, and Mr. Narraway sent me right over."

"Why?" It made no sense. "I've already got a case."

" 'E said this is part of it, sir." Grenville glanced over his shoulder. "I've got a cab waiting. If you'd just like to lock the door, sir, we'll be on our way." The manner in which he said it, his whole bearing, made it apparent he was not a sergeant suggesting something to a senior officer; he was a man who was very sure of his position passing on the order of a superior whose word could not be disobeyed. It was as if Narraway himself had spoken.

Slightly irked and unwilling to intrude on Tellman's first murder case as commander, Pitt did as he was bidden and followed Grenville to the hansom. They rode the short distance along Keppel Street, around Russell Square and a couple of hundred yards down Southampton Row.

"Who is the victim?" he asked as soon as they were moving.

"Maude Lamont," Grenville replied. "She's supposed to be a spirit medium, sir. One of them what says she gets in touch with the dead." His tone and the expressionless look on his face conveyed his opinion of such things, and the fact that he felt it inappropriate to put it into words.

"And why does Mr. Narraway think it has anything to do with my case?" Pitt asked.

Grenville stared straight ahead.

"Don't know that, sir. Mr. Narraway never tells nobody things as they don't need to know."

"Right, Sergeant Grenville, what can you tell me, other than that I am late, I am going to walk in on my erstwhile sergeant and take away his first case, and I have no idea what it's about?"

"I don't know either, sir," Grenville said, glancing sideways at Pitt and then forward again. "Except that Miss Lamont was a spiritualist, like I said, and 'er maid found 'er dead this morning, choked, it seems. Except the doctor says it wasn't an accident, so it looks like one of 'er clients from last night must 'ave done it. I suppose 'e needs you to find out which one, and maybe why."

"And you have no idea what that has to do with my present case?"

"I don't even know what your case is, sir."

Pitt said nothing, and a moment later they pulled up just beyond Cosmo Place. Pitt climbed out, closely followed by Grenville, who led the way to the front door of a very pleasant house which was obviously that of someone in most comfortable circumstances. A short flight of steps led to a carved front door, and there was deep white gravel along the frontage to either side.

A constable answered the bell and was about to turn them away until he looked beyond Grenville to Pitt. "You're back at Bow Street, sir?" he said with surprise, and what seemed to be pleasure.

Before Pitt could reply, Grenville stepped in. "Not for the moment, but Mr. Pitt is taking over this case. Orders from the 'ome Office," he said in a tone which cut off further discussion of the subject. "Where's Inspector Tellman?"

The constable looked puzzled and interested, but he knew how to read a hint. "In the parlor, sir, with the body. If you'll come wi' me." And without waiting for an answer he led them inside across a very comfortable hallway decorated in mock Chinese style, with lacquer side tables and a bamboo-and-silk screen, and into the parlor. This too was of Oriental style, with a red lacquer cabinet by the wall, a dark wooden table with carved abstract designs on it, a series of lines and rectangles. In the center of the room was a larger table, oval, and around it were seven chairs. Double French doors with elaborate curtains looked out into a walled garden filled with flowering shrubbery. A path curved away around the corner, presumably to the front of the house or to a side gate or a door to Cosmo Place.

Pitt's attention was drawn inevitably to the motionless body of a woman half reclined in one of the two upholstered chairs on either side of the fireplace. She seemed in her middle to late thirties, tall and with a fine, delicately curved figure. Her face had probably been handsome in life, with good bones, and framed by thick, dark hair. But at the moment it was disfigured by a terrible, gasping contortion. Her eyes were wide and staring, her complexion mottled and a strange white substance had bubbled out of her mouth and down over her chin.

Tellman, dour as always, his hair slicked back from his brow, was standing in the middle of the room. To his left was another man, older, thicker-set, with a strong, intelligent face. From the leather bag at his feet Pitt took him to be the police surgeon.

"Sorry, sir." Grenville produced his card and held it out to Tellman. "This is a Special Branch case. Mr. Pitt will be taking over. But to keep it discreet, like, it would be better if you were to remain 'ere to work with 'im." It was said as a statement, not a question.

Tellman stared at Pitt. He tried hard to mask his feelings, and the fact that he was taken by surprise, but his chagrin was clear in the rigidity of his body, his hands held tightly at his sides, the hesitation before he was able to master himself sufficiently to think what to say. There was no enmity in his eyes — at least Pitt thought not — but there was anger and disappointment. He had worked hard for his promotion, several

101

years of that work in Pitt's shadow. And now, faced with the very first murder of which he was in charge, with no explanation, Pitt was brought back and given command of it.

Pitt turned to Grenville. "If there's nothing else, Sergeant, you can leave us to get on with it. Inspector Tellman will have all the facts we know so far." Except why Narraway considered this anything whatever to do with Voisey. Pitt could not imagine anything less likely to interest Charles Voisey than spiritual séances. Surely his sister, Mrs. Cavendish, could not have been so credulous as to have attended such a gathering at so sensitive a time? And if she had, and had been compromised by her presence here, was that a good thing or bad?

He felt cold at the thought that Narraway expected him to use it to their advantage. The idea of becoming part of the crime, of using it to coerce, was repellent.

He introduced himself to the doctor, whose name was Snow, then turned to Tellman.

"What do you know so far?" he asked politely and as noncommittally as he could. He must not allow his own anger to reflect in his attitude now. None of this was Tellman's fault, and to antagonize him further would make it more difficult to succeed in the end.

"The maid, Lena Forrest, found her this morning. She's the only servant living in," Tellman replied, glancing around the room to indicate his surprise that in a house of this obvious material comfort there was no resident cook or manservant. "Made her mistress's morning tea and took it up to her room," he continued. "When she found no one there, and the bed not slept in, she was alarmed. She came down here to the last place she had seen her —"

"When was that?" Pitt interrupted.

"Before the start of last night's . . . doings." Tellman avoided the word *séance,* and his opinion of it all was evident in his very slightly curled lip. Otherwise his lantern-jawed face was carefully devoid of expression.

Pitt was surprised. "She didn't see her afterwards?"

"She says not. I pressed her about that. No last cup of tea, no going up, drawing a bath for her or helping her undress? But she says not." His voice allowed no argument. "It seems Miss Lamont liked to stay up as long as she wanted with certain . . .

clients . . . and they all preferred the privacy of no servants around, no one to bump into accidentally or interrupt when . . ." He tailed off, his lips pursed.

"So she came in here, and found her?" Pitt inclined his head towards the figure in the chair.

"That's right. About ten minutes after seven," Tellman responded.

Pitt was surprised. "Early for a lady to get up, isn't it? Especially one who didn't begin work until the evening and frequently stayed late with clients."

"I asked her that, too." Tellman glared. "She said Miss Lamont always got up early and took a nap in the afternoons." His expression suggested the pointlessness of trying to make sense of any of the habits of someone who thought she spoke to ghosts.

"Did she touch anything?"

"She says not, and I can't see any evidence that she did. She said that she could see straight away that Miss Lamont was dead. She wasn't breathing, she had this bluish look, and when the maid put a finger on her neck, it was quite cold."

Pitt turned enquiringly towards the doctor.

Snow pursed his lips. "Died sometime yesterday evening," he said, staring at Pitt with sharp, questioning eyes.

Pitt looked towards the body again, then took a step closer and peered at the face and the strange sticky mess spilling out of her mouth and down over the side of her chin. At first he had thought it vomit from some ingested poison; on closer examination there was a texture to it, a thickness that looked almost like a very fine gauze.

He straightened up and turned to the doctor. "Poison?" he said, his imagination racing. "What is it? Can you tell? Her face looks as if she's been strangled, or suffocated."

"Asphyxia." Snow inclined his head in a very slight nod. "I can't be sure until I get to my laboratory, but I think that's white of egg —"

"What?" Pitt was incredulous. "Why would she swallow white of egg? And what is the — the . . ."

"Some sort of muslin or cheesecloth." Snow's mouth twisted wryly as if he were on the brink of some deeper knowledge of human nature, and afraid of what he would find. "She choked on it. Inhaled it into her lungs. But it wasn't an accident." He moved past Pitt and pulled open the lace front of the bodice to the dead woman's gown. It came away in his hand where it had obviously been torn before in the need to examine her, and closed over again for decency's sake. On the flesh between the swell of her breasts was the beginning of a wide bruise, only just darkening when death had cut off the flow of blood.

Pitt met Snow's eyes. "Force to make her swallow it?"

Snow nodded. "I'd say a knee," he agreed. "Someone put that stuff down her throat and held her nose. You can see the very slight scratch of a fingernail on her cheek. They pinned her down with considerable weight until she couldn't help breathing in, and choking."

"Are you certain?" Pitt tried to rid his mind of the picture, the sense of the thick liquid gagging in her throat, the woman fighting for air.

"As certain as we can be," Snow answered. "Unless on autopsy I find something completely different. But she died of asphyxia. Can tell that from her expression, and from the tiny blood clots in her eyes." He did not show them and Pitt was glad. He had seen it before and was content to accept Snow's word. Instead he picked up one of the cold hands and turned it slightly, looking at the wrist. He found the slight bruises as he had expected. Someone had held her, perhaps only briefly, but with force.

"I see," he said softly. "You'd better tell me if it is egg white, but I'll assume it is. Why would anyone choose such a bizarre, unnecessary way of killing someone?"

"That's your job," Snow said dryly. "I can tell you what happened to her, but not why, or who did it."

Pitt turned to Tellman. "You said the maid found her?"

"Yes."

"Did she say anything else?"

"Not much, only that she did not see or hear anything after she left Miss Lamont when her clients were due. But then she says she took care not to. One of the reasons they liked Miss Lamont was the privacy she offered them . . . as well as her . . . whatever you call it?" He frowned, searching Pitt's face. "What is it?" He had steadfastly refused to call him "sir" right from the first difficult days when Pitt himself was newly promoted. Tellman had resented him because he considered him, as a gamekeeper's son, not to be suitable for command of a station. That was for gentlemen, or returned military or naval men, such as Cornwallis. "What do you call it — a skill, an act, a trick?"

"Probably all three," Pitt replied. Then he went on thinking aloud. "I suppose if it's for entertainment it's harmless enough. But how do you know if someone takes it seriously, whether you mean them to or not?"

"You don't!" Tellman snorted. "I like my conjuring to be strictly a deck of cards or rabbits out of a hat. That way nobody gets taken in."

"Do you know who yesterday evening's clients were, and if they came one at a time or all together?"

"The maid doesn't know," Tellman answered. "Or at least that's what she says, and I've no reason to disbelieve her."

"Where is she? Is she in a fit state to answer questions?"

"Oh yes," Tellman said with assurance. "A little shaken, of course, but seems like a sensible woman. I don't suppose she's realized yet what it will mean for her. But once we've searched the house completely, and maybe locked off this room, there's no reason why she can't stay here for a while, is there? Till she finds another position, anyway."

"No," Pitt agreed. "Better she does. We'll know where to find her if we have more to ask. I'll go and see her in the kitchen. Can't expect her to come in here." He glanced at the corpse as he crossed the room to the door. Tellman did not follow him. He would have his own men to send on errands, searches, perhaps questions of people in the neighborhood, although it was reasonable to suppose that the crime would have taken place after dark and the chances that anyone had observed anything of use were slight.

Pitt followed the passage towards the back of the house, past several other doors, to the one at the end which was open, with a pattern of sunlight on a scrubbed wooden floor. He stopped in the entrance. It was a well-kept kitchen, clean and warm. There was a kettle steaming very slightly on the black cooking stove. A tall woman, a little thin, stood at the sink with her sleeves rolled up above her elbows and her hands in soapy water. She was motionless, as if she had forgotten what she was there for.

"Miss Forrest?" Pitt asked.

She turned slowly. She seemed in her late forties; her brown hair, graying at the temples, was pinned back off her brow. Her face was unusual, with beautiful bones around her eyes and cheeks, her nose straight but not quite prominent enough, her mouth wide and well-shaped. She was not beautiful; in fact, in a way she was almost ugly.

"Yes. Are you another policeman?" She spoke with a very slight lisp, although it was not quite an impediment. Slowly she lifted her hands out of the water.

"Yes, I am," Pitt replied. "I'm sorry to ask you more questions when you must be distressed, but we cannot afford to wait for a better time." He felt a trifle foolish as he said it. She looked completely in control of herself, but he knew that shock affected people in different ways. Sometimes when it was very profound, there were no outward signs at all. "My name is Pitt. Would you sit down please, Miss Forrest."

Slowly she obeyed, automatically drying her hands on a towel left over a brass rail in front of the stove. She sat down on one of the hard-backed chairs near the table, and he sat on one of the others.

"What is it you want to know?" she asked, staring not at him but at some space over his right shoulder. The kitchen was orderly: there was clean, plain china stacked on the dresser, and a pile of ironed linen on one of the broad sills, no doubt waiting to be put away. More hung from the airing rail winched up near the ceiling.

The coke scuttle was full on the floor by the back door. The stove was polished black. Light winked softly over the sides of the copper pans hanging from the cross beam, and there was a faint aroma of spices. The only thing missing was any sight or smell of food. It was a house no longer with any purpose.

"Was Miss Lamont expecting her clients separately or together?" he asked.

"They came one at a time," she replied. "And left that way, for all I know. But they would all be together for the séance." Her voice was expressionless, as if she were trying to mask her feelings. Was that to protect herself, or her mistress, perhaps from ridicule?

"Did you see them?"

"No."

"So they could have come together?"

"Miss Lamont had me lift the crossbar on the side door to Cosmo Place, which she did for some people," she replied. "So I took it that one of the discreet ones came last night."

"People who don't want anyone else to recognize them, you mean?"

"Yes."

"Are there many like that?"

"Four or five."

"So you made arrangements for them to come in from Cosmo Place, instead of the front door on Southampton Row? Tell me exactly how that worked."

She looked up at him, meeting his eyes. "There's a door in the wall that leads into the Place. It has a lock on it, a big iron one, and they lock it behind them when they leave."

"What is the bar you spoke of?"

"That falls across on the inside. It means even with a key you can't get in. We keep it barred except when there is a special client coming."

"And she sees such clients alone?"

"No, usually with one or two others."

"Are there many like that?"

"I don't think so. Mostly she went to clients' houses, or parties. She only had special ones here once a week or so."

Pitt tried to picture it in his mind: a handful of nervous, excited people sitting in the half-light around a table, all filled with their own terrors and dreams, hoping to hear the voice of someone they had loved, transfigured by death, telling them . . . what? That they still existed? That they were happy? Some secrets of passion or money taken with them to the grave? Or perhaps some forgiveness needed for a wrong now beyond recall?

"So these people were special last night?" he said aloud.

"They must have been," she replied with a very slight movement of her shoulders.

"But you saw none of them?"

"No. As I said, they keep it very private. Anyway, yesterday was my evening off. I left the house just after they came."

"Where did you go?" he asked.

"To see a friend, a Mrs. Lightfoot, down in Newington, over the river."

"Her address?"

"Number 4 Lion Street, off the New Kent Road," she replied without hesitation.

"Thank you." He returned to the issue of the visitors. Someone would check her story, just as a matter of routine. "But Miss Lamont's visitors must have seen each other, so they were acquainted at least."

"I don't know," she answered. "The room was always dimly lit; I know how that works from setting up before they come. And putting the chairs right. They sat around the table. It's perfectly easy to stay in the shadows if you want to. I always set the candles at one end only, red candles, and leave the gas off. Unless you knew someone already, you wouldn't see who they were."

"And there was one of these discreet people last night?"

"I think so, otherwise she wouldn't have asked me to lift the bar on the gate."

"Was it back on this morning?"

Her eyes widened a little, grasping his meaning immediately. "I don't know. I never looked."

"I'll do it. But first tell me more about yesterday evening. Anything you can remember. For example, was Miss Lamont nervous, anxious about anything? Do you know if she has ever received threats or had to deal with a client who was angry or unhappy about the séances?"

"If she did, she didn't tell me," Lena replied. "But then she never talked about these things. She must've known hundreds of secrets about people." For a moment her expression changed. A profound emotion filled her and she struggled to hide it. It could have been fear or loss, or the horror of sudden and violent death. Or something else he could not even guess at. Did she believe in spirits, perhaps vengeful or disturbed ones?

"She treated it confidential," she said aloud, and her face was blank again, merely concerned to answer his questions.

He wondered how much she knew of her mistress's trade. She was resident in the house. Had she no curiosity at all?

"Do you clean the parlor where the séances are held?" he asked.

Her hand jerked a tiny fraction; it was not much more than the stiffening of muscles. "Yes. The daily woman does the rest, but Miss Lamont always had me do that."

"The thought of apparitions of the supernatural doesn't frighten you?"

A flash of contempt burned in her eyes, then vanished. When she answered her voice was soft again. "Leave such things alone, and they'll leave you."

"Did you believe in Miss Lamont's . . . gift?"

She hesitated, her face unreadable. Was it a habit of loyalty fighting with the truth?

"What can you tell me about it?" Suddenly that was urgent. The manner of Maude Lamont's death surely sprang from her art, real or sham. It was no chance killing by a burglar surprised in the act, or even the greed of a relative. It was acutely personal, driven by a passion of rage or envy, a will to destroy not only the woman but something of the skills she professed as well.

"I . . . I don't really know," Lena said awkwardly. "I'm a servant here. I wasn't part of her life. I knew there were people who really believed. There were more than the ones she had here. She once said that here was where she did her best work. The things at other people's houses was more like entertainment."

"So the people who came here last night were seeking some real contact with the dead, for some urgent, personal reason." It was more a statement than a question.

"I don't know, but that's the way she said it was." She was tense, her body straight-backed, away from the chair, her hands clenched on the table in front of her.

"Have you ever attended a séance, Miss Forrest?"

"No!" The answer was instant and vehement. There was harsh emotion in her. Then she looked down, away from him. Her voice dropped even lower. "Let the dead rest in peace."

With sudden, overwhelming pity he saw the tears fill her eyes and slide down her cheeks. She made no apology nor did her face move. It was as if for a few moments she were oblivious of him, locked in her own loss. Surely it was for someone dear to her, not for Maude Lamont, lying stiff and grotesque in the next room? He wanted someone who could comfort her, reach across the grief of unfamiliarity and touch her.

"Have you family, Miss Forrest? Someone we could notify for you?"

She shook her head. "I had only one sister, and Nell's long dead, God rest her," she answered, taking a deep breath and straightening up. She made an intense effort to control herself, and succeeded. "You'll be wanting to know who they were that came last night. I can't tell you 'cos I don't know, but she kept a book with all that sort of thing in it. It's in her desk, and no doubt it'll be locked, but she wears the key on a chain around her neck. Or if you don't want to get that, a knife'll break it, but that'd be a shame; it's a handsome piece, all inlaid and the like."

"I'll get the key." He stood up. "I'll need to talk to you again, Miss Forrest, but for the meanwhile, tell me where the desk is, and then perhaps make a cup of tea, for yourself at least. Maybe Inspector Tellman and his men would appreciate it, too."

"Yes sir." She hesitated. "Thank you."

"The desk?" he reminded her.

"Oh! Yes. It's in the small study, second door on the left." She gestured with her hand to indicate where it was.

He thanked her, then went back to the parlor, where the body was, and Tellman standing staring out of the window. The police surgeon had left, but there was a constable standing in the small garden, banked around by camellia and a long-legged yellow rose in full bloom.

"Was the garden door barred on the inside?" Pitt asked.

Tellman nodded. "And you can't get from the French doors to the street. It had to be one of them already in here," he said miserably. "Must have left through the front door, which closes itself. And the maid said she had no idea, when I first asked her."

"No, but she said Maude Lamont kept an engagement diary, and it's in the desk in the small study, and the key is around her neck." Pitt nodded towards the dead woman. "That might tell us quite a bit, even why they came here. Presumably she knew."

Tellman frowned. "Poor devils," he said savagely. "What kind of need draws someone to come to a woman like this and look for the kind of answers you should get from your church, or common sense? I mean . . . what do they ask?" He frowned,

118

making his long face look forbidding. " 'Where are you?' 'What is it like there?' She could tell them anything . . . and how would they know? It's wicked to take money to play on people's grief." He turned away. "And it's daft of them to give it."

It took Pitt a moment to adjust from one subject to the other, but he realized that Tellman was struggling with an inner anger and confusion, and had been trying to evade the conclusion that one of those he pitied, against his will, had to have killed the woman sitting silently in the chair only a few feet away, having put a knee in her chest as she struggled to breathe, choking on the strange substance clogging her throat. He was trying to imagine the fury that had driven the murderer to it. He was a single man, unused to women in other than a formal, police setting. He was waiting for Pitt to touch the body, reach for the key where he would be clumsy and embarrassed to look.

Pitt walked over and gently lifted up the lace front of the gown, and felt under the sides of the plunging fabric of the bodice. He found the fine gold chain and pulled it until he had the key in his fingers. He lifted the chain over her head carefully, trying not to disarrange her hair, which was absurd! What could it matter now? But only a few hours ago she had been alive, lit by intelligence and emotion. Then it would have been unthinkable to have touched her throat and her bosom in such a way.

He moved her hand out of his way, not that crushing it mattered. It was an automatic gesture. It was then that he noticed the long hair caught around the button on her sleeve, quite unlike the rich color of her own. She was dark, and this shone pale for a moment like a thread of spun glass. Then as he moved it became invisible again.

"What has this got to do with Special Branch?" Tellman demanded suddenly, his frustration hard in his voice.

"I have no idea," Pitt replied, straightening up and moving the dead woman's head back to the exact position it had been before.

Tellman stared at him. "Are you going to let me see it?" he challenged.

That was a decision he had not considered. Now he replied without thinking, stung by the absurdity of it. "Of course I am! I want a great deal more out of it than just the names of the people who were here last night. Short of a miracle, we'll need to learn all we can about this woman. Speak to the rest of her clients. Learn all you can. What sort of people came to her, and why? What do they pay her? Does it account for this house?" Automatically, he glanced around at the room with its elaborate wallpaper and intricately carved Oriental furniture. He knew enough to estimate the cost of at least some of it.

Tellman frowned. "How does she know what to tell those people?" he said, biting his lip. "What is it? A mixture of finding out first, then building on good guesses?"

"Probably. She might pick her clients very carefully, only those she already knows something about, or is certain she can research with success."

"I've looked all 'round the room." Tellman stared at the walls, the gas brackets, the tall lacquer cabinet. "I can't see how she did any tricks. What was she supposed to do? Make ghosts appear? Voices? People floating in the air? What? What made anyone believe it was spirits, not just someone telling them whatever they wanted to hear?"

"I don't know," Pitt replied. "Ask her other clients, but tread softly, Tellman. Don't mock another person's faith, however ridiculous you think it is. Most of us need more than the moment; we have dreams that won't come true here, and we need eternity." Without adding anything or waiting for any answer, he went out, leaving Tellman to go on searching the room for something without knowing what it was.

Pitt went to the small study and opened the door. The desk was immediately inside, a beautiful thing, as Lena Forrest had said, golden brown wood inlaid in exquisite marquetry of darker and lighter shades.

He slipped the key into the lock and turned it. It opened easily to form a flat writing surface inlaid with leather. There were two drawers and half a dozen or so pigeonholes. In one of the drawers he found an engagement book and opened it at the page for the previous day's date. He saw two names, both of which he recognized immediately, and with a coldness in the bottom of his stomach: Roland Kingsley and Rose Serracold. Now he understood precisely why Narraway had sent him.

He stood still, absorbing the information and all it could mean. Could it be Rose Serracold's long pale hair on the dead woman's cuff? He had no idea, and he had never seen her, but he would have to find out. Should he show the hair to Tellman or wait to see if he found it for himself, or if the surgeon found it when he removed the clothes for the autopsy? It might mean anything — or nothing.

It was several seconds before he realized that the third line contained not a name at all but a sort of design, like the small drawings the ancient Egyptians had used to signify a word, a name. He had heard them called cartouches. This one was a circle, with a semicircle inside it arched over the top of a figure like a small *F*, but backwards. It was very simple, and to him at least had no meaning whatsoever.

Why would someone be so secretive that even Maude Lamont herself did this odd drawing rather than write his or her name? There was nothing illegal in consulting a spirit medium. It was not even scandalous, or for that matter a subject of ridicule, except for those who had portrayed themselves as otherwise and were thus branded as hypocrites. People of every walk of life had indulged in it, some as serious investigations, others purely as entertainment. And there were always the lonely, the insecure, the grieving who needed the assurance that those they had loved still existed somewhere and cared about them even beyond the grave. Perhaps Christianity, at least as the church preached it now, no longer did that for them.

He riffled through the pages to see if there were any more cartouches, but he saw none, only the same one half a dozen times previously over the months of May and June. The person appeared to have come every ten days or so, irregularly.

Looking again, Pitt saw also that Roland Kingsley had been seven times before, and Rose Serracold ten times. Only three times had they all come to the same session. He looked at the other names and saw many of them repeated over the months, others were there once or twice, or perhaps for three or four weeks in a row, and then not again. Were they satisfied or disillusioned? Tellman would have to find them and ask, learn what it was that Maude Lamont gave them, what it had to do with the strange substance found in her mouth and throat.

Why had a sophisticated woman like Rose Serracold come here to seek for voices, apparitions — answers to what? Surely there was some connection between her presence and that of Roland Kingsley?

He felt rather than saw Tellman just beyond the doorway. He turned towards him.

The question was in Tellman's face.

Pitt passed him the book and saw him look down at it, then up again. "What does it mean?" Tellman asked, pointing to the cartouche.

"I've no idea," Pitt admitted. "Someone so desperate to remain unidentified that Maude Lamont would not write their name even in her own diary."

"Perhaps she didn't know it?" Tellman said. He took a deep breath. "Maybe that's why she was killed? She found out."

"And tried to blackmail him? Over what?"

"Whatever made him keep coming here a secret," Tellman replied. "Maybe he wasn't a client? Perhaps he was a lover? That could be worth killing over." His mouth twisted. "Maybe that's your Special Branch interest. He's some politician who can't afford to be found in an affair at election time." His eyes were challenging, angry to be included in the case against his will and yet told nothing, used but not informed.

Pitt had been waiting for the hurt to show. He felt the stab of it, yet it was almost a relief to have it open between them at last.

"Possibly, but I doubt it," he said bluntly. "At least not that I know. I haven't any idea why Special Branch is involved, but as far as I am aware, Mrs. Serracold is my only interest. And if she turns out to have killed Maude Lamont then I shall have to pursue her as I would anyone else."

Tellman relaxed a trifle, but he did his best to hide the fact from Pitt. He straightened his shoulders a little. "What are we trying to protect Mrs. Serracold from?" If he was aware of having used the plural to include himself he gave no sign of it.

"Political betrayal," Pitt replied. "Her husband is standing for Parliament. His opponent may use corrupt or illegal means to discredit him."

"You mean through his wife?" Tellman looked startled. "Is that what this is . . . a political ambush?"

"Probably not. I expect it has nothing to do with her, except chance."

Tellman did not believe him, and it showed in his face. Actually, Pitt did not really believe it himself. He had tasted Voisey's power too fully to credit any stroke in his favor to luck.

"What is she like, this Mrs. Serracold?" Tellman asked, a slight furrow between his brows.

"I've no idea," Pitt admitted. "I am only

just beginning to learn something about her husband, and more importantly, his opponent. Serracold is very well off, second son of an old family. He studied art and history at Cambridge, traveled considerably. He has great interest in reform and is a member of the Liberal Party, standing for the seat in South Lambeth."

Tellman's face mirrored all his emotions, although he would have been furious to know it. "He's privileged, rich, never worked a day in his life, and now thinks he'd like to get into government and tell the rest of us what to do and how to do it. Or more likely, what not to do," he retaliated.

Pitt did not bother to argue. From Tellman's point of view that was probably close enough to the truth. "More or less."

Tellman breathed out slowly; not having got the argument he had hoped for, he felt no sense of triumph. "What kind of a person comes to see a woman who says she speaks to ghosts?" he demanded. "Don't they know it's all rubbish?"

"People looking for something," Pitt replied. "Vulnerable, lonely, left behind in the past because the future is unbearable for them without whomever they loved. I don't know . . . people who can be used and exploited by those who think they have power, or know how to create a good illusion . . . or both."

Tellman's face was a mask of disgust, pity struggling inside him. "It ought to be illegal!" he said between stiff lips. "It's like a mixture of prostitution and the tricks of a fairground shark, but at least they don't use your griefs to get rich on!"

"We can't stop people believing whatever they want to, or need to," Pitt replied. "Or exploring whatever truth they like."

"Truth?" Tellman said derisively. "Why can't they just go to the chapel on Sundays?" But it was a question to which he did not expect an answer. He knew there was none; he had none himself. He chose not to ask questions where answers lay in the very private realms of belief. "Well, we've got to find out who did it!" he said sharply. "I suppose she's got a right not to be murdered, just like anyone else, even if maybe she looked into things she'd no business to. I wouldn't want my dead disturbed!" He looked away from Pitt.

"How do they do the tricks?" Tellman asked. "I searched that room from floor to ceiling and I didn't find anything, no levers or pedals or wires, anything. And the maid swears she had nothing to do with it . . .

but then I suppose she would!" Tellman paused. "How do you make people think you are rising up into the air, for heaven's sake? Or stretching out and getting longer and longer?"

Pitt chewed his lip. "More important to us, how do you know what they want to hear, so you can tell it to them?"

Tellman stared at him, wonder in his face, then slowly comprehension. "You find out about them," he breathed. "The maid told us that this morning. Said she was very choosy about her clients. You only accept those you can learn about. You pick someone you know, then you listen, you ask questions, you add up what you hear, maybe you have someone go through their pockets or their bags." He warmed to the subject and his eyes glittered with anger. "Maybe you have someone talk to their servants. Maybe you burgle their houses and read letters, papers, look at their clothes! Ask around the tradespeople, see what they spend, who they owe."

Pitt sighed. "And when you have enough about one or two, perhaps try a little carefully chosen blackmail," he added. "We might have a very ugly case here, Tellman, very ugly indeed."

A flicker of pity softened Tellman's

mouth and deliberately he pulled his lips tight to hide it. "Which of those three people did she push too far?" he said quietly. "And over what? I hope it isn't your Mrs. Serracold. . . ." He lifted his chin a trifle, as if his collar were too tight. "But if it is, I'm not looking the other way to please Special Branch!"

"It wouldn't make any difference if you did," Pitt replied. "Because I won't."

Very slowly Tellman relaxed. He nodded fractionally, and for the first time he smiled.

CHAPTER

<u>FOUR</u>

Isadora Underhill sat at the opulently laid out dinner table and toyed with her food, pushing it around her plate with practiced elegance, occasionally eating a mouthful. It was not that it was unpleasant, simply bland, and almost exactly what she had eaten the last time she had been here in this magnificent, mirrored chamber with its Louis Quinze sideboards and enormous gilded chandeliers. Indeed, as far as she could recall it was also the same people, as nearly as made no difference. At the head of the table was her husband, the Bishop. He looked slightly dyspeptic, she thought, a little puffy around the eyes, pale, as if he had slept badly and eaten too much. And yet she saw his plate was still largely untouched. Perhaps he was convinced he was unwell again, or more likely he was, as usual, too busy talking.

He and the archdeacon were extolling the virtues of some long-dead saint she had never heard of. How could anyone speak of true goodness, even holiness, the conquering of fear, and of excuses for the petty vanities and deceits of daily life, the generosity of spirit to forgive the offenses of spite and judgment, kindly laughter and the love of all things living, and yet still manage to make it sound so dull? It should have been wonderful!

"Did she ever laugh?" she said suddenly.

There was silence around the table. Everyone, all fifteen of them, turned and stared at her as if she had knocked over her wineglass or made a rude noise.

"Did she?" she repeated.

"She was a saint," the archdeacon's wife said patiently.

"How can you possibly manage to be a saint with no sense of humor?" Isadora asked.

"Sanctity is a very serious matter," the archdeacon tried to explain, staring at her earnestly. He was a large man with a very pink face. "She was a woman close to God."

"One cannot be close to God without loving one's fellow men," Isadora said stubbornly, her eyes wide. "And how could one possibly love other people without an acute sense of the absurd?"

The archdeacon blinked. "I don't

know what you mean."

She looked at his small brown eyes and careful mouth. "No," she agreed, quite sure that he knew very little. But then she was far from holy, by her own estimation. She could not imagine how anyone, even a saint, could love the archdeacon. She wondered, absently, what his wife really felt. Why had she married him? Had he been different then? Or was it a matter of convenience, or even desperation?

Poor woman.

Isadora looked at the Bishop. She tried to remember why she had married him and if they had both really been so different thirty years ago. She had wanted children, and it had not happened. He had been an honest young man with a good future ahead of him. He treated her with courtesy and respect. But what was it she had imagined she saw in him, his face, his hands that she should let him touch her, his speech that she was prepared to listen to him for the rest of her life? What were his dreams that she had wanted to share them?

If she had ever known, she had forgotten.

They were talking about politics now, rambling on and on, the strengths of this one, the weaknesses of that, how Home Rule for Ireland would be the beginning of the rot which would finally split the Empire, and with that stop the missionary effort to bring the light of Christian virtue to the rest of the world.

She looked around at them and wondered how many of the women were actually listening to the words. They were all dressed in full dinner gowns: puff-shouldered, tight-waisted, high-necked, as was the fashion. Surely at least some of them were staring at the white linen tablecloth, the plates, the cruet sets, the orderly bunches of glasshouse flowers, and seeing moonlight on breaking surf, tumultuous seas with white water racing in and curling under with a ceaseless roar, or the pale sands of some burning desert where horsemen moved black against the horizon, their robes billowing in the wind.

The plates were removed and a fresh course brought. She did not even look to see what it was.

How much of her life had she spent dreaming of somewhere else, even wishing she were there?

The Bishop had declined the course. He must have indigestion again, but it did not stop him from declaiming on the weaknesses, specifically the lack of religious faith, in the Liberal Party's parliamentary candidate for Lambeth South. It seemed the unfortunate man's wife met with his particular disfavor, although he admitted freely that so far as he was aware, he had never met her. But reports had it that she admired a most regrettable kind of person, some of those extraordinary Socialists who called themselves the Bloomsbury set, and had radical and absurd notions of reform.

"Isn't Sidney Webb one of that group?" the archdeacon enquired with a twitch of distaste.

"Indeed he is, if not the leading member," another man replied, hunching his shoulders a little. "He was the man who encouraged those wretched women to go on strike!"

"And the candidate for Lambeth South admires this?" the archdeacon's wife asked incredulously. "But it is the beginning of civil disorder and complete chaos! He is inviting disaster."

"Actually, I believe it was Mrs. Serracold who expressed the opinion," the Bishop corrected. "But of course were he a man of substance and judgment he would not have permitted it."

"Quite. Absolutely." The archdeacon nodded with vigor.

Listening to them, seeing their faces, Isadora warmed to Mrs. Serracold instinctively, although she had never met her, either. If she had had a vote, she would have cast it for the woman's husband, who apparently was standing for Lambeth South. It was no sillier reason than most men had for voting as they did. It was usually based upon whatever their fathers had done before them.

Now the Bishop was talking about the sanctity of women's role as protectors of the home, keepers of a special place of peace and innocence where the men who fought the world's battles could retreat to heal their souls and restore their minds, ready to rejoin the fray the following morning.

"You make us sound like a cross between a hot bath and a glass of warm milk," she said into a moment's silence while the archdeacon drew in his breath to answer.

The Bishop stared at her. "Excellently put, my dear," he said. "Both cleansing and refreshing, a balm to the inner man and to the outer."

How could he so misunderstand her? He had known her for more than a quarter of a century, and he thought she was agreeing with him! Did he not recognize sarcasm when he heard it? Or was he clever enough to turn it against her, disarm her by seeming to take it at face value?

She met his eyes across the table, almost hoping that he was mocking her. It would at least be a communication, an intelligence. But he was not. He looked back at her blankly, and turned to the archdeacon's wife and began wittering on about memories of his blessed mother, who, as Isadora remembered her, had been actually quite fun, and certainly not the characterless creature he was painting with his words.

But how many people she knew tended not to see their parents as the rest of the world did, but rather as stereotypes of mother and father as they held them to be, good or bad? Perhaps she had not known her own parents so very well?

The women at the table said very little. It would be considered rude for them to speak across the men's conversation, and they were not equipped to join in. They believed women to be good by nature — at least the best of them; the worst were at the very roots of damnation. There were not so many in between. But being good and knowing anything about goodness were not the same thing. It was for women to do it, and men to talk about it and, when necessary, to tell women how it should be done.

Since she was neither required nor permitted to contribute to the discussion, other than by a pleasant and interested expression, she allowed her mind to wander. Curious how many of her mental images involved faraway places, especially over the sea. She thought of the vast spaces of the ocean with a level horizon on every side, trying to imagine what it would feel like to have only a deck beneath your feet, constantly moving, the wind and sun on your face, to know that you must have in the tiny wholeness of that ship all that you needed to survive and to find your way across the trackless waste which could rise up in terrible storms to batter you, even to hold and crush you like a mighty hand. Or it could lie so still there was not enough breath across its face to fill your sails.

What lived beneath it? Beautiful things? Fearful things? Unimaginable things? And the only guidance was in the stars above, or of course the sun and a perfect clock, if you had the skill.

". . . really have to speak to someone

about it," a woman in tan and tobacco-brown lace was saying. "We look to you, Bishop."

"Of course, Mrs. Howarth." He nodded sagely, touching his napkin to his lips. "Of course."

Isadora averted her eyes. She did not want to be drawn into the conversation. Why didn't they talk about the ocean? It was the ideal analogy of how alone each person is on the voyage of life, how you have to carry within you everything you need, and only by the understanding of the heavens could you ever know in which direction to steer.

Captain Cornwallis would have understood. Then she blushed at how easily his name had come to her mind, and with what a lurch of pleasure. She felt as if she were transparent. Had anyone else seen her face? Of course she and Cornwallis had never spoken of such things, not directly, but she knew he felt it more completely than any speech. He could say so much in a sentence or two, whereas these men around her were drowning the evening in words, and saying almost nothing.

The Bishop was still talking, and she looked at his complacent, unlistening face, and realized with a horror that rippled right through her, like insects crawling, that she actually disliked him. How long had she felt like that? Since meeting John Cornwallis, or before?

What had her whole life been, spent in the daily presence — she could not say company — of a man she did not even truly like, much less love? A duty? A discipline of the spirit? A waste?

What would it have been like if she could only have met Cornwallis thirty-one years ago?

She might not have loved him then, or he her. They had both been such different people, the lessons of time and loneliness unlearned. Anyway, it was pointless to think of it. No past can ever be undone.

But she could not dismiss the future in the same way. What if she escaped this charade, just walked away? Would it be possible? Go to Cornwallis? Of course they had neither of them ever said as much — it would be unthinkable — but she knew he loved her, as she had slowly realized she loved him. He had the honesty, the courage, the simplicity of mind that was like clear water to her inner thirst. She had to search for his humor, wait for it, but it was there, and without unkindness. It hurt to think of him. It made this ridiculous evening, and her presence in it, even more painful. Had any of them even the remotest idea of where her imagination was? Her face flamed at the thought.

They were still talking about politics, the same subject of how dangerous the extreme Liberal ideas were, already they undermined the values of Christianity. They threatened sobriety, church attendance, the keeping of the Sabbath, the general obedience and respect appropriate, even the very sanctity of the home, safeguarded by the modesty of women.

What would she and Cornwallis have been talking about? Certainly not what other people ought to be doing, saying, or thinking! They would speak of wonderful places, ancient cities on the shores of other seas, cities like Istanbul, Athens, Alexandria, places of ancient legend and adventure. In her mind the sun shone on warm stones, the sky was blue, too bright to look at for more than a moment, and the air was warm. It would be enough even to talk about it with him; she would not ever have to go there, just listen and dream. Even to sit in silence knowing his thoughts were the same would be good enough.

What would happen if she left here and went to him? What would she lose? Her reputation, of course. The condemnation would be deafening! Men would be scandalized, and of course terrified their own wives might be given the idea and the example to do the same thing! Women would be even more furious, because they would envy her and hate her for it. Those who stayed at the call of duty, which would be almost all of them, would positively bristle with virtue.

She would never be able to speak to any of them again. They would cut her dead in the street. She would become invisible. Funny how a scarlet woman was not seen. You would think she would be the most highly visible of all! Isadora smiled at the thought, and saw a look of puzzlement in the face of the woman across the table from her. The conversation was hardly humorous!

Reality came back. It was only a daydream, a sweet and painful way of escaping a tedious evening. Even if she were wild enough to go to Cornwallis, he would never accept her offer. It would be utterly dishonorable to take another man's wife. Would he even be tempted? Perhaps not. He would be embarrassed by her, ashamed of her forwardness, or that she should even think that he might accept such an offer.

Would that hurt intolerably?

No. If he were a man who would have accepted, then she would not have wanted him.

The conversation babbled on around her, getting heated over some difference of theological opinion now.

But if Cornwallis would have accepted her, would she have gone? The answer hovered only a moment on her mind, undecided, then she was afraid that at this instant, hearing the suffocating pomposity around her at this stiff, unhappy table, yes . . . yes! She would have seized the chance and escaped!

But it would not happen. She knew that absolutely; it was more real than the lights of the chandeliers or the hard edge of the table under her hands. The voices ebbed and flowed around her. Nobody noticed that she had said nothing for a while, not even the polite murmuring of agreement.

Going to Cornwallis was a daydream she would never follow through, but suddenly it was intensely important that she know if he would have wished her to, were it possible; if in some way it could have been all right. Nothing else mattered quite as much. She needed to see him again, just to talk, about anything or nothing, but to

143

know that he still cared. He would not say so, he never had. Maybe she would never hear him say the words "I love you." She would have to make do with silence, awkwardness, the look in his eyes and the sudden color in his face.

Where could they meet that would cause no comment? It must be a place where both of them customarily went, so it would look to be chance. An exhibition of some sort, of paintings or artifacts. She had no idea what was showing at the moment. She had not until this moment felt like looking. The National Gallery always had something. She would write to Cornwallis, send him a message, casually worded, an invitation to see whatever it was. It would be simple enough to find out. She would do it in the morning, first thing. She could say something about its being interesting and wondering if he might find it enjoyable also. If it were seascapes no excuse would be needed; if something else, then it hardly mattered whether he believed her or not, what counted was if he came. It was immodest, the very thing the archdeacon had been railing against, but what was there to lose? What had she anyway but this empty game, words without communication, closeness without intimacy, passion, laughter or tenderness?

Her mind was made up. Suddenly she was hungry, and the crème caramel in front of her seemed hardly more than a couple of mouthfuls. She should not have ignored the preceding courses, but it was too late now.

Actually, the National Gallery was showing an exhibition of Hogarth's paintings — portraits, not his political cartoons and commentaries. In his lifetime, some hundred and odd years ago, he had been dismissed by the critics as a miserable colorist, but now his standing had risen considerably. It was something she could quite easily suggest was worth seeing to make one's own judgment, and either confirm the critics or confound them.

She wrote quickly, without giving herself time to become self-conscious and lose her courage.

Dear Captain Cornwallis,

I became aware this morning that the National Gallery has mounted an exhibition of the portraits painted by Hogarth which were much derided in his lifetime, but now have gained far

more favorable attention. It is remarkable how opinion can swing so wildly
upon a single talent. I should now like
to see them for myself and form my
own judgment.

Knowing your interest in art, and
your own ability, I thought you might
also find them thought-provoking.

I appreciate that you have little time
for such things, but in the hope that
duty might allow you half an hour or so
I thought to inform you. I have determined to take at least that long for myself, perhaps towards the end of this
afternoon when I am not required at
home. My curiosity is awakened. Is he
as bad as they first said, or as good as
they say now?

I hope I have not intruded upon your
time.

Sincerely,
Isadora Underhill

No matter how many times she went
over it, it would always be clumsier than
she wished.

She must post it before she read it
through again and felt too abashed to send
it.

A quick walk to the letterbox on the

corner, and it was irretrievable.

At four o'clock she dressed in her most flattering summer costume of old rose with falls of white lace over both sleeves as far as the elbow, and setting her hat on at a more rakish angle than usual, left her home.

It was only when her cab turned into Trafalgar Square that suddenly she felt she was being ridiculous. She leaned forward to tell the driver that she had changed her mind, then said nothing. If she did not now go and Cornwallis was there, he would feel it a deliberate rejection. She would have taken an irrevocable step she did not mean. She could never afterwards withdraw it. He was not a man to whom one could explain. He would simply not open himself up to such hurt again.

She sat back in the seat and waited until the cab stopped near the wide steps up to the immense pillars and the imposing front of the gallery. She alighted and paid her fare. Then she stood in the sun amid the pigeons and the sightseers, the flower sellers, the distant, impressive stone lions, the noise of traffic.

She must have let the boredom addle her wits last night! By writing to Cornwallis she had placed herself in a position where she had either to go back or forward; she could no longer remain where she was, lonely, uncommitted, dreaming but afraid. It was like standing at a gambling table and having cast the dice, waiting for them to stop rolling and decide her fate.

That was overstating it! She had simply written to a friend advising him of an interesting exhibition which she was going to see herself.

Then why were her legs trembling as she walked up the steps and across the stones to the entrance?

"Good afternoon," she said to the man at the door.

"Good afternoon, madam," he replied politely, touching his cap.

"Where is the Hogarth exhibition?" she asked.

"To the left, madam," he said, inclining his head towards a huge notice.

She blushed hotly and almost choked on the words as she thanked him. He must think her blind! How would anyone unable to see a notice a yard high be able to appreciate paintings?

She swept past him and into the first room. There were at least a dozen people in it. At a glance she saw two with whom she was acquainted. Should she speak to them and draw attention to herself? Or not, and perhaps be thought to snub them? That would cause comment, and certainly be repeated.

Before she could reach a decision, years of training overtook her and she spoke, then instantly thought she might have ruined her chance of speaking to Cornwallis other than meaninglessly, in passing. She could hardly say or hear anything she wanted to in company.

But it was too late, the acknowledgment was made. She asked after their health, commented on the weather, and prayed they would leave. She had not the slightest desire to discuss the pictures with them. In the end she lied, claiming to see in the next room some elderly lady she knew and urgently wished to speak with.

There were another dozen people there also, but not Cornwallis. Her heart sank. Why had she supposed he would come, as if he were at her beck and call, with nothing to do but go to art galleries on a whim? She had no doubt whatever that he had been attracted to her, but attraction was not love, not the profound and abiding emotion she felt!

The women were coming in from the previous room. She could not escape. A further half hour's desperate conversation ensued. What did it matter? The whole idea had been ridiculous. She wished more than anything on earth that she had never written to him. If only the post had swallowed her letter, lost it forever!

Then she saw him. He had come! His stance, the set of his shoulders, she would recognize anywhere. In a moment he would turn and see her, then she would have to go forward. Between now and that instant she must control the thumping of her heart, hope to heaven her face did not betray her, and think what to say that opened the way for him to speak, and yet was not too forward, too eager. That would make her look gauche, and it would repel him.

He turned, as if he felt her stare. She saw the pleasure light his face, and then his effort to cover it. For his ease, she forgot herself and went forward.

"Good afternoon, Captain Cornwallis. I am delighted you were able to spare the time to see this for yourself." She gestured delicately towards one of the largest paintings, that of six heads, all facing out of the canvas, looking over the left shoulder of the viewer. It was titled *Hogarth's Servants*. "I think they were mistaken," she said firmly. "Those are real people, and excellently drawn. Look at the anxiety of the one in the middle, poor man, and the calm of the woman on the left."

"The one at the top looks scarcely more than a child," he agreed, but the moment after he had glanced at the picture, his eyes were searching her face. "I'm glad we chanced to meet," he said, then hesitated, as if he had been too elaborately casual. "It . . . it has been a long time . . . at least it seems so. How are you?"

She could not possibly answer with the truth, and yet she longed to say "So lonely I escape into daydreams. I have discovered that my husband not only bores me, but I actually dislike him." Instead she said what she always did. "Very well, thank you. And you?" She looked away from the picture and at him.

There was a very slight color in his cheeks. "Oh, very well," he answered, then he too turned away. He took a step or two to the right and stopped in front of the next picture. It was another portrait, but this time a single person. "It must have been fashion," he said thoughtfully. "One critic mimicking what the others had said. How could anyone with an open mind consider this poor? The face lives. It is highly individual. What more does one wish of a portrait?"

"I don't know," she admitted. "Perhaps they wanted it to tell them something they already believed? Sometimes people wish to hear only what supports the position they would like to maintain." She thought of the Bishop as she said it, and the endless evenings when she had listened to men decrying ideas without looking at them. Maybe the ideas were bad, but then again, maybe not. Without consideration they would never know. "It is so much easier to blame," she said aloud.

He looked at her quickly, his eyes full of questions, but he did not ask her. Of course he didn't! That would be intrusive and improper.

She must not let the conversation die. She had come here to see him, to learn if his feelings were still the same. There was nothing to do . . . almost certainly! But she still needed to know if he longed for her as much as she did for him.

"There is so much in faces, don't you think?" she remarked as they approached another portrait. "Things that can never be said and yet are there if you search for them."

"Yes, indeed." He looked down at the

floor for a moment, then up again at the portrait. "When one has experienced something, one recognizes it in others. I . . . I remember a bosun I had once. Phillips, his name was. I couldn't abide the man." He hesitated, but did not look at her. "Then one early morning, we were off the Azores, terrible weather. Gales whipping up out of the west. Waves twenty, thirty feet high. Any sane man would be frightened, but there was a beauty in it as well. Troughs of the waves were dark still, but early light caught the spume on the tips. I saw the recognition of beauty in his face, just for an instant before he turned away. Can't even remember what he was going to do." His eyes were far away, but in a moment of realization in the past, the magic of understanding.

She smiled, sharing it with him, picturing it in his imagination. She liked to think of him on the deck of a ship. It seemed the right place for him, his element far more than a police desk. And yet she would never have met him were he still there. And if he returned to the sea she would be forever watching the weather, every time the wind blew, fearing for him; every time she heard of a ship in trouble, wondering if it were his.

He looked at her, catching her gaze and the warmth in it. "Sorry," he apologized quickly, blushing and turning away, his neck stiff. "Daydreaming."

"I do a lot of it," she said quickly.

"Do you?" He swiveled back to her, looking surprised. "Where do you go . . . I mean . . . I mean, where would you like to go?"

"Anywhere with you" would have been the truth. "Somewhere I haven't been before," she answered. "Perhaps the Mediterranean. What about Alexandria? Or Greece, somewhere?"

"I think you'd like it," he said softly. "The light is like nothing anywhere else, so brilliant, the sea so blue. And of course there are the Indies . . . West, I mean. As long as you don't go too far south, the danger of fevers is not high. Jamaica, or the Bahamas."

"Do you wish you were still at sea?" She was afraid of the answer. Perhaps that was where his heart really lay.

He looked at her, for a moment without discretion or guard in his face. "No." It was only one word, but the passion in his voice filled it with all she was waiting to hear.

She felt the color burn up inside her, the

relief dizzying. He had not changed. He had said nothing, just answered a simple question about travel, one word, but the meaning was like a huge wave buoying her up, lifting her as if into the air. She smiled back, allowing her other feelings to be unconcealed for an instant, then she turned back to the portrait. She said something meaningless, a remark about color or texture of paint. She was not listening to herself, and she knew he was not, either.

She put off going home for as long as possible. It would be the end of a dream, the return to the daily reality from which she had escaped, and the inevitable guilt because her heart was not where it ought to be, even if her body was.

Eventually, at nearly seven o'clock, she went in through the front door and as soon as she was inside, felt imprisoned in the grayness of it. That was ridiculous. It was really a very pleasant house, full of soft color and most agreeably furnished. The lack of light was inside her. She walked across the floor to the foot of the stairs and reached the bottom just as the Bishop's study door opened and he came out, his hair a little tousled as if he had run his hand through it. His face was pale, his eyes dark-ringed.

"Where have you been?" he demanded querulously. "Do you know what time it is?"

"Five minutes before seven," she replied, glancing at the long case clock against the farther wall.

"The question was rhetorical, Isadora!" he snapped. "I can read a dial as well as you can. And that does not answer where you have been."

"To see the exhibition of Hogarth's paintings at the National Gallery," she replied blandly.

He raised his eyebrows. "Until this hour?"

"I met some acquaintances and fell into conversation," she explained. That was true literally, if not in implication. She resented the fact that she had justified herself to him. She turned away to go up the stairs and remove her hat and change into an appropriate gown for supper.

"That is most unsuitable!" he said sharply. "He painted the sort of person you should have no interest in. *Rake's Progress*, indeed! Sometimes I think you have lost all sense of responsibility, Isadora. It is time you took your position a great deal more seriously."

"It was an exhibition of his portraits!"

she said tartly, turning back to look at him. "There was nothing unsuitable about them at all. There were several of domestic servants with very agreeable faces and dressed right up to the ears. They even had hats on!"

"There is no need to be flippant," he criticized. "And wearing a hat does not make one virtuous! As you should know!"

She was stunned. "Why on earth should I know that?"

"Because you are as aware as I am of the laxity and spiteful tongues of many of the women who attend church every Sunday," he replied. "With hats on!"

"This conversation is absurd," she said, exasperated. "What is the matter with you? Are you unwell?" She did not mean it in any literal way. He bordered on hypochondria and she no longer had patience with it. Then she realized the remarkable change in him. The little color he had bleached out of his skin.

"Do I look ill?" he demanded.

"Yes, certainly you do," she answered honestly. "What did you have for luncheon?"

His eyes widened as if a sudden thought had come to him, a bright and uplifting one. Then anger swept over him, color making his cheeks pink. "Grilled sole!" he snapped. "I prefer to dine alone this evening. I have a sermon to prepare." And without saying anything further, or even glancing up at her, he turned on his heel and went back to his study, closing the door with a sharp snap.

However, at dinnertime he changed his mind. Isadora did not particularly wish to eat, but the cook had prepared a meal and she felt it ungracious not to partake, so she was seated alone at the table when the Bishop appeared. She wondered whether to make any remark on his feeling better, and decided not to. He might construe it as sarcasm, or criticism — or worse, he might tell her, in far more detail than she wished to know, exactly how he was.

For the entire soup course they ate in silence. When the parlormaid brought in the salmon and vegetables the Bishop at last spoke.

"Things are looking dark. I don't expect you to understand politics, but new forces are gaining power and influence over certain parts of society, those easily enamored of new ideas, simply because they are new —" He stopped, apparently having forgotten his train of thought.

She waited, more out of courtesy than interest.

"I am afraid for the future," he said quietly, looking down at his plate.

She was used to pompous statements, so it startled her that she really believed him. She heard fear in his voice, not pious concern for mankind, but real sharp anxiety, the sort that wakens you in the night with sweat on your body and your heart knocking in your chest. What could he possibly know that would shock him out of his habitual complacency? Certitude that he was right was a way of life with him, a shield against all the arrows of doubt that afflict most people.

Could it be anything that mattered? She really did not want to know. It was probably some miserable issue of insult or quarrel within the church hierarchy, or more tragic, someone he cared for fallen from grace. She should have asked him, but tonight she had no patience to listen to some variation on old themes she had heard over and over, in one form or another, all her married life.

"You can only do your best," she said calmly. "I daresay when you tackle it a day at a time, it will not be so bad." She picked up her fork and began to eat again.

They both continued in silence for a while, then she looked up at him and saw panic in his eyes. He was staring at her as if he peered far beyond to something unendurable. His hand holding the fish fork was trembling and there were beads of sweat on his lip.

"Reginald, what has happened?" she said with alarm. In spite of herself she was concerned for him. It angered her. She did not want to have any involvement with his feelings at all, but she could not escape the fact that he was profoundly and mortally afraid of something. "Reginald?"

He gulped. "You are quite right," he said, licking his dry lips. "A day at a time." He looked down at his plate. "It's nothing. I should not have disturbed your dinner. Of course it's nothing. I am seeing" — he took a deep, shuddering breath — "much too far ahead. Trust the divine . . . divine . . ." He pushed himself back from the table and stood up. "I have had sufficient. Please excuse me."

She half rose herself. "Reginald . . ."

"Don't disturb yourself!" he snapped, walking away.

"But . . ."

He glared at her. "Don't make an issue of it! I am going to do some work, reading.

I need to study. I need to know . . . more."
And he closed the door with a bang,
leaving her alone in the dining room confused and just as angry as he was, but with
a growing feeling of unease.

The cottage on the edge of Dartmoor
was beautiful, exactly what Charlotte had
hoped for, but without Pitt it lacked its
heart, and for her its purpose. She had
found the Whitechapel affair very hard to
bear. More than Pitt himself, she had
burned at the injustice of it. She accepted
that it was pointless to fight, but it did not
ease the anger inside her. It had seemed in
Buckingham Palace as if, at a terrible price
for Great-aunt Vespasia, it was all going to
be all right for Pitt. Voisey was robbed of
his chance ever to be president of a Republic of Britain, and Pitt was back in
charge at Bow Street.

Now, inexplicably, it was all gone again.
The Inner Circle had not collapsed, as
they had hoped. In spite of the Queen, it
had had the power to remove Pitt again
and send him back to Special Branch,
where he was junior, unskilled in whatever
arts they required, and responsible to
Victor Narraway, who had no loyalty to
him and, it seemed, no sense of honor to

keep his promises regarding a holiday which had been more than earned.

But again, they were not in a position to fight, or even to complain. Pitt needed the job in Special Branch. It was almost as well paid as Bow Street had been, and they had no resources other than his salary. For the first time in her life, she was aware not just of having to be very careful with money, but of the real danger that they might cease to have any to be careful with.

So she held her peace, and pretended to the children and to Gracie that being here in this wild, sun- and wind-drenched countryside was what she wanted, and the fact that they were alone was only temporary. It was for the excitement and the adventure of it, not because Pitt felt they were safer out of London where Voisey did not know how to find them.

"I never seen so much air in all me life!" Gracie said in amazement as they walked up a long, steep incline to the top of the track and stared out across the vast panorama of the moors, stretching into the distance in hazy greens and sorrels, splashed with gold here and there, cloud-shadowed to people in the distance. "Are we the only ones wot's 'ere?" she said in awe. "Just now nobody else lives 'ere?"

"There are farmers," Charlotte answered, gazing around to the dark rise of the moor itself to the north, and the softer, more vivid slopes of the hills and valleys to the south. "And the villages are mostly on the lee sides of the slopes. Look . . . you can see smoke over there!" She pointed to a slim column of gray smoke so faint one had to peer to make it out.

" 'Ere!" Gracie shouted suddenly. "You look out, Your Lordship!"

Edward grinned at her, then hared over the grass with Daniel after him. They tumbled together in the green bracken and went rolling over and over in a tangle of arms and legs, the sound of laughter quick and happy.

"Boys!" Jemima said in disgust. Then suddenly she changed her mind and went running and jumping easily after them.

In spite of herself, Charlotte smiled. Even without Pitt it could be good here. The cottage was only half a mile from the center of the village, a pleasant walk. People seemed friendly and willing to be helpful. Away from the city the roads were narrow and winding; the views from the upstairs windows seemed to stretch forever. The silence at night was unfamiliar, and once they had blown the candles out, the darkness was total.

But they were safe, and even if that was not what seemed most important to her, it was to Pitt. He had felt the possibility of danger, and to bring the children here was the only way now in which she could help.

She heard a noise behind her and turned to see a pony and trap coming up the winding track just below them. There was a man driving it, face wind-burned, eyes narrowed against the brilliance of the light, as if searching for something. He saw them, and as he drew level he looked at her more closely.

"Arternoon," he said pleasantly enough. "You'll be the lady as 'as come to rent the Garths' cottage over yon." He nodded, but it was a statement that seemed to require an answer.

"Yes," Charlotte agreed.

"That's wot I told 'em," he said with satisfaction, picking up the reins again and urging the pony forward.

Charlotte looked at Gracie. Gracie took a step after the man, then stopped. "Mebbe it's just interest, like?" she said quietly. "There can't be much 'appens 'round 'ere."

"Yes, of course," Charlotte agreed. "All the same, don't let the children go out of

164

sight. And we'll lock the doors at night. Safer, even out here."

"Yeah . . . o' course," Gracie said firmly. "Don't want no wild animals wanderin' in . . . foxes and the like, or wotever. I dunno wot they 'ave 'ere." She stared into the distance. "I'nt it . . . beautiful! D'yer think mebbe I should keep a diary, or summink? I might never see anyfink like this again."

"That's a very good idea," Charlotte said instantly. "We all will. Children! Where are you?" She was absurdly relieved when she heard their answer and all three of them came chasing back over the tussocky grass. She must not allow herself to spoil their happiness with fears for which there was no reason.

CHAPTER FIVE

The day after the murder of Maude Lamont the newspapers gave it sufficient importance to place it on the front page, along with election news and foreign events. There was no question that it had been a crime rather than an accident or natural causes. The police presence confirmed as much, but there had been no statement issued beyond the fact that the housekeeper, Miss Lena Forrest, had summoned them. She had refused to speak, and Inspector Tellman had said only that the matter was being investigated.

Standing by the kitchen table, Pitt poured himself a second cup of tea and offered to do the same for Tellman, who was moving impatiently from one foot to the other. He declined.

"We've seen half a dozen of the other clients," he said, frowning. "They all swear by her. Say she was the most gifted medium they'd ever known. Whatever that means." He threw it out almost as a challenge, as if he wanted Pitt to explain it. He was deeply unhappy with the whole subject, and yet obviously whatever he had been told since Pitt had last seen him had disturbed the simple contempt he had had before.

"What did she tell them, and how?" Pitt asked.

Tellman glared at him. "Spirits coming out of her mouth," he said, waiting for the derision he was certain would follow. "Wavering and sort of . . . fuzzy, but they were quite sure it was the head and face of someone they knew."

"And where was Maude Lamont while this was going on?" Pitt asked.

"Sitting in her chair at the head of the table, or in a special sort of cabinet they had built, so her hands couldn't escape. She suggested that herself, for their belief."

"What did she charge for this?" He sipped his tea.

"One said two guineas, another said five," Tellman answered, biting his lip. "Thing is, if she's just saying it's entertainment, and they won't bring a charge against her, there wouldn't have been anything we could do anyway. Can't arrest a conjurer, and they paid willingly. I suppose it's a bit of comfort . . . isn't it?"

"It probably comes in the same category as patent medicines," Pitt thought aloud. "If you believe it will cure a nervous headache, or make you sleep better, maybe it will? And who's to say you have no right to try it?"

"Because it's nonsense!" Tellman responded with vehemence. "She's making a living out of people who don't know any better. She tells them what they want to hear. Anybody could do that!"

"Could they?" Pitt said quickly. "Send your men back to ask more carefully. We need to know if she was getting real information that wasn't public knowledge, and we can't account for how she heard it."

Tellman's eyes opened wide in disbelief and then a shadow of real alarm.

"If she's got an informant, I want to know about it!" Pitt snapped. "And I mean a flesh-and-blood one."

Tellman's face was comical with relief, then he blushed hot, dull red.

Pitt grinned. It was the first time he had found anything to laugh at since Cornwallis had told him he was back in Special Branch. "I assume you have already made enquiries about anyone seen in the street near Cosmo Place," he went on, "that evening, or any other, who might be our anonymous client?"

"Of course I have! That's what I have sergeants and constables for," Tellman said tartly. "You can't have forgotten that so soon! I'm coming with you to see this Major General Kingsley. I'm sure your judgment of him will be very perceptive, but I want to make my own as well." His jaw tightened. "And he's one of the only two witnesses we have who were there at the . . . séance." He invested the word with all the anger and frustration he felt in dealing with people who exercised their rights to make fools of themselves and involve him in the results. He did not want to be sorry for them, still less to understand, and the struggle to maintain his dispassion was clear in his face, and that he had already lost.

Pitt searched for fear or superstition, and saw not even a shadow. He put down his empty cup.

"What is it?" Tellman said sharply.

Pitt smiled at him, not in humor but in an affection which surprised him. "Nothing," he replied. "Let's go and speak to Kingsley, and ask him why he went to Miss Lamont, and what she was able to do for him, most especially on the night she died." He turned and walked along the passage to the front door, and allowing Tellman to pass him, closed it and locked it behind him.

"Morning, sir," the postman said cheerfully. "Lovely day again."

"Yes," Pitt agreed, not recognizing the man. "Good morning. Are you new on this street?"

"Yes, sir. Just two weeks," the postman replied. "Getting to know people, like. Met your missus a few days ago. Lovely lady." His eyes widened. " 'Aven't seen her since, though. Not poorly, I 'ope? Colds can be wicked to get rid of this time o' year, which don't seem fair, bein' so warm, an' all."

Pitt was about to reply that she was on holiday, but he realized with a sudden chill that the man could be anyone, or pass on gathered information anywhere!

"No, thank you," he responded briskly. "She is quite well. Good day."

"Good day, sir." And whistling through his teeth, the postman moved on.

"I'll get a cab," Tellman offered, looking up and down Keppel Street and seeing none available.

"Why not walk?" Pitt asked, dismissing the postman from his mind and swinging into a long, easy stride eastward towards

Russell Square. "It's not more than half a mile or so. Harrison Street, just the other side of the Foundling Hospital."

Tellman grunted and did a couple of double steps to catch up with him. Pitt smiled to himself. He knew Tellman was wondering exactly how he had discovered where Kingsley lived without the assistance of the police station, which he would know Pitt had not sought. He would be wondering if Special Branch already had an interest in Kingsley.

They walked in silence around Russell Square, across the traffic of Woburn Place, and along Berner Street towards Brunswick Square and the huge, old-fashioned mass of the hospital. They turned right, instinctively avoiding the children's burial ground. Pitt was touched by sadness, as he always was, and glanced sideways to see the same lowered eyes and twist of the lips in Tellman. He realized with a jolt that for all the years they had worked together, he knew very little of Tellman's past, except the anger at poverty which showed naked so often he almost took it for granted now, not even wondering what real pain lay behind it. Gracie probably knew more of the man within the rigid exterior than Pitt did. But then Gracie was a child of the same narrow alleys and the fight for survival. She would not need to be told anything. She might see it differently, but she understood.

Pitt had grown up the son of the gamekeeper on Sir Arthur Desmond's country estate. His parents were servants; his father had been accused and found guilty of poaching and deported, wrongly, Pitt believed. The passion of that conviction had never changed. But he had not been hungry for more than a day, nor walked in danger of attack, except by the boys his own age. A few bruises were his worst affliction, and the odd very sore backside from the head gardener, richly deserved.

In silence they passed the infants' burial place. There was too much to say, and nothing at all.

"He has a telephone," he said at last as they turned into Harrison Street.

"What?" Tellman had been lost in his own thoughts.

"Kingsley has a telephone," Pitt repeated.

"You called him?" Tellman was startled.

"No, I looked him up," Pitt explained.

Tellman blushed hotly. He had never thought of a private person's owning one, although he knew Pitt did. Perhaps one day he could afford it, and maybe even have to, but not yet. Promotion was still fresh and raw to him, uncomfortable as a new collar. It did not fit — most especially with Pitt dogging his footsteps every day, and taking his first case from him, it abraded the tender skin.

They continued side by side until they reached Kingsley's house and were admitted. They were shown through a rather dark, oak-paneled hall hung with pictures of battles on three of the walls. There was no time to look at the brass plates beneath them to see which ones they were. At a glance, most of them looked roughly Napoleonic. One appeared to be a burial. It had more emotion than the others, and better interest of light and shadow, a sense of tragedy in the huddled outline of the bodies. Perhaps it was Moore after Corunna.

The morning room was rigidly masculine also, greens and browns, lots of leather and bookcases with heavy, uniform volumes. On the farther wall hung a variety of African weapons, assegais and spears. They were dented and scarred with use. There was a fine but rather stylized bronze of a hussar on the central table. The horse was beautifully wrought.

When the butler had gone Tellman gazed around with interest, but no sense of comfort. The room belonged to a man of a social class and a discipline alien to him and representing all he had been brought up to resent. One experience in particular had forced him to see a retired army officer as human, vulnerable, even to be deeply admired, but he still regarded that as an exception. The man who owned this room and whose life was mirrored in the pictures and furnishings was eccentric to say the least, almost a contradiction in conceptions. How could anyone who had done that most hideously practical of things, leading men in war, have so lost his grasp on reality as to be consulting a woman who claimed she spoke to ghosts?

The door opened and a tall, rather gaunt man came in. His face had an ashen look, as if he were ill. His hair was clipped short and his mustache was little more than a dark smudge over his upper lip. He stood straight, but it was the habit of a lifetime which kept him so, not any inner vitality.

"Good morning, gentlemen. My butler tells me you are from the police. What may I do for you?" There was no surprise in his voice. Possibly he had read of Maude Lamont's death in the newspapers.

Pitt had already decided not to mention his connection with Special Branch. If he said nothing of it, Kingsley would assume he was with Tellman.

"Good morning, General Kingsley," he replied. "I am Superintendent Pitt, and this is my colleague Inspector Tellman. I am sorry to tell you that Miss Maude Lamont died two nights ago. She was found yesterday morning, in her home. Because of the circumstances, we are obliged to investigate the matter very thoroughly. I believe you were there at her last séance?"

Tellman stiffened at Pitt's bluntness.

Kingsley took in a deep breath. He looked distinctly shaken. He invited Pitt and Tellman to be seated, and then sank into one of the large leather chairs himself. He offered nothing, waiting for them to begin.

"Will you tell us what happened, sir, from the time of your arrival at Southampton Row?" Pitt asked.

Kingsley cleared his throat. It seemed to cost him an effort. Pitt thought it odd that a military man who must surely be accustomed to violent death should be so disturbed by murder. Was not war murder on a grand scale? Surely men went into battle with the express intention of killing as many of the enemy as possible? It could hardly be that this time the dead person was a woman. Women were all too often the victims of the violence, looting and destruction that went with war.

"I arrived at a few minutes after half past nine," Kingsley began. "We were due to begin at a quarter to ten."

"Were the arrangements long-standing?" Pitt interrupted.

"They were made the previous week," Kingsley answered. "It was my fourth visit."

"With the same three people?" Pitt said quickly.

Kingsley hesitated only a moment. "No. It was only the third with exactly the same."

"Who were they?"

This time there was no hesitation at all. "I don't know."

"But you were there together?"

"We were there at the same time," Kingsley corrected. "In no sense were we together, except that . . . that it helps to have the force of several personalities present." He added no explanation as to what he meant.

"Can you describe them?"

"If you know I was there, Superintendent, my name and where to find me, do you not also know the same of them?"

A flash of interest crossed Tellman's face. Pitt saw it in the corner of his vision. Kingsley was at last behaving like the leader of men he was supposed to be. Pitt wondered what shattering thing had happened to him that he had ever thought of turning to a spiritualist. It was painful and repellent intruding into the wounds of people's lives, but the motives of murder were too often hidden within terrible events in the past, and to understand the core of it he had to read it all. "I know the name of the woman," he replied to the question. "Not the third person. Miss Lamont designated him in her diary only by a little diagram, a cartouche."

Kingsley frowned slightly. "I have no idea why. I can't help you."

"Can you describe him to me . . . or her?"

"Not with any accuracy," Kingsley replied. "We did not go there as a social event. I had no desire to be more than civil to anyone else present. It was a man of average height, as far as I recall. He wore an outdoor coat in spite of the season, so I don't know his build. His hair seemed light rather than dark, possibly gray. He remained in the shadows towards the back of the room, and the lamps were red, so the light distorted. I imagine I might know him if we were to meet again, but I am not certain."

"Who was the first to arrive?" Tellman cut across.

"I was," Kingsley replied. "Then the woman."

"Can you describe the woman?" Pitt interrupted, thinking of the long, pale hair around Maude Lamont's sleeve button.

"I thought you knew who she was?" Kingsley retorted.

"I have a name," Pitt explained. "I would like your impression of her appearance also."

Kingsley resigned himself. "She was tall, taller than most women, very elegant, with pale blond hair dressed in a sort of . . ." He gave up.

Pitt felt a knot tighten almost to suffocation inside himself. "Thank you," he murmured. "Please continue."

"The other man was the last to come," Kingsley resumed obediently. "As far as I can recall, he was last on the other occasions as well. He came in through the garden doors, and left before we did."

"Who left last?" Pitt asked him.

"The woman," Kingsley said. "She was still there when I went." He looked unhappy, as if the answer gave him no satisfaction or sense of escape.

"The other man went out of the garden doors?" Tellman asked for confirmation.

"Yes."

"Did Miss Lamont go with him and lock the gate to Cosmo Place after him?"

"No, she remained with us."

"The maid?"

"She left shortly after we arrived. Went out of the kitchen door, I suppose. Saw her walk across the garden just about dusk. She was carrying a lantern, which she left outside the front door."

Pitt visualized the garden path from the back of the house on Southampton Row. It led only to the door in the wall and Cosmo Place. "She went out of the side door?" he said aloud.

"Yes," Kingsley agreed. "Probably why she took the lantern. Left it on the front step. Heard her footsteps on the gravel, and saw the light."

Tellman finished the meaning for him. "So either the woman killed Miss Lamont, or you or the other man came back through the side gate and killed her. Or someone we know nothing about came for a later meeting of some sort and Miss Lamont herself let them in through the front door. But that was unlikely, and according to the maid, Miss Lamont was usually tired after a séance and retired to her bed when her guests left. There was no one else in the diary. No one else has been seen or heard. What time did you leave, General Kingsley?"

"About quarter to midnight."

"Late to have a further client," Pitt remarked.

Kingsley rubbed his hand over his brow as if his head pained him. He looked weary and beaten. "I really have no idea what happened after I left," he said gently. "She seemed perfectly well then, and not in any state of anxiety or distress, certainly not as if she were afraid of anyone, or indeed expected anyone. She was tired, very tired. Calling upon the spirits of those gone before was always a very exhausting experience. It usually left her with barely the strength to wish us good-night and to see us to the door." He stopped, staring miserably into emptiness stretching ahead of him.

Tellman glanced at Pitt and away again. The depth of emotion in Kingsley, and the bizarre subject of the discussion, embarrassed him. It was plain in the rigidity of his body and the way his hands fidgeted on his lap.

"Can you describe the evening for us, please, General Kingsley?" Pitt prompted. "What happened after you arrived and were all assembled? Was there a conversation?"

"No. We . . . we were all there for our own reasons. I had no desire to share mine with others, and I believe they felt the same." Kingsley did not look at him as he said this, as if the matter were still private. "We sat around the table and waited while Miss Lamont concentrated upon . . . summoning the spirits." He spoke hesitantly. He must have been aware at least of Tellman's disbelief and a hovering between pity and contempt. He seemed almost to breathe it in the air.

Pitt was uncertain what he felt, not contempt so much as unease, a kind of oppression. He could not have said why, but he believed it was not right to be attempting to reach the spirits of the dead, whether it was possible or not.

"Where did you sit?" he said aloud.

"Miss Lamont at the head of the table in the tall-backed chair," he replied. "The woman opposite her, the man to her left with his back to the windows, I to her right. We held hands, naturally."

Tellman fidgeted slightly in his seat.

"Is that usual?" Pitt asked.

"Yes, to prevent suspicion of fraud. Some mediums will even sit inside a cabinet to be doubly restrained, and I believe Miss Lamont did that on occasion, but I have not seen her do it."

"Why not?" Tellman asked abruptly.

"There was no need," Kingsley replied with a swift, angry glance at him. "We were all believers. We would not have insulted her with such a . . . a piece of physical nonsense. We were seeking knowledge, a greater truth, not cheap sensations."

"I see," Pitt said quietly, without looking at Tellman. "Then what happened?"

"As far as I can recall, Miss Lamont went into a trance," Kingsley replied. "She seemed to rise in the air several inches above her chair, and after some moments she spoke in a totally different voice. I . . ." He looked down at the floor. "I believe it was her spirit guide speaking to us through her." The words were so quiet Pitt had to strain to hear them. "He wished to know what we had come to find out. He was a young Russian boy who had died in terrible cold . . . in the far north, up near the Arctic Circle."

This time Tellman made no movement at all.

"And what did any of you reply?" Pitt asked. He needed to know what Rose Serracold had attended for, but he was afraid that if Kingsley gave that answer first, and saw or sensed Tellman's response, he would then conceal his own reasons. And perhaps they, too, were relevant. After all, he had written the virulent political attack on Aubrey Serracold, albeit without knowing he was the husband of the woman who sat beside him at Maude Lamont's table. Or had he?

Kingsley was silent for a moment.

"General Kingsley?" Pitt pressed. "What did you wish to learn through Miss Lamont?"

With great difficulty Kingsley answered, still staring at the floor. "My son Robert served in Africa, in the Zulu Wars. He was killed in action there. I . . ." His voice cracked. "I wanted to assure myself that his death was . . . that his spirit was at rest. There have been . . . different accounts of the action. I needed to know." He did not look up at Pitt, as if he did not want to see what was in his face, or reveal the raw need inside him.

Pitt felt some acknowledgment at least

was required. "I see," he said softly. "And were you able to obtain such a thing?" He knew even as he asked that Kingsley had not. The fear in him was tangible in the room, and now too the grief was explained. In Maude Lamont's death he had lost his contact with the only world he believed could give him an answer. Surely he would not willingly have destroyed it?

"Not . . . yet," Kingsley replied, his words so swallowed in his throat Pitt was not sure for a moment if he had heard them at all. He was aware of Tellman beside him and his acute discomfort. Ordinary grief he was accustomed to, but this confounded and disturbed him. He was unsure of his own responses. He ought to feel ridicule and impatience, that was what all his experience of life had taught him. Looking for a moment at Tellman's face, it was compassion that Pitt saw.

"What did the woman want?" Pitt asked.

Kingsley was jerked out of his own thoughts. He glanced up, his eyes puzzled. "I'm not sure. She was very eager to contact her mother, but I was not certain why. It must have been a very private matter, because all her questions were too oblique for me to understand."

"And the answers?" Pitt found himself

tense, afraid of what Kingsley might tell him. Why was Rose Serracold risking the expense and possible ridicule at this extraordinarily sensitive time? Had she no perception at all of what it meant? Or was her search so important to her that all other things were subject to it? What could that possibly be?

"Her mother?" Pitt said aloud.

"Yes."

"And did Miss Lamont contact her?"

"Apparently."

"What did she ask to know?"

"Nothing specific." Kingsley looked puzzled as he recalled it. "Just general family information, other relatives who had . . . gone over. Her grandmother, her father. Were they well."

"When was that?" Pitt pressed. "The night of Miss Lamont's death? Before that? If you can remember exactly what was said it would be most helpful."

Kingsley frowned. "I find it very difficult to imagine that she would have hurt Miss Lamont," he said earnestly. "She seemed an eccentric woman, highly individual, but I saw no anger in her, no unkindness or ill feeling, rather . . ." He stopped.

Tellman leaned forward.

"Yes?" Pitt prompted.

"Fear," Kingsley said quietly, as if it were an emotion with which he had long intimacy. "But there is no point in your asking me of what, because I have no idea. She seemed concerned if her father were happy, if he were restored to health. It was an odd question, I thought, as if disability could be carried beyond the grave. But perhaps when one has loved somebody such concerns are understandable. Love does not always go by the rules of reason." Still he kept his eyes averted, as if it were his only privacy.

"And the other man, who was he seeking?" Pitt asked.

"I don't recall anyone in particular." Kingsley frowned as he said it, as if realizing only now how it puzzled him.

"But he came at least three times that you know of?" Pitt insisted.

"Yes. He was deeply in earnest," Kingsley assured him, looking up now, no more emotion to guard. The man had stirred nothing in him, no specific compassion. "He asked some very telling questions and would not rest until they were answered," he explained. "I did ask Miss Lamont on one occasion if she thought he were a skeptic, a doubter, but she appeared to know his reasons and was quite undisturbed by them. I . . . I find that . . ." He stopped.

"Odd?" Tellman supplied.

"I was going to say 'comforting,'" Kingsley answered.

He did not explain himself, but Pitt understood. Maude Lamont must have been very confident in her skill, whatever its nature, to be unthreatened by the presence of a skeptic at her séances. But then she had apparently not been aware of the hatred which had ended in her death.

"This man did not ask to contact anyone by name?" he persisted.

"Several," Kingsley contradicted him. "But none with particular eagerness. It seemed almost as if he were picking names at random."

"Any subject that he sought?" Pitt would not give up so easily.

"None that I was aware."

Pitt looked at him gravely. "We don't know who he is, General Kingsley. He may be the one who murdered Maude Lamont." He saw Kingsley wince and the lost look return to his eyes. "What did you gather from his voice, his manner, anything at all? His clothes, his deportment! Was he a well-educated man? What were his beliefs in anything, or his opinions? What would you guess his background to be, his income, his place in society? If he has an occupation, what is it? Did he ever mention any family, wife, or where he lives? Did he come far to attend the séances? Anything at all?"

Again, Kingsley waited for so long in thought that Pitt was afraid he was not going to reply. Then he began to speak slowly. "His accent suggested an excellent education. The little he said inclined more towards the humanities than any science. His clothes, so much as I could see them or thought to look, were discreet, dark. His manner was nervous, but I attributed that to the occasion. I cannot remember any specific opinions, but I had the feeling that he was more conservative than I."

Pitt thought of the newspaper article. "Are you not conservative, General Kingsley?"

"No, sir." Now Kingsley looked up directly at Pitt, meeting his eyes. "I have served in the army with all manner of men, and I would dearly like to see a fairer treatment of the ranks than exists at the present moment. I think when one has faced hardship and even death side by side with a man, one sees the worth of him far more clearly than his worldly opportunities may make apparent."

From the candor in his face disbelief was impossible. And yet what he said was deeply at odds with what he had written to four separate newspapers. Pitt was more convinced than ever that Kingsley was involved with Voisey and the election, but whether willingly or not he had no idea. Nor did he know if with sufficient pressure he might have contributed to Maude Lamont's death.

He considered mentioning the articles against Serracold, and telling him that the woman at the séances was Serracold's wife. But he could think of nothing to gain by it now, and once told he could never achieve that possible advantage of surprise.

So he thanked Kingsley and rose to take his leave with Tellman behind him, morose and unsatisfied.

"What do you make of that?" Tellman demanded as soon as they were out on the footpath in the sun. "What makes a man like that go to a . . . a . . ." He shook his head. "I don't know how she did it, but it's got to be a trick. How does anybody with education not see through it in moments? If the leaders of our army believe in that sort of . . . of fairy tale . . ."

"Education doesn't stop loneliness or grief," Pitt replied. There was still a certain innocence in Tellman, in spite of the harsh realism of so many of his views. It irritated Pitt, and yet perversely he liked Tellman the better for it. He was not unwilling to learn. "We all find our own way of easing those wounds," he went on. "We do what we can."

"If I lost someone and tried that way of comforting myself," Tellman said thoughtfully, glancing down at the pavement, "and if I found someone had tricked me, I can't say I wouldn't lose my head and try to choke them. If . . . if someone thought that white stuff was part of a ghost, or whatever it's supposed to be, and they pushed it back into her mouth, is that murder, or would it be accident?"

Pitt smiled in spite of himself. "If that had happened, there were three of them there and at least two of them would have called a doctor, or the police. If all three of them were party to it, then it would be a conspiracy, intended or not."

Tellman grunted and kicked at a small stone in front of him, sending it into the gutter. "I suppose we're going to see Mrs. Serracold now?"

"Yes, if she's in. If not, we'll wait for her."

"I suppose you want to conduct that interview yourself, too?"

"No, but I will. Her husband is standing for Parliament."

"Are the Irish bombers after him?" There was a touch of sarcasm in Tellman's voice, but it was still a question.

"Not so far as I know," Pitt said dryly. "I should doubt it; he's for Home Rule."

Tellman grunted again, and muttered something under his breath.

Pitt did not bother to ask him what it was.

They had to wait nearly an hour for Rose Serracold to come in. They were left in a deep red morning room with a crystal bowl of pink roses on the table in the center. Pitt smiled to himself as he saw Tellman wince. It was an unusual room, almost overpowering at first, with its lush, delicate paintings on the walls and its simple white fireplace. But as he was in the room over a space of time he found it increasingly pleasing. He looked at the scrapbooks set out on the low table. They were beautifully made, put there to while away the time of callers. The first was of botanical specimens, and beside each in neat, rather eccentric handwriting was a short history of the plant, its native habitat, when it was introduced into Britain and by whom, and the meaning of its name. Fond of his own garden, when he had the time, Pitt found it totally absorbing. His imagination was fired by the extraordinary courage of the men who had scaled mountains in India and Nepal, China and Tibet, in search of yet one more perfect bloom, and lovingly brought them back to England.

Tellman paced the floor. He dipped into the other scrapbook, of watercolors of various seaside towns in Britain; very pretty but less interesting to him. Perhaps if it had included the hamlet in Dartmoor where Gracie and Charlotte were staying it would have been a different matter. But Pitt had not told him the name of it anyway. He let his mind wander, trying to picture what they might be doing now, as he was standing here in this alien room. Would Gracie be having to work much, or would she be free to enjoy herself, walk over the hills in the sun? In his mind's eye he saw her, small, very straight, her hair pulled back from her sharp, bright little face, gazing at everything with interest. She would never have seen such a place before, a hundred miles from the narrow city streets in which she had grown up, crowded, noisy, smelling of old cooking, drains, wood rot, smoke. He imagined the countryside around the hamlet would be wide open, almost like a nakedness of the land.

Come to think of it, he had never been in a place like that himself, except in dreams, and while looking at pictures like this.

Would she even think of him while she was there? Probably not . . . or not often. He was still not certain what she felt about him. During the Whitechapel affair it had seemed as if at last she had softened. They still disagreed about a hundred things, important things like justice and society and what it was appropriate for a man or a woman to do. All his teaching and his experience said she was wrong, but he could not put into words any specific instance of precisely in what way. He certainly could not explain it to her. She just looked at him with that withering, impatient air, as if he were an obstreperous child, and went on with whatever she was doing, cooking or ironing, immensely practical — as if women kept the world going while men just argued about it.

Should he write to her while she was away?

That was a difficult question. Charlotte

had taught her to read, but only fairly recently. Might the necessity of replying be an embarrassment to her? Worse, if there were something she could not read, might she show his letter to Charlotte? The thought made him cringe with embarrassment. No! Definitely he would not write. Better not to take the risk. And perhaps better not to have her address written anywhere — just in case.

He still had the scrapbook open when Rose Serracold came in at last and both he and Pitt stood to attention. Tellman did not know what kind of a person he had been expecting, but not the striking woman who stood in the doorway dressed in lilac and navy stripes with huge sleeves and a tiny waist. Her ash-fair hair was dressed in an unusually straight style, swirled around on her head rather than piled in curls, her azure-blue eyes very pale, staring at them both in surprise.

"Good morning, Mrs. Serracold," Pitt said after the first moment's silence. "I am sorry to intrude upon you without notice, but the tragic circumstances of Miss Maude Lamont's death didn't allow me the time to seek an appointment. I realize you must be very busy during the parliamentary election, but this will not wait."

There was a steel in his tone which cut off argument.

She stood strangely motionless, not even turning to notice Tellman, although she could not have been unaware of him only a few feet from her. She stared at Pitt. It was impossible to tell if she had already known of Maude Lamont's death. When she spoke at last it was very softly.

"Indeed. And exactly what is it you think I can say that will help, Mr. . . . . Pitt?" She was obviously remembering his name from what the butler had told her, but with an effort. It was not intended as rudeness, simply that he was not part of her world.

"You were one of the last people to see her alive, Mrs. Serracold," Pitt replied. "And you also saw the others who were present at the séance, and must know what took place."

If she wondered how Pitt was aware of that, she did not say so.

Tellman was curious to see how Pitt was going to speak to this woman to draw everything of use from her. They had not discussed it and he knew it was because Pitt was uncertain himself. She was part of his new role in Special Branch. Her husband was standing for Parliament. Pitt would not share with Tellman exactly what his task was, but Tellman guessed it was to keep her out of scandal, or if that proved to be impossible, then to deal with it discreetly, and perhaps rapidly. He did not envy him. Solving a murder was simple by comparison.

She raised elegant eyebrows very slightly. "I don't know how she died, Mr. Pitt, or if anyone was responsible, or could have acted to prevent it." Her voice was perfectly level but she was very pale and so still that the mastery of emotion in her could be judged simply by the absence of any sign. She dared not allow it to be seen.

Tellman was aware of a very slight air of perfume from her, and that were she to move he would hear the rustle of silks, as he had when she came in. She was a kind of woman who alarmed and disturbed him. He was acutely conscious of her presence, and he understood nothing of her life at all, her feelings or her beliefs.

"Someone was responsible." Pitt's voice cut across his thoughts.

She made no gesture to indicate that they should be seated.

"She was murdered," Pitt finished.

She took a very long, slow breath and let it out in a barely audible sigh. "Did someone break in?" She hesitated a second.

"Perhaps she forgot to lock the side door to Cosmo Place? The last person to arrive came in that way, not through the front door."

"She was not robbed," Pitt replied. "No one had broken anything." He was watching her intently. His eyes never moved from hers. "And the manner in which she was killed seemed to be peculiarly personal."

She brushed past him and sank into one of the dark red chairs, her skirts billowing around her in a soft swish of silk on silk. She was so white Tellman thought that she had at last realized the meaning of what Pitt had told her.

Did it startle her? Or was it that she already knew, and this was remembrance, and the moment of grasping the fact that others knew also, specifically the police?

Or could it be that the knowledge that it had been personal betrayed to her who was responsible?

"I don't think I wish to know about it, Mr. Pitt," she said quickly. She seemed to be completely in command of herself again. "I can tell you only what I observed. It appeared to me a perfectly ordinary evening. There were no quarrels, no ill feeling of any kind that I saw, and I believe I would have seen it had it been there. In spite of what you say, I can't believe it was one of us. It was certainly not I . . ." Now her voice cracked a little. "I . . . I was most indebted to her skill. And I . . . liked her." She seemed about to add something, then changed her mind and stared at Pitt, waiting for him to continue.

He did not wait any longer to be invited, but sat down opposite her, leaving Tellman free to do the same. "Can you describe the evening for me, Mrs. Serracold?"

"I suppose so. I arrived a short while before ten. The soldier was already in the room. I know nothing about him, you understand, but he is most concerned about battles. All his questions are about Africa and war, so I assume he is a soldier, or was." Her face registered momentary pity. "I formed the opinion that he had lost someone he loved."

"And the third person?" Pitt prompted.

"Oh." She shrugged. "The grave robber? He came last."

Pitt looked startled. "I beg your pardon?"

She pulled a little face, an expression of dislike. "I call him that in my mind because I think he is a skeptic, trying to take from us the belief in a resurrection of the spirit. His questions were . . . academic, in a cruel way, as if he were probing a wound. . . ." She searched Pitt's eyes, trying to gauge with what exactness he understood, if he were capable of grasping at least an idea of what she was describing, or if she were laying herself open to unnecessary embarrassment.

Tellman felt a sudden stab of knowledge, as if he saw her in an ordinary dress such as his mother or Gracie would wear, the rustling silks obscured by a clearer sight. She needed to believe in Maude Lamont's powers. There was something she was seeking that had driven her there, compelled her, and now that Maude was dead, she was lost. Behind those bright, pale eyes there was desperation.

Then she spoke again, and shattered the moment. He heard her perfect diction and the brittleness of it, and they were a world apart once more.

"Or perhaps it was my imagination," she said with a smile. "I really hardly saw his face. He might have been afraid of the truth, mightn't he?" Her lips curved as if it were only the inappropriateness of the situation which kept her from actually laughing. "He came and went through the garden door. Perhaps he is a highly important personage who committed a terrible crime and wants to know if the dead will betray him?" Her voice lifted at the fancy. "There's an idea for you, Mr. Pitt." She looked at Pitt steadily, ignoring Tellman, her face calm, vivid, almost challenging.

"It had occurred to me, Mrs. Serracold," Pitt replied, his own face expressionless. "But I am interested that it also came to your mind. Was Maude Lamont a person who was likely to have used such knowledge?"

Her eyelids flickered. The muscles in her throat and jaw tightened.

Pitt waited.

"Used it?" Her voice was a little rough. "Do you mean some sort of . . . of blackmail?" There was surprise in her face, perhaps a little too much.

Pitt smiled very slightly, still polite, as if he thought far more than he could say. "She was murdered, Mrs. Serracold. She had made at least one desperate and very personal enemy."

The blood drained out of her skin. Tellman thought she might even faint. He knew with absolute certainty now that she was the one Pitt was concerned with. It was her presence at the séance which had brought Special Branch into the case and taken it from the police, from him. Did Pitt have some secret reason for believing her guilty? Tellman looked at him, but in spite of all the time they had worked together, the passion and the tragedies they had been involved with, he could not read Pitt's emotions now.

Rose moved her position in the chair. In the silence of the room, even a faint creak of whalebone and taut fabric in her bodice was audible.

"I appreciate that it is terrible, Mr. Pitt," she said quietly. "But I cannot think of anything which will help you. I was aware that one of the men cared intensely about his son and needed to know something of the manner of his death, which occurred in a battle somewhere in Africa." She swallowed, lifting her chin a trifle as if her throat were constricted, although her gown was not high. "The other man I cannot say, except that he gave the impression that he had come to mock or disprove. I don't know why such people bother!" Her delicate eyebrows rose. "If you disbelieve, why not simply leave it alone and allow those who care to pursue knowledge do so in peace? It is surely a decency, a compassion one should allow. Only a complete boor would disturb someone else's religious

201

rites. It is an unnecessary intrusion, a piece of gratuitous cruelty."

"Can you describe what in his manner, or his words, gave you that impression?" Pitt asked, leaning forward a little. "As much as you can remember please, Mrs. Serracold."

She sat without answering for several moments, as if clarifying it in her mind before beginning. "I have a feeling he was trying to catch her in a trick," she said at last. "He moved his head from side to side, always watching just on the edge of his vision, as if not to miss anything. He would not allow his attention to be directed." She smiled. "But there was never anything. I could feel his emotion, but I don't know what it was. I only looked at him now and then because I was naturally far more concerned with Miss Lamont."

"What was there to watch?" Pitt asked, his face perfectly serious.

She seemed uncertain how to reply, or perhaps whether to trust him. "Her hands," she said slowly. "When the spirits spoke through her, she would look quite different. Sometimes she seemed to change shape, her features, her hair. There was a light in her face." Her expression dared him to mock. There was irony in her, as if she would rob his charge of its power by making it first herself. Yet her body was rigid and her hands, on the edge of the chair, were white-knuckled. "A glowing breath came from her mouth, and her voice was utterly unlike her own."

He felt an odd sensation well up inside him, a mixture of fear, almost a desire to believe, and at the same time an impulse to laugh. It was terribly human and vulnerable, so transparent, and yet so easy to understand.

"What did he ask her, as clearly as you can remember?" he said.

"To describe the afterlife, to tell us what there was to see, to do, how it looked and felt," she replied. "He asked if certain people were there and what they were like now. If . . . if his Aunt Georgina were there or not, but I felt as if it were a question intended as a trick. I thought perhaps he didn't even have such an aunt."

"And what was the answer?"

She smiled. "No."

"How did he react?"

"That was the odd thing." She shrugged. "I think he was pleased. It was after that he asked all the questions as to what it was like, what people did, especially if there were any kind of penance."

Pitt was puzzled.

"What were the answers?"

There was a flash of humor in her eyes. "That he was asking things that it was not yet his time to know. That is what I would have answered him had I been the spirit!"

"You disliked him?" he asked. She was sharp in her observation, critical, opinionated, and yet there was a vitality in her that was extraordinarily attractive and her humor appealed to him.

"Frankly, yes." She looked down at the rich silk of her skirt. "He was a frightened man. But we are all frightened of something, if you have any imagination at all, or anything you care about." She raised her eyes and met his. "That does not give you a reason or an excuse to mock the needs of others." A shadow crossed her eyes, as if instantly she had regretted being too candid with him. She stood up and in a graceful movement turned away, keeping her back half towards Pitt and completely towards Tellman. It obliged them both to stand also.

"Unfortunately, I cannot tell you who he was or where to find him," she said quietly. "I regret very much now that I ever went there. It seemed harmless at the time, an exploration of knowledge, a little daring. I believe passionately in freedom of the mind, Mr. Pitt. I despise censorship, the curtailment of learning . . . for anyone at all!" Her voice had a completely different tone; there was no banter in it now, no guard. "I would have absolute freedom of religion built into the law, if I could. We have to behave in a civilized fashion, respect each other's safety — and property, too, I suppose. But no one should set bounds to the mind, above all to the spirit!" She swiveled around, staring at Pitt with color back in her face at last, her chin high and her marvelous eyes blazing.

"And was this third man trying to do that, Mrs. Serracold?" Pitt asked.

"Don't be naive!" she said tartly. "We spend half the energy in our lives trying to dictate what other people will think! That is mostly what the church is about. Don't you listen?"

Pitt smiled. "Are you trying to destroy my belief in it, Mrs. Serracold?" he enquired innocently.

The color glowed up her cheeks.

"I'm sorry," he apologized. "It is just that one person's freedom so easily tramples upon another's. Why did you go to Miss Lamont? Whom did you wish to contact?"

"Why is it your business, Mr. Pitt?" She gestured for him to sit down again.

"Because she was murdered either while you were there or shortly after you left," he answered, relaxing back into the chair and seeing Tellman do the same.

Her body stiffened. "I have no idea who was responsible for that," she said almost under her breath. "Except that it was not I."

"I have been told that you wanted to contact your mother. Is that not true?"

"Who told you?" she demanded. "The soldier?"

"Why should he not? You told me he wished to contact his son, to learn how he died."

"Yes," she conceded.

"What was it you wished to learn from your mother?"

"Nothing!" she said instantly. "I simply wanted to speak with her. Surely that is natural enough?"

Tellman did not believe her, and he knew by the way Pitt's hands stayed motionless and stiff on his knees that he did not, either. But he did not challenge her.

"Yes, of course it is," Pitt agreed. "Have you visited other spirit mediums?"

She waited so long that her hesitation

was obvious, and she gave a slight gesture of capitulation. "No. I admit that, Mr. Pitt. I didn't trust anyone until I met Miss Lamont."

"How did you meet her, Mrs. Serracold?"

"She was recommended to me," she said, as if surprised that he should ask.

His interest quickened. He hoped it did not show in his face. "By whom?"

"Do you imagine it matters?" she parried.

"Will you tell me, Mrs. Serracold, or do I have to enquire?"

"Would you?"

"Yes."

"That would be embarrassing! And unnecessary." She was angry. There were two spots of color high on her smooth cheekbones. "As far as I can recall, it was Eleanor Mountford. I don't remember how she heard of her. She was really very famous, you know — Miss Lamont, I mean."

"She had a lot of clients from society?" Pitt's voice was expressionless.

"Surely you know that." She raised her brows slightly.

"I know what her appointment book says," he agreed. "Thank you for your time, Mrs. Serracold." He rose to his feet again.

"Mr. Pitt . . . Mr. Pitt, my husband is standing for Parliament. I . . ."

"I know that," he said softly. "And I am aware of what capital the Tory press may make of your visits to Miss Lamont, if they become known."

She blushed, but her face was defiant and she made no immediate answer.

"Was Mr. Serracold aware you were seeing Miss Lamont?" he asked.

Her look wavered. "No." It was little more than a murmur. "I went in the evenings he spent at his club. They were regular. It was quite easy."

"You took a very great risk," he pointed out. "Did you go alone?"

"Of course! It is a . . . personal thing." She spoke with great difficulty. It cost her a very visible effort to ask him. "Mr. Pitt, if you could . . ."

"I shall be discreet for as long as possible," he promised. "But anything you remember may be of help."

"Yes . . . of course. I wish I could think of something. Apart from the question of justice . . . I shall miss her. Good day, Mr. Pitt . . . Inspector." She hesitated only an instant, forgetting Tellman's name. But it was not of importance. She did not bother to wait for him to supply it, but sailed out of the room, leaving the maid to show them out.

Neither Pitt nor Tellman commented on leaving the Serracold house. Pitt could sense Tellman's confusion and it matched his own. She was nothing that he could have foreseen in the wife of a man who was running for potentially one of the highest public offices in the country. She was eccentric, arrogant enough to be offensive, and yet there was an honesty about her he admired. Her views were naive, but they were idealistic, born of a desire for a tolerance she herself could not achieve.

Above all she was vulnerable, because there was something she had wanted from Maude Lamont so intensely that she had gone to her séances time after time, even though she was aware of the potential political cost if it became known. And her hair was long and pale silver-gold. He could not forget the hair on Maude's sleeve, which might mean anything, or nothing.

"Find out more about how Maude Lamont acquires her clients," he said to Tellman as they lengthened their pace down the footpath. "What does she charge? Is it the same for all clients? And does it account for her income?"

"Blackmail?" Tellman said with his disgust unconcealed. "It's pathetic to be taken in by that . . . that nonsense. But plenty of people are! Is it worth paying to keep silent about?"

"That depends what she's found out," Pitt replied, stepping off the curb and dodging a pile of horse manure. "Most of us have something we'd prefer to keep private. It doesn't have to be a crime, just an indiscretion, or a weakness we fear having exploited. No one likes to look a fool."

Tellman stared straight ahead of him. "Anyone who goes to a woman who spits up egg white and says it's a message from the spirit world, and believes it, is a fool," he said with a viciousness that sprang from a pity he did not want to feel. "But I'll find out everything about her that I can. Mostly I'd like to know how she did it!"

They stepped up onto the pavement at the far side of the street just as a four-wheeled growler passed by within a yard of them.

"Mixtures of mechanical trickery, sleight of hand, and power of suggestion, I should think," Pitt answered, stopping at the curb to allow a coach and four to pass by. "I assume you know it was egg white from the autopsy?" he said a little caustically.

Tellman grunted. "And cheesecloth," he elaborated. "She choked on it. It was in her throat and lungs, poor creature."

"Anything else you didn't mention?"

Tellman glanced at him with venom. "No! She was a healthy woman of about thirty-seven or eight. She died of asphyxia. You already saw the bruises. That's all there is." He grunted. "And I meant find out the things people don't want known. Was she clever enough to guess from the bits and pieces people asked, like where did Great-uncle Ernie hide his will? Or did my father really have an affair with the girl in the house opposite? Or anything at all!"

"I expect with a lot of listening at parties," Pitt replied, "watching people, asking a few questions, exerting a little pressure now and then, she could piece together enough to make some very good guesses. And people's own conclusions for what she gave them probably supplied the rest. Guilt runs from imaginary threats, as well as real ones. How many times have you seen people betray themselves because they thought we knew, when we didn't?"

"Lots," Tellman said, dodging around a

costermonger's cart of vegetables. "But what if she pushed too hard and somebody turned on her? That'd be the end of it all for her."

"Seems as if it was." Pitt shot him a sideways glance.

"Then what's it to do with Special Branch?" Tellman demanded, anger quick in his voice. "Just because Serracold's running for Parliament? Does Special Branch play party politics? Is that it?"

"No, that's not it!" Pitt snapped, wounded and angry that Tellman should think it a possibility. "I don't care that much" — he snapped his fingers — "who gets in. I care that the fight is fair. I think most of the ideas I've heard from Aubrey Serracold are totally daft. He hasn't got the faintest idea of reality. But if he's beaten I want it done by people who disagree with him, not people who think his wife committed a crime, if she didn't."

Tellman walked in silence. He did not apologize, although he opened his mouth and drew in his breath as if to speak a couple of times. When they came to the main thoroughfare he said good-bye and strode off in the opposite direction, back stiff, head high, while Pitt went to find a hansom to report to Victor Narraway.

"Well?" Narraway demanded, leaning back in his chair and staring up at Pitt unblinkingly.

Pitt sat down without being asked. "So far it seems to have been one of her three clients that evening," he answered. "Major General Roland Kingsley, Mrs. Serracold, or a man whose identity none of them knew, except possibly Maude Lamont herself."

"What do you mean 'none'? You mean neither?"

"No I don't. Apparently, the maid also didn't know who he was. She says she never even saw him. He came in and left through the French doors and the door in the garden wall."

"Why? Was the door in the wall left open? Then anyone could have come or gone."

"The door in the garden wall to Cosmo Place was locked but not barred," Pitt explained. "Other clients had keys. We don't know who. There's no record of it. The French doors were self-closing, so there's no way of knowing if anyone left that way after she was dead. As to why, that's obvious — he didn't wish anyone at all to know he was there."

"Why was he there?"

"I don't know. Mrs. Serracold thinks he was a skeptic, trying to prove Maude Lamont a fraud."

"Why? Academic interest, or personal? Find out, Pitt."

"I intend to!" Pitt retorted. "But first I'd like to know who he is!"

Narraway frowned. "You said 'Roland Kingsley'? Is he the same man who wrote that damning piece about Serracold?"

"Yes . . ."

"Yes, what?" Narraway's clear, dark eyes bored into Pitt's. "There's something more."

"He's afraid," Pitt said tentatively. "Some pain to do with his son's death."

"Find out about it!"

Pitt had been going to say that Kingsley's personal opinions did not seem as virulent as those he had expressed in his letter to the newspapers, but he was not sure enough of it. He had nothing but an impression, and he did not trust Narraway, did not know him well enough to venture something so nebulous. He was uncomfortable working for a man of whom he knew so little. He had no sense of Narraway's personal beliefs; his passions or needs, his weaknesses, even his background before their first meeting, were all shrouded in mystery to him.

"What about Mrs. Serracold?" Narraway went on. "I don't like Serracold's socialism, but anything is better than Voisey with his foot on the ladder. I need answers, Pitt." He sat forward suddenly. "This is the Inner Circle we are fighting. If you doubt what they can do, think back to Whitechapel. Think of the sugar factory, remember Fetters lying dead on his own library floor. Think how close they came to winning! Think of your family!"

Pitt was cold. "I am doing that," he said between his teeth. It cost him an effort precisely because he was thinking of Charlotte and the children and he hated Narraway for reminding him of it. "But if Rose Serracold murdered Maude Lamont, I'm not hiding it. If we do that, then we're no better than Voisey is, and he'll know that as well as we do."

Narraway's face was dark. "Don't lecture me, Pitt!" he spat. "You are not a constable on the beat blowing his whistle if somebody picks a pocket! There's more than a silk handkerchief or a gold watch at stake, there's the government of the nation. If you want simple answers, go back to arresting cutpurses!"

"And precisely what did you say was the difference between us and the Inner Circle, sir?" Pitt exaggerated the last word, and his voice was sharp and brittle as ice.

Narraway's lips tightened, and there was anger deep in his face, but there was a flash of admiration also.

"I haven't asked you to protect Rose Serracold if she's guilty, Pitt. Don't be so damned pompous! Although it sounds as if you think she might be. What did she go to this wretched woman for anyway?"

"I don't know yet." Pitt relaxed into the chair again. "To contact her mother, she admits that, and Kingsley said that was the reason she gave Maude Lamont, but she hasn't told me why, or how it can matter so much she's prepared to deceive her husband and risk his career if some Tory journalist wants to make a fool of her."

"And did she contact her mother?" Narraway asked.

Pitt looked at him with a sudden tingle of shock. Narraway's eyes were clear, without irony. For an instant it was as if he had believed either answer were possible.

"Not to her satisfaction," Pitt replied with certainty. "She is still searching for something, an answer she needs . . . and fears."

"She believed in Maude Lamont's powers." That was a statement.

"Yes."

Narraway breathed in and out silently, very slowly. "Did she describe what happened?"

"Apparently, Maude Lamont's appearance changed, her face shone and her breath seemed luminous. She spoke with a different voice." He swallowed. "She also seemed to rise in the air, and her hands to elongate."

The tension eased out of Narraway's body. "Hardly conclusive. Many of them do that. Vocal tricks, oil of phosphorus. Still . . . I suppose we believe what we want to believe . . . or what we dread to." He looked away. "And some of us feel compelled to find out, however much it hurts. Others leave it forever hanging unknown . . . can't bear to take away the last hope." He straightened up sharply. "Don't underestimate Voisey, Pitt. He won't let desire for revenge get in the way of his ambition. You aren't that important to him. But he won't ever forget it was you who beat him in Whitechapel. He won't forget, and he certainly won't forgive. He will wait for his time, and it will be when you can't defend yourself. He won't be precipitated, but one day he'll strike. I'll watch your back for you as I can, but I'm not infallible."

"I met him . . . in the House of Commons, three days ago," Pitt replied, shivering inside in spite of himself. "I know he hasn't forgotten. But if I walk in fear, then he's won already. My family is out of London, but I can't stop him. I admit, if I thought there were any escape, I might be tempted to take it . . . but there isn't."

"You're more of a realist than I gave you credit for," Narraway said, and there was a grudging respect in his voice. "I resented Cornwallis for wishing you onto me. Took you as a favor to him, but perhaps it wasn't after all."

"Why do you owe Cornwallis any favors?" The words slipped out before he thought about it.

"None of your business, Pitt!" Narraway said tartly. "Go and find out what the devil that woman was doing . . . and prove it!"

"Yes, sir."

It was only when he was outside again in the street in the late sunlight and the roar and rattle of traffic that Pitt stopped to wonder whether Narraway had meant Rose Serracold — or Maude Lamont!

CHAPTER

<u>SIX</u>

When Emily opened the newspaper the day after the discovery of the murder in Southampton Row, her immediate interest was in the political reports. An excellent picture of Mr. Gladstone caught her eye, but for the time being she was more concerned with the London constituencies. There was less than a week to go before voting would begin. She felt a sharp tingle of excitement, more than for the previous election because now she had tasted the possibilities of office and her ambition for Jack was correspondingly higher. He had proved his ability and, perhaps more importantly, his loyalty. This time he might be rewarded with a position of greater importance, and so more power to do good.

He had made an excellent speech yesterday. The crowd had been appreciative. She scanned the pages looking for a report of it. Instead she saw Aubrey Serracold's name, and below it an article which began quite well. Until she was halfway through it she did not read between the lines the sarcasm, the veiled suggestion of the foolishness of his ideas, and that though well-intentioned, they were formed in ignorance, a rich man playing at politics, indescribably condescending in his ambition to change others to his own idea of what was good for them.

Emily was furious. She dropped the paper and stared across the breakfast table at Jack. "Have you seen this?" she demanded, jabbing her finger at it.

"No." He held out his hand and she picked up the fallen sheets and passed them to him. She watched as he read it, the frown deepening between his brows.

"Will it hurt him?" she asked when he looked up. "I am sure it will hurt his feelings, but I mean his chances of being elected," she added quickly.

A flicker of amusement lit his eyes for a moment, and then gentleness. "You want him to win, don't you? For Rose's sake . . ."

She had not realized she was so transparent. It was uncharacteristic of her. She was usually good at revealing only what she wished, totally unlike Charlotte, who could be read by almost anyone. Yet it was not always satisfying to feel so alone. "Yes, I do," she agreed. "I thought it was more or less a certainty. It's been a Liberal seat for decades. Why should it be different now?"

"It's only one article, Emily. If you say anything at all, there's bound to be someone who disagrees with you."

"You disagree with him," she said very seriously. "Jack, can't you defend him anyway? They're making him sound far more extreme than he is. They would listen to you." She saw him hesitate, the shadow in his face. "What is it?" she demanded. "Have you lost confidence in him? Or is it Rose? Of course she's eccentric, she's always been that way. What on earth does it matter? Do our politicians have to be gray to be any good?"

There was laughter in his face for a moment, and then it was gone. "Not gray, but toned down a little. Don't take anything for granted, Emily. Don't take it as certain that I'll win. There are too many issues at stake that could change the way people vote. Gladstone's always on about Home Rule, but I think it's the working day that's going to decide it."

"But the Tories wouldn't grant that!" she protested. "They're even less likely to than we are! Tell them so!"

"I have. But what they say about not granting Home Rule makes sense, at least to the workingman here in London, where our docks and warehouses serve the world." His face tightened. "I've heard what Voisey is saying, and people are listening to him. He's very popular just now. The Queen knighted him for courage and loyalty to the Crown. Nobody knows exactly what he did, but apparently it saved the throne from a very serious threat. He's half won the audience even before he speaks."

"I thought the Queen wasn't very popular," she said dubiously, remembering some of the ugly remarks she had heard, both in society and among more ordinary people. Victoria had been too long absent from public life, still mourning Albert although he had been thirty years dead. She spent her time in her beloved Osbourne, on the Isle of Wight, or at Balmoral, in the Scottish Highlands. People hardly ever saw her. There were no state occasions, no pomp, no excitement or color, no sense of unity that only she could have provided.

"We still don't want her taken from us," Jack pointed out. "We are just as perverse in general as we are individually." He folded his paper and set it on the table, rising to his feet. "But of course I'll support Serracold." He leaned forward and gave her a quick kiss on the brow. "I don't know when I'll be back. Probably for dinner."

She watched him to the door, then poured herself another cup of tea and opened the newspaper again. It was then that she saw the report of Maude Lamont's death, and the fact that the police had no doubt that it was murder. The Bow Street station was mentioned, and apparently Inspector Tellman was in charge. He had made no statement, but speculation was rife. The journalists had invented what they did not know. Who were her clients? Who had been there that night? Who had she claimed to call up from the past and what had they revealed that had ended in murder? Whose secrets were so hideous they would kill to hide them? The whisper of scandal, violence and assault was irresistible.

She read it a second time, but there was no need. She could remember every word, and all the ugly implications. And she could remember very clearly Rose Serracold's saying that she had consulted Maude Lamont. Somehow ragged ends were coming loose in what had seemed to be a simple way ahead. Anxiety gnawed at the back of her mind over Rose, a sense of vulnerability in her, a fear that threatened to escalate and endanger her and Aubrey, and possibly even Jack. It was time Emily did something.

She went straight upstairs to the nursery to spend the morning with her small daughter, Evangeline, who as always was full of questions about everything. Her favorite word was *why*.

"Where's Edward?" Evangeline sat on the floor, her face puckered into a frown. "Why isn't he here?"

"He's gone for a holiday with Daniel and Jemima," Emily answered, offering Evie her favorite doll.

"Why?"

"Because we promised it to him."

"Why?" There was no challenge in her wide eyes.

"He and Daniel are special friends." Thinking on it now, Emily was concerned that Thomas had been prevented from going with them and at almost the same time his reinstatement to Bow Street had been unaccountably withdrawn. Charlotte had suddenly and without explanation been reluctant to take Edward, whereas before she had been more than willing. She had said something halfhearted about Thomas not being there, and hinted at there being possible unpleasantness, but she had not been specific.

"I'm special friends," Evie said, turning the phrase over in her mind.

"Of course you are, darling. You are my special friend," Emily assured her. "Shall we draw a picture? I'll do this part and you can do the house, over there."

Evie began enthusiastically, grasping the crayon in her left hand. Emily thought of changing it to the right, and decided not to.

She was concerned over Charlotte. It was going to be very difficult for her to adapt to having Pitt no longer in a senior police position. It was not exactly a job to be proud of, but it was moderately respectable. Now he did something she could barely mention, and his cases could not be discussed. Of course the money was another matter altogether, and not as good!

The thing that affected Emily the most was the inability to share in any of it herself. She had in the past helped Charlotte when she was involved in Pitt's cases, the more colorful and dramatic of them, where people of the higher social strata were implicated. She and Charlotte had access to the withdrawing rooms of society that Pitt would never have. They had almost solved some of the more bizarre and dreadful murders themselves. Lately that had happened less and less, and Emily was beginning to realize how she missed not only Charlotte's company, and the challenge and excitement of it, but the intrusion into her life of the passions of triumph and despair, danger, judgment, guilt and innocence which had forced her to think more deeply than the comfortable issues of politics which seemed always to do with masses and not individuals, theories and laws rather than the lives of men and women of flesh, dreams, real ability for joy or pain.

If she were to help Charlotte and Thomas again it would be a hard reminder of the urgencies of life and the realities. It would force her to test her beliefs in a way merely thinking never could. She was afraid of it, and for that very reason she also was impelled towards it. Charlotte was away somewhere in Dartmoor. Emily did not have the exact address; Thomas had been very vague. But she would go and see Rose Serracold herself and learn a great deal more about the death of this spirit

medium she had been involved with —
Maude Lamont.

She dressed in an outdoor costume in
the latest fashion from Paris. It was shell
pink with broad diagonal stripes of lavender across the skirt, and a white ruff
high at the throat. The soft colors were unusual, and remarkably flattering to her.

She made all her duty calls to wives of
men with whom it was important to maintain a steady, close connection. She talked
about the weather, the trivial news, exchanging compliments and meaningless
chatter all afternoon, knowing that the
message beneath the words was what mattered.

Then she was free to pursue the questions that had been at the back of her mind
since breakfast. She finally gave her
coachman instructions to go to the Serra-
colds' home. Received by the footman, she
was shown into the sun-filled conservatory,
heavy with the smell of wet earth and
leaves and falling water. She found Rose
sitting alone staring at the lily pool. She
too was dressed as if for calling, in dramatic olive green and white lace, which
with her flaxen hair and extraordinarily
slender body made her look as if she were
some exotic water flower herself.

But as Emily came closer and Rose looked up, Emily saw the tension in Rose stretching the silk of her gown until it hung without her usual extravagant elegance.

"Emily, I'm so pleased to see you!" she said with relief spreading across her face. "I would not have let anyone else in, I swear it!" Her expression crumpled into one of bewilderment. "Maude Lamont has been killed! I suppose you know that; it was in the newspapers. It happened two days ago . . . I was there! At least I was in the house that evening. Emily, I've had the police here this afternoon. I don't know how to tell Aubrey. What am I going to say?"

This was a time for practicality, not gentleness. If she were to learn anything of value, she could not afford to allow Rose to dominate the conversation. She went straight to the first subject which really mattered. "Did Aubrey not know you were seeing a spiritualist?"

Rose shook her head fractionally, the light gleaming on the polished sheen of her hair.

"Why didn't you tell him?"

"Because he wouldn't have liked it!" Rose said immediately. "He doesn't believe."

Emily thought about it for a moment. There was a lie in it, a concealment. She was not sure what it was, but she was quite certain it had to do with Rose's reason for going.

"He would find it a little embarrassing," Rose explained unnecessarily, looking down at the floor, but with a very slight smile on her lips.

"But you went anyway," Emily pointed out. "Even now, just before the election. Which means you had a reason for going that was so strong it outweighed Aubrey's wishes, and any damage it might do him, or he would think it might. Are you really so sure of his winning?" She tried to sound sympathetic and to keep out of her voice the impatience she felt at such naive arrogance.

Rose's eyebrows lifted suddenly. She was about to answer, then the words died on her lips. "I thought I was," she said instead. Then her voice became urgent. "Do . . . do you think this could make any difference? I didn't kill her! Please heaven — I needed her alive!"

Emily knew she was intruding, but there was no time for delicacy. "Why did you need her, Rose? What could she possibly give you that matters so much right now?"

"She was my contact with the other side, of course!" Rose said impatiently. "Now I have to find someone else and start all over again! There isn't time . . ." She bit back the words, knowing she had already said too much.

"Time before what?" Emily pressed. "The election? Is it something to do with the election?" Questions as to why Thomas was still here in London crowded into her mind.

Rose's expression was closed. "Before Aubrey wins his seat and takes up a place in Parliament," she answered. "And I have much less privacy."

She was still lying, or at least telling a half-truth, but Emily could not prove it. Why? Was it a political secret or a personal one? How could she find out? "The man who was here from the police, what did you tell him?" she urged.

"About the other two clients who were there that evening, of course." Rose stood up and walked over to the bowl of peonies and delphiniums on the wrought-iron table. She poked absentmindedly at the stems, rearranging them to no advantage. "The man from Bow Street seemed to think one of them had done it." She gave a shiver and tried to disguise it with a shrug.

"He was not as I would expect a policeman to be," she continued. "He was very quiet and polite, but he made me uncomfortable. I would like to think he wouldn't come again, but I expect he will. Unless, of course, they find very quickly who it was. It must be the man who didn't believe, I should think. It wouldn't be the soldier who wished to speak to his son. He cares just as much as I do."

Emily was confused. She had no idea what Rose was talking about, but this was not the time to admit it. "And if he found something he didn't like?" she said softly. "What then?"

Rose stopped with a delphinium in her hand, still lifted in the air, her face pinched, eyes miserable. "Then he would be crushed," she answered, her voice husky. "He would go away in despair . . . and . . . and try to heal himself, I suppose. I don't know how. What does one do when . . . when you hear the unbearable?"

"Some people would retaliate," Emily answered, watching Rose's stiff back, the silk twisted as she stood half turned. "If nothing else, at least to make sure no one else heard the unendurable thing." Her imagination raced, in spite of the pity she felt for Rose's very obvious distress. Who were the men? What reason could they have had for killing the medium? What secret had Rose stumbled into?

"That's what the policeman suggested," Rose said after a second.

Emily knew that Tellman had been promoted now that Pitt was gone from Bow Street.

"Tellman?" she asked.

"No . . . Pitt, his name was."

Emily breathed out slowly. Now a great deal of it made ugly and frightening sense. There was no doubt anymore that the murder of the spiritualist was a political matter, or Pitt would not have been called. Special Branch could surely not have foreseen it? Could they? Charlotte had told her little of what his new duties were, but Emily knew enough of current affairs to be well aware that Special Branch dealt only with violence, anarchy, threats to the government and the throne, and the ensuing danger to the peace of the nation.

Rose still had her back to Emily. She had seen nothing. Now Emily was torn between one loyalty and another. She had asked Jack to support Aubrey Serracold, and he had been reluctant, even though he would not admit it. Now she understood that he was right. She had taken it for

232

granted that Jack would win his seat again, with all the opportunities and the benefits that it afforded. Maybe she had been hasty in that. There were forces she had not appreciated, or Pitt would not be bothering with one unfortunate crime of passion or fraud in Southampton Row.

One obvious thought crossed her mind. If Rose had unwittingly told this woman of some incident in her past, some indiscretion, a stupid act that would now look ugly, then the possibilities for political blackmail were only too clear. And such a woman could incite motive for murder so easily.

She stared at Rose now, at the wry, eccentric elegance of her, the passion in her face so easy to read behind the thin veneer of sophistication. She pretended she had everything, but there was some wound there, raw and easy to see, even if its nature was not.

"Why did you go to Maude Lamont?" Emily said bluntly. "You're going to have to tell Pitt one day. He'll go on looking until he finds out, and in the process uncover all sorts of other things you might very much rather were kept discreet."

Rose's eyebrows arched. "Really? You sound as if you know him. He hasn't been investigating you, has he?" It was said

233

mockingly, a joke to divert the attention, and with an edge of challenge in it sharp enough to make Emily respond — at least that was what was intended.

"It would be a waste of his time, and hardly necessary," Emily said with a smile. "He's my brother-in-law. He already knows everything about me that he wishes to." It was momentary amusement to watch the shock in Rose's face, the hesitation as she struggled to decide whether Emily was making fun of her or not, and then a surge of anger when she realized it was true.

"That dashed policeman is some kind of a relative of yours?" she said with disgust. "I think in the circumstances you might have mentioned it!" She made a quick little gesture of dismissal. "Although I suppose if I were related to a policeman, I wouldn't tell anyone, either! Not that I would be!" It was said as an insult, and meant as such.

Emily felt the anger rise up inside her, hot and harsh. She rose to her feet with a retort already formed just as the door opened and Aubrey Serracold came in. His long, fair face had its usual air of wry good humor and the slight twist to his mouth as if he would smile were he certain quite when and to whom it was appropriate. His pale hair fell a little forward, lopsidedly, over his brow. As always, he was immaculately dressed, today in a black jacket and faintly striped trousers, his cravat perfectly tied. His valet probably regarded it as an art form. The chill was glaringly apparent in the positions and the stiffness of both women, the distance between them and the way they were half turned. But good manners directed that he affect not to have noticed.

"Emily, how nice to see you," he said with such natural pleasure it was possible to believe for a moment that he was oblivious of the atmosphere. He came towards her, touching Rose on the arm in a gesture of affection as he passed her. "You are standing," he observed to Emily. "I hope that means you have just arrived, not that you are just leaving? I am feeling a trifle bruised around the edges, like an overripe dessert peach that too many people have picked up and then decided against." He smiled ruefully. "I had no idea how terribly tedious it would be arguing with people who are really not listening to a word you say, and have long since decided what you mean, and that it is nonsense. Have you had tea?"

He looked around for signs of a tray or any other evidence of recent refreshment.

"Perhaps it's too late. I think I'll have a whiskey." He reached for the bell cord to fetch the butler. A flash in his eye betrayed that he knew he was talking too much to cover the silence, but he went on anyway. "Jack did warn me that most people have already made up their minds what they believe, which will be either the same as their fathers before them — and grandfathers, too — or in a few instances the direct opposite, and that argument of any sort is so much wind in the trees. I admit I thought he was being cynical." He shrugged. "Give him my apologies, Emily. He is a man of infinite sagacity."

Emily forced herself to smile back at him. She disagreed with Aubrey over a score of things, mostly political, but she could not help herself from liking him, and none of this was his fault. His company was sharp, immediate and very seldom unkind. "Just experience," she answered him. "He says people vote with their hearts, not their heads."

"Actually, he meant their bellies." Laughter lit Aubrey's eyes and then vanished. "How can we ever improve the world if we think no further than tomorrow's dinner?" He glanced at Rose, but she remained grimly silent, still half turned away from Emily as if refusing to acknowledge her presence anymore.

"Well, if we don't have tomorrow's dinner we won't survive into this wonderful future," Emily pointed out. "Nor our children," she added more soberly.

"Indeed," Aubrey said quietly. Suddenly all levity vanished. They were talking about things for which they all cared intensely. Only Rose stood still rigid, her inner fear not swept away.

"More justice would bring more food, Emily," Aubrey said with passionate gravity. "But men hunger for vision as well as bread. People need to believe in themselves, that what they do is better than simply toil in return for enough to survive, and barely that for many."

In her heart Emily wanted to agree with him, but her brain told her he was dreaming too far ahead. It was bright, even beautiful. It was also impractical.

She glanced at Rose and saw the softness in her eyes, the tenderness in her mouth and how very pale she was. Emily could smell lilies and steam rising from the watered earth and feel the heat of the sunlight on the stone floor, but she could sense fear as if it overrode all else. Knowing how fiercely Rose shared Aubrey's beliefs, perhaps was even ahead of them, Emily wondered what did Rose need to know so much that she would now seek another spirit medium, even after what had happened to Maude Lamont?

And what had happened to Maude Lamont? Had she tried political blackmail one time too many, one secret too dangerous? Or was it a domestic tragedy, a lover betrayed, a jealousy over some man's attention stolen or misdirected? Had she promised to relay a command from the next world, perhaps about money, and then reneged on it? There were a hundred possibilities. It did not have to have anything to do with Rose — except that Thomas was there not from Bow Street but from Special Branch!

Could the unknown man have been some politician, a lover, or wished to be? Perhaps he had conceived a passion for her which she had rejected, and in his humiliation he had turned on her and killed her?

Surely, Pitt would have thought of that, wouldn't he?

She looked across at Aubrey now. His expression seemed at a glance to be earnest, but the ghost of humor always hovered in his eyes, as if he could see some enormous comic joke and knew himself a bit player, no more or less important than anyone else, no matter how intensely he might feel. Perhaps that was the greatest reason she liked him.

Rose was still half turned away. She had been listening to Aubrey, but the rigidity of her shoulders made it clear she had not forgotten her quarrel with Emily; she hid it because she would not explain it to him.

Emily gave her light, warm, social smile and said how nice it was to see them both. She wished Aubrey success and reaffirmed her support for him, and Jack's also, even though she was less certain of it, and then took her leave. Rose went as far as the hall with her. She was polite, her voice cheerful, her eyes cold.

On the ride home, sitting in her carriage as it fought its way through the crush of hansoms, coaches, landaus and a dozen other kinds of vehicles, Emily wondered what she should tell Pitt, or if she should speak to him at all. Rose expected her to, and that in itself made her angry, as if she had deceived already, at least in intent. It was untrue, and unfair.

And yet she did instinctively think to tell Pitt all that might be of use to him, all that would explain what had happened, as much for Rose's own sake as anyone else's!

No it wasn't. It was for truth, and for Jack. As she sat and puzzled over the medium's death it was Jack's face that was in her mind all the time, his presence with her as if he were at her shoulder, barely out of sight. She liked Aubrey, she wanted him to win, not only for the good he could do, but intensely, for himself. But it was the fear that he would drag Jack down which drove her to pursue the truth.

She had never seriously considered before that Jack might lose. She had thought only of the opportunities ahead, the privileges and the pleasures. Now she realized with a chill as the carriage lurched forward again, and the shouting of irate drivers cut the warm air, that if he lost there would be a bitter change to get used to, just as harsh as that which Charlotte faced now. Invitations would be different, parties immeasurably more tedious. How would she go back to the idleness of society after the thrill in the blood of politics, the heady dream of power? And sharp and very real, how could she hide her own humiliation that she no longer had anything worthwhile to do?

The resolve that Jack must win tightened in her. She was perfectly aware of her own motives, and it made no difference whatever. Reason did not touch emotion any more than sunlight touches the deep-sea currents. She must do all that was within her ability to help.

She needed someone else to talk to. Charlotte was in Dartmoor; she did not even know precisely where. Her mother, Caroline, was on tour with her second husband, Joshua, an actor presently playing the lead in one of Mr. Wilde's plays in Liverpool.

But even had they been at home, her first choice for confidante would have been Lady Vespasia Cumming-Gould, a great-aunt of her first husband who had remained one of her dearest friends. Therefore she now leaned forward and commanded her coachman to take her to Vespasia's house, even though she had never written or left a card, which was a complete break of etiquette. But then Vespasia had never allowed rules to prevent her from doing what she believed to be right, and would almost certainly forgive Emily for doing the same.

Emily was fortunate in that Vespasia was in and had half an hour since said good-bye to her last visitor.

"My dear Emily, what a pleasure to see you," Vespasia said without rising from her seat by the window of the sitting room. It was all pale colors and full of sunlight. "The more especially at this extraordinary hour," she added, "since it must be something of great interest or urgency which brings you. Do sit down and tell me what it is." She waved impassively at the chair opposite her own, and then regarded Emily's costume with a critical eye. She was stiff-backed, silver-haired, and still had the marvelous eyes and bones which had made her the greatest beauty of her generation. She had never followed fashion, she had always led it. "Very becoming," she gave her approval. "You have been calling upon someone you wish to impress . . . a woman who takes her clothes very seriously, I imagine."

Emily smiled with a sharp sense of pleasure, and relief at being in the company of someone she liked without shadow or equivocation. "Yes," she agreed. "Rose Serracold. Do you know of her?" Vespasia would not be socially acquainted with Rose, since there were the best part of two generations, a gulf of social status, and a considerable degree of wealth, even though Aubrey was more than comfortable, between them. Emily had no idea whether Vespasia would approve of Rose's political opinions. Vespasia could be very extreme herself on occasions, and had fought like a tigress for the reforms in which she believed. But she was also a realist, and fiercely practical. She could very easily see the Socialist ideals as ill-based in the realities of human nature.

"And what in Mrs. Serracold's visit brought you here, rather than home to change for dinner?" Vespasia asked. "Is she related to Aubrey Serracold, who is standing for Lambeth South, and according to the newspapers has expressed some rather foolish ideals?"

"Yes, she is his wife."

"Emily, I am not a dentist to be extracting information from you, like teeth!"

"I'm sorry," Emily said contritely. "It all seems so absurd now I come to put it into words."

"Many things do," Vespasia observed. "That does not mean they are not real. Is it to do with Thomas?" There was a sharp note of concern in her voice, and her eyes were shadowed.

"Yes . . . and no," Emily said quietly. Suddenly it was not ridiculous at all. If Vespasia were afraid, too, then the cause of it was real. "Thomas and Charlotte were going on holiday to Dartmoor, but Thomas's leave was canceled —"

"By whom?" Vespasia interrupted.

Emily swallowed. With a jolt of pain and embarrassment she realized Thomas had not told Vespasia of his dismissal from Bow Street the second time. But she would have to know. Silence was only delaying what was inevitable. "By Special Branch," she said huskily, her voice choked with anger, and now fear as well. She saw the surprise, and then the hardening in Vespasia's face. "He was dismissed from Bow Street again," she went on. "Charlotte told me when she came to pick up Edward to take him with her to Dartmoor. Pitt had been sent back to Special Branch, and his leave rescinded."

Vespasia nodded so fractionally it was barely visible. "Charles Voisey is standing for Parliament. He is head of the Inner Circle." She did not bother to explain any further. She must have seen in Emily's face that she understood the enormity of it.

"Oh God!" Emily said involuntarily. "Are you sure?"

"Yes, my dear, I am perfectly sure."

"And . . . Thomas knows it!"

"Yes. That will be why Victor Narraway has canceled his leave and no doubt ordered him to do all he can to block Voisey's path, although I doubt he will be able to. Only once has anyone ever beaten Voisey before."

"Who was that?" Hope flowed up inside Emily, making her heart pound in her chest.

Vespasia smiled. "A friend of mine named Mario Corena, but it cost him his life. And he had a little assistance from Thomas and myself. Mario is beyond Voisey's reach, but Voisey will not have forgiven Thomas, and perhaps not me, either. I think it would be wise, my dear, if you did not write to Charlotte while she is away."

"Is the danger really so . . ." Emily found her mouth dry, her lips stiff.

"Not as long as he does not know where she is."

"But she cannot stay in Dartmoor forever!"

"Of course not," Vespasia agreed. "But by the time she returns the election will be over, and perhaps we will have found a way to tie Voisey's hands."

"He won't win, will he? It's a safe Liberal seat," Emily protested. "Why is he fighting for that, and not for a Tory seat? It doesn't make sense."

"You are wrong," Vespasia said very quietly. "It is simply sense that we have not yet understood. Everything Voisey does makes sense. I don't know how he will defeat the Liberal candidate, but I believe he will."

Emily was cold in spite of the sun pouring through the windows into the quiet room. "The Liberal candidate is a friend of mine. I came because of his wife. She was one of the last clients of Maude Lamont, the spirit medium who was murdered in Southampton Row. She was there that night. Thomas is investigating it, and I think I may know something."

"Then you must tell him." There was no hesitation in Vespasia's voice, no doubt at all.

"But Rose is my friend, and I learned those things only because she trusted me. If I betray a friend, what have I left?"

This time Vespasia did not answer straightaway.

Emily waited.

"If you have to choose between friends," Vespasia said at last, "and both Rose and Thomas are such, then you must choose neither, but follow your own conscience. You cannot place one set of obligations or loyalties before another with regard to people, their closeness to you, the depth of their hurt, their innocence or their vulnerability, or the degree of their trust in you. You must do what your own conscience dictates to be right. Serve your own truth."

She had not said so, but Emily had no doubt in her mind that Vespasia meant that she should tell Thomas all she knew.

"Yes," she said aloud. "Perhaps I knew that, it was just hard to acknowledge it, because then I have to do it."

"Do you believe Rose may have killed this woman?"

"I don't know. I suppose I do."

They sat without speaking for several minutes, then finally discussed other things: Jack's campaign, Mr. Gladstone and Lord Salisbury, the extraordinary phenomenon of Keir Hardie and the possibility that one day he might actually succeed in reaching Parliament. Then Emily thanked Vespasia again, kissed her lightly on the cheek, and bade her good-bye.

She reached home and went upstairs to change into a suitable gown for dinner, even though she was not going out. She was in her own sitting room when Jack came in. His face was tired and there was a pale film of dust around the bottoms of his trousers, as if he had walked outside on the pavements for some distance.

She stood up to greet him with unaccustomed haste, as if he brought news, although she did not expect anything but the trivia of the campaign, much of which she could gain from the daily papers, had she considered it of sufficient importance.

"How is it progressing?" she asked him, searching his eyes, which were wide and gray with the remarkable lashes she had always admired. She saw in them pleasure at the sight of her, a warmth she had long known and held so dear it still startled her. But too close beneath it for safety she saw anxiety, deeper than before. She said quickly, "What's happened?"

He was reluctant to answer. The words did not come readily to him, and usually they did so easily; that in itself chilled her.

"Aubrey?" she whispered, thinking of Vespasia's warning. "He might lose, mightn't he? Are you going to care very much?"

He smiled, but it was deliberate, a gesture to reassure her. "I like him," he said honestly, sitting down in the chair opposite her, relaxing with his legs out. "And I think with a little more practicality he'd be a fine member. Anyway, we need a few dreamers." He gave a slight shrug. "It would balance out the journeymen who want office only for what it can profit them."

She knew he was hiding the real hurt it would be if Aubrey failed. It was Jack who had encouraged him in the beginning, even opened up much of the pathway for his nomination, and supported him after it. He had made it seem casual, as he did so many things, still keeping that instinctive manner of a man who took things lightly, who dabbled more than he worked, to whom nothing mattered so much as comfort, popularity, good food and good wine, and graciousness around him. He had always appreciated beauty and to flirt was as natural to him as drawing breath. The finality of marriage to a woman who would never turn the other way, or refuse to see what was uncomfortable to her, was the hardest decision he had ever made, and at times he also knew it was the best.

Emily had been careful never to tell him that she was very adept at seeing only what was prudent. She had done it with her first husband, George Ashworth, and when she had thought he had betrayed her, not simply physically but with love of the heart, it had wounded her more deeply than all her sophistication had led her to expect. She had no intention of allowing

Jack to think he could do the same. She knew the strength in him and the hunger for a purpose as consuming as that which drove Pitt. It was the fear he would not match up to it which made him appear to treat it so lightly. She realized now with a startling pain that she would do anything in her power to protect him from failure.

"Rose was at the house of the spirit medium the night she was murdered," she said guardedly. "Thomas went to question her. She's terrified, Jack!"

His face darkened. This time he could not hide the tension tightening inside him. He straightened up in the chair, the ease gone. "Thomas! Why Thomas? He's not in Bow Street anymore."

It was not the response she had expected, but now that she heard it, it was the one she feared. The rest, the questions, the criticism for lack of thought, for selfishness, would come later.

"Emily?" His voice was harsher, afraid she knew something she was not telling him, and for once she did not.

"I don't know!" she said, meeting his eyes squarely. "Charlotte won't tell me. I have to suppose it's political, otherwise Thomas wouldn't be there."

Jack put his hands up over his face, then

ran his fingers through his hair, blinking slowly.

Emily waited, her throat tight. Rose was hiding something. Could it hurt Aubrey, and through Aubrey — Jack? She stared at him, afraid to prompt.

He looked paler, even more tired. It was as if the bloom of youth had gone from him and suddenly she saw how he might look in ten, even twenty, years' time.

He stood up, turning away from her, and took a step or two towards the window. "Davenport advised me today to distance myself a little from Aubrey, for my own good," he said very quietly.

She could hear the silence as if it were tangible. The evening light outside was golden on the trees. "And what did you say?" she asked. She would hate either answer. If he had refused then his name would continue to be linked with Aubrey Serracold, and of course Rose. If Aubrey remained as extreme as he seemed at the moment, if he said more and more what was idealistic but naive, then his opponent would capitalize on it and make him appear an extremist who would at best be useless, at worst a danger. And Jack would be tarred with the same brush, dragged down by association, ideas and principles he could never be charged with so he could refute them, but by which he would be judged just the same, and just as fatally.

And if Rose were in any way involved in the medium's death, then that would damage them all also, never mind what the truth of it was. People would remember only that she was part of it.

Yet if Jack had agreed to Davenport's suggestion and already stepped aside, to save himself, leaving Aubrey to fight alone, what would she think of that? There was a price at which safety cost too much; and loyalty was part of it. Maybe that was even true politically? If you abandoned your friends so easily, on whom could you count when you needed them yourself? And one day you would!

She looked at his broad shoulders, his perfectly tailored coat, the back of his head so familiar she knew every curl of his hair, the way it grew in the nape of his neck, and she realized how little she was certain of what he thought. What would he do to save his seat, if the temptation arose? For a blinding moment she envied Charlotte because she had seen Pitt face so many decisions that drove him to the end of his self-knowledge, his compassion and judgment. She knew already what lay beyond the tested, because it was the pattern of his nature. Jack was charming and funny, gentle with her, and as far as she knew, loyal. He certainly had an honesty she admired, and resolution in a cause. But beyond that — when faced with real loss, what then?

"What did you say to him?" she repeated.

"I told him I can't abandon anyone without a reason," he replied with an edge to his voice. "I think there may be one, but by the time I know it, it will be too late." He looked back at her. "Why in God's name did she go to a medium now? She isn't a fool! She must know what interpretation people will put in it." He groaned. "I can imagine the cartoons! And knowing Aubrey, he might well tell her privately that she's irresponsible and he's furious with her, but he'll not do it in public, even by implication. No matter what it costs him he'll be seen to defend her." He turned back to her. "For that matter, why did she go to a medium at all? I can understand a public entertainment — hundreds of people go — but a private séance?"

"I don't know! I asked her, and she lost her temper with me." She dropped her voice. "Whatever it is, it's not entertainment, Jack. It's not lighthearted. I think she's trying to find out something and it terrifies her."

His eyes widened. "From a spirit medium? Has she taken leave of her senses?"

"Possibly."

He stood still. "You mean that?"

"I don't know what I mean," she said impatiently. "We've only a few days to go before they begin voting. Every day's newspaper matters. There's no time to correct mistakes and win people over again."

"I know." He moved back towards her, putting an arm around her lightly, but she could feel an anger inside him, wound up and aching to burst out, but with no direction in which to strike.

After a few more minutes he excused himself and went upstairs to change, then returned within half an hour and dinner was served. They sat at opposite sides of the table rather than at the ends. The light glittered on the cutlery and glass, and beyond the long windows the fading sun still glinted gold on the windows of the houses opposite.

The footman removed the plates and brought the next course.

"Will you hate it if I lose?" Jack said suddenly.

She stopped with her fork in the air.

She swallowed hard, as if there were an obstruction in her throat. "Do you think you might? Is that what Davenport says will happen if you won't abandon Aubrey?"

"I don't know," he said frankly. "I'm not sure if I'm prepared to pay the price in friendship that power costs. I resent being placed where I have to choose. I resent the hypocrisy of it, the cutting and trimming until you've paid so much you hang on to your prize because you've given up everything else in order to get it. Where is the point at which you say 'I won't do it — I'll let it all go rather than pay this one thing more'?" He looked at her as if he expected an answer.

"When you have to say something you don't believe," she offered.

He gave a sharp laugh, bitter-edged. "And am I going to be honest enough with myself to know when that is? Am I going to look at what I don't want to see?"

She said nothing.

"What about silence?" he went on, his voice rising, his plate forgotten. "What about compromised abstention? Judicious blindness? Passing by on the other side? Or perhaps Pilate washing his hands would be the right image?"

"Aubrey Serracold is not Christ," Emily pointed out.

"My own honor is the point," he said sharply. "What do I have to become to win office? And then what to keep it? If it weren't Aubrey, would it be someone else, or something?" He looked at her challengingly, as if he wanted an answer from her.

"And what if Rose did kill this woman?" she asked. "And if Thomas finds out?"

He said nothing. He looked so wretched for an instant she wished she had not spoken, but the question beat at her mind, echoing all the other things it brought with it. How much should she tell Thomas, and when? Should she make more effort to find out herself? Above all, how could she protect Jack? What was the greatest danger, loyalty to a damaged cause and the risk to his own seat? Or disloyalty and an office perhaps bought at the cost of part of himself? Did he owe it to anyone to go down with him?

Suddenly she was overwhelmingly angry that Charlotte was in some country cottage in Dartmoor with nothing to do but domestic chores, simple, physical things, no decisions to make, and where Emily could not ask her opinion and share all this with her.

But had Aubrey any idea of what was really going on? She saw his face sharp and clear in her mind with its quizzical innocence, the feeling she had that he was so open to pain.

It was not her job to protect him! It was Rose's, and why was she not doing it instead of going on some wild pursuit of voices from the dead? What could she possibly need to know that mattered a damn now?

"Warn him!" she said aloud.

Jack was startled. "About Rose? Doesn't he know?"

"I don't know! No . . . how can I tell? Who ever knows what really happens between two people? I meant warn him about the political realities. Tell him you can't support him if he goes too far with his socialism."

His face tightened. "I tried to. I don't think he believed me. He hears what he wants to —" He was interrupted by the butler coming in discreetly. "What is it, Morton?" Jack asked with a frown.

Morton was standing very straight, his face grave. "Mr. Gladstone would like to see you, sir. He is at the gentlemen's club in Pall Mall. I have taken the liberty of sending Albert for the carriage. I hope I did the right thing." That was not really a question. Morton was an ardent admirer of the Grand Old Man, and the thought of not obeying such a summons instantly was inconceivable to him.

Emily saw Jack stiffen, the muscles in his neck pull taut and the silent intake of breath. Was this the warning about Aubrey from the Liberal Party leader . . . already? Or worse — was it an offer of higher office of real power after the election if Gladstone won? Suddenly she knew that was what she was really afraid of. She felt sick to realize it. Gladstone might be going to offer Jack the chance to achieve what so far he had only cherished in his mind as a dream. But at what price?

Even if that was not what Gladstone wanted at all, she had still feared that Jack could be tempted, misled. Why did she not trust him to see the snare before it closed? Was it his skill she doubted? Or his strength to see the prize in his grasp and turn away from it? Would he rationalize, justify? Wasn't that what politics was all about — the art of the possible?

She had once been the ultimate pragmatist herself. Why was this any different? How had she changed from the brittle, ambitious young woman she used to be? Even as she asked, she knew that the answer had to do with the tragedies, the weakness and the victims of the spirit she had seen in some of the cases Thomas had worked on, and on which she and Charlotte had helped. She had seen ambition bent to evil, the blindness of a vision confuse the ends and the means. It was not as easy as it had once looked. Even those who meant only to do good could so easily be beguiled.

Jack kissed her gently and went to the door, wishing her good-night. He knew he could not say when he would be back. She nodded, agreeing not to wait up for him, knowing that she would. What point was there in trying to sleep while she did not know what Gladstone wanted . . . and how Jack had answered him?

She heard his footsteps cross the hall and the front door open and close.

The footman asked her if she wished to be served the rest of the meal. He had to repeat it before she declined.

"Apologize to Cook for me," she said. "I cannot eat until I know what news there is." She wanted to be civil but not explain herself. She had long ago learned a little courtesy could be returned tenfold.

She decided to wait in the withdrawing room. She had brought a copy of *Nada the Lily*, the very latest book by H. Rider Haggard. It was lying on the table where she had left it nearly a week ago. Perhaps if she read it, it would absorb her attention and the time would pass less painfully.

In snatches it did. For half an hour she would be caught in the passions and the pain of life in Zulu Africa, then her own fear resurfaced and she rose to her feet and paced up and down, her mind darting from one thing to another, nothing resolved. What was the funny, brave Rose Serracold so determined to know that she pursued the services of a spiritualist, even to destruction? She was obviously afraid. Was it for herself, or Aubrey, or someone else? Why could it not wait until after the election? Was she so sure Aubrey would win that she believed she could not find it after that? Or would it then be too late?

It was easier to think of that than to worry about Jack, and why Gladstone had sent for him.

She sat down and opened the book again, and read the same page twice, and still knew nothing of the sense of it.

She must have looked at the clock two dozen times before at last she heard the front door close and Jack's familiar footsteps cross the hall. She picked up her book, so that he should see her lay it aside as he came into the room. She smiled up at him.

"Would you like Morton to fetch you something?" she asked, half stretching her hand towards the bell. "How was the meeting?"

He hesitated for a moment, then he smiled. "Thank you for waiting up."

She blinked, feeling the color warm in her cheeks.

His smile widened; it was the same charm, the slight annoyance mixed with laughter, that she had loved in him in the beginning, even when she had thought him trivial, no more than entertaining.

"I'm not waiting up for you!" she retorted, trying not to let her lips answer the smile, and knowing it was in her eyes. "I'm waiting to hear what Mr. Gladstone had to say. I have a lively interest in politics."

"Then I suppose I had better tell you," he conceded with a sweep of generosity, waving his hand in the air. He turned on his heel and strode back to the door. Then suddenly his body altered, not exactly bending, but lowering one shoulder a trifle forward as if he were, very reluctantly, leaning on a stick. He peered towards her, blinking a little. "The Grand Old Man was very civil to me," he said conversationally.

" 'Mr. Radley, isn't it?' Although he knew perfectly well it was. He had sent for me. Who else would dare come?" He blinked again and put his hand to his ear, as if listening carefully for her reply, making the effort to catch every word. " 'I shall be happy to assist you, Mr. Radley, in any way that I can. Your good efforts have not gone unnoticed.' " In spite of himself there was a touch of pride in his voice, a lift that cut across the mimicry of age.

"Go on!" Emily said impatiently. "What did you say?"

"I thanked him, of course!"

"But did you accept? Don't you dare say you didn't!"

A shadow crossed his eyes and then was gone again. "Of course I accepted! Even if he doesn't actually help me at all, it would be discourteous, and very foolish, not to allow him to believe he has."

"Jack! What will he do?" The surprise was sharp inside her. "You won't let . . ."

He cut across her, aping Gladstone again. He straightened his already immaculate shirtfront and narrow bow tie, then fixing an imaginary pince-nez on his nose he stared at her unblinkingly. He held his right hand up, in a fist almost closed, but as if arthritis prevented him from tightening the swollen joints. " 'We must win!' " he said fervently. " 'In all my sixty years in public office, there has never been more to fight for.' " He coughed, cleared his throat and continued, even more magnificently. " 'Let us go forward in the good work we have to hand, and let us put our trust not in squires and peers . . .' " He stopped. "You are supposed to cheer!" he told Emily sharply. "How can I continue if you don't play your part properly? You are a public meeting. Behave like one!"

"I thought it was only you there," she said quickly, disappointment leaping inside her although she tried to hide it from him. Why had she hoped so much? It was startling how sharply it mattered after all.

"I was!" he agreed, adjusting the imaginary eyeglasses again and peering at her. "Everyone Mr. Gladstone addresses is a public meeting. You are simply a meeting of one."

"Jack!" she said with a slight giggle.

" 'And not in titles or acres,' " he added, pulling his shoulders back, then wincing as if the stiffness of joints had caught him again. " 'I will go further, and say not in men, as such, but in Almighty God, who is the God of justice, and who has ordained the principles of right, of equity and of freedom to be the guides and the masters of our lives.' " He frowned, drawing his brows together. " 'Which means, of course, that His first priority is Home Rule for Ireland, and if we don't grant it immediately we shall all be stricken with the seven deadly plagues of Toryism — or maybe it's Socialism?' "

She started to laugh in spite of herself, the anxiety slipping away like a discarded overcoat now that she was in the warmth. "He didn't say that!"

He grinned at her. "Well, not exactly. But he has said it in the past. What he actually said was that we must win the election because if we don't get Home Rule for Ireland into law then the bloodshed and the loss will follow us down the ages. Everything else we want: a fair working week in all jobs, to prevent at all costs Lord Salisbury's proposed plans for a closer alliance with the court of Rome . . ."

"The court of Rome?" she said in confusion.

"The Pope!" he explained. "Mr. Gladstone is a staunch supporter of the Kirk, for all that they are rapidly failing more and more to return the favor."

She was startled. She had always visualized Gladstone as the epitome of religious rectitude. He was known for his evangelism, and in his younger years for attempting to reform women of the streets, and his wife had given food and assistance to many. "I thought . . ." she began, and then tailed off. The reasons were not important. "He is going to win, isn't he?"

"Yes," he said gently, his body returning into its natural grace. "People laugh at him sometimes, and his political enemies harp on his age . . ."

"How old is he?"

"Eighty-three. But he still has the passion and the energy to go around the country campaigning, and he's the best speaker in front of a crowd that we've ever had. I listened to him a couple of days ago. They cheered him to the echo. There were people who brought their tiny children carried on their shoulders, just so they could tell them one day that they actually saw Gladstone." Almost unconsciously he put his hand up to his eye. "And there are those who hate him as well. A woman in Chester threw a piece of gingerbread at him. I'm glad she's not my cook! It was so hard it actually injured him. It was his better eye, too. But it hasn't slowed him. He's still planning to go up to Scotland and campaign for his own seat . . . and help everyone else he can." There was admiration in his voice, half reluctant. "But he won't give in on the working week! Home Rule before everything."

"Is there any chance of it?"

He gave a little grunt. "None."

"You didn't argue with him, did you, Jack?"

He glanced away from her. "No. But it will cost us dearly. This is an election every man wants to win, and neither party. The burdens are too great, and issues we can't succeed in."

She was momentarily puzzled. "You mean they'd rather be in opposition?"

He shrugged. "The Parliament won't last long. It's all to play for next time. And that could be very soon . . . even within the year."

She caught an edge in his voice, something he was not saying.

He turned away and looked towards the fireplace, staring at the painting over the mantel as if seeing through it. "Someone invited me to join the Inner Circle this evening."

She froze. Like settling ice she remembered what Vespasia had said, and the clashes Pitt had had with the invisible force of secrecy, the power that had no accountability because no one knew who it was. It was they who had cost Pitt his job in Bow Street and sent him almost fugitive into the alleys of Whitechapel. That he had emerged with a desperately hard-won victory, bought with the price of blood, had earned their unrelenting enmity.

"You can't!" she said aloud, her voice harsh with fear.

"I know," he answered, keeping his back to her. The lamplight shone on the black cloth of his jacket, stretching the weave with the tension in his shoulders. Why did he not face her? Why did he not dismiss it with the same anger she felt? For a moment she was not even sure if she had said no again, but she did not move, and the silence in the room was unbroken.

"Jack?" It was almost a whisper.

"Of course." He turned slowly, making himself smile. "It all comes at a high price, doesn't it? The power to do anything useful, make any real changes, the friendship of those you care about, and integrity to yourself. Without the right influence you can play at the edges of politics all your life and not realize until the end, and maybe not even then, that you haven't actually changed a thing, because the real power has eluded you. It was always in the hands of someone else . . . ."

"Someone anonymous," she said very quietly. "Someone who is not what or who you think they are, whose reasons you don't know or understand, who may be the reality behind faces you think are innocent, you think are your friends." She stood up. "You can't make bargains with the devil!"

"I'm not sure you can make political bargains with anyone," he said ruefully, putting one hand on her shoulder and running it lightly down her arm so she could feel it through the silk of her gown. "I think politics is about judgment as to what is possible and what isn't, and having the skill to see as far as you can where each road leads."

"Well, the Inner Circle road leads to giving up your right to act for yourself," she answered.

"Power in government is not about acting for yourself." He kissed her softly and she stiffened for a moment, then pulled away and stared at him. "It's about achieving some real good in making things better for the people who trust you, who elected you," he went on. "That is what honor is — keeping your promises, acting for those who have not the power to do so themselves . . . not for posturing, feeling comfortable or indulging your own conscience."

She looked down, uncertain what to say. She did not know how to put her feelings into words, even to herself, an argument that would make clear the path between helplessness on one hand, and compromise on the other. No one gained anything without a price. How high a price was acceptable? How high was necessary?

"Emily?" he said, a lift of alarm in his voice. It was very slight, but the laughter was false now, a mask. "I refused!"

"I know," she answered, shivering, uncertain he would refuse next time, when the persuasion was stronger, the arguments more passionate, more tilted, the prize greater. And she was ashamed that she was afraid. Had it been Pitt she would not have been. But then Pitt had tasted their power himself, and felt the wounds.

CHAPTER

SEVEN

Charlotte and Gracie worked together in the cottage kitchen. Gracie was cleaning the cooking range after having scrubbed the stone floor, Charlotte was kneading bread, and the butter churn stood on the marble-topped table in the cool of the scullery. Sunlight streamed through the open door; the slight breeze from the moors rising in the distance was sweet and sharp with the aroma of tussock and herbs and the lush grasses of the bogs. The children were playing on the apple tree and every so often they shouted with laughter.

"If that boy rips 'is trousers one more time sliding out o' that tree, I don' know wot you're goin' ter tell 'is mother!" Gracie said exasperatedly, referring to Edward, who was having the time of his life and had torn every piece of clothing he had brought with him. Charlotte had spent time each evening doing her best to repair them. One pair of Daniel's trousers had been sacrificed to make patches for both boys. Even Jemima had rebelled against the restrictions of skirts and tucked them up as she had scrambled over stone walls and loudly declared that there was no natural or moral law that girls should not have just as much fun as boys.

They ate bread and cheese and fruit, raspberries, wild strawberries, and plums, till they were fortunate not to be sick, and fresh sausages from the butcher in the village. It would have been perfect, if only Pitt could have been with them.

Charlotte understood that it was impossible, even if not the details of why. And although Voisey could not know where they were, she was aware all the time of listening to make sure she could hear the children's voices, and every ten minutes or so she went to the door and looked out to see them.

Gracie said nothing about it. Not once did she remark on the fact that they were alone here, but Charlotte heard her going around the windows and doors at night, checking after her that they were locked. Neither did Gracie mention Tellman's name, but Charlotte knew she must be thinking of him, after their closeness during the Whitechapel affair. Her silence was in some ways more telling than words. Perhaps at last her feelings for him were greater than friendship?

Charlotte finished the bread and set it in its tins to rise, then went out to the garden to wash her hands under the pump. She looked up at the apple tree and saw Daniel on the highest branch strong enough to take his weight, and Jemima clinging to the one immediately below. She waited a moment for the stirring of leaves that would tell her where Edward was, and it did not come.

"Edward!" she called. It could only have been minutes. "Edward!"

Silence, then Daniel looked over to her.

"Edward!" she shouted, running towards the tree.

Daniel slid down hand over hand, scrambling into the fork of the branches, and then dropped to the ground. Jemima started to come down a great deal more carefully, hampered by inexperience and the fabric of skirts.

"We can see over the garden wall from up there," Daniel said reasonably. "And there's a patch of wild strawberries that way." He pointed, smiling.

"Is he there?" she demanded, her voice high and sharp beyond her control. Even as she heard it she knew she was being ridiculous, and yet she could not help it. He had only gone to pick fruit, as any child would. There was no need even to be worried, let alone panic. She was allowing imagination to take over her reason. "Is he?" she repeated only a fraction more calmly.

"I don't know." Daniel was looking at her anxiously now. "Do you want me to go up again and look?"

"Yes! Yes, please."

Jemima landed on the grass and straightened up, regarding a small tear in her dress with irritation. She saw Charlotte looking at her and shrugged. "Skirts are stupid sometimes!" she said in disgust.

Daniel went back up the tree, nimbly, hand over hand. He knew exactly the way to go now. "No!" he called from the top. "He must have found another one, maybe better. I can't see him!"

Charlotte felt her heart lurch and the beating of the blood in her ears was deafening. Her vision blurred. What if Voisey had taken revenge on Pitt by hurting Emily's child? Or maybe he didn't even know who was who! What should she do?

"Gracie!" she yelled. "Gracie!"

"Wot?" Gracie flung open the back door

and came running out, fear wide in her eyes. "Wot's 'appened?"

Charlotte swallowed, trying to steady herself. She should not panic and frighten Gracie. It was stupid and unfair. She knew she was doing it and still could not help herself. "Edward has gone . . . gone to pick strawberries," she gulped. "But he's not there anymore." Her mind raced to find a reasonable excuse for the terror which Gracie must see and hear in her. "I'm afraid of the bogs out there. Even the wild animals get caught in them sometimes. I . . ."

Gracie did not wait. "You stay 'ere wi' them!" She waved at Daniel and Jemima. "I'll go look for 'im." And without waiting to see if Charlotte agreed or not, she picked up her skirts and ran with amazing speed across the grass and out of the gate, leaving it swinging behind her.

Daniel turned to Charlotte, his face pale. "He wouldn't go into a bog, Mama. You showed us what they look like, all green and bright. He knows that!"

"No, of course not," she agreed, staring at the gate. Should she take Daniel and Jemima with her and go, too, or were they safer here? She should not leave Gracie alone to look for Edward. What was she thinking of! Don't separate! "Come on!" She darted and grasped Daniel's hand, almost pulling him off balance as she started towards the gate. "Jemima! Come with me. We'll all go and look for Edward. But stay together! We must stay together!"

They were only a hundred yards along the lane, the small, straight-backed figure of Gracie another hundred yards ahead of them, when the dogcart came over the rise and with a flood of relief that brought tears to her eyes, Charlotte saw Edward sitting beside the driver, balancing precariously and grinning with satisfaction.

Now she was so furious with him for the fear she had felt that she would happily have spanked him until he had to eat supper off the mantelpiece — and breakfast, too! But it would be totally unfair; he had not meant harm. Looking at his pleasure, she forced back her emotions, called out to Gracie, then picked her way over the ruts in the track to speak to the driver, who had pulled up in seeing them.

Gracie came back and for a moment her eyes met Charlotte's, and she blinked hard to mask the depth of her own relief. In that instant Charlotte realized just how much they had been hiding from each other, trying to protect, pretend it was not there, and she was filled with gratitude and a startling depth of love for the girl with whom she had so little in common on the surface, and so much in reality.

Pitt's house in Keppel Street was exactly as always, not an ornament or a book out of place. There were even flowers in the vase on the mantel shelf in the parlor, and early sunlight poured through the windows onto the kitchen bench and splashed warm across the floor. Archie and Angus lay curled up together in the clothes basket, purring gently. And yet everything was so different in its emptiness that it seemed more like a painting than a reality. The kettle was beginning to boil on the stove but it only served to elaborate the silence. There were no footsteps on the stairs, no rattle and clatter of Gracie in the larder or the scullery. No one called out asking where a lost shoe or sock was, or a schoolbook. There was no answer from Charlotte, no reminder of the time. The ticking of the kitchen clock seemed to echo.

But Pitt was at ease that they were away from London, safely anonymous in Devon. He had told himself that he did not think anyone in the Inner Circle would revenge themselves on him by hurting his family at

Voisey's command. Voisey would not hire someone he did not trust, he could not afford the risk to himself, and Pitt's turning of the events in Whitechapel had made Voisey appear to betray not only his allies and friends but his cause as well. It should have divided the Circle along lines of personal loyalties and self-interest, but Pitt had no way of knowing if it had.

He could not clear from his mind the look of hatred in Voisey's eyes as he had passed him in Buckingham Palace the moment after the knighthood which he and Vespasia had contrived, using Mario Corena's sacrifice. It had ended forever Voisey's ambitions to be republican president of Britain.

And that same hatred had been there in his eyes again when they had met in the House of Commons. Passion like that did not die. Pitt could sit here at his own kitchen table with some measure of calmness only because he knew his family was hidden and safe, miles away. No matter how much he missed the mere knowledge of their presence in the house, the loneliness was a small price to pay for that.

Was the murder of Maude Lamont connected with Voisey's bid for a parliamentary seat? There were at least two possible connections: the fact that Rose Serracold had been at the séance that night; and the fact that Roland Kingsley, who was also there, had written to the newspapers so vehemently against Aubrey Serracold. Pitt had found nothing in Kingsley's previous political views to lead anyone to expect such an opinion now.

But then elections brought out extreme views. The threat of losing exposed some ugly sides of nature, just as some were surprisingly brash in victory where one had expected grace, even generosity.

Or was the connection the man whose name was concealed by a cartouche, and who might have had a far more personal relationship with Maude Lamont? Was the connection with Voisey even a real one, or was it Narraway's attempt to use any means possible to block his path to power?

If Narraway had been Cornwallis, Pitt would have known every attack he made would be clever but fair. Cornwallis was a man trained by the rigor of the sea who went into battle with his face forward and fought to the end.

Pitt did not know Narraway's beliefs, the motives which drove him, or the experience, the triumphs and the losses which had formed his character. He did not even know whether Narraway would lie to the men under his command in order to make them do whatever would achieve his own ends. Pitt was moving step by step in the dark. For his safety, so he was not manipulated to serve a purpose he did not believe in, he must learn a great deal more about Narraway.

But for the present he needed to discover why Roland Kingsley had proclaimed himself so virulently against Serracold. It was not the opinion he had expressed when Pitt had spoken to him. Had Maude Lamont been manipulating him with the threat of disclosure of something she had learned from his questions to the dead?

What made a man of the successful, practical nature he seemed to possess go to a spirit medium? Tragically, many people lost sons and daughters. Most of them found a fortitude based in the love they shared in the past and an inner belief in some religion, formal or not, that there was a divine power that would reunite them one day. They continued with life the best way they could, with work, the comfort of others they loved, perhaps a retreat into great music or literature, or the solitude of nature, or even exhausting oneself in the care of those less fortunate. They did not turn to notions of Ouija boards and ecto-plasm.

What was there in his son's death that had driven Kingsley so far? And if the answer were blackmail, was it by Maude Lamont herself, or had she only supplied the information to someone else, someone still alive, and who would continue to use it?

Such as a member of the Inner Circle — even Charles Voisey himself?

That was what Narraway would like it to be! And it had nothing to do with whether it was the truth or not. Perhaps Pitt was seeing Voisey where he had no part. Fear itself could be an element of his revenge, maybe better even than the actuality of the blow.

He stood up, leaving his dishes on the table where Mrs. Brody would find them and clear them away. He went outside. He was hot by the time he had walked as far as Tottenham Court Road and stopped on the pavement to hail a hansom.

He spent the morning with the official military records tracing the career of Roland Kingsley. No doubt Narraway would have searched them, if he did not already know the facts, but Pitt wanted to see for himself, in case his interpretation of the records was different.

There was little personal comment. He read through it all quickly. Roland James Walford Kingsley had joined the army at eighteen, like his father and grandfather before him. His career spanned over forty years, from his early discipline and training, his first foreign posting in the Sikh Wars of the late 1840s, the horror of the Crimean War of the mid-1850s, where he had been mentioned several times in dispatches, and the immediately following bloodbath of the Indian Mutiny.

Later he had turned to Africa, the Ashanti Campaign of the mid-1870s, and the Zulu War at the end of the decade, where he had been decorated for extraordinary valor.

After that he had returned to England, seriously injured, and seemingly also wounded in spirit. He never again left the country, although still honoring all his commitments, and retiring in 1890 at the age of sixty.

Pitt then looked up Kingsley's son, seeking his death in those same Zulu Wars, and found it recorded on July 3, 1879, during the fiasco crossing the White Mfolozi. It was the action in which Captain Lord William Beresford had won a Victoria Cross, the highest honor given for supreme gallantry on the field of battle. Two other men had also been killed, and several wounded, in a superbly executed Zulu ambush. But then Isandlwana had proved the Zulu as warriors of not only courage but exceptional military skill. At Rorke's Drift they had brought out the best in British discipline and honor. That action lived in history and fired the imagination of men and boys as they heard the story of how eight officers and a hundred and thirty-one men, thirty-five of whom were sick, had withstood the siege of nearly four thousand Zulu warriors. Seventeen British had been killed, and eleven Victoria Crosses awarded.

Pitt stood in the middle of the floor and closed the book holding the records, the bare words which made little attempt to describe the burning, dusty countryside of another continent, and the men — good and bad, cowardly and brave — who had gone there out of service or adventure, obedience to an inner voice or an outer necessity, and lived and died in the conflicts.

But as he thanked the clerk and walked down the steps and into the clearing air, the pavement cloud and sunshine patterned, he felt emotion constricting his chest, pride and shame and a desperate desire to preserve all that was good in a land and a people he loved. The men who had faced the enemy at Rorke's Drift stood for something far simpler and cleaner than the secrecy of the Inner Circle and political betrayal for ambition's sake.

He took a cab as far as Narraway's office and then paced the floor with mounting anger as he was obliged to wait for him.

When Narraway arrived nearly an hour later he was mildly amused to find Pitt glaring at him. He closed the door. "I assume from your expression that you have found something of interest?" He made it a question. "For heaven's sake, Pitt, sit down and make a proper report. Is Rose Serracold guilty of something?"

"Self-indulgence," Pitt answered, obeying the instruction. "Nothing else, so far as I know, but I have not stopped looking."

"Good!" Narraway said dryly. "That is what Her Majesty pays you for."

"I think Her Majesty, like God, would be horrified at much of what is done in her name," Pitt snapped back. "If she knew about it!" Then, before Narraway could interrupt, he went on. "Actually, I've been looking at Major General Kingsley to see why he went to Maude Lamont and why his letters to the newspapers condemning Serracold are so at odds with the opinions in his ordinary speech."

"Have you indeed?" Narraway's eyes were very sharp and still. "And what have you found?"

"Only his military record," Pitt replied guardedly. "And that he lost his son in a skirmish in Africa in the same Zulu Wars in which he himself was highly distinguished. It was a bereavement from which he doesn't seem to have recovered."

"It was his only son," Narraway said. "Only child, actually. His wife died young."

Pitt searched his face, trying to read the man's feelings behind the repeating of simple and terrible facts. He saw nothing he was sure of. Did Narraway deal in death so often, in other people's grief, that it no longer marked him? Or could he not afford to feel, in case it swayed judgments that had to be made in the interest of all, not simply those for whom he cared? The closest look at Narraway's clever, line-seamed face told him nothing. There was passion there, but was it of the heart or only the mind?

"How did he die?" Pitt asked aloud.

Narraway raised his eyebrows in surprise that Pitt should want to know. "He was one of the three who was killed during the reconnaissance at White Mfolozi. They ran straight into a rather well-laid Zulu ambush."

"Yes, I saw that in the records. But why is Kingsley pursuing it through a woman like Maude Lamont?" Pitt asked. "And why now? Mfolozi was thirteen years ago!"

Anger flashed in Narraway's eyes, then pain. "If you had lost anyone, Pitt, you would know that the hurt doesn't go away. People learn to live with it, to hide it, most of the time; but you never know what is going to wake it again, and suddenly, for a space, it is out of control." His voice was very quiet. "I've seen it many times. Who knows what it was? The sight of a young man whose face reminded him of his son? Another man who has the grandchildren he doesn't? An old tune . . . anything. The dead don't go away, they just fall silent for a while."

Pitt was aware of something intensely personal in the room. These words were not practical, they were from the passion of the moment. But the shadow in the eyes, the set of Narraway's lips, forbade the intrusion of any words that touched them.

Pitt affected not to have noticed.

"Is there any connection between Kingsley and Charles Voisey?" he asked.

Narraway's dark eyes widened suddenly. "For God's sake, Pitt, don't you think I'd tell you that if I knew?"

"You might prefer me to find it for myself . . ."

Narraway jerked forward, the muscles of his body locked. "We haven't time for games!" he said between his teeth. "I can't afford to give a damn what you think of me! If Charles Voisey gets into Parliament there'll be no stopping him until he has the power to corrupt the highest office in the land. He's still head of the Inner Circle." A shadow crossed his face. "At least I think he is. There is another power there. I don't know who it is . . . yet."

He held up his hand, finger and thumb an inch apart. "He came that close to losing it! We did that, Pitt! And he won't forget it. But we didn't finish him. He will have a new Number Two, and Three, and I haven't the faintest idea who they are. It is a disease eating at the bowels of the true government of the land, whichever party sits in Westminster. We can't deal without power — and we can't deal with it! It's a balancing act. If we stay one step ahead, keep changing often enough, weed out the infection of madness as soon as we recognize it, the delusion that you can do anything and get away with it, that you're infallible, untouchable, then we win — until next time. Then we start all over again, with new players and a new game."

He threw himself back in the chair suddenly. "Find the connection between Kingsley and Charles Voisey yourself, whether it has to do with that woman's death or not. And be careful, Pitt! You were a detective before for Cornwallis, a watcher, a judge. For me you're a player. You too will win — or lose. Don't forget that."

"And you?" Pitt asked a little huskily.

Narraway flashed him a sudden smile that lit his face, but his eyes were hard as coal. "Oh, I intend to win!" He did not say he would die before letting loose his hold, like an animal whose jaws do not unlock even in death. He did not need to.

Pitt rose to his feet, muttered a few words of acknowledgment, and went outside, his mind whirling with unanswered questions, not about Kingsley or Charles Voisey, but about Narraway himself.

He returned home briefly, and on the

footpath at the end of Keppel Street heard a voice addressing him.

"Afternoon, Mr. Pitt!"

He turned around, startled. It was the postman again, smiling, holding out a letter for him.

"Good afternoon," he replied hastily, a sudden excitement inside him, hope surging that it was from Charlotte.

"From Mrs. Pitt, is it?" the postman asked cheerfully. "Somewhere nice, is she?"

Pitt looked down at the letter in his hand. The writing was so like Charlotte's, and yet it was not, and the postmark was London. "No," he said, unable to keep the disappointment out of his voice.

"She's only been gone a day or two," the postman comforted him. "Takes a while from farther off. You tell me where she's gone, I'll tell you 'ow long it'll take for 'er letter ter get 'ome."

Pitt drew in his breath to say "Dartmoor," and then looked at the man's smiling face, and sharp eyes, and felt the coldness well up inside him. He forced himself to remain calm, and it took such an effort that it was a moment before he could reply.

The postman waited.

"Thank you," Pitt said then answered with the first place that came to his mind: "Whitby."

"Yorkshire?" The man looked extraordinarily pleased with himself. "Oh, that shouldn't be more than two days at the most this time of year, maybe only one. You'll 'ear soon, sir. Maybe they're 'aving too much fun ter get down ter writing. Good day, sir."

"Good day." Pitt swallowed, and found his hands shaking as he tore open the letter. It was from Emily, dated the previous afternoon.

Dear Thomas,
Rose Serracold is a friend of mine, and after visiting her yesterday I feel that I know certain things which may be of some meaning to you.
Please call upon me when you have the opportunity.

Emily

He folded it up and slipped it back into the envelope. It was the middle of the afternoon, a time when she would normally be out visiting, or receiving calls, but there would be no better opportunity, and perhaps what she had to say would help. He could not afford to decline any chance at all.

He turned around and walked back to-wards Tottenham Court Road again. Half an hour later he was in Emily's sitting room and she was telling him, with awk-ward phrases and some self-consciousness, of her quarrel with Rose Serracold. She spoke of her growing conviction that Rose was so deeply afraid of something that she was impelled to visit Maude Lamont in spite of the danger of ridicule, and that she had, if not deceived him, at least omitted to tell Aubrey anything about it.

Emily's warning had produced anger in her to the point of endangering their friendship.

When she finished she stared at him, her eyes filled with guilt.

"Thank you," he said quietly.

"Thomas . . ." she began.

"No," he answered before she could ask any further. "I don't know whether she killed her or not, but I cannot look the other way, no matter who gets hurt. All I can promise is that I will cause no more pain than I have to, and I hope you knew that already."

"Yes." She nodded, her body stiff, her face pale. "Of course I did." She took a breath as if to say something more, then changed her mind and offered him tea, which he did not accept. He would have liked to accept — he was tired and thirsty, hungry also if he thought about it — but there was too much emotion between them, too much knowledge for it to be comfortable. He thanked her again and took his leave.

That evening Pitt telephoned Jack's political offices to find out where he was going to speak, and on being informed of the place, he set out to join him, first to listen, feel the political temper of the crowd, then maybe to judge from it more accurately what Aubrey Serracold faced.

And he admitted he was also increasingly concerned for Jack himself. It was going to be a far closer election than last time. Many Liberals could lose their seats.

He arrived as some two or three hundred people were gathering, mostly men from the nearby factories, but also a good number of women, dressed in drab skirts and blouses grained with the sweat and dirt of hard work. Some were even as young as fourteen or fifteen, others with skins so tired and gaunt, bodies so shapeless, that it was hard to tell how old they were. They might have been the sixty that they looked, but Pitt knew very well it was more likely they were still under forty, just exhausted and poorly fed. Many of them would have borne too many children, and the best would have been given to them, and to the men.

There was a low murmur of impatience, a couple of catcalls. More people drifted in. Half a dozen left, grumbling loudly.

Pitt shifted his weight from one foot to the other. He tried to overhear conversations. What did these people think, what did they want? Did anything make any difference to the way they voted, except to a handful of them? Jack had been a good constituency member, but did they realize that? His majority was not large. On a wave of Liberal success he would have had no cause to worry, but this was an election even Gladstone did not wholly desire to win. He fought it from passion and instinct, and because he had always fought, but his reasoning mind was not in it.

There was a sudden flurry of attention and Pitt looked up. Jack had arrived and was walking through the crowd, clasping people by the hand, men and women alike, even one or two of the children. Then he climbed onto the tail of a cart which had been drawn up to form a makeshift platform for him, and began to speak.

Almost immediately he was heckled. A semibald man in a brown coat waved his arm and demanded to know how many hours a day he worked. There was a roar of laughter and more catcalls.

"Well, if I don't get returned to the House, I'll be out of work!" Jack called back at him. "And the answer will be none!"

Now the laughter was directed the other way — humor, not jeering. There followed immediately an argument about the working week. Voices grew harsher and the underlying anger had an ugly edge. Someone threw a stone, but it went yards wide and clattered off the warehouse wall and rolled away.

Looking at Jack's face, handsome and easy-natured as it seemed to be, Pitt could see he was holding his temper with an effort. A few years ago he might not even have tried.

"Vote for the Tories," Jack offered with an expansive gesture. "If you think they'll give it to you."

There were curses and hoots and whistles of derision.

"None of yer's any good!" a scrawny

woman yelled, her lips drawn back from broken teeth. "All yer do is bleed us fer taxes and tie us up in laws no one understands."

And so it continued for another half hour. Slowly, Jack's patience and occasional banter began to win over more of them, but Pitt could see in the growing tension in his face and the tiredness of his body the effort it cost him. An hour later, dusty, exhausted and hot from the press of the crowd and the stale, clinging air of the dockside, he climbed down from the cart and Pitt caught up with him as he walked towards the open street where he would be able to find a hansom. Like Voisey he had had the tactical sense not to bring his own carriage.

He turned to Pitt with surprise.

Pitt smiled at him. "An accomplished performance," he said sincerely. He did not add any facile words about winning. As close to Jack as he was, he could see the exhaustion in his eyes and the grime in the fine lines of his skin. It was dusk and the street lamps were glowing. They must have passed the lamplighter without noticing him.

"Are you here for moral support?" Jack asked dubiously.

"No," Pitt admitted. "I need to know more about Mrs. Serracold."

Jack looked at him in surprise.

"Have you eaten?" Pitt asked.

"Not yet. Do you think Rose could be involved in this wretched murder?" He stopped, turning to face Pitt. "I've known her for a couple of years, Thomas. She's eccentric, certainly, and has some idealistic beliefs which are highly impractical, but that's a very different thing from killing anyone." He pushed his hands into his pockets, which was uncharacteristic in him; he cared too much about the cut of his suits to so misuse them. "I don't know what on earth possessed her to go to this medium now, of all times." He winced. "I can imagine how the press would ridicule it. But honestly, Voisey's making pretty heavy inroads into the Liberal position. I started off believing Aubrey would get in as long as he didn't do anything totally stupid. Now I'm afraid Voisey's winning is not as impossible as it seemed even a couple of days ago." He continued walking, looking straight ahead of him. They were both dimly aware of supporters, out of uniform, twenty yards behind.

"Rose Serracold," Pitt reminded him. "Her family?"

"Her mother was a society beauty, as far as I know," Jack replied. "Her father was from a good family. I did know who, but I forget. I think he died quite young, but it was illness, nothing suspicious, if that's what you're thinking."

Pitt was reaching after every possibility. "A lot of money?"

They crossed the alley and turned left, feet echoing on the cobbles.

"I don't think so," Jack answered. "No. Aubrey has the money."

"Any connection with Voisey?" Pitt asked, trying to keep his voice light, free from the emotion that surged up in him at even the mention of his name.

Jack glanced at him, then away again. "Rose, you mean? If she has, then she's lying, at least by implication. She wants Aubrey to win. Surely if she knew anything about him at all, she would say so?"

"And General Kingsley?"

Jack was puzzled. "General Kingsley? You mean the fellow who wrote that harsh piece in the newspaper about Aubrey?"

"Several harsh pieces," Pitt corrected. "Yes. Has he any personal enmity against Serracold?"

"None that Aubrey knows of, unless he's concealing something as well, and I'd swear he isn't. He's actually quite transparent. He was pretty shaken by it. He's not used to personal attack."

"Could Rose know him?"

They were halfway along a stretch of narrow pavement outside a warehouse wall. The single street lamp lit only a few yards on either side, cobbles and a dry gutter.

Jack stopped again, his brows drawn together, his eyes narrow. "I presume that is a euphemism for having an affair?"

"Probably, but I mean any kind of knowing," Pitt said with rising urgency. "Jack, I have to find out who killed Maude Lamont, preferably show beyond any doubt at all that it was not Rose. Mocking her for attending séances will be nothing compared with what Voisey will see that the newspapers do to her if any secret emerges which suggests she committed murder to hide it."

They were still under the light. Pitt saw Jack wince, and he seemed almost to shrink into himself. His shoulders drooped and the color ebbed from his face.

"It's a hell of a mess, Thomas," he said wearily. "The more I know of it the less I understand, and I can explain almost nothing at all to people like those." He jerked a hand backwards to indicate the crowd near the dockside, now out of sight beyond the jutting mass of the warehouse.

Pitt did not ask him to explain; he knew he was going to.

"I used to imagine the election rested on some kind of argument," Jack went on, starting to walk again. Ahead of them, the Goat and Compasses public house was glowing invitingly in the rapidly thickening dusk. "It's all emotion," he went on. "Feeling, not thought. I don't even know if I want us to win . . . as a party, I mean. Of course I want power! Without it we can't do anything. We might as well pack up and leave the field to the opposition!" He glanced at Pitt quickly. "We were the first country in the world to be industrialized. We manufacture millions of pounds worth of goods every year, and the money that earns pays most of our population."

Pitt waited for the rest of it after they entered the Goat and Compasses, found a table and Jack sank into a chair and requested a large ale. Pitt fetched his usual cider and returned with both tankards.

Jack drank for several moments before continuing. "More and more goods all the time. If we are to survive, then we need to sell all those goods to someone!"

Pitt had a sudden perception where Jack was reaching. "The Empire," he said quietly. "Are we back to Home Rule again?"

"More than that," Jack replied. "We're on the whole moral subject of should we have an empire at all!"

"Bit late for that, isn't it?" Pitt asked dryly.

"Several hundred years. As I said, it isn't based on thought. If we divest ourselves of the Empire now, who do we sell all our goods to? France and Germany and the rest of Europe, not to mention America, are all manufacturing now as well." He bit his lip. "The goods are growing more and the markets less. It's a wonderful ideal to give it all back, but if we lose our markets, untold numbers of our own people will starve. If the country's economy is ruined there'll be no one with the power to help them, for all the good intentions in the world." A wet glass slipped from someone's hand and splintered on the floor. They cursed fluently. A woman laughed too loudly at a joke.

Jack gave an abrupt, angry little gesture. "And try campaigning by telling people, 'Vote for me and I'll free you of the Empire you are so against. Of course, unfortunately it will cost you your jobs, your homes, even your town. The factories will go out of business because there'll be too few customers being courted to buy too many goods. The shops will close, and the factories and the mills. But it's a high-minded thing to do, and must surely be morally right!' "

"Are our manufactured goods not competitive against the rest of the world?" Pitt asked.

"The world doesn't need them." Jack picked up the second half of his beer. "They're making their own. Can you see anybody voting you in on that?" He raised his eyebrows, his eyes wide. "Or do you think we should tell them we won't, and then do it anyway? Lie to them all in the name of moral righteousness! Isn't it up to them whether they want to save their souls at that price?"

Pitt said nothing.

Jack did not expect an answer. "It's all in the uses and balances of power, isn't it?" he went on softly, staring into the distance of the crowded tavern. "Can you pick up the sword without cutting yourself? Someone must. But do you know how to use it any better than the next man? Don't you believe anything enough to fight for it? And what are you worth if you don't?" He looked at Pitt again. "Imagine not caring for anything sufficiently to take a risk for it! You'd lose even what you had. I can imagine what Emily thinks of that." He stared down at the mug in his hand, smiling a trifle twistedly. Then suddenly he looked up at Pitt. "Mind, I'd sooner face Emily than Charlotte."

Pitt winced, a new set of images in his mind, racing away, one melting into another. For an instant he missed Charlotte so much it was a physical ache. He had sent her away to be safe, but he was not stepping forward to fight some noble battle by choice. Looking at it now with hindsight, if he could have evaded Voisey, perhaps he would have. "Are you thinking of what will happen if you are given office?" he said suddenly.

A swift color stained Jack's cheeks, making a lie impossible. "Not exactly. They asked me to join the Inner Circle. Of course I won't!" He spoke a little too quickly, his eyes fixed on Pitt's. "But it was very clearly pointed out to me, if I were not with them, then my opponents would be. You can't step outside it all . . ."

Pitt felt as if someone had opened the doors onto a winter night. "Who was it that asked you?" he said softly.

Jack shook his head, only a tiny movement. "I can't tell you."

It was on the edge of Pitt's tongue to demand if it had been Charles Voisey, but he remembered at the last moment that Jack did not know what had happened in Whitechapel, and for his own safety it was better it should remain so. Or was it? He looked at Jack now, sitting at the other side of the table with the beer tankard between his hands, his expression still carrying some of the charm and a kind of innocence he had had when they had first met. He had been so worldly wise in the manners and rules of society, but naive of the truly darker alleys of life, the violence of the mind. The facile betrayals of country house parties, the selfishness of the idle, was an uncomplicated thing compared with the evil Pitt had seen. Would knowledge be a greater protection? Or a greater danger? If Voisey guessed Jack was aware of his position as leader of the Inner Circle, it might mark Jack as another he had to destroy!

And yet if Jack did not know, was Pitt leaving him without shield against the seduction of twisted reason? Was Jack more than just another Liberal candidate? Disarmed, was he also another way to wound

Pitt? Corruption would be infinitely more satisfying than mere defeat.

Or perhaps it was coincidental, and Pitt was creating his own demons?

He pushed his chair back and stood up, drinking the last of his cider and setting the glass down. "Come on. We've both got a long way to go home, and there'll be all sorts of traffic on the bridges at this time of night. Don't forget Rose Serracold."

"Do you think she killed that woman, Thomas?" Jack climbed to his feet also, ignoring the dregs of his ale.

Pitt did not answer until they had pushed their way through the crowd and were outside in the street, which was almost completely dark.

"It was she, General Kingsley, or the third person, who kept his identity secret," Pitt replied.

"Then it was the third person!" Jack said instantly. "Why would any honest man hide his identity over what is an eccentric pursuit, perhaps a trifle absurd, even pathetic, but quite respectable and far from any kind of crime?" His voice picked up enthusiasm. "There was obviously more to it! He was probably slipping back after the others left and having an affair with her. Perhaps she blackmailed him, and he killed her to keep her quiet. What better way to conceal his visits than in the open, going to a séance with other people. He's looking for his great-grandfather, or whoever. Foolish, but innocent."

"Apparently he wasn't looking for anyone in particular. He appeared to be a skeptic."

"Better still! He's trying to discredit her, prove her a fraud. That shouldn't be difficult. The very fact that he didn't expose her suggests another motive."

"Perhaps," Pitt agreed as they passed under the street lamp again. The wind was rising a little, blowing up from the river, carrying loose sheets of old newspapers, drifting over the cobbles and settling again. There were beggars in the doorways; it was too early to huddle down for the night. A street woman already kept an eye hopeful for custom. The air was sour in the throat as they walked abreast towards the bridge.

Pitt slept badly. The silence in the house was oppressive, an emptiness, not a peace. He woke late with a headache and was sitting at the kitchen table when the doorbell rang. He stood up and went in his stocking feet to answer it.

Tellman stood on the step looking cold

although the morning was mild and the high clouds were already thinning. By midday it would be bright and hot.

"What is it?" Pitt asked, stepping back in tacit invitation. "Judging by your face, nothing good."

Tellman stepped in, frowning, his lantern jaw set tight and hard. He glanced around as if for a moment he had forgotten that Gracie would not be there. He looked forlorn, as if he too had been abandoned.

Pitt followed him back to the kitchen. "What is it?" he repeated as Tellman went to the far side of the table and sat down, ignoring the kettle and not even looking for cake or biscuits.

"We might have found the man written in the diary as a picture . . . what did you say . . . a cartouche?" he replied, his voice flat, struggling to keep all expression out of it, leaving Pitt to make all his own judgments.

"Oh?"

The silence in the room was heavy. A dog was barking somewhere in the distance, and Pitt could hear the slithering sound of a bag of coal being emptied into a cellar chute next door. He felt a curious, sinking sensation. There was a premonition of tragedy in Tellman's face, as if already a weight of darkness had settled inside him.

Tellman looked up. "He fits the description," he said quietly. "Height, age, build, hair, even voice, so the informant says. I suppose he would, or Superintendent Wetron wouldn't have passed it on to us."

"What makes him think it's this man rather than any of a thousand others who also fit the description?" Pitt asked. "All we have is middle height, probably in his sixties, neither thin nor fat, gray hair. There must be thousands of men like that, tens of thousands within train distance of Southampton Row." He leaned forward across the table. "What is the rest, Tellman? Why this man?"

Tellman did not blink. "Because he's a retired professor, apparently, who just lost his wife after a long illness. All their children died young. He has nobody else, and he's taken it very hard. Sort of . . . started behaving oddly, wandering around talking to young women, trying to recapture the past. His dead children, I suppose." He looked wretched, as if he had been caught intruding on someone's acute private embarrassment, like a voyeur. "He's got himself talked about . . . a bit."

"Where does he live?" Pitt asked unhappily. Why on earth did Wetron think this unfortunate man had anything to do with Maude Lamont's death? "Is it near Southampton Row?"

"No," Tellman said quickly. "Teddington."

Pitt thought he had misheard. Teddington was a village miles up the Thames, beyond Kew, beyond even Richmond. "Where did you say?"

"Teddington," Tellman repeated. "He could come in on the train quite easily."

"Why on earth should he?" Pitt asked incredulously. "Aren't spirit mediums common enough? Why Maude Lamont? She's rather expensive for a retired teacher, isn't she?"

"That's it." Tellman was totally miserable. "He's still noted as a deep thinker and very highly respected. Writes the definitive textbooks on some things. Obscure, but then it would be, to most of us. But his own people think the world of him."

"Having the means doesn't explain coming all the way into the city to consult a spirit medium whose sessions go on till nearly midnight," Pitt argued.

Tellman took in a deep breath. "It might if you were a senior sort of clergyman whose reputation rested on your insight into the Christian faith." Again the pity and contempt struggled in his face. "If you took to looking for answers from women who spit up eggs and cheesecloth and tell you it's ghosts, I should think you'd be looking to go as far away from home as possible. Personally, I'd want it to be another country! I'm not surprised he came and went by the garden door, and wouldn't even tell Miss Lamont his name."

Suddenly it was tragically clear to Pitt. It answered all the anomalies of secrecy, evasion, and why he was so frightened of anyone guessing his identity that he would not even name those spirits he wanted to find. It was tragic, yet so fallible and, with a little imagination, easily understood. He was an old man left bereaved of all things he had loved. The final blow of his wife's death had been too much for his balance. Even the strongest have a dark night of the soul somewhere in the long journey of life.

Tellman was watching him, waiting for his response.

"I'll go to see him," Pitt said unhappily. "What's his name, and where in Teddington does he live?"

"Udney Road, just a few hundred yards from the railway station. London and

South West Line, that is."

"And his name?"

"Francis Wray," Tellman replied, watching Pitt's eyes.

Pitt thought of the cartouche with its bent letter inside the circle, like a reversed *f*. Now he understood more of Tellman's unhappiness and why he could not cast it aside, much as he would prefer to. "I see," he acknowledged.

Tellman opened his mouth to speak, then closed it again. There really was nothing to say that they did not both know already.

"What have your men found on the other clients?" Pitt asked after a moment or two.

"Nothing very much," Tellman replied dourly. "All kinds of people; about the only thing they have in common is enough money and time to spend chasing after signs of those already dead. Some of them are lonely, some confused and needing to feel their husband or father still knows what's going on and loves them." His voice was getting lower and lower. "A lot of them are just interested, looking for a bit of excitement, want to be entertained. Nobody has a grudge worth doing something about."

"Did you learn anything about the other ones who came through the garden door from Cosmo Place?"

"No." There was a flicker of resentment in his eyes. "Don't know any way of finding them. Where would we begin?"

"About how much did Maude Lamont earn for this?"

Tellman's eyes were wide. "About four times as much as I do, even with promotion!"

Pitt knew exactly what Tellman would earn. He could imagine the volume of business Maude Lamont could take if she worked four or five days a week. "That is still rather less than running that house must have cost her, and maintaining a wardrobe like hers."

"Blackmail?" Tellman said without hesitation. His face tightened to a mask of disgust. "It isn't enough she dupes them, she has to make them pay for silence over their secrets?" He was not looking for any answer, he simply needed to find words for his bitterness. "There are some people who look to be murdered so hard it makes you wonder how they escaped it before!"

"It doesn't make any difference to the fact that we must find out who killed her," Pitt said quietly. "The fact of murder cannot go unanswered. I wish I could say that justice would always visit every act fairly and apportion punishment or mercy as it was deserved. I know it won't. It will be mistaken in both directions. But allowing private vengeance, or escape from anything except threat to life, would be the gateway to anarchy."

"I know!" Tellman said curtly, angry with Pitt for pointing out to him the helplessness he already understood quite clearly, as if he could not have found the words so easily to express it.

"Anything more from the maid?" Pitt ignored his tone.

"Nothing helpful. Seems a sensible sort of woman on the whole, but I think she may know more about those séances and how they were rigged than she's telling us. Had to. She was the only one close. All the other staff, cook and laundress and gardener, all came in by the day and were gone before the private sessions ever began."

"Unless she was equally deceived?" Pitt suggested.

"She's a sensible woman," Tellman argued, his voice sharper as he repeated himself. "She wouldn't be taken in by tricks like pedals and mirrors and oil of phosphorous, all that kind of thing."

"Most of us have a tendency to believe what we want to," Pitt replied. "Especially if it matters very much. Sometimes the need is so great we don't dare disbelieve, or it would break our dreams, and without them we die. Sense has little to do with it. It is survival."

Tellman stared at him. He seemed on the point of arguing again, then he changed his mind and remained silent. It obviously had not occurred to him that Lena Forrest might also have doubts and loves, people now dead who were woven into the meaning of her life. He flushed very faintly at his omission, and Pitt liked him the better for it.

Pitt stood up slowly. "I'll go and see this Mr. Wray," he said. "Teddington! I suppose Maude Lamont was good enough to bring someone all the way from Teddington to Southampton Row?"

Tellman did not answer.

Pitt wasted no time thinking about how to approach the Reverend Francis Wray when he should find him. It was going to be wretched no matter what he said. It was best to do it before apprehension made him clumsier and even more artificial.

He made his way to the railway station and enquired about the best route to Teddington, and was told that he would have to change trains, but that the next train to begin his journey was due to leave in eleven minutes. He purchased a through ticket, thanked the man, and went to get a newspaper from the vendor at the entrance. Most of the space was taken up with election issues and the usual virulent cartoons. He did notice an advertisement for the upcoming exhibition of costermongers' ponies and donkeys to be held at the People's Palace in Mile-End Road in a couple of weeks' time.

On the platform with him were two elderly women and a family obviously on a day out. The children were excited, hopping up and down and unable to stop chattering. He wondered how Daniel, Jemima and Edward were enjoying Devon, if they liked the country, or if they found it strange, if they missed their usual friends. Did they miss him? Or was it all too full of adventure? And of course Charlotte was with them.

He had been away from them too often lately, first in Whitechapel, and now this! He had hardly spoken to either Daniel or Jemima in a couple of months, not with time to reach towards the more difficult subjects, to listen to what was unsaid as well as the surface words. When this matter of Voisey was over, whether they knew who had killed Maude Lamont or not, he must make sure he took a day or two every so often just to spend with them. Narraway owed him at least that much, and he could not live the rest of his life running away from Voisey. That would be giving him victory without even the effort of a fight.

He dared not even think too closely of Charlotte; missing her left an ache in him too big to fill with thought or action. Even dreams left an ache that hurt too much.

The train came in in a roar of steam and the clatter of iron wheels on iron rails, with flying smuts, the smell and heat of power, and the moment of parting with her was as sharp as if she had left barely a moment ago. He had to force himself into the present, to open the carriage door and hold it for two elderly women, then follow them up the step and inside and find a seat.

It was not a long journey. Forty minutes and he was in Teddington. As Tellman had told him, Udney Road was only a block away from the station, and a few minutes' walk took him to the neat gate of number four. He stared at it in the sun for several moments, breathing in the scents of a dozen flowers and the sweet, clean odor of hot earth newly watered. It was so full of memory, so domestic, that for an instant it overwhelmed him.

At a glance the garden looked random, almost overgrown, but he knew the years of care that had gone into its nurture and upkeep. There were no dead heads, nothing out of place, no weeds. It was a blaze of color, new with long familiar, exotic and indigenous side by side. Simply staring at it told him much of the man who had planted it. Was it Francis Wray himself, or an outdoor servant paid for the task? If it were the latter, whatever he earned, his real reward was in his art.

Pitt unfastened the gate and went in, closing it behind him, and walked up the path. A black cat lay stretched on the windowsill in the sun, a tortoiseshell strolled through the dappled shade of late crimson snapdragons. Pitt prayed he was here on a fool's errand.

He knocked on the front door, and was admitted by a girl in a maid's uniform, but who could not have been more than fifteen years old.

"Is this the home of Mr. Francis Wray?" Pitt enquired.

"Yes sir." She was obviously concerned because he was someone she did not know. Perhaps Wray was usually visited only by fellow clergymen or members of the local community. "Sir . . . if you'd wait there, I'll go an' see if 'e's at 'ome." She stepped back, then did not know whether to ask him in, leave him on the step, or even close the door in case he might have designs on the gleaming horse brasses hanging behind her in the hall.

"May I wait in the garden?" he asked, glancing back at the flowers.

Her face flooded with relief. "Yes sir. 'Course yer can. 'E keeps it a real treat, don't 'e?" She blinked suddenly as tears came to her eyes. Pitt gathered that Wray had thrown himself into its care since his bereavement. Perhaps it was a physical labor that eased some of the emotion inside. Flowers were a kind of company that absorbed all your ministrations, yet gave back only beauty, asking no questions and intruding nowhere.

He had not long to stand in the sun watching the tortoiseshell cat before Wray himself came out of the front door and along the short path. He was of average height, at least four inches shorter than Pitt, although in his youth he might have been less so. Now his shoulders sank, his back was a little bent, but it was his face that carried the indelible marks of inner pain. There were shadows around his eyes, deep lines from nose to mouth and more than one razor nick on his papery skin.

"Good afternoon, sir," he said quietly in a voice of remarkable beauty. "Mary Ann tells me you wish to see me. I am Francis Wray. What may I do for you?"

For a moment Pitt even thought of lying. What he was about to do could only be painful and grossly intrusive. The thought vanished again. This man could be "Cartouche," and if nothing more, he could supply another recollection not only of the evening, but of the other occasions on which he had been at Maude Lamont's with Rose Serracold and General Kingsley. With a lifetime spent in the church, surely he was a profound observer of human nature?

"Good afternoon, Mr. Wray," he replied. "My name is Thomas Pitt." He hated approaching the subject of Maude Lamont's death, but he had no other reason for taking Wray's time or intruding into his home. But not all the truth was necessary yet. "I am endeavoring to be of some assistance in a recent tragedy which has occurred in the city, a death in most unpleasant circumstances."

Wray's face tightened momentarily, but the sympathy in his eyes was unfeigned. "Then you had better come in, Mr. Pitt. If you have come from London, perhaps you have not had luncheon yet? I'm sure Mary Ann could find enough for both of us, if simple fare would suffice for you?"

Pitt had no choice but to accept. He needed to speak with Wray. To have gone in but refused the hospitality would have been churlish and hurt the man's feelings for no reason but to ease his own conscience, and quite artificially. Putting distance between them would not make his act any less intrusive or his suspicions less ugly. "Thank you," he accepted, following Wray back up the path and in through the front door, hoping he would not be placing more pressure on young Mary Ann.

He glanced at the hall as he passed through it towards the study, waiting a moment while Wray spoke to Mary Ann. Other than the horse brasses there was an elaborate brass stick and umbrella stand, a carved wooden settle that looked at a glance to be Tudor, and several very lovely drawings of bare trees.

Mary Ann scurried off to the kitchen and Wray returned, seeing the direction Pitt was looking.

"You like them?" he said gently, his voice charged with emotion.

"Yes, very much," Pitt answered. "The beauty of a bare trunk is quite as great as that of a tree in full leaf."

"You can see that?" For an instant Wray's face lit with a smile, like a shaft of sunlight on a spring day. Then it vanished again. "My late wife did them. She had a gift for seeing a thing as it really is."

"And a gift to translate that beauty for others," Pitt responded, then wished he had not. He was here to find out if this man had gone to a spirit medium in a bid to recapture something of those he had loved, but in contradiction of all that his life and faith had taught him. Pitt might even have to entertain the idea that Wray had murdered the confidence artist who had betrayed that trust.

"Thank you," Wray murmured, turning quickly aside to give himself a moment's privacy as he led the way to his study, a small room with too many books, a plaster bust of Dante on a plinth, a watercolor painting of a young woman with brown hair smiling out shyly at the viewer. There was a silver vase of roses of all colors mingled together balanced on the desk, rather too near the edge. Pitt would have liked to read the titles of a score or so of the books to see what they were, but he had time to notice only three: Flavius Josephus's *Histories*, *Thomas à Kempis*, and a commentary on Saint Augustine.

"Please sit down and tell me how I can help," Wray offered. "I have plenty of time, and nothing in the world more useful to do with it." He attempted a smile, but it was more of warmth than any happiness within him.

It was no longer possible to evade the issue entirely. "Are you by any chance acquainted with Major General Roland Kingsley?" Pitt began.

Wray thought for a moment. "I seem to recall the name."

"A tall gentleman, returned from military service largely in Africa," Pitt elaborated.

Wray relaxed. "Ah yes, of course. Zulu Wars, wasn't it? Served with great distinction, as I recall. No, I've never met him, but I have heard him referred to. I am very sorry to hear he has had another tragedy. He lost his only son, I do know that." His eyes were bright and seemed almost blind for a moment, but he controlled his voice, and his attention was set entirely upon what he could do to assist Pitt.

"This is not about his bereavement," Pitt said quickly, before thinking as to whether he was contradicting himself or not. "He was present shortly before someone died . . . someone to whom he had been going in an effort to find solace for his son's death . . . or the manner of it." He swallowed, watching Wray's face. "A spirit medium." Had he read of it in the newspapers? They were mostly overrun by coverage of the election.

Wray frowned, his expression darkening. "You mean one of those people who claim to be in touch with the spirits of the dead, and take money from the vulnerable in order to produce voices and signs?"

He could hardly have more clearly worded his contempt for them. Did it spring from his religious views or his own betrayal? There was real anger in his eyes; the gentle, courteous man of a few moments ago was temporarily gone. Perhaps noticing Pitt's attention, he went on. "It is a very dangerous thing to do, Mr. Pitt. I would wish no one harm, but it is better that such activities cease, although I would not have had it by violent means."

Pitt was puzzled. "Dangerous, Mr. Wray? Perhaps I misled you. She was killed by entirely human means, there was nothing occult about it. It was your possible knowledge of the other people who were present that I wanted, not of the divine."

Wray sighed. "You are a man of your time, Mr. Pitt. Science is the idol we worship now, and Mr. Darwin, not God, the begetter of our race. But the power of good and evil is still there, whatever the mask of the day we set over them. You assume that this medium had no powers to touch beyond the grave, and you are probably right, but that does not mean to say that they do not exist."

Pitt felt a chill in the warmth of the room and knew it was inside himself. He had been too quick to like Wray. He was old, charming, gentle and generous in manner, and he was lonely and he had invited Pitt in to luncheon. He loved his garden and his cats. He also believed in the possibilities of calling up the spirits of the dead, and was deeply and profoundly angry with those who attempted to do so. Pitt must at the very least find out why.

"It was the sin of Saul," Wray continued

earnestly, as if Pitt had spoken his thoughts aloud.

Pitt was completely blank. Nothing returned from schoolroom memories.

"King Saul of the Bible," Wray said with sudden gentleness, almost apology. "He sought the ghost of the Prophet Samuel through the witch of Endor."

"Oh." It was the intensity in Wray's face, the fixity of his eyes, that held Pitt. There was an almost uncontrollable emotion in the man. Pitt was compelled to ask him the next question. "And did he find him?"

"Oh yes, of course," Wray replied. "But it was the beginning of that seed of defiance in his nature, the pride against God which in the end was rage and envy, and sin unto death." His face was intensely earnest, a tiny muscle in his temple flickering uncontrollably. "Never underestimate the danger of seeking to know what should not be known, Mr. Pitt. It carries with it a monstrous evil. Shun it as you would a plague pit!"

"I have no desire whatever to enquire into such things," Pitt said honestly, and then realized with a rush of gratitude and guilt how easy it was to say that when he had no insupportable grief, no loneliness that wrapped around him as this man had, no real temptation. He could not bear even to think of it, to believe that the threat in Voisey's eyes was anything but emotion, the rage at his defeat in Whitechapel, blind, incapable of action.

"I hope that if I lost someone profoundly dear to me I would seek my comfort in the faith of a resurrection according to the promises of God," he said to Wray, embarrassed to find his voice trembling. A sudden shivering cold seized hold of him as thoughts of Charlotte and his children forced themselves into his mind, without him, and in a place he had never even seen. Were they safe? He had not heard from them yet! Was he protecting them the best way, and was it good enough? What if it wasn't? What if Voisey did take that way to exact his vengeance? It might be crass, obvious, unrefined and too quick in its execution, dangerous for him — but it would also be the most exquisitely painful for Pitt . . . and final. If they were dead, what would there be left of value in life?

He looked at the elderly, broken man in front of him, so filled with his loss it seemed to bleed out of him into the air of the room, and Pitt could feel the ache of it himself. In such a situation would he be different? Was it not foolish and unbelievably arrogant, the sign of complacent stupidity, to be so sure that he would never turn to mediums, tarot cards, tea leaves, anything at all that would fill the void in which he dwelt alone in a universe crowded with strangers he could touch in no way of the heart?

"At least I hope so," he said again. "But of course I don't know."

Wray's eyes filled with tears which spilled down his cheeks without his blinking. "Do you have family, Mr. Pitt?"

"Yes. I have a wife and two children." Was it compounding the pain to tell him that?

"You are fortunate. Say to them all that you mean, while there is time for you. Never let a day go by without thanking God for what He has given you."

Pitt struggled to bring his mind back to his reason for being here. He should satisfy himself once and for all that Wray could not have been the man represented by the cartouche in Maude Lamont's diary.

"I will try," he promised. "Unfortunately, I still need to do what I can to understand the death of Maude Lamont and prevent the wrong person from being blamed for having killed her."

Wray looked at him with incomprehension. "If it was unlawful, surely that is a matter for the police, distressing as that is. I understand perfectly that you may not wish to have them involved, but I am afraid you have no moral choice."

Pitt felt a stab of shame at willfully misleading this man. "They are already involved, Mr. Wray. But one of the people present on that last evening is the wife of a man standing for a seat in Parliament, and a third is someone who wishes to keep his identity a secret, and so far has succeeded."

"And you wish to know who he is?" Wray said in a moment of startling clarity. "Even if I knew, Mr. Pitt, if it were told me as a matter of confidence, I could not pass on that secret to you. The best I could do would be to counsel him with all my strength to be honest with you. But then I would already have counseled him with every argument and plea within my power to have nothing to do with such an evil and dangerous practice as meddling with knowledge of the dead. The only righteous knowledge of such things is gained through prayer." He shook his head a little. "Why is it you were led to believe that I might be of service to you? I do not understand that."

Pitt improvised with a flash of invention.

"You have a name for knowledge on the subject, and for your powerful feelings against it. I thought you might have some information on the nature of mediums, particularly Miss Lamont, which would help. She has a very wide reputation."

Wray sighed. "I am afraid my knowledge, such as it is, is general and not particular. And lately my memory is not as keen as it used to be. I forget things, and I regret to say I have a tendency to repeat myself. I tell the jokes that I like rather too many times. People are very kind, and I would almost prefer that they were not. Now I never know if I have already said before what I am saying now, or if I haven't."

Pitt smiled. "You have said nothing twice to me!"

"I have not told you any jokes," Wray said sadly. "Nor have we had luncheon yet, and no doubt I will show you every flower at least twice."

"A flower is worth looking at at least twice," Pitt replied.

A few moments later Mary Ann came in to tell them somewhat nervously that the meal was ready, and they removed to the small dining room, where she had obviously gone to some trouble to make it look even more attractive. There was a china jug of flowers in the center of the table and a carefully ironed cloth set with blue-ringed china and old, well-polished silver. She served a thick vegetable soup with crusty bread, butter and a soft, crumbling white country cheese, and a homemade pickle that Pitt guessed to be rhubarb. It all made him realize how much he missed the domestic touches in his own home with Charlotte and Gracie both away.

Pudding was plum pie with clotted cream. He refrained only with the greatest difficulty from actually asking for more.

Wray seemed to be happy to eat in silence. Perhaps simply to have someone opposite him at the table was sufficient.

Afterwards they rose to go and admire the garden. It was only then that Pitt saw on the side table a folder advertising the powers of Maude Lamont, in which she offered to bring back to the bereaved the spirits of loved ones departed and to give them the opportunity to say all those precious and important things that untimely death had taken from them.

Wray was ahead of him, walking out into the sun, dazzling as it was reflected off the blaze of flowers and the clean white of the painted fence. Almost stumbling on the sill of the French doors, Pitt went after him.

CHAPTER
EIGHT

Bishop Underhill did not spend a great deal
of time in speaking with individual parishio-
ners. When he did it was largely on formal
occasions, weddings, confirmations, now
and then baptisms. However, it was part of
his calling to be available to counsel the
clergy within the boundaries of his see, and
when they had spiritual burdens of any sort
it was right that it was to him they came for
help and comfort.

Isadora was used to seeing anxious men
of all ages, from curates overwhelmed by
their responsibilities or their ambitions to
acquire more, to senior clergy who found
administration and the care of those in
their charge sometimes more than they felt
equipped to handle.

The ones she dreaded most were the bereaved, those who had lost a wife or child
and came seeking a greater comfort and
strength to their faith than their daily rit-
uals could offer them. They could give so

much support to others, and yet their own grief sometimes overwhelmed them.

Today it was the Reverend Patterson, who had lost his daughter in childbirth. He sat in the Bishop's study, an elderly man with gaunt body, his head bent, his face half covered by his hands.

Isadora brought in the tray of tea and set it on the small table. She did not speak to either of them, but silently filled both cups. She knew Patterson well enough not to need to ask him if he wished for milk or sugar.

"I thought I would understand," Patterson said desperately. "I've been a minister in the church for almost forty years! God knows how many people I've comforted in their loss, and now all those words I've said so carefully mean nothing to me." He peered up at the Bishop. "Why? Why don't I believe them when I say them to myself?"

Isadora waited for the Bishop to reply that it was shock, anger at pain, and he must give himself time to heal. Even expected death is a huge and strange thing and takes courage to face, no less by a man dedicated to God's service than by any other. Faith is not certainty, and belief does not take away the hurt.

The Bishop seemed to be floundering

for words. He drew in his breath, and then let it out again in a sigh. "My dear man, we will all experience great trials of faith during our lives. I am sure you will rise to this with all your usual fortitude. You are a good man, rest in the knowledge of that."

Patterson stared up at him, the agony in his face as naked as if he were oblivious of Isadora's presence. "If I am a good man, why has this happened to me?" he begged. "And why do I feel nothing but confusion and pain? Why can I see no hand of God in it, no whisper of the divine anywhere?"

"The divine is an infinite mystery," the Bishop answered, staring across Patterson's head at the far wall, his face intensely troubled, his eyes fixed. He looked as if he saw no more comfort than Patterson did himself. "It is beyond us to comprehend. Perhaps we are not meant to."

Anguish contorted Patterson's features, and it seemed to Isadora, afraid to move in case she drew attention to herself, that he was on the edge of screaming with the sheer frustration that boiled up inside him, unanswered by anything he could ever reach towards.

"There's no sense in it all!" he cried out, his voice strangled in his throat. "One day she was alive, so alive, her child within her.

She glowed with the joy of her time coming . . . and then nothing but suffering and death. How could it be? How? It's senseless! It's cruel and wasteful, and stupid, as if there is no meaning in the universe." He drew in a great sob. "Why have I spent my life telling people there is a just and loving God, that it all makes a perfect pattern that we will see one day, and then when I need to know that myself . . . there's nothing but darkness . . . and silence? Why?" His voice grew more demanding, angrier. "Why? Was my whole life a farce? Tell me!"

The Bishop hesitated, shifting his weight to the other foot, his body awkward.

"Tell me!" Patterson shouted.

"My dear man . . ." the Bishop sputtered. "My dear . . . man, these are dark times . . . we all have them, times when it seems the world is monstrous. Fear covers everything like a descending night and no dawn is . . . is imaginable . . ."

Isadora could not bear it. "Mr. Patterson, of course your sense of loss is terrible," she said urgently. "If you truly love anyone then their death has to hurt, but most especially if they are young." She moved forward a step, ignoring the Bishop's startled expression. "But to lose is part of our human experience, as God intended it to be. The fact that it hurts to the very limit of our ability to bear is the whole point. In the end it comes down to one question, do you trust God, or not? If you do, then you endure the pain until you can come through to the other side of it. If you don't, then you had better begin to think exactly what you do believe, and exercise yourself to your very soul." She lowered her voice very gently. "I think you will find that your life experience tells you that your faith is there . . . not all the time, but most of it. And most of it is enough."

Patterson looked up at her in amazement. The anguish eased out of him as he began to consider what she had said.

The Bishop turned towards her, incredulity slackening his face until it held exactly the same expression he had when he was asleep, an uncanny vacancy waiting to be filled by thought.

"Really, Isadora . . ." he started, then stopped again. It was desperately apparent that he was at a loss to know how to deal with her or with Patterson, but above either was some emotion deep within himself which overpowered even his anger or his embarrassment. His usual complacency had vanished, the polished certainty in his own power to answer everything which she was so accustomed to, and its absence was like a raw wound.

She turned to Patterson. "People do not die because they are good or bad," she said firmly. "And it is certainly not to punish anyone else. That thought is monstrous and would destroy all reality of good or evil. There are scores of reasons, but many of them are simply mischance. The only thing we know to cling to, all the time, is that God is in control of the greater destiny, and we do not need to know what that is. Indeed, we could not understand it if we were told. What we need to do is trust Him."

Patterson blinked. "You make it sound as if it were simple, Mrs. Underhill."

"Perhaps." She smiled with a sudden bleakness at the force of the knowledge inside her of her own prayers unanswered, the loneliness which at times was almost unbearable. "But that is not the same thing as saying it is easy. That is what should be done; I do not say that I can do it, any more than you or anyone else."

"You are very wise, Mrs. Underhill." He looked up at her gravely, trying to read in her face what experience it was that had taught her such things.

She turned away. It was too vulnerable to share, and if he understood anything at all, it would betray Reginald completely. No woman who was happy in her marriage had such a desolation inside her. "Do drink your tea while it is still hot," she advised. "It doesn't solve problems, but it makes us better able to attempt them." And without waiting for any response she left the room, closing the door softly behind her.

Out in the hall, she was overcome with a profound sense of having intruded. Never in all her married life had she usurped her husband's role in such a way. Hers was to support, sustain, to be loyal and discreet. She had just violated almost every rule there was. She had made him look hopelessly inadequate in front of one of his own juniors.

No! That was unfair. He *had* been inadequate. She had not caused that. He had dithered when he should have been decisive, full of quiet confidence, an anchor when Patterson was tossed by storms, at least temporarily, beyond his control.

Why? What on earth was wrong with Reginald? Why could he not have stated with passion and certainty that God loved every man, woman and child, and when understanding failed then trust must take over? That is what faith means. Most of us can cling to our faith, or at least seem to cling to it, when we have all we want. Nothing is measured until faith is tested.

She walked back to the kitchen to speak to the cook about dinner the following day. Tonight she and the Bishop were going to another one of the interminable political receptions. Still, it was only days till the election now, and then at least this part of it would be over.

What lay ahead? Only variations of the same, stretching on into loneliness infinite.

She was in the sitting room again when she heard Patterson leave and knew that within minutes the Bishop would be through to face her for her intrusion, and she waited, wondering what she would say. Would it be simplest in the long run merely to apologize? Nothing would justify what she had done. She had undermined him by offering the comfort that he should have given.

She was still waiting a quarter of an hour later when at last he came into the room. He looked pale, and she expected the explosion of outrage any moment. But the apology still stuck in her throat.

"You look exhausted," she observed with

less sympathy than she knew she ought to feel, of which she was truly ashamed. She should have cared. In fact, he sank into a chair as if he felt really quite ill. "What have you done to your shoulder?" She tried to make up for her indifference, noticing that he winced and rubbed his arm as he shifted position a trifle.

"A touch of rheumatism," he replied. "It's most painful." He smiled, a forced gesture which disappeared almost instantly. "You must speak to Cook. She has allowed her standards to slip lately. I have never had so much indigestion in my life."

"Perhaps a little milk and arrowroot?" she suggested.

"I can't live on milk and arrowroot for the rest of my days!" he snapped. "I need a household that is properly run with a kitchen that serves edible food! If you paid attention to your own duties instead of interfering in mine, then we would not have the problem. You are responsible for my health, and you should concern yourself with it, not attempting to console someone like poor Patterson, who is crumbling before the vicissitudes of life."

"Death," she corrected.

"What?" His hand jerked up and he glared at her. He really was very pale, and there was a sheen of sweat on his lip.

"It is death that he is finding impossible to accept," she pointed out. "She was his daughter. It must be the most terrible thing to lose a child, although heaven knows it happens to enough people." She buried the empty ache inside herself because it could never happen to her. She had dealt with most of that years ago; only now and then did it return, unexpectedly, and surprise her.

"She was not a child," he replied. "She was twenty-three."

"For heaven's sake, Reginald, what on earth has her age got to do with it?" She was finding it more and more difficult to keep her temper. "Anyway, it really makes no difference what was the cause of his distress; it is our task to try to comfort him, or at least offer him the assurance of our support and remind him that in time faith will ease his grief." She drew in her breath deeply. "Even if the time in question is beyond this life. Surely that is one of the main purposes of the church, to offer the strength for those losses and afflictions that the world cannot ease?"

He rose suddenly to his feet, coughing and putting his hand to his chest. "It is the church's task, Isadora, to point the moral pathway so that those who are faithful may reach the . . ." He stopped.

"Reginald, are you ill?" she asked, now prepared to believe that he really was.

"No, of course I'm not ill!" he said angrily. "I am simply tired and have indigestion . . . and a spot of rheumatism. I wish you would keep the windows either open or closed, not this ajar manner which causes so many drafts!" His voice was sharp, and she caught something she thought with amazement was an edge of fear. Was it because he had so signally failed to help Patterson? Was he afraid of a weakness in himself, of being seen to fall short?

She tried to think back to any other time when she had heard him comfort the bereaved, or indeed the dying. Surely he had been stronger than this; the words had come to him fluently, quotations from scriptures, past sermons, the words of other great churchmen. His voice was beautiful; it was the one physical characteristic that had never failed to please her, even now.

"Are you sure you are . . ." She was not certain what she meant to say. Was she about to press for an answer she did not want?

"What?" he demanded, turning in the doorway. "Ill? Why do you ask? I've already told you, it is indigestion and a touch of stiffness. Why? Do you think it is more, something worse?"

"No, of course not," she said quickly. "You are quite right. I apologize for making a fuss. I shall see that Cook is more careful with spices and pastries. And goose — goose is very rich."

"We haven't had goose in years!" he said in disgust, and went out of the door.

"We had it last week," she said to herself. "At the Randolphs'. It didn't agree with you then!"

Isadora prepared for the reception with great care.

"Is it something special, ma'am?" her lady's maid asked with interest and just an edge of curiosity as she wound Isadora's hair up to show off the white streak from the brow just to the right of her widow's peak. It was startling and she did not try to disguise it.

"I am not expecting it to be," Isadora replied with a touch of self-mockery. "But I would dearly like something remarkable to happen. It promises to be unutterably tedious."

Martha was not quite sure what to say, but she caught the idea very well. Isadora was not the first lady she had worked for who hid a deep restlessness under a mask of good behavior. "Yes, ma'am," she said obediently, and proceeded to make the hairstyle a little more extreme, and really very flattering.

The Bishop made no comment upon Isadora's appearance, either the dramatic hair or the ocean-green gown with its daringly swathed bodice crossed very low over the bosom and filled in with exquisite white lace, the same as that shown where the skirt was slashed so the silk fell to a point at the floor in front, and then in wide, sweeping folds all around the back. He looked at her, and then away again as he helped her up into the carriage and bade the coachman be on his way.

She sat beside him in the dim light and wondered what it would be like to dress for a man who looked at her with pleasure, enjoying the color, the line of what she wore, seeing how it flattered her, above all finding her beautiful. There is something of loveliness in most women, be it no more than a grace of moment, a tone of voice, but to find someone who delighted in it was like spreading your wings and feeling

341

the sun on your face.

The fact that he never spoke with intimacy or joy shriveled her up inside so it was an effort to hold her head high, to smile, to walk as if she believed in herself.

Again she allowed herself to daydream. Would Cornwallis have liked this gown? Had it been he she was dressing for, would he have stood at the bottom of the stairs and watched her come down with amazement in his eyes, even a little awe at how beautiful a woman could look, at silks and lace and perfume, all things with which he was so unfamiliar?

Stop it! She must control her imagination. She blushed hot at her own thoughts, and deliberately turned towards the Bishop to say something, anything to break the spell.

But all through the journey he sat uncharacteristically silent, as if he were unaware of her beside him. Usually he would speak about who was to be present at a function and rehearse to her their virtues and their weaknesses and what might be expected of them in terms of their contribution to the welfare of the church in general, and his see in particular.

"What do you think we can do to help poor Mr. Patterson?" she said at last when

342

they were almost at their destination. "He seems in very great distress."

"Nothing," he replied without turning. "The woman is dead, Isadora. There is nothing anyone can do about death. It is there, inescapable, before us and around us. Whatever we say in the light of day, come the night, we don't know where we come from, and we have no idea where we go — if anywhere at all. Don't condescend to Patterson by telling him otherwise. If he finds faith, he will do it himself. You cannot give him yours, assuming you have it and are not merely saying what you yourself wish to hear, like most people. Now, you had better prepare yourself, we are about to arrive."

The carriage pulled up and they alighted and climbed the steps as the front door opened and they were welcomed. As usual they were formally announced. Once Isadora had been excited hearing Reginald spoken of as His Grace the Bishop. It had seemed a title with infinite possibilities, more worthy than a peerage because it was not inherited but rather bestowed by God. Now she stared at the sea of noise and color in front of her as she came into the room on his arm. It seemed no more than an accolade given by men to someone who had fitted most closely the pattern they desired, who had pleased the right people and avoided offending anyone. He was not the finest in a bold and courageous way, to change lives, but merely the least likely to endanger the existing way, the known and comfortable. He was the ultimate conserver of what was already here, good and bad.

They were introduced and she followed a step behind him, acknowledging people with a smile and a polite response. She tried to be interested in them.

"Mr. Aubrey Serracold," she was told by Lady Warboys. "He is standing for the South Lambeth seat. Mrs. Underhill. Bishop Underhill."

"How do you do, Mr. Serracold," Isadora replied dutifully, then suddenly found that after all there was something in him that caught her attention. He responded to her with a smile and his eyes met hers with a secret amusement, as if they were both privy to the same rather absurd joke which honor obliged them to play out in front of this audience. The Bishop passed on to the next person, and she found herself smiling back at Aubrey Serracold. He had a long face and fair hair which flopped forward over one side of his brow. She remembered now that she had heard somewhere he was the second son of a marquis, or some such, and could have used a courtesy title of Lord, but preferred not to. She wondered what his political beliefs were. She hoped he had them, and was not merely looking for a new pastime to fill his boredom.

"Indeed, Mr. Serracold," she said with interest she did not have to feign. "And which party are you representing?"

"I am not entirely sure that either is willing to take responsibility for me, Mrs. Underhill," he replied with a slight grimace. "I have been candid enough to express a few of my own opinions, which have not been universally popular."

In spite of herself she was interested, and it must have shown in her face, because he immediately elaborated in explanation. "For a start I have committed the unpardonable sin of preferring the Eight-Hour Bill in urgency before Home Rule for Ireland. I see no reason why we cannot commit to them both, and by so doing be far more likely to win the support of the greater mass of the people, and a base of power from which to accomplish other much-needed reform, beginning with yielding up the Empire to its natural citizens."

"I am not certain about the Empire, but the rest sounds eminently reasonable," she agreed. "Far too much so to become law."

"You are a cynic," he said with mock despair.

"My husband is a bishop," she replied.

"Ah! Of course . . ." He was prevented from saying more by the need to acknowledge being joined by three further people, including Serracold's wife, whom Isadora had not met, although she had heard her spoken of with both alarm and admiration.

"How do you do, Mrs. Underhill." Rose returned the introduction with barely feigned interest. Isadora was not involved with politics, nor was she truly fashionable, in spite of the ocean-green gown. She was a woman of conservative grace and that kind of beauty which does not change.

Rose Serracold, on the other hand, was outrageously avant-garde. Her gown was a mixture of burgundy satin and guipure lace which, in combination with her startlingly fair coloring, was all the more dramatic, like blood and snow. Her brilliant aqua-colored eyes seemed to survey everyone in the room with something like hunger, as if looking for a particular person she did not find.

"Mr. Serracold has been telling me of

the reforms he desires to effect," Isadora said conversationally.

Rose flashed her a dazzling smile. "I am sure you must have your own knowledge of such needs," she responded. "No doubt in your husband's ministry he becomes painfully aware of the poverty and injustice there is which could be eased with more equitable laws?" She said it as a challenge, daring Isadora to claim ignorance and so brand herself a hypocrite in the Christianity which, through the Bishop, she professed.

Isadora responded without stopping to measure her words.

"Of course. It is not the changes I find trouble in imagining, but how we can effect them. For a law to be any good it must be enforceable, and there must be a punishment we are willing and able to inflict if it is broken, as it assuredly will be, even if only to test us."

Rose was delighted. "You have actually thought about it!" Her surprise was palpable. "I apologize for slighting your sincerity." She lowered her voice so it was audible only to those closest to them, and then went on speaking in spite of the sudden hush as others strained to hear what she was going to say. "We must talk together, Mrs. Underhill." She put out an elegant hand, long-fingered, jeweled with rings, and drew Isadora away from the group in which they had found themselves more or less by chance. "Time is terribly short," she went on. "We must go far beyond the core of the party if we are to do any real good. Abolishing fees for elementary schooling last year has already had wonderful effects, but it is only a beginning. We must do much more. Education for all is the only lasting answer to poverty." She drew in her breath and then plunged on. "We must make a way for women to be able to restrict their families. Poverty and exhaustion, both physical and mental, are the unavoidable outcomes of having child after child whom you have not strength to care for nor money to feed and clothe." She regarded Isadora with candid challenge in her eyes again. "And I am sorry if that is against your religious convictions, but being a bishop's wife with a residence provided for you is a far cry from being in one or two rooms with no water and little fire and trying to keep a dozen children clean and fed."

"Would an eight-hour day help or hurt that?" Isadora asked, willing herself not to take offense at things which were, after all, irrelevant to the real issue.

Rose's arched eyebrows rose. "How could it possibly make it worse? Every laborer, man or woman, should be protected against exploitation!" The anger flared up in her face, pink color across her white skin.

Isadora was intending to ask Rose's opinion rather than express any of her own, but was prevented in either by their being joined by a friend of Rose who greeted her with affection. She was introduced to Isadora as Mrs. Swann, and in return presented her companion, a woman of perhaps forty, with the confidence of maturity and still sufficient of the bloom of youth to attract the eye of most men. There was a grace in the way she held her dark head, and her deportment was that of someone who is quite certain of herself, yet interested in others.

"Mrs. Octavia Cavendish," Mrs. Swann said with a touch of pride.

Isadora realized only just before speaking that the newcomer must be a widow to be so addressed. "Are you interested in politics, Mrs. Cavendish?" she asked. Since the evening was to that end it was a natural assumption.

"Only so far as it changes laws, I hope to

the benefit of all," Mrs. Cavendish replied. "It takes great wisdom to see ahead what will be the results of our actions. Sometimes the most nobly inspired paths are disastrous in their unforeseen ends."

Rose opened her remarkable eyes very wide. "Mrs. Underhill was about to tell us how the eight-hour day could be ill," she said, staring at Mrs. Cavendish. "I fear perhaps she is a Conservative at heart!"

"Really, Rose," Mrs. Swann cautioned her with a quick glance of apology towards Isadora.

"No!" Rose said impatiently. "It is time we were less mealymouthed and said what we really mean. Is honesty too much to ask — indeed, to demand? Have we not the duty to pose questions and challenge the answers?"

"Rose, eccentricity is one thing, but you risk going too far!" Mrs. Swann said with a nervous hiccup. She placed a hand on Rose's arm but it was impatiently shaken off. "Mrs. Underhill may not —"

"Don't you?" Rose asked, her flashing smile returning briefly.

Before Isadora could answer, Mrs. Cavendish stepped in. "It is very hard to be overworked, and quite unjust," she said smoothly. "But it is still better than having no work at all . . ."

"That is extortion!" Rose said with a wild anger cutting in her voice.

Mrs. Cavendish kept her temper admirably. "If it is done deliberately, then of course it is. But if an employer is facing falling profits and more intense competition, then he cannot afford to increase his costs. And if he does, then he will lose his business altogether and his employees will lose their places. We need to keep an Empire, now that we have one, whether we want it or not." She smiled to rid her words of sting but none of their power of conviction. "Politics is what is possible, not always what we wish," she added. "I think that is part of the responsibility."

Isadora looked from Mrs. Cavendish to Rose, and saw the sudden amazement in Rose. She had encountered someone of equal and opposite conviction, and her own power could not override the logic of the argument. In spite of herself, she was temporarily beaten. It was a new experience.

Isadora looked at Aubrey Serracold and saw the tenderness in his eyes, and a kind of sadness, a knowledge that precious things can be broken.

Isadora might have felt like that about John Cornwallis. There was a heart and mind in him, a hunger for honor, a revulsion from the tawdry, that she would have suffered any wound to protect. It was of infinite value, not just to her, but in and of itself. There was nothing in Reginald Underhill which awoke that fierce ache in her that was half pain, half joy.

The moment was broken by the arrival of another man, the familiarity of his glance at Mrs. Cavendish making it apparent that he was with her. Isadora was not surprised that she should have at least one admirer. She was a remarkable woman in far more than mere physical beauty. There was character, intelligence, and a clarity of mind in her which was most unusual.

"May I introduce my brother," Mrs. Cavendish said quickly. "Sir Charles Voisey. Mrs. Underhill, Mr. and Mrs. Serracold." She added the last two with a slight grimace, and Isadora remembered with a jolt that of course Voisey and Serracold were contesting the same seat for Parliament. One of them had to lose. She looked at Voisey with quickened interest. He did not resemble his sister that she could see. His coloring was slightly auburn, while her skin was clear and her hair dark, shining brown. His face was long, his nose a little crooked as if at some time it had been broken and badly set. The only thing they had in common was their agile intelligence and a sense of inner power. In him it was so intense she almost expected to feel a heat in the air.

She murmured something polite and sensible. She was acutely aware that Aubrey Serracold was now hiding his feelings, the knowledge that his opponent was a different kind of man, that there could be no holds or blows barred in the battle. This courteous exchange now was a matter of form, and not intended to deceive anyone.

There was anger in Rose's stiff, elegant body with her long back and slender hips encased in bright taffeta, her fingers glittering as she moved her hands. The skin of her neck and throat looked almost blue-white in the light from the chandeliers above them, as if peering a little closer one might see the veins. There was also fear of something. Isadora could sense it as if it were a perfume in the air amongst the lavender, jasmine and the numerous scents from the bowls of lilies on the tables. Did it matter to her so much to win? Or was it something else?

They were shown in to dinner, all in the

correct order of precedence. As a bishop's wife, Isadora went in early, after the most senior of the nobility, long before such ordinary men as mere parliamentary candidates. The tables were laden with crystal and porcelain. Ranks of knives, forks and spoons gleamed by every setting.

The ladies took their seats, and then the gentlemen. The first course was served immediately and the business of the evening continued, the conversation, the weighing and judging, the bright chatter disguising the bargains made, the weaknesses tested and, when found, exploited. This was where future alliances were born, and future enmities.

Isadora only half listened. She had heard most of the arguments before: the economics, the moral issues, the finances, the religious difficulties and justifications, the political necessities.

She was startled and her attention was drawn, her mind suddenly clear, when she heard the Bishop mention Voisey's name and his tone altered to one of enthusiasm. "Innocence does not protect us from the errors of well-meaning men whose knowledge of human nature is far less than their desire to do good," he said earnestly. He did not look at Aubrey Serracold, but

Isadora saw at least three others around the table who did. Rose stiffened, her hand on her wineglass motionless.

"I have begun to appreciate lately what a complex study it is to govern wisely," the Bishop went on, his face set as if determined to follow his train of thought to the end. "It is not a job for the amateur gentleman, no matter how noble his intent. We simply cannot afford the cost of error. One unfortunate experiment with the forces of trade and finance, the abandonment of laws we have obeyed for centuries, and thousands will suffer before we can reverse the moment and regain the balance we have lost." He shook his head sagely. "This is a far deeper issue than ever before in our history. For the sake of those we lead and serve, we cannot afford to be self-indulgent or sentimental." His eyes flickered, and he glanced at Aubrey and away again. "That is our duty above all, or else we have nothing."

Aubrey Serracold looked pale, his eyes glittering. He didn't bother to argue. He realized the folly of it and remained silent, his hands clenched on his knife and fork.

For a moment no one answered, then half a dozen people spoke at once, apologized, and then started again. But looking at them one by one, Isadora could see that what Reginald had said had made a mark on them. Suddenly charm and ideals were less bright, less effective.

"A very unselfish vision, my lord," Voisey said, turning to look at the Bishop. "If all spiritual leaders had your courage we should know where to turn for our moral leadership."

The Bishop glanced at him, his face white, his chest rising and falling as if he found breathing unaccountably difficult.

He has indigestion again, Isadora thought. He has taken too much of the celery soup. He should have left it; he knows it does not agree with him. One would think from his speech it had been laced with wine!

The evening dragged on, promises were made, others abandoned. Shortly after midnight the first guests left. The Bishop and Isadora were among them.

Outside, as they stepped up into their carriage and drew away, she turned to him. "What on earth possessed you to speak against Mr. Serracold like that? And in front of the poor man! If his ideas are extreme, no one will accept them into law."

"Are you suggesting I should wait until they are presented in Parliament before I speak against them?" he asked with a touch of asperity. "Perhaps you would like me to wait until the Commons have passed them and they are before the Lords, where I can debate the issue? I have no doubt the Lords Temporal will override most of them, but I have no such faith in my brother Lords Spiritual. They confuse the ideal with the practical." He coughed. "Time is short, Isadora. No one can afford to put off the day of his actions. Tomorrow may not be given him in which to make amends."

She was taken aback. It was a completely uncharacteristic remark. She had never known him so driven to leap to words, to committing himself to anything at all without leaving a way to extricate himself if circumstances should change.

"Are you feeling quite well, Reginald?" she asked, then instantly wished she had not. She did not want to hear a catalog of what was wrong with the dinner, the service, other people's opinions or expressions of them. She wished she had bitten her tongue and simply made some unemotional murmur of agreement. Now it was too late.

"No," he said rather loudly, his voice rising to a note of distress. "I do not feel well at all. They must have put me in a draft. My rheumatism is most powerful, and I have severe pain in my chest."

"I think the celery soup was not a wise choice," she said, trying to sound sympathetic and knowing she was failing. She heard the indifference in her own voice.

"I fear it is more serious than that." Now there was definite panic in him, barely concealed. If she could have seen him in the darkness inside the carriage she was certain his face would have betrayed a real fear running close to losing control. She was glad she could not. She did not want to be drawn into his emotions. That had happened too many times before.

"Indigestion can be very unpleasant," she said quietly. "Anyone who makes light of it has never suffered. But it does pass and leaves no harm behind but the tiredness of being unable to sleep. Please don't worry."

"Do you think so?" he asked. He did not turn his head towards her, but she heard the eagerness in him.

"Of course," she responded soothingly.

They rode in silence the rest of the way home, but she was acutely aware of his discomfort. It sat like a third entity between them.

★ ★ ★

She woke in the night to find him sitting on the edge of the bed, his face ashen, his body bent forward, his left arm hanging loose as if he had no power in it. She closed her eyes again, willing herself to sink back into the dream. It had been something to do with wide seas and the gentle rush of water past the hull of a boat. She pictured John Cornwallis there, his face set towards the wind, a smile of pleasure on his lips. Every now and then he would turn to her and meet her eyes. Perhaps he would say something, but probably not. The silence between them was one of total peace, a joy shared too deeply to need the intrusion of words.

But her conscience would not allow her to remain with the sea and sky. She knew Reginald was sitting a few feet from her in pain. She opened her eyes again and sat up slowly. "I'll get you a little boiled water," she said, pushing back the covers and getting out of bed. Her fine linen nightgown came to the floor and in the summer night she needed no more for warmth, or for modesty. There would be no servants about at this hour.

"No!" The cry was almost strangled in his throat. "Don't leave me!"

"If you sip the water it will help," she said, sorry for him in spite of herself. He looked wretched, his skin pallid and beaded with sweat, his body locked in a huddle of pain. She knelt down in front of him. "Do you feel sick? Perhaps something in the meal was not fresh, or not well cooked."

He said nothing, staring at the floor.

"It will pass, you know," she said gently. "It is fearful for a while, but it always goes. Perhaps in future you should think less of your hostess's feelings and decline all but the simplest dishes. Some people don't realize how often you are obliged to eat as others' guest, and it can become excessive after a while."

He raised dark, frightened eyes to hers, pleading without words for some kind of help.

"Would you like me to send Harold for the doctor?" It was an offer simply for something to say. All the doctor would give him would be peppermint water, as he had in the past. It would be an indignity to send for him for a case of wind, no matter how fierce. The Bishop had always refused before, feeling it robbed him of the gravity of his high office. How can one look with awe up to a man who cannot control his digestive organs?

"I don't want him!" he said with desperation. Then he caught his breath in a sob. "Do you think it is something in the dinner?" There was a wild note of hope in him, as if he were begging her to assure him that it was.

She realized he was terrified that it was not merely indigestion, that after all the years of petty complaints at last he really was ill. Was it pain he was so deeply frightened of? Or distress and the embarrassment of vomiting, losing control of his bodily functions and having to be cared for, cleaned up after? Suddenly she was truly sorry for him. Surely that was a secret dread of everyone, but especially a man to whom power and self-importance were everything. In his heart he must suspect how desperately fragile was his hold on respect. He did not really imagine she loved him, not with the passion and tenderness that would bind her to him through such a time. Duty would hold her, but that would almost be worse than the ministration of strangers, except to the outside world, who would see only a wife at her husband's side, where she should be. What really passed between them, anything or nothing at all, would never be known to anyone else.

He was still staring at her, waiting for her to assure him that his fear was unnecessary, that it would all go away. She could not. Even had he been a child, not a man older than herself, she could not have given him that. Illness was real. It could not always be warded off.

"I'll do all I can to help," she whispered. Tentatively, she reached out her hand and put it over his where it lay gripping his knee. She felt the terror in him as if it had flooded through his skin and into hers. Then like fire she recognized what it was: he was afraid of dying. He had spent his life preaching the love of God, the obedience to commands that permitted no question or explanation, the acceptance of affliction on earth with the absolute trust in an eternity of heaven . . . and his own belief in it was only word deep. When he faced the abyss of death there was no light, no God at the end of it for him. He was as alone as a child in the night.

She heard herself with amazement, letting go of her own dreams. "I'll be with you. Don't worry." Her grip tightened on his hand and she took hold of his other arm. "There is nothing to fear. It is the path of all mankind, only a gateway. This is the time for faith. You are not alone,

Reginald. Every living thing is with you. This is just one step in eternity. You've seen so many people do it well, with courage and grace. You can too . . . you will."

He remained sitting on the edge of the bed, but gradually his body eased. The pain must have subsided, because at last he allowed her to help him back into bed and within moments he fell asleep, leaving her to get up and go around to her own side and climb in also.

She was tired, but the blessing of oblivion escaped her until it was almost morning.

He rose as usual. He was a little pale, but otherwise apparently quite normal. He made no reference to the episode. He did not actually meet her eyes.

She was overwhelmingly angry with him. It was a meanness of heart not at least to have thanked her, acknowledged her, even if only by a smile. She did not have to have words. But he was furious that she had seen his abandonment of dignity, his naked fear. She understood that, but she still despised him for his poverty of spirit.

He was ill. She accepted that now. Even if he chose to forget it today, it was the reality. He needed her; whether it was affection, pity, respect, or simply duty that held her, she was imprisoned with him for as long as it lasted. And that might be years. She could see it like a road stretching to the horizon across a flat, gray plain. She would have to paint her own dreams on it, but never reach for them.

Perhaps they had never been more than dreams anyway. Nothing had changed except in her knowledge.

CHAPTER

NINE

"I don't believe it!" Jack Radley exploded, holding the newspaper up at the breakfast table, his face pale, his hands shaking.

"What is it?" Emily demanded, her first thoughts flying to the murder of Maude Lamont, now just a week ago. Had Thomas found something damning that incriminated Rose? Only now did she realize how much she had been dreading it. Guilt overwhelmed her. "What have you seen?" Her voice was sharp with fear.

"Aubrey!" Jack said, laying the paper down so he could see her. "He's written to the editor. I suppose it's in rebuttal of what General Kingsley said about him, but it's very ill thought."

"Ill thought? You mean carelessly written? That's not like Aubrey." She could recall his beautiful voice, not just a matter of diction but his choice of words also. "What does he say?"

Jack drew in a deep breath and bit his

lip, reluctant to answer, as if reading it aloud would give it a greater reality.

"Is it so very bad?" she asked with a chill of anxiety biting deep into her. "Will it matter?"

"I think it might."

"Well, either read it to me or pass it!" she directed. "For heaven's sake, don't tell me it's bad and then keep it!"

He looked down at the page and began, his voice low and almost expressionless.

" 'I have in this newspaper recently been accused by Major General Roland Kingsley of being an idealist with little grasp upon reality, a man who would discard the glories of our nation's past, and with it the men who fought and died to protect us and extend the rule of law and liberty to other lands. Normally I would be content to allow time to prove him mistaken. I would trust my friends to know me better, and strangers to be honest in their judgment.

" 'However, I am standing for the seat of South Lambeth in the present parliamentary election, and the date of that does not permit me the luxury of time.

" 'Our past has many glorious events I cannot and would not change. But the future is ours to mold as we will. Let us by all means write great poetry about military disasters like the Charge of the Light Brigade at Sebastopol, where brave men died uselessly at the command of incompetent generals. Let us pity the survivors of such desperate actions when they hobble past us in the streets, blind or maimed, or lie in hospital beds. Let us lay flowers on their graves!

" 'But let us also act to see that their sons and grandsons do not fall the same way. This we have not only the power but the obligation to change.' "

"That's not ill thought!" Emily argued. "As far as I can see, it is true, a perfectly fair and honorable assessment."

"I'm not finished yet," Jack said grimly.

"Well, what else does he say?"

He looked down at the page again. " 'We need an army to fight in time of war, should we be threatened by a foreign nation. We do not need adventurers who are tarred with the brush of Imperialism, and believe that as Englishmen we have the right to attack and conquer any other land we choose to, either because we believe profoundly that our way of life is superior to theirs and they would benefit from our laws and our institutions imposed upon their own, by force of arms, or because they have land, minerals, or any other natural resources that we may exploit.' "

"Oh, Jack!" Emily was appalled.

"There's more of the same," he said bitterly. "He doesn't exactly accuse Kingsley of being a self-interested glory seeker at the expense of the ordinary man, but the implication is clear enough."

"Why?" she said with a sinking feeling deepening in her. "I thought he had more . . . more sense of reality. Even if that were all true, it won't win any friends he needs! Those who agree will be on his side anyway, and those who don't will hate him for it!" She put her hands up to her face. "How could he be so naive?"

"Because Kingsley must have rattled him," Jack replied. "I think Aubrey's always hated opportunism, the idea that the strongest have the right to take what they want, and he sees Imperialism that way."

"That's a little narrow, isn't it?" she asked, not really as a question. She did not defer to Jack, or anyone else, in her beliefs. Actual knowledge was another thing, but this was emotion and the understanding of people. "I am coming to think more and more that political fighting is only a good understanding of human nature and the sense to keep your mouth closed when speaking would not help. Tell no lies in which you will be caught, and never ever lose your temper or promise something you may be seen not to have given."

He smiled, but there was no pleasure in it at all. "I wish you had told Aubrey that a couple of days ago."

"Do you think it will really make a difference?" She was clinging on to hope. "That is the *Times*, isn't it? Yes. How many of the voters in Lambeth South will read it, do you suppose?"

"I don't know, but I'll wager you anything you like that Charles Voisey will!" he responded.

She thought for a moment of making the wager and asking for a new parasol if she won, then realized how futile it was. Of course Voisey would see it — and use it.

"Aubrey talks about the military as if the generals were fools," Jack went on with a note of despair in his voice. "Heaven knows we've had enough of them who were, but planning the tactics of battle is harder than you think. You can have clever enemies, inadequate arms, supply lines cut, a change in the weather! Or just plain bad luck. When Napoleon got a new marshal he didn't ask if he was clever, he asked if he was lucky!"

"What did Wellington ask?" she returned.

"I don't know," he admitted, rising to his feet. "But he wouldn't have had Aubrey. This is not dishonesty or even bad politics at heart, but it is the most appalling tactic against a man like Charles Voisey!"

Emily went with Jack to listen to Voisey speak to a large crowd in the early afternoon. It was in Kennington, and the park was full of people walking in the hot sun, eating ice creams and peppermint sticks and toffee apples, drinking lemonade, and eager for a little heckling and entertainment. To begin with, nobody cared greatly what Voisey had come to say. It was a good way to spend an hour or so, and far more interesting than the halfhearted game of cricket a score of boys were playing at the farther end. If he wanted their attention he would have to say something to amuse them, and if he did not know that now, he would soon learn.

Of course, only some of the listeners had the right to vote, but everyone's future was affected, so they crowded around the empty bandstand Voisey climbed onto with supreme confidence and began to talk to them.

Emily stood in the sun with her hat shading her face, looking first at the crowd, then at Voisey, then sideways at Jack. She was not really listening to the words. She knew it was about patriotism and pride. It was very subtle, but he was praising them in a very general sense, making them feel part of the accomplishment of Empire, although he never gave it that name. She watched as they stood a little straighter, unconsciously smiling, shoulders squared and chins a trifle higher. He was making them feel as if they belonged, they were part of the victory, among the elite.

She looked at Jack and saw the corners of his mouth pinch. His face was tight with dislike, but there was admiration in him also, no matter how reluctant; he could not hold it back.

Voisey went on. He never mentioned Serracold's name. Serracold might not have existed. Voisey did not put the choice before them: vote for me or for the other candidate, vote Tory or Liberal; he just spoke to them as if the decision had already been made. They were of one mind because they were of one race, one people, one shared destiny.

Of course that would not persuade everyone. She saw stubbornness in the set of many faces, disagreement, anger, indifference. But then he did not need all of them, only enough to make a majority, along with those who were natural Tory voters anyway.

"He's winning, isn't he?" she said quietly, searching Jack's face and seeing the answer in his expression. He was angry, helpless, frustrated, and yet acutely aware that if he spoke to defend Aubrey Serracold as he wished to, he would achieve nothing but demonstrate the loyalty of a friend, and he would jeopardize his own seat. Nothing was as certain as he had imagined it to be only a week ago.

She watched him as Voisey went on and the crowd listened. They were with him now, but she knew what a fickle thing popularity was. Give people laughter, praise, hope of benefit, a shared belief, and they were yours. A breath of fear, a perceived insult, even boredom, and they were lost again.

What would Jack do?

Part of her wanted him to honor friendship, say what he could to right the inequity between Aubrey and this man who was manipulating the situation with such skill. Aubrey's letter to the editor had played right into Voisey's hands. Why had

Aubrey been so foolish? She felt a sinking weight inside her as the answer came unbidden to her mind. Because he was idealistic but naive. He was a good man with an honest dream, but he was no politician yet, and circumstances would give him no time to become one. There were no rehearsals, only reality.

She looked at Jack again, and saw the indecision still in him. She said nothing. She was not yet ready for the answer, whatever it was. He was right, there were some prices that were very high to pay for power. And yet without power one could achieve little, perhaps nothing. Battles were costly; that was the nature of fighting for any principle, any victory at all. And if you retreated from the struggle because it hurt, then the prize went to someone else, someone like Voisey. And what was the price of that? If good men did not take up the sword, literal and figurative, then the victory would go to whoever would. Where did the right lie?

If it were easy to see, maybe more people would find it, and fewer be beguiled along the way.

She moved a step closer to Jack and linked her arm in his. Then he turned to her, but she did not meet his eyes.

★ ★ ★

There was a reception that evening which Emily had considered earlier would promise a certain enjoyment. It was less formal than a dinner and offered much more opportunity to speak with a greater variety of people of one's choice, simply because one was not seated around a table. As usual at such events there would be some form of entertainment, either a small orchestra, with a soloist to sing, or possibly a string quartet, or an exceptional pianist.

However, she already knew that Rose and Aubrey Serracold would also be there, and word of this afternoon's speech would have reached at least some of the guests, so in a matter of an hour or so all would be aware not only of Aubrey's extraordinary breach of sense in the newspapers but of the superb response to Voisey's speech. The evening now promised to be awkward, even embarrassing. And whatever Jack was going to do about it, time would not allow him any more latitude in which to make up his mind.

It was unfair, but she was angry with Charlotte for not being here to discuss it with. There was no one else in whom she could have confided exactly the same feelings, the doubts and the questions.

As always, she dressed carefully. Impressions mattered a great deal, and she had long known that a pretty woman can charm a man's attention when a plainer one cannot. She had also learned more recently that careful grooming, a shade and line of gown that flattered, a direct smile with an air of confidence, could make others believe one was far more beautiful than was the bare fact. Accordingly, she wore a tight-waisted, flaring gown of natural-colored sheer printed in green, a shade which had always become her. The effect was so dramatic that even Jack, in a wretched mood over Voisey, widened his eyes and was obliged to compliment her.

"Thank you," she said with satisfaction. She was dressed for battle, but he was still the conquest which mattered the most.

They arrived sixty minutes after the hour stated on the invitation, which was about as early as was decently acceptable. A score of other people arrived either immediately before or after them, and for a few moments the hall was a crush of guests all exchanging greetings. The ladies divested themselves of capes. Though the evening was mild, they would not be leaving until after midnight, when it would be chilly.

Emily saw several social acquaintances

and political wives it was wise to befriend, and a few she actually liked. She knew that Jack had his own duties for the evening which he could not afford to ignore. This was not an occasion purely for pleasure.

She set about listening with charm and attention, passing the appropriate, well-thought compliment, exchanging a word or two of gossip which if repeated would not come back to haunt her.

It was two hours later, after the musical entertainment had begun — the soloist was one of the plainest women Emily had ever seen, but had the effortless soaring voice of a true operatic diva — that Emily saw Rose Serracold. She must only just have arrived, since she was so strikingly dressed no one could possibly have missed her. Her gown was vermilion and black stripes, richly draped over the sleeves and bust in black lace, which flattered her extreme slenderness. There was a vermilion flower on the skirt to match the ones at bosom and shoulder. She was sitting on one of the chairs at the edge of the group, her back stiff, the light gleaming on her pale hair like the sun on corn silk. Emily looked for Aubrey beside her, or beyond, and did not see him.

The singer was so very excellent she

commanded the mind and the senses, her voice so lovely it would have been vandalism of the ear to speak through her performance. But as soon as it was over Emily stood up and went to Rose. There was a small group already gathered around, and before anyone stood a little to one side to allow her to join, she heard the conversation. She knew instantly with a cold sinking in her stomach exactly what they were referring to, even though no names had been mentioned.

"He is far cleverer than I thought, I admit," a woman in gold was saying ruefully. "I fear we have underestimated him."

"I think you overestimate his morality," Rose said sharply. "Perhaps that was our error."

Emily opened her mouth to intervene, but someone else spoke first.

"Of course he must have done something remarkable to have been knighted by the Queen. I suppose we should have taken that into better account. I'm so sorry, my dear."

Perhaps it was the condescension in the voice, but it was to Rose a goad she could not ignore. "I'm sure he did something very special indeed!" she retorted. "Probably to the tune of several thousand pounds — and contrived to do it while there was still a Tory Prime Minister to recommend him."

Emily froze. Her throat was tight and the room glittered and swam around her, the lights in the chandeliers multiplying in her vision as if she were going to faint. Everyone knew that wealthy men had donated massively to both political parties and been given knighthoods or even peerages for it. It was one of the ugliest scandals, and yet it was the way both parties funded themselves. But to say specifically that anyone had been rewarded in such a way was inexcusable, and wildly dangerous, unless one was both able and willing to prove it. Emily knew Rose was lashing out in every direction she could because she was afraid Aubrey was not going to win after all. She wished it for all the good she knew he could do, and believed in passionately, but also for him because she loved him and it was what he had set his heart on.

Perhaps also she was afraid of the guilt that would consume her for her own part in the loss, if it should happen. Whether the newspapers ever heard of her connection with Maude Lamont or not, or whether they used it, she would always know that she had cared more for her own necessity than for Aubrey's career.

But the urgency now was to stop her before she made it any worse.

"Really, my dear, that is a very extreme thing to say!" the woman in gold warned with a frown.

Rose's fair eyebrows shot up. "If the battle to win a place in the government of our country is not extreme, then what prize is it we are waiting for before we really say what we mean?"

Emily's mind raced for something, anything to rescue the situation. Nothing came to her. "Rose! What a marvelous gown!" It sounded inane, forced, even to her own ears. How idiotic it must sound to the others.

"Good evening, Emily," Rose replied coolly.

Emily had not forgotten a word of their previous clash. All the warmth of friendship was gone. And perhaps she was already realizing that Jack was not going to defend Aubrey if it looked like doing so would jeopardize his own seat. And even if it did not cost that price, it might well mean any offer of position that Gladstone was considering making him would be reconsidered in the light of his unwise friendship. Aubrey would be marked as an unreliable man, like a cannon loose on the deck of a pitching ship. If she could not save his seat for this election, at least she could save his honor and reputation for the next, which by all accounts would not be too far away.

Emily forced a smile to her face which she feared might look as ghastly as it felt. "How discreet of you not to say what it was he did!" She heard her voice high and a trifle shrill, but certainly drawing the complete attention of the others in the circle. "But I fear that in so doing you have created the misimpression that it was a donation of money, rather than a service of great worth to equal such an amount . . . conservatively." She tried to scrape together in her mind the pieces of information Charlotte, or Gracie, had let slip of the Whitechapel affair and Voisey's part in it. They had, for once, been remarkably discreet. Damnation! She widened her smile and stared around at the other women, all startled and fascinated to know what else she was going to say.

Rose breathed in sharply.

Emily must be quick before Rose spoke and ruined it. "Of course, I don't know it all myself," she hurried on. "I know something, but please don't ask me! It was most certainly an act of great physical courage, and violence . . . I cannot say what, I should not like to misrepresent anyone, perhaps malign them . . ." She left that suggestion lingering in the air. "But it was of great worth to Her Majesty, and to the Tory government. It is very natural that he should be rewarded for it . . . and quite right." She shot a jaggedly warning glance at Rose. "I am sure that is what you meant!"

"He is an opportunist," Rose snapped back. "A man seeking office for himself, not to pass laws that will bring social justice for more people, for the poor and ignorant and dispossessed, who should be our greatest charge. I would have thought a little time listening to what he says, with thought rather than simply emotion, would have made that abundantly clear." It was an accusation, and directed at all of them.

Emily began to panic. Rose seemed bent on self-destruction, and of course that meant taking Aubrey with her, which would cause endless guilt and pain afterwards. Could she not see what she was doing?

"All politicians are tempted to say whatever they think will get them elected,"

Emily answered a little too loudly. "And it is so easy to respond to a crowd and to try to please them."

Rose's eyes were wild and hard, as if she felt Emily were deliberately attacking her and it was yet another betrayal of friendship. "It is not only politicians who have succumbed to the temptation to play to the gallery, like a cheap actress!" she retaliated.

Emily lost her temper. "Indeed? Your simile escapes me. But then apparently you know more about cheap actresses than I do!"

One woman gave a nervous giggle, then another. Several looked acutely uncomfortable. The quarrel had reached the pitch where they were no longer happy to be witnessing it and were desperate to find any excuse to withdraw and join some other group. One by one they left, murmuring unintelligible excuses.

Emily took Rose by the arm, feeling her resist with rigid body. "What on earth is the matter with you?" she hissed. "Are you mad?"

Rose's face lost the shred of color it had had, as if every drop of blood had drained out of her.

Emily clasped Rose's arm, afraid she was

going to fall. "Come and sit down!" she ordered. "Quickly! This chair, before you faint." She dragged her the few yards to the nearest seat and forced her onto it, against her will, pushing her until her head was forward, almost to her knees, and shielding her from the rest of the room with her own body. She would have liked to fetch her something to drink, but she dared not leave her.

Rose remained motionless.

Emily waited.

No one approached them.

"You can't sit like that forever," Emily said at last, quite gently. "I can't help you if I don't know what is wrong. This calls for sense, not tantrums. Why is Aubrey behaving like such a fool? Is it something to do with you?"

Rose jerked up, two spots of furious color in her cheeks, her eyes brilliant like blue glass. "Aubrey is not a fool!" she said very quietly but with an intensity of feeling that was almost shocking.

"I know he isn't," Emily said more gently. "But he is behaving like one, and you are even more so. Haven't you any idea how ugly it looks to attack Voisey as you are doing? Even if everything you say is true, and you could prove it, which you can't, it would still not gain you any votes. People don't like having their heroes torn down or their dreams burst. They hate the people who deluded them, but they hate the ones who made them realize it just as much. If they want to believe he's a hero then they will. All you look is desperate and spiteful. The fact that you may be right has nothing to do with anything."

"That's monstrous!" Rose protested.

"Of course it is," Emily agreed. "But it is idiotic to play the game by the rules you would like there to be. You will lose every time. You must play within the rules there are . . . better if you like, but never worse."

Rose said nothing.

Emily went back to her first question in the whole miserable affair, which she still thought might be at the heart of it. "Why did you go to the spirit medium? And don't tell me it was simply to contact your mother for a comforting talk. You would never do that at election time, or deceive Aubrey about it. You're tormented with guilt over it, and yet you kept on going. Why, Rose? What do you need to resolve from the past at that price?"

"It has nothing to do with you!" Rose said miserably.

"Of course it has," Emily contradicted

her. "It's going to affect Aubrey — in fact, it already has, and that will affect Jack, if you expect him to try and help, to support Aubrey at the election. And you do, don't you? His backing away now would be pretty obvious."

Rose looked for a moment as if she were going to argue, her eyes hot and angry, then she said nothing after all, as if the words were useless even as she thought of them.

Emily pulled another chair closer, opposite Rose, and sat down, leaning forward a little, her skirts around her. "Was the medium blackmailing you because you went to her?" She saw Rose wince. "Or over whatever it was you found out from your mother?" she pressed.

"No, she wasn't!" It was not a lie, but Emily knew it was not entirely the truth, either.

"Rose! Stop running away!" she begged. "The woman was murdered! Somebody hated her enough to kill her. It wasn't a chance lunatic who wandered in off the street. It was someone who was there at the séance that night, and you know that!" She hesitated, then plunged on. "Was it you? Did she threaten you with something so terrible that you stayed behind and rammed that stuff down her throat? Was it to protect Aubrey?"

Rose was ashen, her eyes almost black. "No!"

"Then why? Something in your family?"

"I didn't kill her! Dear God! I wanted her alive, I swear!"

"Why? What did she do for you that matters so much?" She did not believe it, but she wished to jolt Rose into telling the truth at last. "Did she share the secrets about other people with you? Was it power?"

Rose was appalled. There was anguish, fury and shame in her face. "Emily, how can you think such things of me? You are vile!"

"Am I?" It was a challenge, a demand for the truth.

"Nothing I did harmed anyone else . . ." She dropped her eyes. "Except Aubrey."

"And have you the courage to face it?" Emily refused to give up. She could see that Rose was shivering and close to the breakdown of her self-control. She reached out and took Rose's hands in hers, still shielding them both from the rest of the room, all busy talking, gossiping, flirting, making and breaking alliances. "What did you need to know?"

"If my father died insane," Rose whispered. "I do wild things sometimes; you asked me just now if I were mad. Am I? Am I going to end up mad, as he was, to die alone somewhere in an asylum?" Her voice cracked. "Is Aubrey going to have to spend the rest of his life worrying about what I'm going to do? Am I going to be an embarrassment to him, someone he has to watch and continually apologize for, terrified of what awful thing I shall say or do next?" She gulped. "He wouldn't have me put away, he's not like that, not able to save himself by hurting someone else. He'd wait until I ruined him, and I couldn't bear that!"

Emily was overwhelmed with a pity that rendered her speechless. She wanted to put her arms around Rose and hold her so tightly she could force warmth and comfort into her, which was impossible. And in this crowded room it would have caused even these busy, absorbed people to turn and stare. Anything she offered could only be words. They must be the right ones.

"It is fear that's making you behave wildly, Rose, not inherited madness. What you have done is no more stupid than the things any of us do at one time or another. If you need to know what your father died from, there must be ways of finding out from the doctor who attended him."

"Then everyone else would know!" Rose said with panic rising in her voice, her hands gripping Emily's. "I can't bear that!"

"No, they don't have to —"

"But Aubrey . . ."

"I'll come with you," Emily promised. "We'll say it is a day out together, and we'll go and ask the doctor who attended him. He'll not only tell you whether your father was mad or not, but if he was, whether it is something that happened to him alone, because of an accident or a disease, or if it is something you might inherit. There are lots of different kinds of madness, not just one."

"And if the newspapers find out? Believe me, Emily, learning that I went to a séance will be nothing compared with that!"

"Then wait until after the election."

"I need to know before! If Aubrey becomes a member, if he's called into some office in the government, the Foreign Office . . . I am . . ." She tailed away, unable to say the words.

"Then it will be terrible," Emily said for her. "And if you are not, but are driven mad by fear, then you will have sacrificed all your chances for good for nothing at all.

And not knowing won't change it anyway."

"Will you?" Rose asked. "Come with me, I mean?" Then her face changed and the hope died out of it and it became bleak and full of pain again. "Then I suppose you will go and tell your policeman brother-in-law!" It was an accusation born out of despair, not a question.

"No," Emily replied. "I will not come in with you, and I will have no idea what answer you receive from the doctor. And it is certainly no business of the police what manner of illness your father died from — unless it caused you to kill Maude Lamont, because she knew?"

"I didn't! I . . . I never got to asking the spirit of my mother." She sank her head into her hands again, lost in misery, fear and embarrassment.

The exquisite voice of the singer floated through from the other room again, and Emily realized they were alone, except for a dozen or so men all talking earnestly together in the farther corner near the doors to the hallway. "Come," she said firmly. "A little cold water on your face, a hot cup of tea, which they are serving in the dining room, and we shall rejoin the others. Let them assume we are planning a garden party, or some such. But we had better tell the same story. A fête . . . to raise money for a charity. Come!"

Slowly, Rose climbed to her feet, straightened her shoulders, and obeyed.

CHAPTER
<u>TEN</u>

Pitt and Tellman returned to the house in Southampton Row. Pitt was increasingly certain that he was being observed each time he came and went in Keppel Street, although he had never actually seen anyone but the postman and the man who sold milk from the cart which usually stood at the corner of the mews leading through to Montague Place.

He had received two brief letters from Charlotte saying that all was well; they were missing him profoundly, but other than that having an excellent time. There was no return address on either of them. He had written to her, but made sure that he dropped the letters in boxes far from Keppel Street where the inquisitive postman would never see them.

The house in Southampton Row looked peaceful, even idyllic in the hot, still summer morning. There were errand boys in the street as usual, whistling as they carried messages, fish and poultry, or other small grocery items. One of them called out a cheeky compliment to a housemaid shooing a cat up the area steps and she giggled and told him off soundly.

"Get on wi' yer, yer daft 'aporth! Flowers, indeed!"

"Violets!" he shouted after her, waving his arm.

Once inside the house it was a different matter. The curtains were half drawn as was appropriate for a death, but then many people did that anyway, simply to protect the rooms from the strong light, or to offer a greater privacy.

The parlor where Maude Lamont had died was undisturbed. Lena Forrest received them civilly enough, although she still looked tired and there was a greater air of strain about her. Perhaps the reality of Maude's death had become apparent to her, and in a short while the necessity of finding another position. It cannot have been easy to live alone in the house where a woman whom you knew, saw every day in the most intimate circumstances, had been murdered only a week ago. It said a great deal for her fortitude that she had managed to remain in control of herself.

Except that no doubt she had seen death

many times before, and the fact that she served Maude Lamont did not in itself mean that she had any personal affection for her. She might have been a hard mistress, demanding, critical or inconsiderate. Some women thought their maids should be on duty at any hour of the day or night that they might be sent for, whether it was really necessary or not.

"Good morning, Miss Forrest," Pitt said courteously.

"Good morning, sir," she replied. "Is there something further I can do for you?" She included Tellman in her glance. They were standing in the parlor now, uneasily, each of them aware of what had happened there, if not why. Pitt had been thinking profoundly about that, and had discussed it briefly on the way over.

"Please sit down," he invited her, then he and Tellman did also.

"Miss Forrest," Pitt began. Her attention was unwavering. "Since the front door was closed and locked, the French doors to the garden" — he glanced at them — "were closed but not locked, and the only way out from the garden is through the door into Cosmo Place, which was locked but unbarred, it is the inevitable conclusion that Miss Lamont was killed by one of the people in the house during the séance. The only alternative is that it was all three in some collusion, and that does not seem even remotely likely."

She nodded silently in agreement. There was no surprise in her face. Presumably she had already realized as much herself. She had had a week in which to think of it, and it must have crowded almost everything else out of her mind.

"Have you had any further thought as to why anyone should wish Miss Lamont any harm?"

She hesitated, doubt in her face. It was clear some deep emotion worked within her.

"Please, Miss Forrest," he urged. "She was a woman who had opportunity to discover some of the most profound and vulnerable secrets in people's lives, things that they may well have been desperately ashamed of, past sins and tragedies too raw to forget." He saw the instant compassion in her face, as if her imagination reached out to such people and saw the horror of their memories in all their terrible detail. Perhaps she had served other mistresses with griefs, children dead, unhappy marriages, love affairs that tormented them. People did not always realize just how much a lady's maid was privy to, and sometimes how much she knew of a woman's most intimate life. Some might like to think of her as a silent confidante, others might be appalled that anyone else saw their most private moments and understood too much. Just as no man was a hero to his valet, so no woman was a mystery to her maid.

"Yes," Lena said very quietly. "There are not many secrets from a good medium, and she was very good."

Pitt looked at her, trying to read in her face, her eyes, whether she knew more than the bare words she was offering. It would have been difficult for Maude Lamont to have hidden from her maid any regular accomplice, either to fake manifestations or to gain personal information about prospective clients. A lover would also have given himself away sooner or later, even if only in Maude's demeanor. Was Lena Forrest keeping such secrets out of loyalty to a dead woman, or self-preservation because if she betrayed them then who would employ her in such a sensitive position in the future? And she had to think very carefully about that. Maude Lamont was not here to give her a good reference as to her character or skills. Lena was coming from a house where a murder had been committed. Her outlook was, if not desperate, at the least extremely poor.

"Did she have regular callers who were not to do with séances?" Tellman asked. "We're looking for those who gave her the information about people that she told them . . . things they wanted to hear."

Lena looked down, as if embarrassed. "You don't need a lot. People give themselves away. And she was very good at reading faces, understanding the things people don't say. She was a terribly quick guesser. I can't count the number of times I was thinking something, and she'd know what it was before I said it."

"We've searched the house for diaries," Tellman said to Pitt. "We found nothing other than lists of appointments. She must have committed everything to memory."

"What did you think of her gifts, Miss Forrest?" Pitt said suddenly. "Do you believe in the power to contact the spirits of the dead?" He watched her closely. She had denied helping Maude Lamont, but surely there had been some assistance, and there was no one else here.

Lena took in a long, very deep breath and let it out in a sigh. "I don't know. Seeing as I've lost my mother and my

sister, I'd like to think they were somewhere I could speak to them again." Her
face was blurred with the depth of her
emotion, which she kept only barely in
control. It was profoundly obvious that her
loss still racked her, and Pitt loathed
having to reawaken it, and in front of
others. Such grief should be afforded privacy.

"Have you ever seen manifestations
yourself?" he asked. The answer to Maude
Lamont's murder lay at least in part in this
house, and he had to find it, whether it affected Voisey or the election, or anything
else. He could not let murder go, whoever
the victim and whatever the reason.

"I used to think so," she said hesitantly.
"Long ago. But when you want something
bad enough, like these people did . . ." She
glanced sideways at the chairs where
Maude's clients sat at the séances. "Then
perhaps you see it anyway, don't you?"

"Yes, you can," he agreed. "But you had
no interest in the spirits these people
wanted to contact? Think back to all you
heard, all you know of what Miss Lamont
was able to create. We've heard from other
clients of voices, music, but the levitation
seems to have happened only here."

She looked puzzled.

"Rising up in the air," Pitt explained. He saw a sudden flash of understanding in her eyes. "Tellman, take another look at the table," he ordered. He turned back to Lena Forrest. "Do you ever remember seeing something different on the mornings after a séance, anything misplaced, a different smell, dust or powder, anything at all?"

She was silent for so long he was not sure if she was concentrating on something or if she simply did not intend to answer.

Tellman was sitting in the chair where Maude sat. Lena's eyes were steady on him.

"Did you ever move the table?" Pitt asked suddenly.

"No. It's fixed to the floor," Tellman replied. "I tried to move it before."

Pitt stood up. "What about the chair?" As he said it he walked over and Tellman rose and picked it up. He saw with surprise that there were four slight indentations on the floorboards where the feet had rested. Surely even the most continual use could not have made them. He moved to one of the other chairs and lifted it. There were no marks. He looked up quickly at Lena Forrest and caught the knowledge in her face.

"Where's the lever?" he said grimly. "Your

position is a very precarious one, Miss Forrest. Don't jeopardize your future by lying to the police." He hated making the threat, but he had no time to waste in trying to dismantle the woodwork to find the mechanism, and he needed to know how far she was involved. It might be crucial later.

She stood up, white-faced, and came around to the opposite side of the chair. She leaned over and touched the center of one of the carved flowers on the table edge.

"Press it," he ordered.

She did, and nothing happened.

"Do it again!" he ordered.

She stood perfectly still.

Very gradually the chair began to rise, and glancing down Pitt saw that the floorboards immediately under it rose also, just those actually supporting the four feet. The rest remained where they were. There was no sound whatever. The machinery was so perfectly oiled it happened easily. When the chair was about eight inches above the rest of the floor it stopped.

Pitt stared at Lena Forrest. "So you knew that at least this much was trickery."

"I only just found out," she said with a quiver in her voice.

"When?"

"After she was dead. I started to look. I

didn't tell you because it seemed . . ." She looked down, then quickly up again. "Well, she's gone. I suppose she can't be hurt. She doesn't know anything now."

"I think you'd better tell us what else you learned, Miss Forrest."

"I don't know anything else, just the chair. I . . . I heard of the things she did from someone who came by . . . with flowers, to say how sorry they were. So I looked. I never sat in on a séance. I was never there!"

Pitt could not draw anything more from her. Minute examination of the chair and the table, and a journey to the cellar, exposed a very fine mechanism, kept in perfect repair, also several bulbs for electric light, with which the house was fitted, and which worked from a generator also in the cellar.

"Why so many bulbs?" Pitt said thoughtfully. "Electric isn't even in most of the house, only the parlor and the dining room. All the rest is gas, and coal for heat."

"No idea," Tellman confessed. "Looks like she used the electricity for the tricks more than anything else. In fact, come to think of it, there are only three electric lights altogether. Maybe she meant to get more?"

"And got the bulbs first?" Pitt raised his eyebrows.

Tellman shrugged his square, thin shoulders. "What we need to find out is what she knew about those three people that made one of them kill her. They all had secrets of one sort, and she was blackmailing them. I'd lay odds on that!"

"Well, Kingsley came because of his son's death," Pitt replied. "Mrs. Serracold wanted to contact her mother, so presumably hers is a family matter lying in the past. We have to be certain who Cartouche is, and why he came."

"And why he wouldn't even tell her his name!" Tellman said angrily. "For my money, that means he's someone we'd recognize. And his secret is so bad he won't risk that." He grunted. "What if she recognized him? And that was why he had to kill her?"

Pitt thought about it for a few moments. "But according to both Mrs. Serracold and General Kingsley, he didn't want to speak to anyone in particular . . ."

"Not yet! Perhaps he would have, once he'd really believed she could do it!" Tellman said with rising certainty. "Or perhaps when he was convinced she was genuine, he would have asked for someone.

What if he was still testing her? From both witnesses, it sounds as if that was what he was trying to do."

Tellman was right. Pitt acknowledged it, but he had no answer. The suggestion that it had been Francis Wray was not one that he believed, not if it included the possibility that it was he who had deliberately knelt on Maude Lamont's chest and forced the egg white and cheesecloth down her throat, then held her until she choked to death, gasping and gagging as it filled her lungs, fighting for life.

Tellman was watching him. "We've got to find him," he said grimly. "Mr. Wetron insists it's this man in Teddington. He says the evidence will be there, if we look for it. He half suggested I send a squad of men over there and —"

"No!" Pitt cut across him sharply. "If anyone goes, I will."

"Then you'd better go today," Tellman warned. "Otherwise Wetron may —"

"Special Branch is in charge of this case." Again Pitt interrupted him.

Tellman stiffened, his resentment still clear in his eyes and the hard set of his face. His jaw was tight and there was a tiny muscle ticking in his temple. "Don't have a lot to show for it, though, do we?"

Pitt felt himself flush. The criticism was fair, but it still hurt, and the fact that in Special Branch he was out of his depth, and aware of it, and someone else had his position in Bow Street, made it worse. He did not dare to think of failure, but it was always at the back of his mind, waiting for an unguarded moment. When he was at home in the empty house, weary and without any clear idea where to look next, it was a black hole at his feet and falling into it was a possibility all too real.

"I'll go," he said curtly. "You'd better do more to find out how she got her blackmail material. Was it all watching and listening, or did she do some active research? It may help to know."

Tellman appeared undecided, one emotion conflicting with another in his face. It looked like anger and guilt, perhaps regret for having said aloud what was in his mind. "I'll see you tomorrow," he muttered, and turned to leave.

Sitting in the train to Teddington, Pitt turned over in his mind all the possible lines of enquiry about Francis Wray. Always at the forefront was the leaflet he had seen on the table advertising Maude Lamont, and the fury in Wray's face at

403

mention of spirit mediums. He denied to himself that the old man was so emotionally disturbed by the death of his wife he had lost mental balance, and perhaps he had, in the first depth of his grief, abandoned a lifetime's faith and gone to a medium. He certainly would not be unique in that, not even unusual. And with the vehemence of his conviction that it was sin, he would then have equated the medium with the offense, and have tried to rid himself of his self-loathing by destroying her! And the more that thought intruded into Pitt's mind, the more fiercely he tried to deny it.

When he reached Teddington he got off the train, but this time he avoided Udney Road and went to High Street. He loathed asking the villagers about Francis Wray, but there was no choice left to him. If he did not, then Wetron would send others who would be even clumsier, and cause more pain.

He had to use an invention. He could hardly say outright, "Do you think Mr. Wray has lost the hold of his sanity?" He framed instead questions as to things having been lost, lapses of memory, other people's concern that Wray was unwell. It was not as difficult as he had expected simply to find the words, but forcing himself to pry into the way the old man's grief had affected him was one of the most offensive things he had ever done, not to the people he spoke to, but to himself.

The answers all carried the same elements. Francis Wray was deeply liked and admired, perhaps *loved* would not have been too strong a word. But those who answered Pitt were also anxious for Wray, aware that his loss had left him more vulnerable than they were sure he could deal with. Friends had been uncertain whether to call in to see him or not. Was it intrusive, disturbing a private emotion, or was it a much-needed respite from the utter loneliness of the house with no one to speak to but young Mary Ann, who was devoted to his welfare but hardly a companion to him.

Pitt did manage to draw something from one of these friends, another man roughly Wray's age, and also a widower. Pitt found him in his garden tying up the most magnificent pink hollyhocks, well above the height of his own head.

"It's only a matter of concern," Pitt explained himself. "There is no complaint."

"No, of course," Mr. Duncan answered, pulling off a length of string from the ball and cutting it awkwardly with his secateurs. "I am afraid when we get old and lonely we tend to make nuisances of ourselves without realizing it." He smiled a little ruefully. "I daresay I did so myself the first year or two after my wife died. Sometimes we can't bear to speak to people, and others we can't leave them alone. I'm glad you see no need to do more than ascertain that there was no offense intended." He cut off another length of string, and looked apologetically at Pitt. "Young ladies can misunderstand the desire for their company, no doubt with cause, now and again."

Reluctantly, Pitt introduced the subject of séances.

"Oh dear, how unfortunate!" Mr. Duncan's face filled with alarm. "I am afraid he feels very strongly against that kind of thing. He was here when we had a local tragedy, quite a number of years ago now." He chewed his lip, ignoring the hollyhocks. "A young woman had a child — out of wedlock, you know. Penelope, her name was. The child died almost immediately, poor little thing. Penelope was distraught with grief and went to a spirit medium who promised to put her in touch with her dead child." He sighed. "Of course, the woman was a complete fraud, and when she discovered it, poor Penelope went quite wild with grief. It seems she thought she had spoken with the child, and that it had gone on to a far better place. She was comforted." The muscles in his face tightened. "And then the deception drove her right out of her senses. I am afraid she took her own life. It was very dreadful, and poor Francis saw it all and was helpless to prevent any of it.

"He argued to have the child buried properly, but of course he lost, since it was illegitimate and unbaptized. He was very put out with the local minister over that. The feeling lasted for quite a while. Francis would have baptized the child regardless, and taken the consequences. But of course he didn't have the power."

Pitt tried to think of something to say that expressed the emotions boiling up inside him, and found nothing that touched the anger or the futility he felt.

"And of course he comforted her the best he could," Duncan continued. "He knew the wretched medium was a fraud, but Penelope wouldn't listen. She was desperate to have any belief at all that her child still existed somewhere, poor creature. She wasn't very old herself. Of course, Francis has had something of a passion against all kinds of spiritualist activity ever since then. From time to time he has launched something of a crusade."

"Yes," Pitt said, pity twisting inside him with a hard, empty pain. "I can understand his feelings. There can be little more bitterly cruel, even if possibly it is not meant so."

"Yes." Duncan nodded. "Yes, indeed. One cannot blame his anger. I think I felt much the same myself at the time."

Pitt thanked him and excused himself. There was nothing more to learn from other people. It was time he faced Wray again and pressed him further to account more precisely for his whereabouts on the evenings Cartouche was recorded in Maude Lamont's diary as having been at Southampton Row.

At Udney Road, Mary Ann welcomed him in without question, and Wray himself met him in the study doorway with a smile. He did not even ask Pitt if he would stay for tea, but sent Mary Ann straightaway to prepare it, with sandwiches and fruit scones with greengage jam. "It was an excellent crop last year," he said enthusiastically, leading the way back into the study and offering Pitt a chair. He blinked and his voice dropped and became suddenly very gentle. "My wife was extremely good at making jam. Greengage was one of her favorites."

Pitt felt wretched. He was sure guilt must be written in his face at the thought of probing the grief of this man who so obviously liked and trusted him, and had not the remotest suspicion that Pitt was here not in friendship but in pursuit of his job.

"Perhaps I should not take it?" he said unhappily. "Would you not rather keep it for . . ." He was not sure what he wanted to say.

"No, no," Wray assured him. "Not at all. I am afraid the raspberry is all gone. I rather indulged myself. I should be delighted to share this with you. She really was very good." Sudden concern filled his eyes. "Unless, of course, you do not care for it?"

"Oh, I do! I like it very much!"

"Good. Then we shall have it." Wray smiled. "Now, tell me why you are here, and how you are, Mr. Pitt. Have you found this unfortunate man who was consulting the medium who died?"

Pitt was not ready to pursue it yet. He had thought his plan was clear, and now it was not. "No . . . no, I haven't," he replied. "And it is important that I do. He may have knowledge which would make it much plainer why she was killed, and by whom."

"Oh dear." Wray shook his head. "How very sad. Evil always comes of such things, you know. We should not meddle with them. To do so, even in the imagination of innocence, is to awaken the devil to our weaknesses. And never doubt it, Mr. Pitt, it is an invitation he will not pass by."

Pitt was embarrassed. It was an area of thought he had never considered, perhaps because his faith was more of morality than the metaphysics of God or Satan, and certainly he had never considered belief in calling upon spirits. Yet Wray was in deadly earnest; no one looking at the passion in his face could mistake it.

Pitt compromised. "It seems likely that she was in the practice of a very human evil, Mr. Wray, namely that of blackmail."

Wray shook his head. "A kind of moral murder, I think," he said very quietly. "Poor woman. She has forfeited a great deal of herself, I fear."

He was prevented from saying any more on the subject by a knock on the door, and a moment later Mary Ann appeared with their tea. The tray was so laden with plates that it looked precariously heavy, and Pitt shot to his feet to take it from her in case in her efforts to hold both it and the door, she should drop it.

"Thank you, sir," she said uncomfortably, flushing a little. "But you shouldn't!"

"It is no trouble," Pitt assured her. "It looks excellent, and very generous. I had not realized I was hungry, but now I definitely am."

She bobbed a little curtsy of satisfaction and almost ran out, leaving Wray to pour, smiling at Pitt as he did so. "A nice child," he said with a nod. "She does everything she can to care for me."

There was no answer to make that would not have been trite. The contents of the tray were stronger evidence of her care than any words could have been.

They ate in silent appreciation for several minutes. The tea was hot and fragrant, the sandwiches delicious, and the fresh scones crumbled at the touch, rich with butter and the sharp, sweet jam.

Pitt bit into it, and looked up. Wray was watching him intently, waiting to see if he truly liked the greengage jam, and he could not bear to ask.

Pitt did not know whether to praise it highly, if that would sound artificial, in the end a condescension worse than silence. Pity could be the ultimate offense. And yet if he were lukewarm that would be wrong, too, insensitive and of little use.

"I hate to eat the last of it," he said with his mouth full. "You won't get the like of it again. There is a richness and a delicacy to it. It must be exactly the right amount of sugar because there is no cloying sweetness to mar the taste of the fruit." He took a deep breath and thought of Charlotte, and Voisey, and everything he could lose and how it would destroy all that was good and precious in his world. "My wife makes the best marmalade I've ever tasted," he said, and was horrified to hear his voice husky.

"Does she?" Wray struggled to keep control, to speak with something like normality. They were two men who were barely acquaintances, sharing afternoon tea, and thoughts of preserves, and the women they loved more profoundly than any words about anything at all could say.

The tears brimmed in Wray's eyes and slid down his cheeks.

Pitt swallowed the last mouthful of scone and jam.

Wray bent his head and his shoulders trembled, and then began to shake. He struggled for a moment or two.

Pitt stood up quietly and went around the table, and sat sideways on the arm of

412

the old man's chair. Tentatively at first, then with more assurance, he put his hand on Wray's shoulder, feeling it startlingly frail, then around him, and as he relaxed his weight, allowed him to weep. Perhaps it was the first time Wray had permitted himself to do so since his wife's death.

Pitt had no idea how long they sat like that, until at last Wray ceased to move, to shake, and finally straightened himself up.

He must be allowed dignity. Without looking at him, Pitt rose to his feet and walked out of the French doors into the garden and the sun. He would give him ten minutes at least to compose himself, wash his face, and then they could both pretend nothing had happened.

He was standing facing the road when he saw the carriage coming. It was a very handsome vehicle with excellent horses and a coachman in livery. To his great surprise it stopped at the gate and a woman alighted carrying a basket covered with a cloth. She was of very striking appearance, dark-haired, with a face not immediately beautiful, but of powerful intelligence and character. She walked with unusual grace, and appeared to notice him only as her hand was on the latch. Perhaps at first she had assumed he was a gardener, until she looked more clearly and saw his clothes.

"Good afternoon," she said calmly. "Is Mr. Wray at home?"

"Yes, but he is a little unwell," he answered, moving towards her. "I daresay he will be pleased to see you, but in courtesy I think we should allow him a few minutes to recover himself, Mrs. . . ."

"Cavendish," she replied. Her look was very direct. "I know his doctor, and you are not he. Who are you, sir?"

"My name is Pitt. I am merely a friend."

"Should we call his doctor? I can send my carriage immediately." She half turned. "Joseph! Dr. Trent . . ."

"It is not necessary," Pitt said quickly. "A few minutes and he will be much better."

She looked doubtful.

"Please, Mrs. Cavendish. If you are a friend then your company may be the thing most helpful." He glanced down at her basket.

"I brought him some books," she said with a faint smile. "And some jam tarts. Oh! Not greengage . . . this is merely ordinary raspberry."

"That is kind of you," he said sincerely.

"I am very fond of him," she answered. "As I was of his wife."

They stood together in the sun for a few

minutes longer, then the French doors opened and Wray himself came out, walking carefully as if a trifle uncertain of his balance. His skin was very pink and his eyes red-rimmed, but he had obviously dashed a little water over his face and was almost composed. He looked startled to see Mrs. Cavendish, but not in the least displeased, only perhaps embarrassed that she should find him in such a barely concealed emotional state. He did not meet Pitt's eyes.

"My dear Octavia," he said with warmth. "How kind of you to call on me again, and so soon. You really are very generous."

She smiled at him with affection. "I think of you very often," she replied. "It seemed the natural thing to do. We are all extremely fond of you." She turned her shoulders away from Pitt, as if to exclude him from the remark. She took the cloth off the basket. "I have brought a few books you may care to read, and some tarts. I hope you will enjoy them."

"How thoughtful," he said with an immense effort to sound pleased. "Perhaps you will come in and have some tea?"

She accepted, and with a sharp look at Pitt, started to walk towards the French doors.

Wray turned to Pitt. "Mr. Pitt, do you care to come back also? You are most welcome. I do not feel as if I have helped you very much, although I confess I have no idea how I can."

"I am not at all sure that there is any way," Pitt said before he considered the defeat implicit in the remark. "And you have given me most excellent hospitality. I shall not forget it." He did not mention the jam, but he knew by the sudden brightness of Wray's eyes, and the way he blushed, that he understood perfectly.

"Thank you," Wray said with overwhelming emotion, and before he was overcome again, he turned and followed Mrs. Cavendish back towards the French doors and went inside after her.

Pitt walked through the flowers to the gate, and out into Udney Road.

CHAPTER
<u>ELEVEN</u>

The air blowing down off the moor was
sweet, barely stirring the leaves of the apple
tree in the cottage garden, and the silence
and darkness were unbroken. It ought to
have been a perfect night for deep, untrou-
bled sleep. But Charlotte lay awake, aware of
her loneliness, ears straining as if expecting
to hear a sound, a footfall somewhere, a
loose stone disturbed on the track beyond
the gate, perhaps wheels, or more likely
simply a horse's hoof striking a sudden hard
surface.

When at last she did hear it, the reality
shot through her blood like fire. She threw
back the bedcovers and stumbled the mere
three steps to the window, and peered out.
In the starlight there was nothing but a
variance of depth in the shadows. Anyone
could have been there, and she would not
have seen.

She stayed until her eyes ached, but
there was no movement, just another slight

sound, no more than a rustle. A fox? A stray cat, or a night hunting bird? She had seen an owl at dusk yesterday evening.

She crept back to bed, but still lay awake, waiting.

Emily also found it hard to sleep, but it was guilt that disturbed her, and a decision she did not want to make but knew now was inevitable. Of all the possibilities she had considered for the fear that haunted Rose, insanity had never been among them. She had thought of an unfortunate romance before Aubrey, or even after, possibly a lost child, someone in her family with whom she had quarreled and who had died before she had had the chance to repair the rift. Not once had she imagined something as terrible as madness.

She could not commit herself to telling Pitt, and yet in her heart she knew she had to, she was just not prepared yet to admit it to herself. She still wanted to believe that somehow she would be able to protect Rose from . . . what? Injustice? Judgment that knew only some of the facts? The truth?

She toyed with the idea of going to Pitt in the morning, an hour or so after breakfast, when she had had time to compose herself, think exactly what she was going to say and how to word it.

But honesty compelled her to acknowledge that if she waited, then Pitt would almost certainly have left the house, and she was only thinking of doing it so she could pretend to herself that she had tried, when in actuality she had quite deliberately gone when she knew it was too late.

So she rose at six, when her maid brought her the requested cup of hot tea, which made her feel rather more like facing the day. She dressed and was out of the house by half past seven. Once you have made up your mind to do something that you know will be difficult and unpleasant, it is better to do it immediately, before too much thinking of it can fill your mind with the fears of all that can hurt and go wrong.

Pitt was startled to see her. He stood in the doorway in Keppel Street in shirt-sleeves and stocking feet, his hair untidy as ever. "Emily!" His concern was instant. "Has something happened? Are you all right?"

"Yes, something has happened," she replied. "And I am not sure whether I will be all right or not."

He stood aside, inviting her in, allowing

her to lead the way to the kitchen. She sat down on one of the hard-backed chairs, sparing only a glance at the familiar surroundings, so subtly different without either Charlotte or Gracie there. The room had a vaguely unused feel, as if only the necessities were being done, no baking of cakes, no smell of richness or warmth, too little linen on the airing rail strung up to the ceiling. Only Archie and Angus, stretching themselves awake on the hearth of the cooking range, looking totally comfortable.

"Tea?" Pitt asked, indicating the pot on the table and the kettle whistling gently on the back of the hob. "Toast?"

"No, thank you," she declined.

He sat down, ignoring his own half-finished drink. "What is it?"

She had passed the point of changing her mind . . . well, almost. There was still time to say something else. He was looking at her, waiting. Perhaps he would draw it out of her whether she wanted him to or not. If she hesitated long enough he might do that, and relieve her of the guilt.

Except that was a lie to herself. She was here. At least do what needed doing with some integrity! She raised her eyes and stared at him. "I saw Rose Serracold yesterday evening and talked with her as if we were alone. It can be like that sometimes at a big party, find yourself sort of . . . islanded in noise, so no one overhears you. I bullied her into telling me why she went to Maude Lamont." She stopped, remembering how she had forced Rose into an emotional corner. *Bullied* was the right word.

Pitt waited without prompting her.

"She is afraid her father died insane —" She stopped abruptly, seeing Pitt's amazement, and then instant horror. "She is terrified that she might have inherited the same taint in the blood," she went on quietly, as if whispering could lessen the pain of it. "She wanted to ask her mother's spirit if it was true, if he really was mad. But she didn't have the chance. Maude Lamont was killed too soon."

"I see." He sat staring at her without moving. "We can ask General Kingsley to confirm that at least she had not contacted her mother by the time she left."

She was startled. "You think she might have gone back afterwards and had a private séance?"

"Someone went back, whatever for," he pointed out.

"Not Rose!" she said with more conviction than she felt. "She wanted her alive!" She leaned forward across the table. "She's still so afraid she can hardly keep control of herself, Thomas. She doesn't know yet! She's hunting for another medium so she can go on searching."

The kettle shrilled more insistently on the hob, and he ignored it. "Or Maude Lamont told her something she doesn't want to believe," he said gently. "And she is terrified that it will be discovered."

She looked at him, wishing he did not understand her so well, read in her the racing thoughts she would so much rather have concealed. And yet if she could dupe him that would not be any comfort, either. She had always believed that her own skill with people was her greatest asset. She could charm and beguile and so often make people do what she wished them to without their even being aware that what they embraced so eagerly was actually her idea.

And the use of it left her oddly dissatisfied. She had realized that more and more lately. She did not want to see further than Jack could, or be stronger or cleverer than he was. Ahead was a very lonely place. One had to take the burden sometimes, it was part of love, part of responsibility — but only sometimes, not always. And it was a pleasure only because it was right, fair, an act of giving, not because it afforded any comfort to oneself.

So while she resented Pitt's pressure on her to tell him more than she wished to, she also felt a sense of comfort that she could not fob him off with half an answer. She needed him to be cleverer than she was, because she had not the power to help Rose, or even to be certain what help would be. She might only make it worse. She realized now that she was not absolutely sure that Rose was not touched with the edge of madness, and could in her panic have thought Maude Lamont knew her secret and would endanger her, and then Aubrey. She remembered how quickly Rose had turned on her when she was afraid. Friendship had vanished like water dropped on the hot surface of a griddle, evaporated before her sight.

"She swore she did not kill her," she said aloud.

"And you want to believe her," Pitt finished the unsaid thought. He stood up and went to the stove, moving the kettle off the heat. He turned back to face her. "I hope you are right. But somebody did. I don't want it to be General Kingsley, either."

"The anonymous person," Emily concluded. "You still don't know who he was . . . do you?"

"No."

She looked at him. Something was closed and hurt in his eyes. He was not lying. She had never known him to do that. But there was a world of feeling and of fact that he was not willing to tell her.

"Thank you, Emily," he said, coming back to the table. "Did she say if anyone else knew of this fear? Does Aubrey know?"

"No." She was quite certain. "Aubrey doesn't know, and if you are thinking Maude Lamont blackmailed her, I don't think so." She was aware of a sudden lurch of anxiety as she said it, and that it was only partially true. Could Pitt see that in her face?

He gave a slight shrug. "Perhaps Maude Lamont didn't know yet," he said dryly. "Someone may have affected a very lucky escape for Rose."

"Aubrey doesn't know, Thomas! He really doesn't!"

"Probably not."

He walked with her to the front door, collecting his jacket on the way, and outside he accepted a lift in her carriage as far as Oxford Street, where she turned west to go back home. He went south towards the War Office, to again search its records for whatever it was that had forced General Kingsley to attack the political party whose values he had always believed. Surely it had to have some connection with the death of his son or some action shortly before it.

He had been there over an hour, reading one report after another, when he realized that he still had no flavor of the man, no sense of anything other than a torrent of formal, fleshless words. It was like seeing the skeleton of a man and trying to imagine the look of his face, his voice, his laughter, the way he moved. There was nothing here. Whatever it had been was covered over. He could read this all day and learn nothing.

He copied out the names of most of the other officers and men who had been at Mfolozi to see if any of them were here in London, and perhaps willing to tell him more than this. Then he thanked the clerk and left.

He had already given the cabbie the address of the first man on the list when he changed his mind, and gave Lady Vespasia Cumming-Gould's address instead. Perhaps it was an impertinence to call on her uninvited, but he had never found her unwilling to help in any cause in which she believed. And after Whitechapel, where they had shared not only the battle itself but a depth of emotion, a fear and a loss, and a victory at terrible price, there was a bond between them unlike any other.

Therefore it was with confidence that he presented himself at the front door of her house and told the maid who answered it that he wished to speak with Lady Vespasia on a matter of some urgency. He would await her convenience, however long that might be.

He was left in the morning room, but it proved to be only for a matter of minutes, then he was shown into her sitting room, which faced onto the garden and always seemed to be full of peace and a soft light, whatever the season or the weather.

She was wearing a shade of clover pink, so subtle it was hardly pink at all, and the usual pearls around her neck. She smiled to greet him, and held out her hand very slightly, not for him to take, merely as a gesture that he should come in.

"Good morning, Thomas. How pleasant to see you." Her eyes searched his face. "I have been half expecting you ever since

Emily called. Or perhaps 'half hoping' would be more accurate. Voisey is standing for Parliament." She could not even say his name without the emotion thickening her voice. She had to be remembering Mario Corena, and the sacrifice which had cost Voisey so dearly.

"Yes, I know," he said softly. He wished he could have spared her being aware of it, but she had never evaded anything in her life, and to protect her now would surely be the ultimate insult. "That is why I am here in London rather than with Charlotte in the country."

"I am glad she is away." Her face was bleak. "But what is it you believe you can do, Thomas? I don't know much about Victor Narraway. I have asked, but either the people I spoke to know little themselves or they are not prepared to tell me." She looked at him steadily. "Be very careful that you do not trust him more than is wise. Don't assume that he has the concern for you, or the loyalty, that Captain Cornwallis had. He is not a straightforward man —"

"Do you know that?" Pitt said, cutting across her unintentionally.

She smiled very slightly, a gesture that barely moved her lips. "My dear Thomas,

Special Branch is designed and created to catch anarchists, bombers, all kinds of men, and I suppose a few women, who plan in secret to overthrow our government. Some of them intend to replace it with another of their own choosing, others simply wish to destroy without the slightest idea what will follow. Some, of course, have loyalties to other countries. Can you imagine John Cornwallis organizing a force to prevent them before they succeed?"

"No," Pitt admitted with a sigh. "He is brave and profoundly honest. He would expect to see the whites of their eyes before he would shoot."

"He would invite them to surrender," she amended. "Special Branch requires a devious man, subtle, full of imagination, a man seen only in the shadows, and never by the public. Do not forget that."

Pitt was cold, even in the sun. "I think General Kingsley was being blackmailed by Maude Lamont, at least on the surface it was by her."

"For money?" She was surprised.

"Possibly, but I think more likely to attack Aubrey Serracold in the newspapers, sensing his inexperience and the probability that he would react badly, damaging himself further."

"Oh dear." She shook her head very slightly.

"One of them killed her," he continued. "Rose Serracold, General Kingsley, or the man denoted in her diary by a cartouche, a little drawing rather like a reversed small f with a semicircle over the top of it."

"How curious. And have you any idea who he may be?"

"Superintendent Wetron believes he is an elderly professor of theology who lives in Teddington."

Her eyes widened. "Why? That seems a very perverse thing for a religious man to do. Was he seeking to expose her as a fraud?"

"I don't know. But I . . ." He hesitated, not sure how to explain either his feelings or his actions. "I really don't believe it was he, but I am not certain. He recently lost his wife and is deeply grieved. He has a passion against spirit mediums. He believes they are evil, and acting contrary to the commandments of God."

"And you are afraid that this man, deranged by his grief, may have taken it into his head to finish her intervention permanently?" she concluded. "Oh, Thomas, my dear, you are too softhearted for your profession. Sometimes very good men can make the most terrible mistakes, and bring untold misery while convinced they are bent upon the work of God. Not all the inquisitors of Spain were cruel or narrow-minded men, you know. Some truly believed they were saving the souls of those in their charge. They would be astounded if they knew how we perceived them now." She shook her head. "Sometimes we see the world so differently from each other you would swear we could not possibly be speaking of the same existence. Have you never asked half a dozen witnesses to an event in the street, even the description of a person, and received such conflicting answers, told in all sincerity, that they cancel each other out entirely?"

"Yes, I have. But I still do not think he is guilty of having killed Maude Lamont."

"You do not want to think it. What can I do to help you, more than simply listen?"

"I must discover who killed Maude Lamont, even though that is really Tellman's job, because the people she blackmailed are part of the effort to discredit Serracold . . ."

Sadness and anger filled her eyes. "They have already succeeded, with the poor man's own help. You will have to perform a miracle if you are to rescue him now."

Then she brightened. "Unless, of course, you can demonstrate that Voisey had a hand in it. If he obtained her murder . . ." She stopped. "I think that would be good fortune beyond our reach. He would not be so foolish. Above all, he is clever. But he will be behind the blackmail; it just depends how far behind! Can you prove that?"

He leaned forward a little. "I may be able to." He saw her eyes shine, and he knew she was thinking of Mario Corena again. She could not weep. She had already shed all her tears for him, first in Rome in '48, then here in London only a few weeks ago. But the loss was still raw. Perhaps it always would be. "I need to know why Kingsley was being blackmailed," he went on. "I think it was to do with the death of his son." Briefly, he told her what he had learned, first about Kingsley himself and his part in the Zulu Wars, and then the ambush at Mfolozi, so soon after the heroism of Rorke's Drift.

"I see," she said when he had finished. "It is very hard to follow in the steps of a father or brother who has succeeded in the eyes of the world, most especially in the world of military courage. Many young men have thrown away their lives rather than be thought to fail in what was expected of them." There was a weight of sadness in her voice, and memory sharp and painful in her eyes. Perhaps she was thinking of the Crimea, of Balaclava, and the Alma, or of Rorke's Drift, Isandlwana, or the Indian Mutiny and God knew how many other wars and losses. Her memory might even have stretched back as far as her girlhood, and Waterloo.

"Aunt Vespasia . . . ?"

She brought herself back to the present with a jolt. "Of course," she agreed. "It will not be too difficult for me to learn from one friend or another what really happened to young Kingsley at Mfolozi, but I think it hardly matters, except to his father. No doubt what was used to blackmail him was the possibility of a coward's death. It did not have to be the fact. It is not only the wicked who run where no man pursues, it is also the vulnerable, those who care more than they are able to govern, and who have raw wounds they cannot defend."

Pitt thought of Kingsley's bent shoulders and the haggard lines of his face. It took a particular kind of sadism to torture a man in such a way for one's own profit. For a moment he hated Voisey with a passion that would have exploded in physical violence, had he been there to lash out at.

"Of course it may be that the incident of his death is so blurred that the truth cannot be known, or a lie dismissed," Vespasia went on. "But I shall do all I can to find out, and if it is of any ease at all, I shall inform General Kingsley of it."

"Thank you."

"Which is not a great deal of use in tying the blackmail to Voisey," she continued with a trace of anger. "What hope have you of discovering the identity of this third person? I assume you know it is a man? You refer to him as 'he.' "

"Yes. It is a man of late middle years, fair or gray hair, average height and build. He seems to be well educated."

"Your theologian," she said unhappily. "If he went to a spirit medium with the intent of proving her a fraud and unmasking her in front of her clients, that would not please Voisey very much. I think we may assume he could retaliate, perhaps with extreme pressure."

That was impossible to argue against. Pitt remembered the look in Voisey's eyes as they had passed each other in the House of Commons. Voisey forgot nothing and forgave nothing. Again Pitt found himself sitting in the light of the sun, and cold inside.

Vespasia was frowning.

"What is it?" he asked.

Her silver-gray eyes were troubled, her body not merely straight-backed with the disciplined posture of decades of self-control, but her shoulders stiff with an inner tension.

"I have given it much thought, Thomas, and I still do not understand why you were dismissed a second time from command of Bow Street . . ."

"Voisey!" he said with a bitterness that startled him. He had thought himself in control of his anger, his burning sense of injustice on the subject, but now it came back in a drowning wave.

"No," she said, half under her breath. "No matter how much he may hate you, Thomas, he will never act against his own interest. That is his greatest strength. His head always governs his heart." She stared straight ahead of her. "And it is not in his interest to have you in Special Branch, which is where he must have known you would go if dismissed from Bow Street again. In the police, unless he commits a crime, you have no jurisdiction in his affairs. If you involve yourself with him he

434

can charge you with harassment and have you disciplined. But in Special Branch your duties are far more fluid. Special Branch is secret, not answerable to the public." She turned to look at him. "Always keep your enemies where you can see them. He is not fool enough to forget that."

"Then why would he do it?" he asked, confused by her logic.

"Perhaps it was not Voisey?" she said very carefully.

"Then who?" he asked. "Who else but the Inner Circle would have the power to go behind the Queen's back and undo what she had done?" The thought was dark and frightening. He knew of no one else he had offended, and certainly no other secret societies with such tentacles winding into the heart of government.

"Thomas, how hard have you thought about the effect on the Inner Circle of Voisey's knighthood, and the reason for it?" Vespasia asked.

"I hope it shattered his leadership," he said honestly. He tried to swallow down his anger and the gall of disappointment inside him. "It hurts that it hasn't."

"Few of them are idealists," she replied ruefully. "But have you considered that it might have fractured the power within the Circle? A rival leader who has arisen may have taken with him sufficient of the old Circle to form a new one."

Pitt had not thought of it, and as the idea ballooned in his mind he saw all sorts of possibilities, dangerous to England but also exquisitely dangerous to Voisey himself. Voisey would know who the rival leader was, but would he ever be certain whose loyalty was where?

Vespasia saw all these thoughts in Pitt's face. "Don't rejoice yet," she warned. "If I am right, then the rival is powerful, too, and no more a friend of yours than Voisey. It is not always true that my enemy's enemy is my friend. Is it not possible that it was he who removed you again from Bow Street, either because he believes you will be more of a thorn in Voisey's flesh in Special Branch, possibly in time even destroy Voisey for him? Or else it matters to him to have Superintendent Wetron in charge of Bow Street rather than you?"

"Wetron in the Inner Circle?"

"Why not?"

There was no reason why not. The deeper it sank into his mind the more it clarified into a picture he could not disbelieve. There was an exhilaration to it, a beating of the blood as at the knowledge of danger, but there was fear as well. An open battle between the two leaders of the Inner Circle might leave many other victims in its wake.

He was still considering the implications of this when the maid appeared at the door looking alarmed.

"Yes?" Vespasia asked.

"M'lady, there's a Mr. Narraway to see Mr. Pitt. He said he would wait, but that I was to interrupt you." She did not apologize in words, but it was there in her gestures and her voice.

"Indeed?" Vespasia sat very straight. "Then you had better ask him to come in."

"Yes, m'lady." She dropped the very slightest curtsy and withdrew to obey.

Pitt met Vespasia's eyes. A hundred ideas flashed between them, all wordless, all touched with fear.

Narraway appeared a moment later. His face was bleak with misery and defeat. It dragged his shoulders in spite of the fact that he stood straight.

Pitt climbed to his feet very slowly, finding his legs shaking. His mind whirled with thoughts of horror; the most hideous and persistent, crowding all the rest, was that something had happened to Charlotte.

His lips were dry, and when he tried to speak his voice caught in his throat.

"Good morning, Mr. Narraway," Vespasia said coolly. "Please sit down and inform us what it is that brings you personally to speak to Thomas in my house."

He remained standing. "I am sorry, Lady Vespasia," he said very softly, merely glancing at her before turning to Pitt. "Francis Wray was found dead this morning."

For a moment Pitt could not grasp it. He was light-headed, his senses swimming. It was nothing to do with Charlotte. She was safe. It was all right! The horror had not happened. He was almost afraid he was going to laugh out of sheer hysteria of relief. It cost him an intense effort to control himself.

"I'm sorry," he said aloud. He meant it, at least in part. He had liked Wray. But considering the depth of grief that Wray had been in, perhaps death was not a hard thing but a reunion?

Nothing changed in Narraway's face, except a tiny twitch of muscle near his mouth. "It appears to have been suicide," he said harshly. "It seems he took poison some time yesterday evening. His maid found him this morning."

"Suicide!" Pitt was appalled. He refused to believe it. He could not imagine Wray doing anything he would regard as so deeply against the will of the God in whom all his trust lay, the only pathway back to those he loved so intensely. "No . . . there has to be another answer!" he protested, his voice harsh and high.

Narraway looked impatient, as if a fearful anger lay only just under the surface of his control. "He left a message," he said bitterly. "In a poem by Matthew Arnold." And without waiting, he went on and quoted by heart:

Creep into thy narrow bed,
Creep, and let no more be said!
Vain thy onset! All stands fast.
Thou thyself must break at last.

Let the long contention cease!
Geese are swans, and swans are geese.
Let them have it how they will!
Those art tired; best be still.

Narraway's eyes did not move from Pitt's. "Close enough to a suicide note for most people," he said softly. "And Voisey's sister, Octavia Cavendish, who has been a friend of Wray's for some time, called by to visit him just as you were leaving yesterday afternoon. She found him in a state of some distress; in her opinion, he had been weeping. You had made enquiries about him in the village."

Pitt felt the blood drain from him. "He wept for his wife!" he protested, but he heard the note of despair in his voice. It was the truth, but it sounded like an excuse.

Narraway nodded very slowly, his mouth a thin, tight line.

"This is Voisey's revenge," Vespasia whispered. "He has not minded sacrificing an old man in order to blame Thomas for hounding him to his death."

"I didn't . . ." Pitt began, then stopped, seeing the look in her eyes. It was Wetron who had given him Wray's name and suggested he was the man behind the cartouche. And according to Tellman, it was Wetron who had insisted Pitt go out again and follow up his first enquiry, or else he himself would send a force of men, surely knowing Pitt would go before he would allow that. Was he with Voisey, or against him? Or either way as it suited his own purposes?

Vespasia turned to Narraway. "What are you going to do?" she asked him, as if it

440

were inconceivable he should do nothing.

Narraway looked beaten. "You are quite right, my lady, it is Voisey's revenge, and it is exquisite. The newspapers will crucify Pitt. Francis Wray was deeply revered, even loved, by all who knew him. He had suffered many reverses of fortune with courage and dignity, first the loss of his children, then of his wife. Someone has already told the newspapers that Pitt suspected him of having consulted Maude Lamont and then having murdered her."

"I did not!" Pitt said desperately.

"That is irrelevant now," Narraway dismissed it. "You were trying to determine if he was Cartouche, and Cartouche is among the suspects. You are arguing the depth of the water in which you will drown. It is deep enough. What does it matter if it is two fathoms or thirty, or a hundred?"

"We had afternoon tea," Pitt said, almost to himself. "With greengage jam. He hadn't much of it left. It was an act of friendship that he shared it with me. We talked of love and loss. That was why he wept."

"I doubt that is what Mrs. Cavendish will say," Narraway replied. "And he was not Cartouche. Someone else has come forward to say exactly where Wray was on the evening of Maude Lamont's last séance. He had a late supper with the local vicar and his wife."

"I believe I already asked you, Mr. Narraway, what you intend to do about it?" Vespasia said a little more sharply.

He turned to look at her. "There is nothing I can do, Lady Vespasia. The newspapers will say what they wish, and I have no power over them. They believe that an innocent and bereaved old man has been hounded to death by an overzealous policeman. There is considerable evidence to that effect, and I cannot prove it false, even though I believe it is." There was no conviction in his voice, just a flat despair. He looked at Pitt. "I hope you will be able to continue with your job, although it seems inevitable now that Voisey will win. If you need anyone to help you, other than Tellman, let me know." He stopped, his face pinched with misery. "I'm sorry, Pitt. No one crosses the Inner Circle and wins for long . . . at least not yet." He went to the door. "Good day, Lady Vespasia. I apologize for my intrusion." And he left as easily as he had come.

Pitt was stunned. In a matter of a quarter of an hour his world had been shattered. Charlotte and the children were safe; Voisey had no idea where they were, but then possibly he had never tried to find out! His vengeance was subtler and more appropriate than simple violence. Pitt had ruined him in the eyes of the republicans. And in return he had ruined Pitt in the eyes of the people he served and who had once thought so well of him.

"Courage, my dear," Vespasia said gently, but her voice cracked. "I think this is going to be very hard, but we will not cease to fight. We will not allow evil to triumph without giving everything we have in the cause against it."

He looked at her, frailer now than she used to be, her back ramrod stiff, her thin shoulders square, her eyes burning with tears. He could not possibly let her down.

"No, of course not," he agreed, though he had not the faintest idea even where or how to begin.

CHAPTER

<u>TWELVE</u>

The next morning was one of the worst in Pitt's life. He had finally gone to sleep holding on to his gratitude that at least Charlotte, the children and Gracie were safe. He awoke with them pictured in his mind and found himself smiling.

Then memory returned and he knew that Francis Wray was dead, possibly by his own hand, alone and in despair. He could remember him so clearly sitting at the tea table, apologizing for having no cake or raspberry jam to offer, and giving Pitt the precious greengage instead, with such pride.

Pitt lay on his back staring up at the ceiling. The house was silent. It was shortly after six, two hours before Mrs. Brody would come. He could think of nothing to get up for, but his mind would not let him go back to sleep. This was Voisey's revenge, and it was perfect. Had Wetron known he was helping to accomplish it for him when he had sent Tellman to prompt Pitt to go back to Teddington a second time and ask around the village?

Wray was the perfect victim, a bereaved and forgetful old man, too honest to guard his tongue in his hatred of what was to him a sin against God in the calling up of the dead. Voisey would certainly have known the story of the young woman, Penelope, who had lost her child and in her grief sought a spirit medium who had used her, duped her, taken her money and then been caught in a cheap fraud. After all, it had happened in the very village where his sister lived! A situation too ideal to pass by.

Perhaps it was even Octavia Cavendish who had left the tract on Maude Lamont in Wray's house. Simple enough to do, and right where Pitt would see it. They had both been led like lambs to the slaughter . . . and in Wray's case it was literal. In Pitt's it would be slower, more exquisite. He would suffer and Voisey would watch, taking his pleasure sip by sip.

It was stupid lying here thinking about it. He got up quickly, washed, shaved and dressed, then went downstairs in the silence to make himself a cup of tea and feed Archie and Angus. He did not feel like eating.

What would he tell Charlotte? How could he explain to her yet another disaster in their fortunes? His mind was almost numb with pain at the thought.

He was not aware of time as he sat letting his tea go cold, before finally standing up, fishing in his pockets to see what change he had, and going out to buy a newspaper.

It was still not yet eight o'clock, a calm summer morning, the light pale through the haze of the city, but the sun already high. It was the middle of summer, and the nights were short. There were many people up and busy, errand boys, delivery carts, peddlers looking for early business, maids banging around in the areaways as they put out rubbish, bossed around the bootboys and scullery maids, or told the tweenies what to do and how to do it. Every now and again he heard the hard thwack of someone beating a rug and saw a fine cloud of dust rise in the air.

There was a newsboy on the corner, the same one he knew from every other day, but this time there was no smile, no greeting.

"Yer'll not be wantin' it, I should think," he said grimly. "I'm surprised, I'll say that for yer. Knew yer was a rozzer, for all yer live in a nice area 'n all. Never thought yer'd 'ound an old man ter 'is death. That'll be tuppence, if yer please."

Pitt held the money and the newsboy took it without a word, half turning his back as soon as the exchange was made.

Pitt walked home without opening the paper. Two or three other people passed him. None of them spoke. He had no idea whether they would have normally. He was too dazed to think.

Once inside he sat down at the kitchen table again and spread the paper open. It was not in the front pages — they were dominated by the election, as he had expected them to be — but as soon as he was past that, on page 5, it was there at the top, in the middle.

We are deeply sorry to report the death of the Reverend Francis W. Wray, discovered at his home in Teddington yesterday. He was seventy-three years old, and was still grief-stricken at the recent death of his beloved wife, Eliza. He leaves no children, all having died in their early years.

The police, in the person of Thomas Pitt, lately relieved of his command of the Bow Street station, and with no acknowledged authority, called upon Mr. Wray several times, and spoke to other residents in the area, asking them many intrusive and personal questions regarding Mr. Wray's life and beliefs and his recent behavior. He denied that this was in his so-far-unsuccessful pursuit of the murder in Southampton Row, Bloomsbury, of the spirit medium and conductor of séances, Miss Maude Lamont.

After Mr. Pitt's latest enquiries in the village he visited Mr. Wray in his home, and a later caller found Mr. Wray in a state of extreme distress, as if he had been reduced to weeping.

The next morning Mr. Wray's housekeeper, Mary Ann Smith, found Mr. Wray dead in his armchair, leaving no letter, but a book of poetry marked at the verse by the late Matthew Arnold which appears his tragic, despairing farewell to a world he could no longer endure.

The doctor was called, and gave his opinion that the cause of death was poison, most likely of the type that creates damage to the heart. Speculation has occurred that it might have been something from the wide variety of plants within Mr. Wray's garden, because it is known that he did not leave home after Mr. Pitt's call.

Francis Wray had an outstanding academic career . . .

It then went on to list the achievements of Wray's life, followed by tributes from a number of prominent people, all of whom mourned his death and were shocked and grieved by the manner of it.

Pitt closed the paper and made himself another cup of tea. He sat down again, nursing his tea between his hands, trying to think exactly what he had said to the people in Teddington that could have gone back so quickly to Wray, and how it could possibly have hurt him so deeply. Had he really been guilty of such crass clumsiness? Certainly he had said nothing to Wray himself. The distress Octavia Cavendish had seen was the grief for his wife . . . but of course she could not know that, nor in the circumstances would she be likely to believe it. No one would. That Wray had grieved for his wife only added to Pitt's sin.

How could he fight Voisey now? The election was too close. Aubrey Serracold was losing ground, and Voisey gaining it with each hour. Pitt had made not the slightest mark in Voisey's success. He had watched it all happen and had about as much effect on it as a member of the audience has on a play on the stage in front of him, visible, audible, but totally beyond his reach.

He did not even know which one of her three clients had killed Maude Lamont. All he felt certain of was that the motive had been the blackmail she was exercising over them because of their different fears: Kingsley that his son had died a coward's death; Rose Serracold that her father had died insane, and the truth or falsity of that was still unknown; and the man represented by the cartouche, and Pitt had no idea who that was or what his vulnerability might be. Nothing he had heard from Rose Serracold or Kingsley shed any light on it. There was not even a suggestion. Those already dead could in theory know anything at all. It could be a family secret, a dead friend betrayed, a child, a lover, a crime concealed, or simply some foolishness that would embarrass by its intimacy. All it had to be was sufficient for the knowledge of it to be worth paying a price to keep hidden.

Perhaps if he started at the other end of the reasoning it would make more sense?

What was the price? If it was connected with Voisey, then it was something that provided fuel in his campaign for power. He had all the help he needed in his own speeches, his funds, the issues to address. What could help him was to undermine Serracold. That is what he had had Kingsley do. His own supporters were already won; the victory lay in turning those who would be natural Liberals, holding the balance of power. Who had attacked Serracold to any effect . . . who that one would not have expected?

Reluctantly, he picked up the newspaper again and looked through the political commentary, the letters to the editor, the reports of speeches. There were plenty praising and blaming candidates on both sides, but most of them were general, aimed more at party than individual. There were several barbed comments about Keir Hardie and his attempt to create a new voice for the workingman.

Underneath one such Pitt found a personal letter criticizing the immoral and potentially disastrous views of the Liberal candidate for Lambeth South and praising Sir Charles Voisey, who stood for sanity rather than socialism, the values of thrift and responsibility, self-discipline and

Christian compassion rather than laxity, self-indulgence and untried social experiment which took away the ideals of worth and justice. It was signed by Reginald Underhill, Bishop in the Church of England.

Of course Underhill was entitled to political opinions, and to express them as fiercely as he wished, like any other man, regardless of whether they were logical, or even honest. But was he doing so from his own conviction or because he was being blackmailed into it?

Except what reason could there possibly be for a bishop of the church ever to have consulted a spirit medium? Surely, like Francis Wray, he would have abhorred the very idea.

Pitt was still considering the possibility when Mrs. Brody arrived. She said good morning to him civilly enough, then stood moving her weight from one foot to the other, obviously embarrassed.

"What is it, Mrs. Brody?" he asked. He was in no mood to care about a domestic crisis today.

She looked miserable. "I'm sorry, Mr. Pitt, but arter wot's in the papers this mornin', I can't keep on comin' ter do for yer. Me 'usband says it in't right. There's plenty o' work goin' 'round about, an' 'e says I gotta find another place. Tell Mrs. Pitt I'm very sorry, like, but I gotta do like 'e says."

There was no point in arguing with her. Her face was set in unhappy defiance. She had to live with her husband, whatever her own opinions. She could walk away from Pitt.

"Then you'd better go," he said flatly. He took half a crown out of his pocket and put it on the table. "That's what I owe you for this week so far. Good-bye."

She did not move. "I can't 'elp it!" she accused.

"You have made your decision, Mrs. Brody." He stared at her with equal anger, all the hurt and helplessness boiling up inside him. "You have worked here for over two years, and you have decided to believe what is written in the newspapers. That's an end of the matter. I'll tell Mrs. Pitt that you left without notice. Whether she gives you a character or not is her decision. But then as you are believing ill of her by inference because she is my wife, I doubt that as my wife her recommendation would be of much value to you anyway. Please close the front door as you leave."

"It in't my doing!" she said loudly. "I

don't go out ter some poor old man an' 'ound 'im ter 'is death!"

"You think I suspected him without grounds?" he asked, his own voice louder than he had meant it to be.

"That's wot it says!" She stared back at him.

"Then if that is sufficient for you, you had better judge me equally without grounds, and leave. As I said, please make sure the front door is closed behind you. It is the kind of day when anyone might come in off the street with ill will. Good-bye."

She snorted loudly, picked up the money off the table, then swiveled on the heel of her boot and went marching down the passage. He heard the front door bang loudly, no doubt so he would entertain no question as to whether she had left.

It was another miserable quarter of an hour before the doorbell rang. Pitt very nearly ignored it. It rang again. Whoever it was did not intend to accept refusal lightly. It rang a third time.

Pitt stood up and walked the length of the passage. He opened the door, ready to defend himself. Cornwallis stood on the step looking miserable but resolute, his face set grimly, eyes meeting Pitt's.

"Good morning," he said quietly. "May I come in?"

"What for?" Pitt asked less graciously than he meant. He would find criticism from Cornwallis harder to take than from almost any other man. He was surprised and a little frightened by how vulnerable he felt.

"Because I'm not going to talk to you standing here on the step like a peddler!" Cornwallis said tartly. "I've no idea what to say, but I'd rather try to think of something sitting down. I was so damned angry when I read the newspapers I forgot to have any breakfast."

Pitt almost smiled. "I've got bread and marmalade, and the kettle's on. I'd better stoke the stove. Mrs. Brody's just given her notice."

"The daily?" Cornwallis asked, stepping inside and closing the door behind him as he followed Pitt back down the passage.

"Yes. I'll have to start fetching for myself." In the kitchen he offered tea and toast, which Cornwallis accepted, making himself reasonably comfortable sitting on one of the hard-backed chairs.

Pitt stoked the stove with coal and poked it until it was burning brightly, then put a slice of bread on the toasting fork and held it to brown. The kettle started to whistle gently on the hob.

When they had a piece of toast each and the tea was brewing, Cornwallis began to talk.

"Did this man Wray have anything to do with Maude Lamont?" he asked.

"Not so far as I know," Pitt replied. "He had a hatred of spirit mediums, especially those who give false hope to the bereaved, but so far as I know not to Maude Lamont in particular."

"Why?"

Pitt told him the story of the young woman in Teddington, her child, her consulting of the spirit medium at the time, the violence of her grief and then her own death.

"Could it have been Maude Lamont?" Cornwallis asked.

"No." Pitt was quite certain. "When that happened she could not have been more than about twelve years old. There's no connection, except the one Voisey created to trap me. And I did everything to help him."

"So it would seem," Cornwallis agreed. "But I'm damned if I'm going to let him get away with it. If we can't defend ourselves, then we must attack."

This time Pitt did smile. Surprise and

gratitude welled up inside him that Cornwallis should so fully and without question take his part. "I wish I knew how," Pitt answered. "I have been considering the possibility that the real man behind the cartouche was Bishop Underhill." He was startled to hear himself say it aloud, and without fear that Cornwallis would dismiss it as absurd. Cornwallis's friendship was the only decent thing in the day. He knew inside himself that Vespasia would react similarly. He was relying on her to help Charlotte in what would be a very difficult time to bear — not only for herself, both in her anger and inability to help, and her pain for him, but also for the cruelty the children would endure from school friends, even people in the street, barely knowing why, only that their father was hated. It was something they had never known before and would not understand. He refused to think about it now. Terrible enough when he had to, no need to anticipate the pain when he could do nothing about it.

"Bishop Underhill," Cornwallis repeated thoughtfully. "Why? Why him?"

Pitt told him his line of reasoning based upon the assistance the Bishop had given Voisey.

Cornwallis frowned. "What would take him to a spirit medium?"

"I've no idea," Pitt replied, too lost in his own unhappiness to catch the emotion in the other man's voice.

Further discussion was interrupted by the sound of the doorbell again. Cornwallis stood up immediately and went to answer it without giving Pitt the opportunity. He returned a few moments later with Tellman behind him, looking like the chief mourner at a funeral.

Pitt waited for one of the other two to speak.

Tellman cleared his throat, then sank back into a wretched silence.

"What did you come for?" Pitt asked him. He heard his voice edgy and accusing, but it was beyond his control.

Tellman looked at him, glaring. "Where else would I be?" he challenged. "It was my fault! I told you to go to Teddington! You'd never have heard of Wray if it weren't for me!" His face was filled with anguish, his body rigid, his eyes hot.

Pitt saw with a rush of surprise that Tellman really did blame himself for what had happened. He was scalded with a shame too deep to find words. At another time, if Pitt were hurting even a little less

458

himself, he would have been moved by Tellman's loyalty, but now his own fear was too deep. It all stemmed back to his evidence before Whitechapel. If only he hadn't been so sure of himself, so pig-headed in giving evidence because he wanted his idea of justice served!

He had been right, of course, but that was not going to help now.

"Who told you about Francis Wray?" Cornwallis asked Tellman. "And for heaven's sake sit down. We're standing around as if we were at the graveside. The battle is not over yet."

Pitt wanted to believe that, but there was no rational hope that he could grasp.

"Superintendent Wetron," Tellman answered. He glanced at Pitt.

"Why?" Cornwallis persisted. "What reason did he give? Who suggested Wray to him? He didn't know him himself, so who told him about Wray? Who made the connection between Wray and the un-known man who visited Maude Lamont?"

Absentmindedly, Pitt thought how Cornwallis had grown in his knowledge of detection. He looked at Tellman.

"He never said," Tellman replied, his eyes widening. "I did ask him, but somehow he never really answered. Voisey?

It must have been." There was a thin thread of hope in his voice. "All the information about Wray came from Superintendent Wetron, so far as I know." His mouth tightened. "But if he believes in Voisey, or . . . or maybe he is Inner Circle himself?" He said it with disbelief, as if even now the thought of his superior's being one of that terrible society was too monstrous to be more than a bad idea, something to be said and discarded.

Pitt thought of Vespasia. "When we disgraced Voisey we may have fractured the Inner Circle," he said, looking from Cornwallis to Tellman and back again. Tellman knew all about the Whitechapel matter; Cornwallis knew something, but there were still large gaps in his knowledge, although even as Pitt watched him he saw his understanding leap forward. He asked no questions.

"Fractured?" Tellman said slowly. "You mean like in two parts?"

"At least," Pitt answered.

"Voisey and someone else?" Cornwallis's eyebrows rose. "Wetron?"

Tellman's sense of decency was outraged. "Oh no! He's a policeman!" But even as he protested he was entertaining the idea. He shook his head, pushing it away. "A small member, maybe. People do, to get on, but . . ."

Cornwallis chewed his lip. "It would make a lot of sense. Someone with a great deal of power, a very great deal, had you dismissed from Bow Street a second time," he said to Pitt. "Perhaps it was Wetron? After all, he was the one who took charge from you. Superintendent of Bow Street is a very nice place for the head of the Inner Circle." He looked rueful, even for an instant aware of fear. "There'll be no end to his ambition."

No one laughed, and no one denied it.

"He's an ambitious man," Tellman said very seriously.

Cornwallis leaned forward a little across the table. "Could they be rivals?"

Almost as if he had spoken it aloud, Pitt knew what he was thinking. It was the first spark of real hope, wild as it was. "Use it?" he asked, almost afraid to put words to it.

Cornwallis nodded very slowly.

Tellman stared at them, his face pale. "One against the other?"

"Can you think of anything else?" Cornwallis asked him. "Wetron is ambitious. If he thinks he can challenge Voisey for leadership of half the Inner Circle, and I think we can assume he is the one who led the

461

breakaway, if not at first, then at least by the time it achieved its independence, then he is very ambitious indeed. And he cannot be fool enough to think Voisey will forgive him for it. He will have to live the rest of his life watching his back. If you know you have an enemy, better make a preemptive strike. If you believe you can do it effectively, finish your man."

"How?" Pitt asked. "Tie Voisey in to the Southampton Row murder?" The idea strengthened as he was speaking. "There must be a continuous connection: Voisey goes to Maude Lamont with social connections, money, whatever it is she wants, and in return she blackmails certain of her clients to speak out against Voisey's opponent in the election, Aubrey Serracold. Which in turn helps Voisey."

"Ties up," Tellman agreed. "Voisey to Maude Lamont to her clients, who do what she tells them, which helps Voisey. But we can't prove it! Maude Lamont was the link, and she's dead." He took in a deep breath. "Just a minute! Did the blackmail stop? Did they stop helping Voisey?" That question was asked of Pitt.

"No," he said. "No. So Maude didn't do the blackmailing, she just provided the information as to where they were vulnerable." Then the chill returned. "But we found no connection to Voisey. We searched all her papers, letters, diaries, banking accounts, everything. There is no trace of a link between them. But then he wouldn't leave one. He's far too clever for that. For a start, she could have used it herself!"

"You are looking at the wrong enemy," Cornwallis said with a rising note of excitement in his voice. It was almost as if he was reliving one of his battles at sea, lining up the opposing ship to fire the broadside that would hole her below the waterline. "Wetron! We shouldn't aim at either one, but make them attack each other."

Tellman scowled. "How?"

Pitt felt a leap of triumph again and turned to stifle it in case it flared up out of control, and the darkness afterwards was too deep to bear.

"Wetron is an ambitious man," Cornwallis said again, but this time with a new intensity. "If he could solve the Southampton Row murder in a spectacular way, personally taking the credit for it, it would enhance his position, make him strong enough no one could challenge him in Bow Street, and perhaps build a rung higher in the ladder."

The next major step up would be Cornwallis's own job. Pitt felt a tug of emotion that Cornwallis could not have been unaware of such a risk, and yet looking at him leaning his elbows on the kitchen table, there was not a shadow of hesitation in him.

"Find Cartouche!" Cornwallis said. "If it was Wetron who worked out who he was, and trapped him, and forced from him the secret of the blackmail, perhaps even to implicate Voisey — which might be possible with Rose Serracold being one of the other victims and Kingsley the third."

"Dangerous . . ." Pitt warned, but the blood was beginning to beat in his pulses and he felt alive again, quickened inside, and something like hope at the edge of his mind.

Cornwallis smiled very slightly, more a baring of the teeth. "He used Wray. Let us use him again. The poor man is beyond being hurt anymore. Even his reputation is ruined if they bring in a verdict of suicide. His life will be rendered almost meaningless in the sense he valued."

A black rage hardened in Pitt at that thought. "Yes, I should very much like to use Wray," he said between clenched jaws. "No one knows what I said to him, or he to me. And since I cannot prove I did not threaten him, neither can they deny anything I say he told me!" He too leaned forward across the table. "He had no idea who Cartouche was, but no one else knows that. What if I say that he did, and he told me, and that it was Cartouche's identity which so distressed him?" His mind was racing now. "And that Maudc herself knew, in spite of all his precautions? And she left a note of it somewhere hidden in her papers? We searched the house, but we did not understand what we saw. Now, with Wray's information, we will . . ."

"Then Cartouche will come to look for it and destroy it . . . if he knows!" Tellman finished. "Except how will we make sure he hears? Will Wetron tell him? Wetron doesn't know who he is, or he'd . . ." He stopped, confused.

"Newspapers," Cornwallis replied. "I'll make sure the newspapers print it, tomorrow. The case is still headlines because of Wray's death. I can make Cartouche think he has to get back Maude Lamont's notes on him or he'll be exposed. It doesn't matter what his secret is."

"What are you going to tell Wetron?" Tellman asked, frowning. He was puzzled, but the eagerness to act burned in him.

His eyes were bright.

"You are," Cornwallis corrected. "Report back to him, as you ordinarily would, that the circle is about to be completed: Voisey through money to Maude Lamont through blackmail to Kingsley and Cartouche, to destroy Voisey's opponent, back to Voisey, and that you are about to get the proof. Then he will call the press. But he must believe it, or they won't print it."

Tellman swallowed, and nodded slowly.

"Wray will still be buried as a suicide," Pitt said, and found even putting words to it painful. "I . . . I find it hard to believe that he would . . . not after he had endured his grief and . . ." But he could imagine it. No matter how brave one was, there were some pains that became unendurable in the darkest moments of the night. Maybe he could manage most of the time, when there were people around, something to do, even sunlight, the beauty of flowers, anyone else who cared. But alone in the dark, too tired to fight anymore . . .

"He was deeply loved and admired." Cornwallis was struggling to find a better answer himself. "Perhaps he will have friends in the church who will use influence to see that he is never named as such."

"But you didn't hound him!" Tellman protested. "Why would he give in now? It's against his faith!"

"It was some kind of poison," Pitt told him. "How could he do that by accident? And it wasn't natural causes." But another thought was stirring in his mind, a wild possibility. "Perhaps Voisey wasn't using a perfect chance given him? Perhaps he murdered Wray, or at least caused him to be murdered? His revenge was only complete if Wray was dead. With Wray miserable, haunted by gossip and fear, violated, I appear a villain. But if he is dead that is far better. Then I am irredeemable. Surely Voisey would not hesitate at the final act? He didn't in Whitechapel."

"His sister?" Cornwallis said with genuine horror. "He used her to poison Wray?"

"She may have had no idea what she was doing," Pitt pointed out. "And there was virtually no chance of her getting caught. As far as she knew, she was no more than a witness to my cruelty to an old and vulnerable man."

"How do we prove it?" Tellman said, thin-lipped. "Us knowing it is no good! It only adds to the flavor of his victory if we actually know what happened and still can't do a damn thing about it!"

"An autopsy," Pitt said. It was the only thing that seemed an answer.

"They'd never do it." Cornwallis shook his head. "No one wants it. The church will be afraid it would prove suicide, which they'll do all they can to protect him from, and Voisey will be afraid it will prove murder, or at least raise the question."

Pitt stood up. "There'll be a way. I'll make one. I'll go to see Lady Vespasia. If anyone can force the issue, she will know who it is and how to find him." He looked at Cornwallis, then at Tellman. "Thank you," he said with sudden over-whelming gratitude. "Thank you for . . . coming."

Neither of them answered, each in his own way confused for words. They did not seek or want gratitude, only to help.

Tellman went straight back to Bow Street. It was a quarter past ten in the morning. The desk sergeant called out to him, but he barely heard. He went straight up the stairs to Wetron's office, which had once been Pitt's. It was extraordinary to think that had been only a few months ago. Now it was an alien place, the man in it an enemy. That idea had come easily. He was startled to realize that it had taken no effort of mind to accommodate it.

He knocked, and after a few moments heard Wetron's voice telling him to come in.

"Good morning, sir," he said when he was inside and the door closed behind him.

"Morning, Tellman." Wetron looked up from his desk. At first sight he seemed an ordinary man, middle height, mousy coloring. Only when you looked at his eyes did you realize the strength in him, the undeviating will to succeed.

Tellman swallowed. He began the lie. "I saw Pitt this morning. He told me what he actually said to Mr. Wray, and why Wray was so distressed."

Wetron looked up at him, his face bleak. "I think the sooner you dissociate yourself, and this police force, from Mr. Pitt, the better, Inspector. I shall issue a statement to the newspapers that he no longer has anything whatever to do with the Metropolitan Police, and we take no responsibility for his actions. He's Special Branch's problem. Let them get him out of this, if they can. The man's a disaster."

Tellman stood rigid, the fury inside him ready to explode, every injustice he'd ever seen like a red haze inside him. "I'm sure you're right, sir, but I think you ought to know what he learned before you do that." He ignored Wetron's impatience, signaled in his flicking fingers and the crease between his brows. "It seems Mr. Wray knew who the third visitor was at Maude Lamont's the night she was murdered." He took a shaky breath. "Because it was someone of his acquaintance. Another churchman, I think."

"What?" Now he had Wetron's entire attention, even if not his belief.

Tellman met his eyes without flinching. "Yes sir. Apparently, there's something in the woman's notes, Miss Lamont I mean, which could prove it, now we know who she meant."

"What is it, man?" Wetron demanded. "Don't stand there talking in riddles!"

"That's it, sir. Mr. Pitt can't be sure until he sees the papers in Miss Lamont's home." He hurried on before Wetron could interrupt him again, forcing his voice to rise as if in excitement. "It'll still be hard to prove it. But if we were to tell the newspapers that we have the information . . . of course, we don't need to mention Mr. Pitt, if you don't think it's a good idea . . . then whoever this man is, and he is probably the one who killed her, then he may very well betray himself by going to Southampton Row."

"Yes, yes, Tellman, you don't need to spell it out for me!" Wetron said sharply. "I understand what you are suggesting. Let me give it some thought."

"Yes sir."

"We'll keep Pitt out of it, I think. You should go to Southampton Row. After all, it's your case." He made the point deliberately, watching Tellman's face.

Tellman made himself smile. "Yes sir. I don't know why Special Branch got involved with it at all. Unless, of course, it was because of Sir Charles Voisey?"

Wetron sat very still. "What has it to do with Voisey? You're not imagining the man implicated by the cartouche was Voisey, are you?" There was heavy ridicule in his tone, and the curl of his smile was bitter, tinged with mockery and regret.

"Oh no, sir," Tellman said quickly. "We're pretty sure that Maude Lamont was blackmailing at least some of her clients, certainly the three that were there the night she was killed."

"Over what?" Wetron asked carefully.

"Different things, but not for money, for certain behavior in the present political campaign that was helpful to Sir Charles Voisey."

Wetron's eyes widened.

"Indeed? That's a rather odd accusation, Tellman. I suppose you are aware of exactly who Sir Charles is?"

"Yes sir! He's a most distinguished appeal court judge who is now standing for a seat in Parliament. He was recently knighted by Her Majesty, but I don't know exactly what for, except word has it that it was something remarkably brave." He said it with reverence, and watched Wetron's lips tighten and the muscles stand out cord-hard on his neck. Perhaps Lady Vespasia was right?

"And has Pitt got some reason to believe all this?" Wetron asked.

"Yes sir." Tellman kept his voice perfectly level, not too assured. "There is some very definite connecting link. It all makes a lot of sense. We're that far from it!" He held up his finger and thumb about an inch apart. "We just need to flush this man out, and then we can prove it. Murder's a very nasty crime indeed, any way you want to look at it, and this one especially. Choked the woman. Looks like he put his knee in her chest and forced this stuff down her throat until she died."

"Yes, you don't need to be graphic, Inspector," Wetron said tartly. "I'll call the press and tell them. You get on with finding the proof you need." He bent to the paper he had been reading before he was interrupted. It was dismissal.

"Yes sir." Tellman stood to attention, then turned on his heel. He did not breathe a sigh of relief, or allow his body to let go of the tension and shiver until he was halfway down the stairs again.

CHAPTER

<u>THIRTEEN</u>

Pitt returned immediately to Vespasia, this time writing a note which he handed to the maid, then he waited in the morning room. He believed Vespasia was one person who would refrain from judging his part in Wray's death, but he could not bring himself to assume it before he had seen her. He waited, pacing the floor, his hands sweating, his breath ragged.

He spun around when the morning room door opened, expecting the maid to tell him either that Lady Vespasia would see him or that she would not. But it was Vespasia herself who was there. She came in and closed the door behind her, shutting out the servants and, from the look on her face, the rest of the world.

"Good morning, Thomas. I assume you have come because you have some plan of battle, and a part in it for me? You had better tell me what it is. Are we to fight alone, or do we have allies?"

Her use of the plural was the most heartening thing she could have said. He should never have doubted her, regardless of what the press wrote or what the odds against them might be. It was not modesty on his part, it was lack of faith.

"Yes, Captain Cornwallis and Inspector Tellman."

"Good, and what are we to do?" She sat down in one of the large rose-pink morning room chairs and indicated another for him.

He told her the plan, such as it was, which they had formulated around his kitchen table. She listened in silence until he had finished.

"An autopsy," she said at last. "That will not be easy. He was a man not only revered but actually loved. No one, apart from Voisey, will wish to see him named a suicide, even though that is already the assumption. I imagine the church will endeavor to leave the exact verdict open, and at least tacitly assume some kind of misadventure, in the belief that the less that is said the sooner it will be forgotten. And there is considerable discretion and kindness in that." She looked at him very steadily. "Are you prepared for the discovery that he did, in fact, take his own life, Thomas?"

"No," he said honestly. "But nothing I feel about it is going to alter the truth, and I think I need to know it. I really don't believe he took his own life, but I admit it is possible. I think Voisey contrived his death, using his sister, almost certainly without her knowledge."

"And you believe an autopsy will indicate that? You may be right. Anyway, as you will no doubt agree, we have little else." She rose to her feet stiffly. "I do not have the influence to force such a thing myself, but I believe Somerset Carlisle does." The faintest smile flickered over her face and lit her silver-gray eyes. "You no doubt remember him from that farcical tragedy in Resurrection Row among the thugs." She did not go on to mention his bizarre part in it. It was something neither of them would forget. If any man on earth would be willing to risk his reputation for a cause in which he believed, it was Carlisle.

Pitt smiled back, for a moment memory erasing the present. Time had bleached the horror from those events and left only the black humor, and the passion which had compelled that extraordinary man to act as he had.

"Yes," he agreed with fervor. "Yes, we'll ask him."

Vespasia rather liked the telephone. It was one of several inventions to have become generally available to those with the means to afford it, and it was reasonably useful. In a mere quarter of an hour she was able to ascertain that Carlisle was at his club in Pall Mall — where, of course, ladies were not admitted — but that he would leave forthwith and go to the Savoy Hotel, where he would receive them as soon as they arrived.

Actually, with the state of the traffic as it was, and the time of the day, it was almost an hour later when Pitt and Vespasia were shown into the private sitting room that Carlisle had engaged for the purpose. He rose to his feet the instant they were shown in, elegant, a little gaunt now, his unusual eyebrows still giving his face a faintly quizzical look.

As soon as they were seated and appropriate refreshments had been ordered, Vespasia came straight to the point.

"No doubt you have read the newspapers and are aware of Thomas's situation. You may not be aware that it has been carefully and extremely cleverly arranged by a man whose intense desire is to be revenged for a recent very grave defeat. I cannot tell you what it was, only that he is powerful and dangerous, and has managed to salvage from the wreck of his previous ambition a new one only slightly less ruinous to the country."

Carlisle asked no questions as to what it might be. He was well acquainted with the need for absolute discretion. He regarded Pitt levelly for several moments, perhaps seeing the weariness in him and the marks of the despair so close under the surface. "What is it you want from me?" he asked very seriously.

It was Vespasia who answered. "An autopsy of the body of the Reverend Francis Wray."

Carlisle gulped. For an instant he was thrown off balance.

Vespasia gave a tiny smile. "If it were easy, my dear, I should not have needed to ask for your assistance. The poor man is going to be regarded as a suicide, although of course the church will never permit it to be said in so many words. They will speak of unfortunate accidents, and bury him properly. But people will still believe he took his own life, and that is necessary to the plan of our enemy, otherwise his revenge upon Thomas fails to have effect."

"Yes, I see that," Carlisle agreed. "No one can have driven him to suicide unless there is believed to have been one. People will assume the church is concealing it as a matter of loyalty, which will probably be the truth." He turned to Pitt. "What do you believe happened?"

"I think he was murdered," Pitt replied. "I doubt there was an accident which timed itself to the hour to suit their purposes. I don't know if an autopsy will prove that, but it is the only chance we have."

Carlisle thought in silence for several minutes, and neither Pitt nor Vespasia interrupted him. They glanced at each other, and then away again, and waited.

Carlisle looked up. "If you are prepared to abide by the result, whatever it is, I believe I know a way to persuade the local coroner that it must be done." He smiled a little sourly. "It will entail a certain elasticity of the truth, but I have shown a skill in that area before. I think the less you know about it, Thomas, the better. You never had any talent in that direction at all. In fact, it worries me more than a little that Special Branch is desperate enough to employ you. You are the last man cut out to succeed in this kind of work. I heard you may have been drafted merely to give them a more respectable face."

"In that case they have failed spectacularly," Pitt replied with a considerable edge to his voice.

"Nonsense!" Vespasia snapped. "He was dismissed out of Bow Street because the Inner Circle wanted one of their own men there. There is nothing subtle or devious about it at all. Special Branch was simply available, and not in a position to refuse." She rose to her feet. "Thank you, Somerset. I assume that as well as the necessity for this autopsy, you are also aware of the urgency? Tomorrow would be good. The longer this slander against Thomas is around, the more people will hear it and the work of undoing it will become a great deal more difficult. Also, of course, there is the matter of the election. Once the polls close there are certain things it becomes very difficult to abrogate."

Carlisle opened his mouth, and then closed it again. "You are utterly reliable, Lady Vespasia," he said, rising also. "I swear you are the only person since I was twenty who can totally wrong-foot me, and you never fail to do it. I have always admired you, but it completely escapes me why I also like you."

"Because you have no desire to be comfortable, my dear," she replied without hesitation. "More than a month or two and you become bored." She smiled at him, utterly charmingly, as if she had given him a great compliment, and extended her hand for him to kiss, which he did with grace. Then she took Pitt's arm and, with head high, walked out into the corridor and the main foyer.

They were about halfway across when Pitt quite clearly saw Voisey excuse himself from a group of passersby and walk towards them. He was half smiling, supremely confident. Pitt knew from his face that he had come to taste victory, to savor it and roll it around his tongue. He had very possibly arranged to be here precisely for that purpose. What was revenge worth if you did not see your enemy's pain? And in this instance he not only had Pitt, he had Vespasia as well.

Voisey could never have forgiven her for the crucial part she had played, not only in the Whitechapel defeat, but in using all her influence to gain him his knighthood. Perhaps ruining Pitt was as much to hurt her as it was to hurt him? And now he could watch them both.

"Lady Vespasia," he said with extreme courtesy. "What a pleasure to see you. How loyal of you to take Mr. Pitt to luncheon so publicly at this unfortunate time.

I do admire loyalty, and the more expensive it is, the more valuable." Without waiting for her to reply, he turned to Pitt. "Perhaps you will be able to find a position away from London. I would advise it after your recent unfortunate behavior with poor Francis Wray. Somewhere in the country? If your wife and family have taken a liking to Dartmoor, perhaps that would do? Although Harford is much too small to require a policeman. It is barely a village, more of a hamlet, a mere two or three streets, and very isolated up there on the edge of Ugborough Moor. I doubt they have ever seen a crime, let alone a murder. It was murder you specialized in, wasn't it? Still, I suppose that might change." He smiled, turned to Vespasia, and then continued on his way.

Pitt stood frozen, the cold running through him like a tide, drowning from the inside. He was barely aware of the room around him, even of Vespasia's hand on his arm. Voisey knew where Charlotte was! He could reach out at any time and destroy her. Pitt's heart contracted inside him. He could barely breathe. He heard Vespasia's voice from a long way off, her words indistinct.

"Thomas!"

Time had no meaning.

"Thomas!" The grip tightened on his arm, fingers digging into him. She spoke his name for the third time.

"Yes . . ."

"We must leave here," she said firmly. "We are beginning to draw attention to ourselves."

"He knows where Charlotte is!" He turned to look at her. "I've got to get her away! I've got to —"

"No, my dear." Her hand held on to him with all her strength. "You have got to stay here and fight Charles Voisey. If you are here then his attention will remain here. Send that young man, Tellman, to take Charlotte and your family somewhere else, as discreetly as possible. Voisey needs to win the election, and he also needs to guard himself against your effort to find out the truth of Francis Wray's death, and to watch and see what you learn about the man you have named as Cartouche. If Voisey is indeed connected with Maude Lamont's death, he cannot afford to delegate that to someone else. You already know that he does not trust anyone to hold that power over him of having known the ultimate secret."

She was right, and when Pitt's mind

cleared again and he faced reality, he knew it also. But there was no time to waste. He must find Tellman immediately and be sure that he would go to Devon. Even as the thoughts were in his mind he put his hand into his pocket to see what money he had. Tellman would need his rail fare to Devon and back again, certainly. And he would need money to move the family also, and to find a new and safer place for them. They could not come back to London yet. He had no idea when that would be. It was impossible to plan that far ahead, or to see how he could even make it safe for them.

Vespasia understood the gesture, and the need. She opened her reticule and took out all the money she had. He was startled how much it was, nearly twenty pounds. With the four pounds, seventeen shillings he had, plus a few odd pennies, it would be enough.

Wordlessly, she passed it to him.

"Thank you," he accepted. This was no time for pride or burden of gratitude. She must know that he felt it more profoundly than could be conveyed.

"My carriage," she directed. "We must find Tellman."

"We?"

"My dear Thomas, you are not leaving me in the Savoy penniless to find my own way home while you go pursuing the cause!"

"Oh, no. Do you . . ."

"No, I do not," she said decisively. "You may require every penny. Let us proceed. We also should use every minute. Where will he be? What is his most urgent task? We have not time to search half of London for him."

Pitt disciplined his mind to remember exactly what Tellman had been sent to do. First he would have gone to Bow Street to speak with Wetron. That might have taken no more than an hour, at the most, unless Wetron were not there. Then, since ostensibly his greatest concern was the identity of Cartouche, he would have done something to appear to be following that. Pitt had not mentioned Bishop Underhill to Tellman. It was only a deduction based upon the Bishop's attacks against Aubrey Serracold.

"Where to?" Vespasia enquired as he handed her up into her carriage and then climbed in after her and sat down.

He must answer with something. Would Tellman have told anyone in Bow Street where he was going? Perhaps not, but it was a chance he should not overlook. "Bow Street," he replied.

When they got there he excused himself and went straight to the desk sergeant. "Do you know where Inspector Tellman is?" he asked, trying to keep the panic out of his voice.

"Yes sir," the man replied immediately. It was clear in his face that he had seen the newspapers and his concern was genuine, and more than that, sympathetic. He had known Pitt many years, and he believed what he knew, not what he read. " 'E said as 'e were goin' ter see some o' that spirit medium's other clients. 'E said as if yer was ter come by for any reason an' ask, sir, as I was ter tell yer where 'e wos." He regarded Pitt anxiously and produced a list of addresses written on a sheet torn from a notebook.

Pitt gave a prayer of thanks for Tellman's intelligence, then thanked the desk sergeant so sincerely the man colored with pleasure.

Back in the carriage, weak with mounting relief, he showed the paper to Vespasia and asked her if she would rather be taken home before he began to follow the trail.

"Certainly not!" she said briskly. "Please get on with it!"

★ ★ ★

Tellman had already checked on Lena Forrest's story of visiting her friend in Newington and found that she had indeed been there, although Mrs. Lightfoot had only the vaguest ideas of time. Now he was retracing his steps with Maude Lamont's other clients simply in the vague hope of learning something more about her methods which might lead him to Cartouche. He had little expectation of success, but he must appear to Wetron to be following it with urgency. Previously he had regarded Wetron as no more than the man who had replaced Pitt, by chance more than design. He resented him for it, but knew that it was not Wetron's fault. Someone had to take the position. He did not like Wetron; his personality seemed to be calculating and too remote from the emotions of anger and pity that Tellman was used to in Pitt. But then whoever it had been would not have pleased him.

Now he suddenly perceived Wetron in an entirely different way. He was not a colorless career officer; he was a dangerous enemy to be regarded in an acutely personal light. Any man who could rise to leadership in the Inner Circle was brave, ruthless and extremely ambitious. He was also clever enough to have outwitted even Voisey, or he would be no threat to him. Only a fool would leave any act or word unguarded.

Therefore, Tellman set about appearing to pursue Cartouche, after having left a list of the places he would be with the desk sergeant, in case Pitt should want him for anything to do with the real issues that mattered.

He was listening to a Mrs. Drayton recounting her last séance, which had produced manifestations so dramatic as to astound Maude Lamont herself, when the butler interrupted them to say that a Mr. Pitt had called to see Mr. Tellman and the matter was so urgent that he regretted it could not await their convenience.

"Send him in," Mrs. Drayton said before Tellman could excuse himself to leave.

The butler naturally obeyed, and a moment later Pitt was in the room looking white-faced and hardly able to keep still.

"Really completely remarkable, Mr. Tellman," Mrs. Drayton said enthusiastically. "I mean, Miss Lamont had not expected such a display herself! I could see the amazement in her face, even fear." Her voice rose with excitement. "It was at that moment that I absolutely, truly knew she had the power. I confess I had wondered once or twice before if it could have been faked, but this wasn't. The look in her eyes was proof to me."

"Yes, thank you, Mrs. Drayton," Tellman said rather abruptly. It all seemed terribly unimportant now. They had found the lever on the table, a simple mechanical trick. He stared at Pitt, knowing that something of great and terrible urgency had happened.

"Excuse me, Mrs. Drayton," Pitt said, his voice husky. "I am afraid I require Inspector Tellman to undertake something else . . . now."

"Oh . . . but . . ." she began.

Pitt probably had no intention of dismissing her, but he was beyond the point of patience. "Thank you, Mrs. Drayton. Good day."

Tellman followed him outside and saw Vespasia's carriage at the curb, and the glimpse of her profile inside.

"Voisey knows where Charlotte and the family are." Pitt could contain himself no longer. "He named the village."

Tellman felt the sweat break out on his body and his chest tighten until he could hardly breathe. He cared about Charlotte, of course he did, but if Voisey sent anyone after Charlotte it would mean Gracie would be hurt as well, and it was the thought of that which filled his mind and drenched him with horror. The idea of Gracie hurt, crushed . . . the specter of a world without her was so terrible he could not bear it. It was as if happiness would never again be possible.

He heard Pitt's voice as if from miles away. He was holding out something in his hand.

"I wish you to go down to Devon, today, now, and take them somewhere safe."

Tellman blinked. It was money Pitt was giving him. "Yes!" he said, grasping it. "But I don't know where they are!"

"Harford," Pitt replied. "Take the Great Western as far as Ivybridge. From there it's only a couple of miles to Harford. It's a small village. Ask and you'll find them. You'd better take them to one of the nearby towns, where you'll be anonymous. Find lodgings where there are lots of other people. And . . . stay with them, at least until after the election results for Voisey. It won't be very long." He knew what he was asking, and what it might cost Tellman when Wetron found out, and he asked anyway.

"Right," Tellman agreed. It did not even

occur to him to question it. He took the money, then climbed into the carriage beside Vespasia, and as soon as Pitt was in also, they drove to the railway terminus for the Great Western. With the briefest farewell, Tellman was on his way to purchase his ticket and get onto the next train.

It was a nightmare journey simply because it seemed to take forever. Mile after mile of countryside rattled past the windows of the carriage. The sun began to sink in the west and the late-afternoon light deepened, and still they were nowhere near their destination.

Tellman stood up and stretched his cramped legs, but there was nothing to do except sway, adjusting his weight and balance, watch the hills and valleys steepen and then flatten out again, then sit down and wait longer.

He had not stopped to pack clean shirts or socks or linen. In fact, he did not even have a razor, a comb, or a toothbrush. None of that mattered; it was just easier to think of the small things than of the larger ones. How would he defend them if Voisey sent someone to attack them? What if when he got there they were already gone? How would he find them? That was too terrible to bear, and yet he could not drive it from his thoughts.

He stared out of the window. Surely they were in Devon by now? They had been traveling for hours! He noticed how red the earth was, quite unlike the soil around London that he was used to. The land looked vast, and in the distance ahead, even in high summer, there was something forbidding about it. The tracks stretched over the graceful span of a viaduct. For a moment the sheer daring of having built such a thing amazed him. Then he realized the train was slowing, they were reaching a station.

Ivybridge! This was it. At last! He threw the door open and almost tripped in his haste to reach the platform. The evening light was long, shadows stretching two and three times the length of the objects that cast them. The horizon to the west burned in a blaze of color so brilliant it hurt his eyes to look at it. When he turned away he was blinded.

"Can I help you, sir?"

He blinked and swiveled around. He was facing a man in the extremely smart uniform of a stationmaster, and who obviously took his position with great seriousness.

"Yes!" Tellman said urgently. "I have to

get to Harford as soon as possible. Within the next half hour. It is an emergency. I must hire a vehicle of some sort, and have the use of it for a day at least. Where can I begin?"

"Ah!" The stationmaster scratched his head, setting his cap crooked. "What sort of a vehicle would you be wanting, sir?"

Tellman could barely contain his impatience. It took a monumental effort not to shout at the man. "Anything. It's an emergency."

The stationmaster seemed to remain unmoved. "In that case, sir, Mr. Callard down at the end of the road." He pointed helpfully. "He might have something. Otherwise there's old Mr. Drysdale up the other way, 'bout a mile and a half. He has the odd dray, or the like, that he can sometimes spare."

"Something faster than that would be better, and I haven't time to walk in both directions to find it," Tellman replied, trying to keep the panic and the temper out of his voice.

"Then you'd best walk to the left, down that way." The stationmaster pointed again. "Ask Mr. Callard. If he doesn't have anything, he'll maybe know someone who does."

"Thank you," Tellman called over his shoulder as he already began moving away.

The road was downhill slightly, and he strode out as fast as he could, and kept up the pace. When he reached the yard it took him another five minutes to locate the proprietor, who seemed as unmoved by any sense of haste as the stationmaster had been. However, the sight of Vespasia's money drew his attention, and he found he did have a fairly light cart, still capable of carrying half a dozen people, and a good enough horse to pull it. He took an exorbitant deposit, which Tellman resented, until he realized that he had no idea how or when he was going to return the vehicle, and that his skill at driving it was absolutely minimal. In fact, even climbing up onto the seat was awkward, and he heard Callard muttering under his breath as he turned away. Tellman very gingerly encouraged the horse to move, and then guided the cart out of the yard and along the road he had been told led to the village of Harford.

Half an hour later he was knocking on the door of Appletree Cottage. It was dark and he could see the lights on through the cracks in the curtains at the window. He had met no one else on the road except one man in a dray cart, from whom he had asked directions. Now he stood on the step, acutely aware of the intense darkness around him, the sharp smell of the wind off the open stretch of the moor he could no longer see away to the north. It was no more than a denser black against the occasional stars. It was a different world from the city, and he felt alien to it, at a loss to know what to do or how to cope. There was no one else to turn to. Pitt had entrusted him with rescuing the women and children. How on earth was he going to be equal to it? He had no idea what to do!

"Who is it?" a voice demanded from behind the door.

It was Gracie. His heart leaped.

"It's me!" he shouted, then added self-consciously, "Tellman!"

He heard bolts withdrawn and the door open with a crash, showing a candlelit interior with Gracie standing in the doorway and Charlotte just behind her, the poker from the fireplace hanging loosely in her hand. Nothing could have told him more vividly that something had frightened them far more than the mere knocking on the door of a stranger.

He saw the fear and the question in Charlotte's face.

"Mr. Pitt's all right, ma'am," he said in answer to it. "Things are hard, but he's quite safe." Should he tell her about Wray's death and all that had happened? There was nothing she could do about it. It would only worry her when she should be concerned with herself, and escaping from here. And should he even tell them how urgent that was? Was it his job to protect them from fear, as well as actual physical danger?

Or would lying by omission make them act less urgently? He had thought about that on the train, and vacillated one way and then the other, making up his mind, and as quickly unmaking it.

"Why are yer 'ere, then?" Gracie's voice cut across his thoughts. "If nothin's wrong, why aren't yer in the city doin' yer job? 'Oo killed the ghosty woman? Yer get that all sorted?"

"No," he answered, moving inside to allow her to close the door. He looked at her pale, set face and the rigidity of her body inside her hand-me-down country dress, and he had to fight to keep the emotion down, stop it from tightening his throat until he couldn't get the words out. "Mr. Pitt's working on it. There's been another death he needs to prove isn't suicide."

"So why aren't yer doin' summink about it, too?" Gracie was far from satisfied. "Yer look like summink the cat drug in. Wot's the matter wif yer?"

He could see she was going to fight him all the way. It was infuriating, and yet so characteristic of her he felt tears sting his eyes. This was ridiculous! He should not allow her to do this to him!

"Mr. Pitt isn't satisfied this is a safe place for you," he said tartly. "Mr. Voisey knows where you are, and I'm to take you somewhere else straightaway. There's probably no danger, but best be safe." He saw the fear in Charlotte's face and knew that for all Gracie's bravado, they were just as aware as Pitt that the danger was real. He swallowed. "So if you'll get the children up and dressed we'll go tonight, while it's dark. Doesn't stay long, this time of year. We need to be well out of the area in three or four hours, because it'll be daylight by then."

Charlotte stood motionless. "Are you sure Thomas is all right?" Her voice was sharp, edged with doubt, her eyes wide.

If he told her, it would relieve Pitt from having to try to find a way when they finally got back to London. And perhaps it would ease her physical fear for him.

Voisey would never damage him now, he was too precious alive, to watch him suffer.

"Samuel!" Gracie demanded sharply.

"Well, he is and he isn't," he replied. "Voisey's made it look like it was Mr. Pitt's fault that this man committed suicide, and he was a churchman, very well liked. Of course it wasn't, and we'll get to prove it . . ." That was a pretty wild piece of optimism. "But for now the newspapers are giving him a hard time. But will you please go and get the children up, and put your things into cases, or whatever you brought them in. We haven't got time to stand here and argue it out!"

Charlotte moved to obey.

"I suppose I'd better pack up the kitchen," Gracie said, darting Tellman a fierce look. "Well, don't just stand there! Yer look as starved as an alley cat! Come 'ave a slice o' bread an' jam while I pack up wot we got. No sense leaving it 'ere! An' yer can carry it out ter wotever kind o' cart yer got out there. Wot 'ave yer got, anyway?"

"It'll do," he answered. "Make me a slice, and I'll eat it on the way."

She shivered, and he noticed that her hands were clenched, knuckles white.

"I'm sorry!" he said with a wave of

feeling so intense his voice was husky. "There's no need to be afraid, Gracie. I'll look after you!" He reached out to touch her, a stab of physical memory bringing back the moment he had kissed her when they were following after Remus in the Whitechapel affair. "I will!"

She looked away from him and sniffed. "I know yer will, yer daft 'aporth," she said savagely. "An' all of us! One-man army, y'are. Now do summink useful an' get these things inter a box an' take 'em out to yer cart, or wotever it is. An' wait! Put that light out 'afore yer open the door!"

He froze. "Is someone watching you?"

"I dunno! But they could be, couldn't they?" She started to take things out of the cupboards and put them into a wicker laundry basket. In the dim candlelight he saw two loaves of bread, a large pot of butter, a leg of ham, biscuits, half a cake, two jars of jam, and other tins and boxes he couldn't name.

When the basket was full enough he shaded the candle with his hand, opened the door, and then, blowing out the flame and picking up the basket, he stumbled his way to the cart, several times barely missing tripping over the uneven path.

Fifteen minutes later they were all sitting

wedged in, Edward shivering, Daniel half asleep, Jemima sitting awkwardly between Gracie and Charlotte, her arms gripped tightly around herself. Tellman urged the horse forward and they began to move, but the feeling was extremely different from when he had driven in. Now the cart was heavily laden and the night was so black it was hard to know how even the horse could find its way. He also had very little idea where they were going. Paignton was the obvious place, the first that anyone Voisey employed would think to look. Perhaps the opposite direction was equally obvious? Maybe there was somewhere off to the side? Where else was there a station? By train they could go anywhere! How much money had he left? They had to pay for lodgings and food as well as tickets.

Pitt had said a town, somewhere with lots of people. That meant Paignton or Torquay. But back at the Ivybridge station they would be remembered all standing together waiting for the first train. The stationmaster would be able to tell anyone who asked exactly where they went.

As if reading his thoughts, even in the dark, Gracie spoke. "Where are we goin', then?"

"Exeter," he said without hesitation.

"Why?" she asked.

"Because it isn't really a holiday place," he replied. It seemed as good an answer as any other.

They drove in silence for a quarter of an hour. The darkness and the weight of the cart made them slow, but he could not urge the horse any more. If it slipped, or went lame, they were lost. They must be over a mile from Harford and the cottage by now. The road was not bad and the horse was finding its way with more ease. Tellman began to relax a little. None of the difficulties he had feared had come to pass.

The horse pulled up abruptly. Tellman nearly fell off the seat, and saved himself only by grabbing hold of it at the last moment.

Gracie stifled a shriek.

"What is it?" Charlotte said sharply.

There was someone on the road ahead of them. Peering forward, Tellman could just make out the dark shape in the gloom. Then a voice spoke quite clearly, only a yard or so away.

"Now, where are you going at this time o' the night? Mistress Pitt, isn't it? From Harford way? You shouldn't be out at this hour. Get lost, you will. Or have an accident." It was a man's voice, deep and with a lift of sarcasm to it.

Tellman heard Gracie gasp with fear. The fact that the man had used Charlotte's name meant that he knew them. Was it intended as a threat? Was he the watcher who had told Voisey where they were?

The horse shook its head as if someone were holding its bridle. The darkness prevented Tellman from seeing. He hoped it also prevented the man from seeing him. How did he know who they were? He must have been watching and ridden ahead, knowing they would come this way. If he had seen Tellman go to the cottage door and then carry the boxes out, then it meant he had been there all the time. He had to be Voisey's man. He had come ahead of them here into this lonely stretch of road between Harford and Ivybridge to catch them where there was no one to see, or to help. And there was no one — except Tellman. Everything rested with him.

What could he use for a weapon? He remembered packing a bottle of vinegar. It was half empty, but there was enough in it still to give it weight. But he daren't ask Gracie for it aloud. The man would hear him. And he did not know how she had stacked the basket!

He leaned over and whispered in her ear. "Vinegar!"

"Wha . . . oh." She understood. She slid back a little and started feeling for the bottle. Tellman made some move himself to cover the sounds, climbing off the box and slithering down the side of the cart until his feet touched the ground. He felt his way around to the back, hand over hand on the rough wood, and was coming around on the other side when he made out in the gloom the figure of a man ahead of him. Then he felt a smooth weight against his forearm and Gracie's breath on his cheek. He took the vinegar bottle from her hand. He could see the dark shape of Charlotte, with her arms around the children.

"It's you again!" Gracie's voice came clearly from just beside him, but she was speaking to the man at the horse's head, drawing his attention. "Wot yer doin' out 'ere in the middle o' the night, then? We're goin' 'cos we got a family emergency. Yer got one, too, 'ave yer?"

"That's a shame," the man replied, the expression in his voice impossible to read. "Going back to London, then?"

"We never said we come from London!" Gracie challenged him, but Tellman could hear the fear in her, the slight quiver, the higher pitch. He was only a yard away from the man now. The vinegar bottle was heavy in his hand. He swung it back, and as if he had caught the movement in the corner of his eye, the man swiveled and shot out his fist, sending Tellman sprawling backwards onto the ground, the vinegar bottle flying out of his grasp and rolling away on the grass.

"Oh, no you don't, mister!" the man said, his voice suddenly altered to a vicious anger, and the next moment Tellman felt a tremendous weight on top of him, knocking the air out of his lungs. He was no match for the man in strength and he knew it. But he had grown up in the streets and the instinct to survive was above almost everything else; the only thing greater was the passion to protect Gracie . . . and of course Charlotte and the children. He kneed the man in the groin and heard him gasp, then poked at his eyes with stiff fingers, or at any piece of flesh he could reach.

The fight was short, intense and absolute. It was only moments later that his hands reached the unbroken vinegar bottle and he finished the job, cracking the man over the head with it and laying him senseless.

He scrambled to his feet and staggered around to where the other horse was standing with a dogcart pulled across the track, and led it off onto the side. Then he ran back and with difficulty in the dark, took the bridle of their own horse and led it past, before climbing up onto the box again and urging it forward as fast as it was capable of going. The east was already fading a little ahead of them and dawn would not be far away.

"Thank you," Charlotte said quietly, holding a shivering Jemima close to her and Daniel by the other hand. Edward was clinging on at the farther end. "I think he has been watching us almost since we got here." Charlotte did not add anything further, or mention Voisey's name, or the Inner Circle. It was in all their minds.

"Yes," Gracie agreed, a quiet pride in her voice and in the stiff, square-shouldered way she sat. "Thank you, Samuel."

Tellman was bruised, his blood was beating so hard he was dizzy, but above all he was astounded by the savagery which had driven him. He had behaved like something primitive and it was exhilarating, and frightening.

"You're going to stay in Exeter until the election is over and we know whether

Voisey has won or lost," he answered.

"No, I think I shall return to London," Charlotte contradicted. "If they are blaming Thomas for this man's death then I should be there with him."

"You're to stay here," Tellman said flatly. "That's an order. I'll send a telephone message to Mr. Pitt to say as you're all right and safe."

"Inspector Tellman, I . . ." she began.

"It's an order," he said again. "Sorry, but that's the end of it."

"Yes, Samuel," Gracie murmured.

Charlotte tightened her arms around Jemima and said nothing more.

CHAPTER

<u>FOURTEEN</u>

Isadora sat at the breakfast table across from the Bishop and watched him toy with his food, pushing bacon, eggs, sausage and kidney around his plate. He did not look well, but then he so often complained of some minor ailment, and she knew that if she asked him he would tell her. She would be required, in ordinary civility, to listen and to offer some condolence. Kindness dictated she do more than that, and she could not bring herself to feel such a thing. So she ate her own breakfast of toast and marmalade, and avoided his eyes.

The butler brought in the morning newspaper and the Bishop motioned him to lay it on the table at his end, where he could reach it in a moment or two when he was ready.

"Take my plate away," he directed.

"Yes, my lord. Is there something else you would prefer?" the butler asked solicitously, doing as he was bidden. "I am sure

Cook would oblige."

"No, thank you," the Bishop declined. "I'm not hungry. Just pour the tea, would you."

"Yes, my lord." Again he did as he was bidden, and then discreetly withdrew.

"Are you feeling unwell?" Isadora asked before checking herself. It was so much habit with her that it required a conscious effort not to do so.

"The news is depressing," he answered, but without picking up the paper. "The Liberals will win and Gladstone will form a government again, but it won't last. But then nothing does."

She must make the effort. She had promised him, and she sensed the fear in him across the table as if it were an odor in the air. "Governments don't last, but neither should they," she said gently. "The good things do. You've preached that all your life. You know it's true. And the things that are destroyed, but in righteousness, God can rebuild. Isn't that what the resurrection is all about?"

"That is the idea, the hope," he replied, but his voice was flat, and he did not look up at her.

"Is it not the truth?" She thought that by provoking him into arguing it, the sound of his own words would strengthen him. He would realize that he did believe it.

"Really . . . I have no idea," he answered instead. "It is a habit of thought. I repeat it over and over every Sunday because it is my job. I can't afford to stop. But I don't know that I believe it any more than the members of my congregation who come because it is the thing to be seen to do. Kneel in your pew every Sunday, repeat all the prayers, sing all the hymns and look as if you are listening to the sermon, and you will seem to be a good man. Your mind can be anywhere . . . on your neighbor's wife, or his goods, or relishing his sins, and who will know?"

"God will know," she said, startled by the anger in her voice. "And quite apart from that, you will know yourself."

"There are millions of us, Isadora! Do you suppose God has nothing better to do than listen to our witterings? 'I want this' and 'Give me that,' 'Bless so and so, which will release me of the necessity of doing anything about him.' Those are the sort of orders I give my servants, which is why we have them in the first place, so we don't have to do everything ourselves." His face twisted with disgust. "That isn't worship, it's a ritual performed for ourselves, and to impress each other. What kind of a God wants that, or has any use for it at all?" There was contempt in his eyes, and anger, as if he had been let down unfairly and was just realizing the fullness of it.

"Who decided that it was what God wanted?" she asked.

He was startled. "It is what the church has done for the best part of two thousand years!" he retorted. "In fact, always!"

"I thought it was only meant to be the instrument of our growth," she replied to him. "Not an end in itself."

His brow creased with irritation. "Sometimes you talk the most arrant nonsense, Isadora. I am a bishop, ordained of God. Don't try to tell me what the church is for. You make yourself ridiculous."

"If you are ordained of God, then you should not doubt Him," she snapped. "But if you are ordained of man, then perhaps you should be looking for what God wishes instead. It may not be the same at all."

His face froze. He sat motionless for a moment, then leaned over and picked up the newspaper, holding it high enough to hide behind.

"Francis Wray committed suicide," he said after a few moments. "It seems that damned policeman Pitt was hounding him over the murder of the spirit medium, imagining he knew something about it. Stupid man!"

She was horrified. She remembered Pitt; he had been one of Cornwallis's men, one he was particularly fond of. Her first thought was for how it would hurt Cornwallis, for the injustice if it were not true, and for the disillusion, if by some terrible chance it were.

"Why on earth would he think that?" she said aloud.

"Heaven knows." He sounded final, as if that closed the matter.

"Well, what do they say?" she demanded. "You've got it in front of you."

He was irritated. "That was yesterday's paper. There's very little about it today."

"What did they say?" she insisted. "What are they blaming Pitt for? Why would he think Francis Wray, of all people, would know anything about a spirit medium?"

"It really doesn't matter," he replied without lowering the paper. "And Pitt was quite wrong anyway. Wray had nothing to do with it, that has been proved." And he refused to say anything further.

She poured a second cup of tea and drank it in silence.

Then she heard his suddenly indrawn

breath and a gasp. The paper slid from his hands and fell in loose sheets in his lap and over his plate. His face was ashen.

"What is it?" she said with alarm, afraid he was having some kind of attack. "What's happened? Have you pain? Reginald? Shall —" She stopped. He was struggling to his feet.

"I . . . I have to go out," he mumbled. He thrashed at the newspaper, sending the sheets slithering to the floor, rattling together.

"But you have the Reverend Williams coming in half an hour!" she protested. "He's come all the way from Brighton!"

"Tell him to wait." He flapped a hand at her.

"Where are you going?" She was on her feet also. "Reginald! Where are you going?"

"Not far," he said from the doorway. "Tell him to wait!"

There was no use asking anymore. He was not going to tell her. It had to be something in the newspaper which had created such a panic of emotion in him. She bent and picked it up, starting her search on the second page, roughly where she guessed he had been reading.

She saw it almost immediately. It was an announcement by the police on the Maude

Lamont case. There had been three clients at her house on Southampton Row for the last séance she had given. Two of them were named in her diary of engagements, the third had been represented by a little drawing, a pictograph or cartouche. It was like a small *f* hastily written, under a half circle. Or to Isadora's eye, a bishop's crozier under a roughly drawn hill — Underhill.

The police said that there was something in Maude Lamont's papers which indicated that she had known who the third man was, and that he, like the other two, had been blackmailed by her. They were close to a breakthrough, and when they read her diaries again, with this new understanding, they would have the identity of Cartouche, and of her murderer.

The Bishop had gone to Southampton Row. She knew it as surely as if she had followed him there. He was the one who had gone to Maude Lamont's séances, hoping to find some kind of proof that there was life after death, that his spirit would live on in a form he could recognize. It was not extinction that awaited him, but merely change. All the Christian teachings of his lifetime had built no sure faith in him. In his desperation he had turned to a

513

spirit medium, with her table rappings, levitation, ectoplasm. Far worse than that, which held more horror, doubt and weakness, and which she could understand only too easily, he had known fear, loneliness soul-deep, even the hollow, consuming well of despair. But he had done it secretly, and even when Maude Lamont had been murdered, he had not come forward. He had allowed Francis Wray to be suspected of being the third person, and to have his reputation ruined, and now Pitt's as well.

Her anger and her contempt for him burned in a pain that ran through her mind and body, consuming her. She sat down suddenly in his chair, the newspaper dropped onto the table, still open at the article. It had been proved that Francis Wray was not the third person, but too late to save his grief, or his sense that all his life's meaning had been denied as far as those who had loved and cherished him could see. Too late, above all, to prevent him from committing the irretrievable act of taking his own life.

Could she ever forgive Reginald for his part in letting that happen, for his utter cowardice?

What was she going to do? Reginald was

even now going to Southampton Row to see if he could find and destroy the evidence that implicated him. What loyalty did she owe him?

He was doing something she believed to be profoundly wrong. It was hypocritical and ugly, but it was largely his own destruction rather than anyone else's. Worse, he had allowed Francis Wray to be blamed for long enough to destroy him, to be the last weight of misery on top of his grief, which had broken him, perhaps not only for this life but for the life to come. Although she could not accept that God would condemn forever any man, or woman, who had finally broken, perhaps only for one fatal instant, beneath something too great for them to bear.

It could not be undone. Wray was gone. The degree of sin in his death was beyond anyone to alter. If the church concealed it and gave him a decent burial that would redeem him to the world, but it altered none of the truth.

What was her deepest loyalty now? How far along the road of his cowardice did she have to go with her husband? Not all the way. You did not owe it to anyone to drown yourself along with him.

And yet she was perfectly sure that he

would regard it as betrayal whenever she left him.

Did he know who had killed Maude Lamont? Was it even imaginable that he had done it himself? Surely not! No! He was shallow, self-important, condescending, totally absorbed in his own feelings and oblivious of the joy or the pain of anyone else. And he was a coward. But he would not have committed any of the open sins, the ones that even he could not deny because they were against the law of the land, and he would be forced to conceal them. Even he could not justify murdering Maude Lamont, no matter what she had blackmailed him for.

But he might know who had, and why. The police must know the truth. She had no idea how to contact Pitt at Special Branch, and the new commander of Bow Street was a stranger to her. She needed to speak to someone she knew. This was going to be agonizing enough without trying to explain to a stranger. She would go to Cornwallis. He would begin halfway towards understanding.

Now that she had made up her mind she did not hesitate. It hardly mattered what she wore, simply that she composed her mind to speak sensibly and to tell only the truth she knew and allow him to make all deductions. She must not permit her anger or her contempt to show through, or the bitterness that welled up inside her. There must be no manipulation of emotions. She must tell him as one person to another, no more, and with no reminder, however subtle, of what either of them might feel.

Cornwallis was in his office but occupied with someone. She asked if she might wait, and nearly half an hour later she was taken up by a constable and found Cornwallis standing in the middle of his room waiting for her.

The constable closed the door behind her and she remained standing.

Cornwallis opened his mouth to say something, the conventional greeting, to give himself time to adjust to her presence. And then before he could speak, he saw the pain in her eyes.

He took half a step forward. "What is it?"

She stood where she was, keeping the distance between them. This must be done carefully, and without ever losing her self-control.

"This morning something occurred which makes me believe that I know who

517

the third person was who visited Maude Lamont on the night of her death," she began. "He was indicated only by the little drawing which looks rather like a small *f* with a semicircle over the top." Now it was too late to retreat. She had committed herself. What would he think of her? That she was disloyal? He probably regarded that as the ultimate human sin. One does not betray one's own, no matter what the circumstances. She stared at him, and could read nothing of what was in his face.

He looked at the chair as if to invite her to sit down, then changed his mind. "What was it that happened?" he asked.

"The police have issued a statement saying that they believe Maude Lamont knew the identity of that person," she replied. "She was blackmailing him, and there are papers still in her house in Southampton Row, together with the information that Mr. Pitt gathered from the Reverend Francis Wray." Her voice dropped at mention of Wray's name, and for all her intentions not to allow it, her anger came through. "It will make his identity plain."

"Yes," he agreed, frowning. "Superintendent Wetron told the press."

She took a deep breath. She wished she

could control the lurching of her heart and the dizziness in her, the sheer physical reactions that were going to let her down. "When my husband read that at the breakfast table he went completely white," she continued. "And then he rose and said that he was canceling his appointments this morning, and has left the house." Put like that it sounded absurd, as if she wanted to believe it was Reginald. That was proof of nothing at all, except what was going on in her own mind. No wife who loved her husband would have leaped to such a conclusion. Cornwallis must see that — and despise her for it! Did he think she was trying to create some excuse to leave Reginald?

That was terrible! She must make him understand that she truly believed it, and that it had come to her only slowly, and reluctantly.

"He is ill!" she said jerkily.

"I'm sorry," he murmured. He looked terribly awkward, not knowing whether to offer any more sympathy, as if it were an irrelevance.

"He is afraid he is dying," she hurried on. "I mean really very afraid. I suppose I should have realized years ago." Now she was speaking too quickly, words falling over each other. "All the signs were there if I'd been looking, but it never occurred to me. He preached so vividly . . . sometimes . . . with such power . . ." That was true, at least it was how she remembered it. Her voice dropped. "But he has no belief in God. Now, when it really matters, he is not sure if there is anything beyond the grave. That is why he went to a spirit medium, to try to contact a dead person, any dead person, just to know they were there."

He looked stunned. She could see it in his face, his unblinking eyes, the line of his lips. He had no idea what to say to her. Was it pity that silenced him, or disgust?

She felt both herself, and shame because Reginald was her husband. However far apart they were in thought or care, they were still tied together by the years they had been married. Perhaps she could have helped him if she had loved him enough? Perhaps the depth of the love she longed for had nothing to do with it; common humanity for a fellow being should have reached across the gulf and offered something!

It was too late now.

"Of course when she knew who he was, that gave her the means to blackmail him."

Her voice was now little more than a whisper. She felt the color hot in her cheeks. " 'Church of England Bishop goes to spirit medium to seek proof of life after death!' He'd be a laughingstock. It would ruin him." As she said it she realized just how much that was true. Would he have killed to prevent it? She had started out quite sure that that was impossible — but was it? If his reputation were gone, what had he left? How far had his illness, and the fear of death, unbalanced his mind? Fear can warp almost anything, only love was strong enough to overcome it . . . and did Reginald really love anything well enough for that?

"I'm so sorry," Cornwallis said with a break in his voice. "I . . . I wish I could . . ." He stopped, staring at her helplessly, not knowing what to do with his hands.

"Aren't you going to . . . to do something?" she asked. "If he finds the evidence he'll destroy it. That's what he's gone for."

He shook his head. "There isn't any," he answered quietly. "We put it in the paper to try to make Cartouche show himself."

"Oh . . ." She was stunned. Reginald had betrayed himself unnecessarily. He would be caught. The police would be waiting for him. But that was what she had come here for, it had to be. She could never have imagined Cornwallis would simply listen and not act, and yet now that it was going to happen, she realized the enormity of it. It would be the end of her husband's career, a complete disgrace. He would not ever be able to retire behind excuses of ill health, because the police would be involved. He might even be charged with something — obstruction, or concealing evidence. She refused to think, even in the very back of her mind, of a charge of murder.

Suddenly, Cornwallis was standing in front of her, his hands holding her arms, steadying her as if she had swayed and were about to fall over.

"Please . . ." he said urgently. "Please . . . sit down. Let me send for tea . . . or something. Brandy?" He slid his arm around her and led her to the chair, still holding her as she sank down into it.

"The drawing," she said, gulping a little. "It wasn't an *f*, it was a bishop's crozier, under a hill. It's very clear when you think about it. I don't want brandy, thank you. Tea would be quite all right."

Pitt knew that if he went to Southampton Row alone he could not prove anything satisfactorily, either about the identity of Cartouche or about his involvement in the death of Maude Lamont. Tellman was in Devon, and Pitt did not trust anyone from Bow Street, even supposing Wetron would give him somebody, which was unlikely without an explanation. And of course he could not explain, not knowing Wetron's own involvement in any of it.

Therefore he went straight to Narraway, and it was Narraway himself who came with Pitt to Southampton Row in the bright, early sunlight of the July morning. They traveled in mere silence, each absorbed in his own thoughts.

Pitt could not rid his mind of his memory of Francis Wray. He hardly dared allow himself to hope that an autopsy would somehow show that Wray had not taken his own life, even if only to Pitt. Whether they could ever prove it to the rest of the world was another matter.

He repeated in his mind all that he thought he had asked of the people in the village. Were the questions so open, so accusatory, that anyone would have supposed from them that Wray was suspected of being involved in Maude Lamont's death? And if he went to see her with the intent of exposing her manifestations as fraud, then where was there any fault or hypocrisy in that?

And it was very easy to believe that in his outrage at the damage spirit mediums could do, he might well have used all his energy to expose them. Pitt thought back to the story of the young woman Penelope, who had lived in Teddington, and whom Wray must have known. She had lost her child and been tricked and misled by séances and manifestations, and when she had seen through them, in despair she had taken her own life.

He already knew that Maude Lamont had used mechanical tricks, at least some of the time — the table, for example — and he could not help feeling that the collected electric light bulbs were part of an illusion also. That number of them was certainly not for ordinary domestic use.

Was it conceivable she had some real power, of which she herself was only partly aware? More than one of her clients had said she seemed startled by some of the manifestations, as if she had not engineered them herself. And she had no helper. Lena Forrest denied all knowledge of her arts or how they were exercised.

Then another thought occurred to him, new and extraordinary, but the more he weighed it and measured it against all he knew, the more it seemed to make some kind of sense.

When they reached Southampton Row he climbed out of the hansom, with Narraway at his heels. Narraway paid the cabbie and they waited until he had driven away before they turned into the short alley of Cosmo Place.

Narraway looked at the door into the garden of Maude Lamont's house.

"It'll be locked," Pitt observed.

"Probably." Narraway squinted at it. "But I'm not climbing that damn wall and then finding I didn't have to." He put out his hand and tried the iron ring, turning it a quarter of a circle until it stopped. He grunted.

"I'll give you a lift up," Pitt offered.

Narraway shot him a malicious glance, but considering their relative heights, and Narraway's slender build, it would have been absurd for him to have tried to lift Pitt. He regarded his trousers, his lips forming a thin line as he considered what the mossy stone would do to them, then turned to Pitt impatiently. "Get on with it, then! I would greatly prefer not to be caught doing this and trying to explain myself to the local constable on the beat."

Pitt grinned at the idea, but it was brief, and there was little pleasure in it. He bent and made a cradle of his hands and Narraway stepped gingerly onto it. Pitt straightened up and in seconds Narraway was on top of the wall, scrambling for a moment, until he found his balance and sat astride, then he leaned forward and offered Pitt his hand. It was an effort to haul himself up, but after a few very undignified wriggles he breasted the wall, and a moment later swung his legs over and down onto the earth at the far side, immediately followed by Narraway.

He brushed as much of the moss stain and dust off himself as he could, then stared around. It was the reverse of the view he had seen from the strip of grass in front of the French windows of the parlor. "Keep back." He waved. "Another couple of yards and we can be seen from the house."

"Then what, exactly, are we doing here?" Narraway retorted. "We can't see the front door and we can't see the parlor. And now we can't even see the street!"

"If we keep to the bushes we can make our way to the back of the house, and once we've seen where Lena Forrest is, we'll know if she goes to answer the door, and we can get inside through the back," Pitt replied softly. He moved over to shelter behind the laurels as he spoke, motioning Narraway to follow him. "Since Cartouche always came through the side door anyway, I think that's probably the way he'll come now, if he's still got the key."

"Then we'd better make sure the bar is up," Narraway observed, looking back over his shoulder at the door. "And it's not!" He strode rapidly over to it and in a single movement lifted the bar up and laid it back off the rests that kept it closed. Then he drew back behind the shelter of the bushes beside Pitt.

Pitt's mind was still half occupied with the idea which had come to him. He looked up at the branches of the silver birch trees above the laurels. There would probably be nothing to see, no mark now, but he could not help searching.

"What is it?" Narraway said crossly. "He's hardly going to come down from the sky!"

"Can you see any notches up there, notches rubbed bare of moss or scraping on the bark?" Pitt said softly.

Narraway's face was tense, interest flaring in his eyes. "Like a rope burn? Why?"

"An idea. It may be . . ."

"Of course it's an idea!" Narraway snapped. "What?"

"To do with the night Maude Lamont was killed, and tricks, illusion that there might have been."

"We'll discuss it when we're watching the woman. I don't care how brilliant your theory is, it'll do us no good if we miss Cartouche arriving . . . assuming he comes."

Obediently, Pitt started to creep along the wall, as much as possible keeping concealed behind the various bushes and shrubs until they were fifteen yards away from the door in the wall, and only four yards from the scullery windows and the back door. They could see the shadowy figure of Lena Forrest moving about in the kitchen. Presumably she was getting herself breakfast and perhaps beginning whatever chores she had for the day. It must be a long, drawn-out, boring time for her with no mistress in the house to care for. They could not expect her to remain here much longer.

"Why were you looking for rope marks?" Narraway said insistently.

"Did you see any?" Pitt countered.

"Yes, very slight, a mark more like twine

than rope. What was on it? Something to do with Cartouche?"

"No."

They heard the sound at the same instant, the scraping of a key in the lock of the garden door. As one they shrank back behind the heavy leaves, and Pitt found himself holding his breath.

There was no sound until the key scraped again and then the slight clunk of the bar being dropped back. There were no footfalls across the grass.

They waited. Seconds ticked by. Was the visitor waiting also, or had he passed by soundlessly and might already be inside?

Narraway moved very carefully until he could see the side of the house. "He's gone in through the French windows," he said softly. "I can see him in the parlor." He straightened up. "There's no cover outside here. We'd better go around the back. If we run into the woman we'll have to tell her." And without waiting for Pitt to argue, he sprinted across the open space towards the scullery door and stopped just outside.

Pitt wondered for an instant if perhaps they should have left a constable at the front door, just in case Cartouche tried to escape that way. But then if he had seen anyone in the street he might not have risked coming in at all, and the whole exercise would have been useless.

Another alternative was for one of them to wait in the garden now, but then if Cartouche said anything, or Lena did, there needed to be more than one witness to it. He ran across the open lawn and joined Narraway at the scullery door.

Narraway looked cautiously in through the window. "There's no one there," he said, pushing the door. Inside was a small, tidy room with vegetable racks, rubbish bins, a sack of potatoes and several pots and pans, as well as the usual sink and low tub for laundry.

They went up the step into the kitchen, and still there was no one in sight. Lena must have heard the intruder and gone through to the parlor. On tiptoe, Pitt and Narraway crept along the passage and stopped just short of the doorway. It was ajar. They could hear the voices inside. The first was male, rich and melodious, only slightly sharpened by emotion. His diction was still perfect.

"I know that there are other papers, Miss Forrest. Don't try to mislead me."

Then Lena's voice in reply, surprised and a trifle edgy. "The police already took everything that has to do with her appointments. There's nothing here now but household bills and accounts outstanding, and that's just the ones that have come in through the last week. The lawyers have all the old ones. It's part of her estate."

Now there was fear in his voice, and anger. "If you imagine you can continue where Miss Lamont was obliged to desist, and that you can blackmail me, Miss Forrest, you are most deeply mistaken. I will not permit it. I will do not another thing by coercion, do you hear me? Not one more word, written or spoken."

There was a moment of silence. Narraway was standing in front of Pitt, blocking his view through the crack between the door and the jamb. His eye was about level with the top of the hinge.

"She was blackmailing you!" Lena said with consuming disgust. "You were so afraid of what she knew about you that you'd rather remove her papers for good or ill than have people know about you."

"I no longer care, Miss Forrest!" There was a wild note in him now, as if he would overbalance out of control any moment.

Pitt stiffened. Was she in possible danger? Had Cartouche murdered Maude Lamont over this blackmail, and if Lena pressed him too far, would he kill again, once he knew where the papers were? And of course she could not tell him because they did not exist.

"Then why are you here?" Lena asked. "You've come for something!"

"Only her notes that would tell who I am," he replied. "She's dead. She can't say anything further now, and it's my word against yours." There was an element of confidence creeping in. "There's no question which of us they would believe, so don't be foolish enough to try blackmail of your own. Just give me the papers and I'll not trouble you again."

"You aren't troubling me now," she pointed out. "And I never blackmailed anyone in my life."

"A sophistry!" he sneered. "You were helping her. I don't know if there's a legal difference, but morally there isn't."

There was real anger in her voice; it shook with something close to fury. "I believed her! I worked in this house for five years before I had any idea she was a fraud! I thought she was honest." She choked on a sob and caught her breath painfully. Her voice sank so low Pitt leaned forward to hear her. "It was only after someone else made her blackmail certain people that I found her out in tricks . . .

with the magnesium powder on the wires of the light bulbs . . . and that table. She never used them before . . . that I know of."

Another moment's silence. This time it was he who was urgent, choked with feeling. "Wasn't it all . . . tricks?" It was a cry of the heart, desperate.

She must have heard it. She hesitated.

Pitt could hear Narraway's breath and felt the tension in him when they stood almost touching each other.

"There are real powers," Lena said very softly. "I discovered that myself."

Silence again, as if he could not bear to put it to the test.

"How?" he said at last. "How would you know? You said she used tricks! You discovered it. Don't lie to me! I saw it in your face. It shattered you!" That was almost an accusation, as if somehow it were her fault. "Why? Why do you care?"

Her voice was almost unrecognizable, except that it could be no one else. "Because my sister had a baby out of wedlock. He died. Because he was illegitimate they wouldn't baptize him. . . ." She was gasping for breath, choking on her pain. "So they wouldn't bury him in hallowed ground. She went to a spirit medium . . .

to know what happened to him after . . . after death. That medium was a fake as well. It was more than she could bear. She killed herself."

"I'm sorry," he said softly. "The child, at least, was innocent. It would have done no harm to . . ." He tailed off, knowing it was all too late, and a lie anyway. The church's rules on illegitimacy and suicide were beyond his power to break, but there was pity in his voice, and contempt for those who built rules without compassion. He obviously saw no kind of God in it.

Narraway turned and stared at Pitt.

Pitt nodded.

There was a rustle inside the room.

Narraway swiveled back.

"You weren't here the night she was killed," the man said. "I saw you go myself."

She snorted. "You saw the lantern and the coat!" she retorted. "You think I learned nothing the weeks I worked here after I knew she was a fraud? I watched. I listened. It's not very hard with ropes."

"I heard you replace the lantern outside the front door when you got 'round to the street!" He made it an accusation.

"A few stones dropped on the ground," she said with scorn. "I let another lantern down on a string. I went out afterwards . . . to see a friend who has no clock. The police checked. I knew they would."

"And you killed her . . . after we'd gone? Leaving us to take the blame!" Now he was angry again, and frightened.

She heard it. "No one's been blamed yet."

"I will be, when they find those papers!" He sounded shrill, the pity gone.

"Well, I don't know where they are!" she retorted. "Why . . . why don't we ask Miss Lamont?"

"What?"

"Ask her!" she repeated. "Don't you want to know if there's life after death, or if this is the end? Isn't that why you came here in the first place? If anyone should be able to come back to tell us, it's her!"

"Oh yes?" His tone was razor-edged with sarcasm, and yet he could not keep the thin thread of hope out of it. "And how are we going to do that?"

"I told you!" Now she was sharp, too. "I have powers."

"You mean you learned some of her tricks!" The voice was filled with contempt.

"Yes, of course I did!" she said witheringly. "I already told you that. But I've been looking ever since Nell died. I'm not easily taken in. There was some truth as well, before the blackmailing started. Spirits can be called up, if the circumstances are right. Draw the curtains. I'll show you."

There was silence.

Narraway turned and looked at Pitt, questioning in his eyes.

Pitt had no idea what Lena was going to do, or if they should allow it to go ahead.

Narraway pursed his lips.

They heard the very slight sound of fabric against fabric, then footsteps. Pitt grasped Narraway by the shoulders and half dragged him backwards, and they were in the drawing room opposite, still with the door open, only just in time to avoid being seen by Lena as she came out of the parlor and disappeared towards the kitchen.

She was gone for several minutes. There was no sound from Cartouche, in the parlor.

Lena returned and went into the room again, closing the door.

Pitt and Narraway resumed their listening position, but could make out only the occasional word.

"Maude!" That was Lena's voice.

Then nothing.

"Maude! Miss Lamont!" That was Cartouche, unmistakable, even though his voice was higher pitched with urgency.

Narraway swung around to look at Pitt, his eyes wide.

"Miss Lamont!" It was Cartouche again, but this time with excitement, almost awe. "You know me! You wrote my name down! Where are the papers?"

There was a long moan, impossible to tell if it was a man or a woman. In fact, it could even have been an animal, so strange and stifled in the throat was it.

"Where are you? Where are you?" he begged. "What is it like? Can you see? Can you hear? Tell me!"

There was a loud bang, and a shriek, and an even louder crash as if something made of glass had broken.

Narraway put his hand on the door just as an explosion shook the whole house, and there was a roaring like a sheet of flame and the smell of burning was thick in the air.

Pitt threw himself at Narraway and dragged him away from the door handle, Narraway kicking and struggling against him.

"They're in there!" he shouted furiously. "The stupid woman has set fire to something. They'll suffocate! Let go of me, damn it! Pitt! Do you want them to burn?"

"Gas!" Pitt yelled back at him, just as the whole side of the house erupted, hurling them backwards to land sprawled on the floor a couple of yards from the front door, which now hung crazily on its hinges, gaping open. Pitt scrambled to his feet.

The parlor door had gone altogether, and the room was full of flame and smoke. A gust from the hall blew across it and it cleared for a moment. Bishop Underhill lay on his back with his head towards the doorway, a look of amazement on his face. Lena Forrest was slumped in the chair at the end of the table, blood on her head and shoulders.

Then the fire took renewed hold as the flames roared upwards, consuming the curtains and the woodwork.

Narraway was on his feet now, too, his face ashen under the dust and smoke.

"We can't do anything for them," Pitt said shakily.

"The whole house could go up any moment." Narraway coughed and choked. "Come on out! Pitt! Run!" And he yanked him around by the arm and plunged for the front door.

They went careering out over the step and fell into the street side by side just as the third explosion rent the air and a gout of flame shot out through the windows with glass flying everywhere.

"Did you know?" Narraway demanded, on his hands and knees. "Did you know it was Lena who killed Maude Lamont?"

"I did by this morning," Pitt replied, rolling over to sit. His knees were scraped, his hands scarred and he was scorched and filthy. "When I realized it was her sister who died in Teddington. Nell is short for Penelope." He bared his teeth savagely. "Voisey missed that one!"

There were several people in the street now, running, shouting. In a little while the fire engines would be here.

"Yes," Narraway agreed, his smoke-grimed face splitting into a white-toothed grin. "He did — didn't he!"

CHAPTER

FIFTEEN

There was little to be salvaged from the ruins of the house on Southampton Row, but the fire engines did at least stop the flames from spreading to the house to the south, or across Cosmo Place to the north.

There was no question that it was the curtains catching fire and the flames spreading to the gas brackets which had caused the first explosion, which had then cracked other gas mains throughout the north part of the house. Gas had leaked out, and as soon as the open flame had reached it, it had made a bomb out of the parlor and its immediate surrounds.

Pitt and Narraway were fortunate to be no more seriously hurt than a few scratches and bruises, and clothing that would never again be fit to wear. It would be late tonight, or even tomorrow morning, before it would be safe for anyone to go into the ruins to look for what was left of Lena Forrest and Bishop Underhill.

And unless there was a connection between Maude Lamont and Voisey in the papers they already had, there was no way in which they could prove such a thing now. Certainly there would be nothing in Southampton Row, nor would Lena Forrest be able to speak again.

"The solution, for what it's worth," Narraway said when the firemen had asked them all they wished and were satisfied there was nothing more to add.

Pitt knew what he meant. There was little satisfaction in it, except that of the mind, and perhaps that Rose Serracold was not guilty. But there was none of the connection to Voisey they had hoped for. It was there, but impossible to prove, which made it more acutely painful. Voisey could look at them and know they knew very clearly what he had done, and why, and that he would succeed.

"I'm going to Teddington," Pitt said after a moment or two as they walked along the footpath out of the way of the horses and the fire engines. "Even if there's nothing I can prove, I want to know that Francis Wray didn't kill himself."

"I'll come with you," Narraway said flatly. He gave a thin smile. "Not for your sake! I want to catch Voisey enough to take any chance there is, no matter how slight. But first one of us had better tell Bow Street what's happened here. We've solved their case for them!" He said that with considerable satisfaction. Then he frowned. "Why the devil isn't Tellman here?"

Pitt was too tired to bother with a lie. "I sent him to Devon to move my family." He saw Narraway start. "Voisey knew where they were. He told me so himself."

"Did he get there?"

"Yes." Pitt said it with infinite satisfaction. "Yes, he did!"

Narraway grunted. There was no comment worth making. The darkness seemed to be gathering on all sides around Pitt, and facile remarks would be worse than useless. "I'll tell Wetron about this," he said instead. "You might tell Cornwallis. He deserves to know."

"I will. And someone has to tell the Bishop's wife. It will be a while before the firemen get to know who he is."

"Cornwallis will find someone," Narraway said quickly. "You haven't time. And you can't go looking like that anyway."

They reached the end of the pavement at the corner of High Holborn. Narraway hailed the first empty hansom that passed.

Isadora returned home after having told Cornwallis about the Bishop's going to Southampton Row. She arrived in the house feeling miserable and horribly ashamed because the step she had taken was irrevocable. She had made her husband's secret public, and Cornwallis was a policeman; he could not keep such a thing in confidence.

It was possible the Bishop was actually the person who had killed the unfortunate spirit medium, although the more she thought about it, the less did she actually believe he had done it. But she had not the right to conceal information on the strength of her own beliefs when they were not knowledge. Somebody had killed Maude Lamont, and the other people there that evening seemed equally unlikely.

She had thought she knew her husband, but she had been completely unaware of his crisis of faith, the terror inside him. It could not have arisen suddenly, even if it had seemed so to him. The underlying weakness must have been there for years, perhaps always?

How much do we ever know other people, especially if we don't really care, not deeply, not with compassion and the effort to watch, to listen, to stretch the imagination and to stop placing self to the front? The fact that he did not know her, or particularly want to, was not an excuse.

She sat thinking all these things, not moving from her chair, not finding anything to comfort herself with or even anything there was purpose in doing until he should return, either with or without the proof he sought.

What would she say to him then? Would she have to tell him that she had been to Cornwallis? Probably. She would not be able to lie to him, to live in the same house, sit across the meal table and make idiotic conversation about nothing, all the time hiding that secret.

She was still sitting doing nothing, her mind consumed in thought, when the maid came to say that Captain Cornwallis was in the morning room and said he must see her.

Her heart lurched, and for a moment she felt so dizzy she could not stand up. So it was Reginald who had killed the medium! He had been arrested. She told the maid that she would come, and then as the girl stood staring at her, she realized she had spoken only in her mind.

"Thank you," she said aloud. "I shall see

him." Very slowly she stood up. "Please do not interrupt unless I send for you. I . . . I fear it may be bad news." She walked past the girl and out of the door, across the hall and into the morning room, closing the door behind her before she faced Cornwallis.

At last she looked at him. He was very pale, his eyes fixed as if something had shocked him so profoundly he was slow to react in the most physical sense. He took a step towards her, then stopped.

"I . . . I know of no gentle way to tell you . . ." he began.

The room swam around her. It was true! She had not even really thought it could be, not even a moment ago.

She felt his hands on her arms, holding her, almost supporting her weight. It was ridiculous, but her legs were buckling under her. She staggered back and sank into one of the chairs. He was leaning over her, his face tense with overwhelming emotion.

"Bishop Underhill went to Southampton Row and spoke for some time to the housekeeper, Lena Forrest," he was saying. "We do not know exactly what was the cause, but there was a fire, and then an explosion which broke the gas lines."

She blinked. "Is he . . . hurt?" Why did she not ask what really mattered: Is he guilty?

"I am afraid there was another, bigger explosion," he said very quietly. "They were both killed. There is very little left of the house. I'm so sorry."

Dead? Reginald was dead? That was the one thing she had not thought of. She should be feeling horror, loss, a great aching hollow inside herself. The pity was all right, but not the sense of escape!

She closed her eyes, not for grief, but so Cornwallis would not see in her the confusion, the great rise of overwhelming relief that she would not have to watch Reginald suffer shame, humiliation, rejection by his fellows, the confusion and pain that would follow. Then perhaps a long and debilitating illness, and the fear of death that would go with it. Instead, death had found him suddenly, with no time for him even to recognize its face.

"Will they ever know the real reason he went there?" she asked, opening her eyes and looking at him.

"I know of no reason why they should," he replied. "It was the housekeeper who killed Maude Lamont. It seems her sister had had a tragic experience with a medium years ago, and took her own life as a result. Lena never got over it. She believed in Maude Lamont until just recently. At least that is what Pitt explained to me." He dropped to his knees in front of her, taking her stiff hands in his. "Isadora."

It was the first time he had used her name.

Suddenly she wanted to weep. It was shock, the warmth of him close to her. She felt the tears flood her eyes and spill over.

For a moment he was at a loss, then he leaned forward and put his arms around her, holding her and allowing her to weep as long as she needed to, safe, very close, his cheek against her hair. And she stayed there long after the shock had worn itself out, because she did not wish to move, and she knew in her heart that he did not, either.

Pitt met Narraway again at the railway station, waiting for the train to Teddington. Narraway had a tight, hard smile on his face, still savoring the satisfaction of telling Wetron the conclusion of the case and handing it to him.

"Cornwallis will tell Mrs. Underhill," Pitt said briefly. His mind was leaping ahead to the coroner, and the thin thread of hope that in examining Wray's body he would find something that would show any truth better than the one Pitt feared.

There was little to say on the train journey. Both men had been bruised physically and emotionally by the tragedy of the morning. Pitt at least felt a mixture of compassion and revulsion for the Bishop. Fear was too familiar not to understand it, whether it was of physical pain and then extinction, or of emotional humiliation. But there had been too little in the man to admire. It was a pity without respect.

Lena Forrest was different. He could not approve what she had done. She had murdered Maude Lamont in revenge and outrage, not to save her own life, or anyone else's, at least not directly. She may have believed it so in her own imagination. They would never know.

But she had planned it with great care and ingenuity, and after carrying it out, had been perfectly willing to allow the police to suspect others.

Still, he felt sorry for the pain she must have endured over the years since her sister's death. And they had suspected others of having killed Maude Lamont only because there were those she had given real cause to hate and fear her. She was a woman prepared to act with extraordinary cruelty and to manipulate the tragedies of the most vulnerable for her own personal gain.

He would have guessed Cornwallis might have felt similarly. Of Narraway's thoughts he had no idea at all, and no intention of asking. If after this he was still able to work in London at all, it would be for Narraway. He could not afford anger or contempt for him.

They sat in silence all the way to Teddington, and to Kingston beyond. The noise of the train was sufficient to make conversation difficult, and neither had any desire to discuss either what had passed or what might be to come.

At Kingston they took a hansom from the station to the mortuary where the autopsy had been conducted. Narraway's position was sufficient to command an almost immediate attention from a highly irritated doctor. He was a large man with a snub nose and receding hair. In his youth he had been handsome, but now his features had coarsened. He regarded the two bruised, filthy men with extreme distaste.

Narraway retained his look with a level stare.

"I can't imagine what Special Branch

wants with the death of an unfortunate old man of such distinction in his life," the doctor said tartly. "Good thing he has only friends, and no family to be distressed by all this!" He flicked his hand, indicating the room behind him, where presumably autopsies were carried out.

"Fortunately, your imagination, or lack of it, does not matter," Narraway replied frostily. "We are concerned only with your forensic skill. What was the cause of Mr. Wray's death, in your opinion?"

"It is not an opinion, it is a fact," the doctor snapped back at him. "He died of digitalis poisoning. A slight dose would have slowed the heart; this was sufficient to stop it altogether."

"Taken in what form?" Pitt asked. He could feel his own heart racing as he waited for the answer. He was not certain if he wanted it.

"Powder," the doctor said without hesitation. "Crushed up tablets, probably, in raspberry jam, almost certainly in a pastry tart. It was eaten very shortly before he died."

Pitt was startled. "What?"

The doctor looked at him with mounting annoyance. "Am I going to have to say everything again for you?"

"If it matters enough, yes you are!" Narraway told him. He turned to Pitt. "What's wrong with raspberry jam?"

"He didn't have any," Pitt replied. "He apologized for it. Said it was his favorite and he had eaten it all."

"I know raspberry jam when I see it!" the doctor said furiously. "It was barely digested at all. The poor man died within a very short time of eating it. And it was unquestionably in pastry. You would have to produce some very remarkable evidence, and I cannot imagine what it would be, to make me believe other than that he went to bed with jam tarts and a glass of milk. The digitalis was in the jam, not the milk." He looked at Pitt with withering disgust. "Although from Special Branch's point of view, I can't see why it matters either way. In fact, I can't see why any of it is even remotely your business."

"I want the report in writing," Narraway told him. He glanced at Pitt, and Pitt nodded. "Time and cause of death, specifically that the digitalis which killed him was in the raspberry jam, in pastry. I'll wait."

Muttering to himself, the doctor went out of the door, leaving Pitt and Narraway alone.

"Well?" Narraway asked as soon as they

were out of earshot.

"He had no raspberry jam," Pitt insisted. "But Octavia Cavendish came with a basket of food for him just as I was leaving. There must have been raspberry jam tarts in it!" He tried to crush the leap of hope inside himself. It was too soon, too fragile. The weight of defeat was still closed down hard. "Ask Mary Ann. She'll remember whatever she unwrapped and put out for him. And she'll tell you there were no jam tarts in the house before that."

"Oh, I will!" Narraway said vehemently. "I will. And when we have the autopsy report in writing, he can't go back on it."

The doctor returned a few moments later, handing over a sealed envelope. Narraway took it from him, tore it open and read every word on the paper inside while the doctor glared at him, offended that he had not been trusted. Narraway looked at him with contempt. He trusted no one. His job depended upon being right to the last detail. A mistake, one thing taken for granted, a single word, could cost lives.

"Thank you," he said, satisfied, and put the paper in his pocket. He led the way out, Pitt following closely behind.

It was necessary to go to the station to

catch the next train back towards London. The first stop would be Teddington, and from there it was only a short distance to Wray's house.

From the outside it looked just the same, the flowers brilliant in the sun, tended with love but not discipline. The roses still tumbled around the doors and windows and ran riot over the arch above the gate. Pinks spilled over the pathways, filling the air with perfume. For a moment it was hard to remember that Wray was gone from here forever.

And yet there was a blind look to the windows, a sense of emptiness. Or perhaps that was only in his mind.

Narraway glanced at him. He seemed about to say something, then kept silent. They walked one behind the other up the flagstoned path and Pitt knocked on the door.

It was several moments before Mary Ann came. She looked at Narraway, then at Pitt, and her face lit with remembrance.

"Oh, it's you, Mr. Pitt! It's nice o' yer to 'ave come, 'specially after the rotten, stupid things some folk are saying. Sometimes I give up! Yer know 'bout poor Mr. Wray, o' course." She blinked, and the tears welled up in her eyes. "Did yer know as 'e left yer the jam? 'E didn't actually write it down, like, but 'e said it to me. 'Mary Ann, I must give Mr. Pitt some more o' the jam, 'e was so kind to me.' I meant to, an' then Mrs. Cavendish came an' the chance rather slipped away. Yer know the way 'e used to talk." She sniffed and searched for a handkerchief, blowing her nose hard. "I'm sorry, but I miss 'im summink terrible!"

Pitt was so touched by the gesture, so overwhelmingly relieved that even if Wray had taken his own life, it was not with ill thought towards him, that he felt his throat tighten and a sting in his eyes. He would not betray it by speaking.

"That's very kind of you," Narraway spoke for him, whether he sensed the need or simply was accustomed to taking control. "But I think that there may be other claimants to his possessions, even those of the kitchen, and we would not wish you to be in any difficulty."

"Oh no!" she said with certainty. "There in't no one else. Mr. Wray left everything to me, an' the cats, o' course. The lawyers came and told me." She gulped and swallowed. "This whole house! Everything! Can you imagine that? So the jam's mine, except 'e said as Mr. Pitt should 'ave it."

Narraway was startled, but Pitt saw with surprise a softness in his face, as if he also were moved by some deep emotion.

"In that case, I am sure Mr. Pitt would be very grateful. We apologize for intruding, Miss Smith, but in light of knowledge we now have, it is necessary we ask you certain questions. May we come in?"

She frowned, looking at Pitt, then back at Narraway.

"They are not difficult questions," Pitt assured her. "And in nothing are you to blame, but we do need to be sure."

She pulled the door and stepped backwards. "Well, I s'pose yer'd better. Would yer like a cup o' tea?"

"Yes, please," Pitt accepted, not bothering to see whether Narraway did or not.

She would have had them wait in the study, where Pitt had met with Wray, but partly from haste, mostly out of revulsion at the idea of sitting where he had talked so deeply with a man now dead, they followed her into the kitchen.

"The questions," Narraway began, as she put more water in the kettle and opened the damper in the stove to set the flames burning inside again. "When Mr. Pitt was here for tea, the day Mr. Wray died, what did you serve them?"

"Oh!" She was startled and disconcerted. "Sandwiches, and scones and jam, I think. We 'adn't any cake."

"What kind of jam?"

"Greengage."

"Are you sure, absolutely certain?"

"Yes. It was Mrs. Wray's own jam, 'er favorite."

"No raspberry?"

"We didn't 'ave any raspberry. Mr. Wray'd eaten it all. That was 'is favorite."

"Could you swear to that, before a judge in court, if you had to?" Narraway pressed.

"Yes. 'Course I could. I know raspberry from greengage. But why? What's 'appened?"

Narraway ignored the question. "Mrs. Cavendish came to visit Mr. Wray just as Mr. Pitt was leaving?"

"Yes." She glanced at Pitt, then back at Narraway. "She brung him some tarts with raspberry jam in them, an' a custard pie an' a book."

"How many tarts?"

"Two. Why? What's wrong?"

"And did he eat them both, do you know?"

"What's wrong?" She was very pale now.

"You didn't eat one?" Narraway insisted.

" 'Course I didn't!" she said hotly. "She

brung them for 'im! What d'yer think I am, to go eating the master's tarts what a friend come with?"

"I think you are an honest woman," Narraway answered with sudden gentleness. "And I think that honesty saved your life to inherit a house a generous man wished you to have in appreciation for your kindness to him." She blushed at the compliment.

"Did you see the book Mrs. Cavendish brought?" Narraway asked.

She looked up quickly. "Yes. It were poems."

"Was it the book that was found beside him when he died?" Narraway winced very slightly at the baldness of the question, but he did not retreat from it.

She nodded, her eyes filling with tears. "Yes."

"Are you certain?"

"Yes."

"Can you write, Mary Ann?"

"O' course I can!" But she said it with sufficient pride that the possibility of her not having been able to was very real.

"Good," Narraway said with approval. "Then will you please find a paper and pen and write down exactly what you have told us — that there was no raspberry jam in the house that day, until it was brought in by Mrs. Octavia Cavendish, and that she came with two raspberry jam tarts, both of which Mr. Wray ate. Also, if you please, that she brought the book of poetry found beside him. And put the date on it, and sign your name."

"Why?"

"Please do it, then I shall explain to you. Write it first. It is important."

She saw something of the gravity in his face, and she excused herself and went to the study. Nearly ten minutes later, after Pitt had taken the kettle off the stove, she returned and offered Narraway a piece of paper very carefully written on and signed and dated.

He took it from her and read it, then gave it to Pitt, who glanced at it, saw that it was wholly satisfactory, and put it away.

Narraway gave him a sharp look but did not demand it back.

"Well?" Mary Ann asked. "You said you'd tell me if I wrote that for you."

"Yes," Narraway agreed. "Mr. Wray died as a result of eating raspberry jam that had poison in it." He ignored her pale face and her gasp of breath. "The poison, to be specific, was digitalis, which occurs quite naturally in the foxglove plant, of which you have several very fine specimens in your garden. It has been supposed by certain people that Mr. Wray took some of the leaves and made a potion which he drank, with the intention of ending his life."

"He'd never do that!" she said furiously. "I know that, even if there's some as don't!"

"No," Narraway agreed. "And you have been most helpful in proving that to be the case. However, you would be very wise, in your own safety, not to say so to anyone else. Do you understand me?"

She looked at him with fear in her eyes and in her voice. "You're saying as Mrs. Cavendish gave 'im tarts what was poisoned? Why would she do that? She was real fond of 'im! It don't make no sense! 'E must 'ave 'ad a 'eart attack."

"It would be best that you think so," Narraway agreed. "By far the best. But the jam is very important, so no one ever supposes that he took his own life. That is a sin in his church, and they would bury him in unhallowed ground."

"That's wicked!" she cried furiously. "It's downright vicious!"

"It is wicked," Narraway said with profound feeling. "But when did that ever stop men who consider themselves righteous from judging others they think are not?"

She swung around to Pitt, her eyes burning. " 'E trusted yer! Yer got to see they don't do that to 'im! You've got to!"

"That is what I am here for," Pitt said softly. "For his sake, and for my own. I have enemies, and as you know, some of them are saying that I was the one who drove him to it. I tell you that so I have not misled you; I never believed he was the man who went to Southampton Row, and I did not even refer to it the last time I was here. The man who visited the spirit medium was called Bishop Underhill, and he is dead too."

" 'E never . . ."

"No. He died by accident."

Her face creased with pity. "Poor man," she said softly.

"Thank you very much, Miss Smith." No one could have mistaken Narraway's sincerity. "You have been of the greatest help. We will take care of the matter from here. The coroner will bring in a verdict of death by misadventure, because I will see to it that he does. If you have any care for your own safety, you will agree to that, regardless to whom you speak or in what circumstances, unless brought to a court of law by me, or by Mr. Pitt, and questioned on the subject under oath. Do you understand me?"

She nodded, swallowing hard.

"Good. Then we shall leave you and be on our way to the coroner."

"Yer don't want a cup o' tea? Anyway, yer got to take your jam," she added to Pitt.

Narraway looked at the kettle. "Actually, yes, we can stay for tea, just a cup. Thank you. It has been an unusually trying day."

She glanced at the dirt and the tears in his clothes, and in Pitt's, but she made no remark. She would have considered it rude. Anyone can fall on hard times, and she knew that very well. She did not judge people she liked.

Pitt and Narraway walked as far as the station together.

"I am going back to Kingston to the coroner," Narraway announced as they crossed the road. "I can enforce the verdict we wish. Francis Wray will be buried in hallowed ground. However, there is little purpose in proving that Mrs. Cavendish's tarts poisoned him. She would be charged with murder, on unarguable circumstantial evidence, and I doubt very much that she had the slightest idea of what she was doing. Voisey either gave her the jam, or more probably the tarts themselves, in order to make sure no one else was affected, both for his own safety in case it was traced back to him, and because insofar as he cares for anyone, it is she."

"Then how in God's name did he bring himself to use her as an instrument of murder?" Pitt demanded. Such callousness was utterly beyond him. He could not conceive of a rage consuming enough to use any innocent person as a weapon of death, let alone someone you loved, and above all who trusted you.

"Pitt, if you are to be any damned use to me at all, then you must stop imagining everyone else operates on the same moral and emotional plane as you do!" Narraway demanded. "They don't!" He glared savagely at the footpath ahead of him. "Don't be so bloody stupid as to think what you would do in a situation! Think what they would do! You are dealing with them . . . not a hundred mirror images of yourself. Voisey hates you with a passion you can't even think of. But believe it! Believe it every day and every hour of your life . . . . because if you don't, one day you will pay for it." He stopped and held out his hand, causing Pitt to all but collide with him. "And I will have Mary Ann's testimony. That, and the autopsy result, are going where even Voisey will never find them. He needs to know that, and he needs to know that if anything happens to you, or to your family, then they will become public, which would be very unfortunate for Mrs. Cavendish, very unfortunate indeed, and ultimately for Voisey himself, whether she were prepared to testify against him or not."

Pitt hesitated only a moment. It was safety for his family, and bought without compromise, without surrender. He put his hand in his pocket and pulled out Mary Ann's testimony. If he could not trust Narraway then he had nothing.

Narraway took it and smiled, thin-lipped. "Thank you," he said with mild sarcasm. He knew Pitt had doubted, for an instant. "I am perfectly happy to have a photograph made of both papers and lodged wherever you wish. The originals must remain where even Voisey can never reach them, and it is best you also do not know where that is. Believe me, Pitt, they will be safe."

Pitt smiled back. "Thank you," he accepted. "Yes, a photograph of each would be nice. I daresay, Commissioner Corn-wallis would appreciate that."

"Then he shall have it," Narraway answered. "Now, catch your train back to the city and see what election results have come in. There should be some by now. I would suggest the Liberal Club. They will have news as fast as anyone, and they put it up in electric lights for all to see. If I didn't have to speak to the coroner, I'd go myself." A flicker of pain crossed his face. "I think the fight between Voisey and Serracold may be far closer than we wish, and I won't call it. Good luck, Pitt." And before Pitt could answer, he turned and walked smartly away.

Pitt, exhausted, stood in the crowd on the pavement outside the Liberal Club staring up at the electric lights which flashed the latest news of the results. He cared about Jack, but the Voisey-Serracold contest filled his mind, and he refused to let go of the last hope that Serracold could still ride the Liberal tide and win, by however narrow a majority.

The result at the moment was one in which he had no interest, a safe Tory seat somewhere in the north of the city.

Two men were standing a yard or two from him.

"Did you hear?" one of them demanded incredulously. "That fellow got in! Would you believe it?"

"What fellow?" his companion asked irritably.

"Hardie, of course!" the first man replied. "Keir Hardie! Labor Party indeed!"

"You mean he won?" The questioner's voice was high with disbelief.

"I told you!"

Pitt smiled to himself, although he was not sure what it would mean for politics, if anything. His eyes were fixed on the electric lights, but he began to realize it was pointless. Results were coming in as they were known, but Jack's seat, or the Lambeth South seat, might already have been declared. He needed to find someone who could tell him. If there were time, he could even get a hansom and go to Lambeth and hear the result in person.

He moved away from the group watching the lights and went to the doorman. He had to wait a moment or two before the man was free to speak to him.

"Yes sir?" he enquired patiently, politely ignoring Pitt's appearance. Everyone was seeking him tonight and it was a highly satisfying feeling.

"Is there any news on Mr. Radley's result in Chiswick?" he asked.

"Yes sir, came almost quarter of an hour ago. Close, but 'e's nicely in, sir."

Pitt felt a burst of relief warm inside him. "Thank you. What about Lambeth South, Mr. Serracold and Sir Charles Voisey?"

"Don't know, sir. 'Eard it's a bit tighter there, but couldn't say for sure. Might be either way."

"Thank you." Pitt stepped back to make room for the next eager enquirer, and hurried to find a cab. Unless he came across an extraordinary traffic jam, he would be able to get to Lambeth's town hall in less than an hour. He could see the result come in himself.

It was a fine evening, warm and humid. Half of London seemed to be out taking the air, walking or riding, choking the streets. It was ten minutes before he found a free hansom and climbed in, calling to the driver to take him over the river to the Lambeth town hall.

The hansom turned and headed back the way it had come, fighting against the stream. There were lights everywhere, people calling out, the sound of hooves on cobbles and the clash and jingle of harness. He wanted to shout to the driver to hurry, to push his way through, but he knew it was pointless. For his own sake the man would already be doing all he could.

Pitt sat back, forcing himself to be patient. He veered between believing Aubrey Serracold could still win and the sick doubt in his stomach that anyone could beat Voisey. He was too clever, too certain.

They were crossing the Vauxhall Bridge now. He could smell the damp of the river and see the lights reflected from the shore. There were still pleasure boats out, laughter floating on the air.

On the far side there were people in the streets, but a little less traffic. The hansom picked up speed. Perhaps he would be there in time to hear them announce the result. Part of him hoped it would be all over when he got there. Then he could simply be told, and that would be it. Was there anything at all even Narraway could do to curb Voisey's power if he were to win? Would he end up Lord Chancellor of England one day, perhaps even before the next government was out?

Or would Wetron be the one to stop him?

No — Wetron had neither the skill nor the nerve. Voisey would crush him, when he was ready.

" 'Ere y'are, sir!" the cabbie called. "This is as close as I can get!"

"Right!" Pitt scrambled out, paid him and pushed his way through the rest of the traffic to the town hall steps. Inside was full of more people, jostling each other, cramming forward to see.

The returning officer was on the platform. The noise abated. Something was about to happen. The light shone on Aubrey Serracold's pale hair. He looked stiff, tense, but his head was high. Pitt saw Rose in the crowd, smiling. She was excited, but the fear seemed to have gone from her. Perhaps she had found the answer to the question she had asked Maude Lamont in a far better, more certain way than any medium could give?

Voisey was on the other side of the returning officer, standing to attention, waiting. Pitt realized with a particle of pleasure that he did not yet know if he had won or not. He was not sure.

Hope welled up inside Pitt like a spring, making him gasp.

There was silence in the room.

The returning officer read out the figures, Aubrey first. There was a tremendous shout. It was high. Aubrey flushed with pleasure.

The officer read out Voisey's figure; it was nearly a hundred higher. The noise was deafening.

Aubrey was white, but he had been born and bred to accept defeat as graciously as victory. He turned to Voisey and offered his hand.

Voisey took it, then that of the returning officer. Then he stepped forward to thank his supporters.

Pitt stood frozen. He should have known, but he had hoped, right to the bitter end he had hoped. Defeat was crushing like a weight in his chest.

The words went on, the cheers. Then at last Voisey left the platform and pushed his way through the crowd. He was bent on savoring the last drop of his victory. He must see Pitt, look at him and be certain he knew.

A moment and he was there, standing in front of him, close enough to touch.

Pitt offered his hand. "Congratulations, Sir Charles," he said levelly. "In a sense you deserved it. You paid a far higher price than Serracold ever would have."

The amusement was sharp in Voisey's eyes. "Indeed? Well, the big prizes do cost, Pitt. That is the difference between the men who reach the top and those who don't."

"I imagine you know that Bishop Under-hill and Lena Forrest both died in the explosion in Southampton Row this morning?" Pitt went on, standing in front of Voisey, blocking his way.

"Yes. I heard. An unfortunate business." He was still smiling. He knew he was safe.

"Perhaps you have not yet heard that they performed an autopsy on Francis Wray," Pitt continued. He saw Voisey's eyes flicker. "Digitalis poisoning." He pronounced the words very clearly. "In raspberry jam tarts . . . quite unmistakably. I don't have the autopsy report myself, but I have seen it."

Voisey was staring at him incredulously, fighting against belief in what he had heard. A bead of sweat formed on his lip.

"The odd thing is" — Pitt smiled very slightly — "there was no raspberry jam in the house, except in two tarts brought as a gift by a Mrs. Octavia Cavendish. Why on earth she should wish to murder such a gentle and harmless old man, I have no idea. There must be some reason we have not yet discovered."

There was panic in Voisey's eyes; his breath was ragged, beyond his control.

"It seems probable," Pitt said, "that someone who trusted Mrs. Cavendish implicitly enlisted her help with the express purpose of killing Wray in a manner that would look like suicide, regardless of what it might cost her!" He moved his hand very slightly, dismissing the subject. "The reason doesn't matter . . . let us say it was a complicated scheme of personal revenge. That is as good a story as any."

Voisey opened his mouth to speak, then gulped air and closed it again.

"We have the coroner's report," Pitt continued. "And Mary Ann Smith's testimony signed and witnessed, and there will be photographs of both kept in separate and extremely safe places, to be made public should anything unpleasant happen to me, or to any member of my family — or, of course, to Mr. Narraway."

Voisey stared at him, his skin pasty white. "I'm sure . . ." he said between dry lips. "I'm sure nothing will happen to them."

"Good," Pitt said with intense feeling. "Very good." And he stood back for Voisey to pass, unsteadily, ashen-faced, on his way.

We hope you have enjoyed this Large Print book. Other Thorndike Press or Chivers Press Large Print books are available at your library or directly from the publishers.

For more information about current and upcoming titles, please call or write, without obligation, to:

Publisher
Thorndike Press
295 Kennedy Memorial Drive
Waterville, ME   04901
Tel. (800) 223-1244

OR

Chivers Press Limited
Windsor Bridge Road
Bath BA2 3AX
England
Tel. (0225) 335336

All our Large Print titles are designed for easy reading, and all our books are made to last.